Soul Blade

BOOK SEVEN

Lindsay Buroker

Soulblade
(Dragon Blood, Book 7)

by Lindsay Buroker

Copyright @ Lindsay Buroker 2016

Cover and Formatting: Deranged Doctor Design

No part of this book may be reproduced, scanned, or distributed in any printed or electronic form without permission. Please do not participate in or encourage piracy of copyrighted materials in violation of the author's rights. Thank you for respecting the hard work of this author.

This is a work of fiction. Names, characters, places, and incidents either are the product of the author's imagination or are used fictitiously, and any resemblance to locales, events, business establishments, or actual persons—living or dead—is entirely coincidental.

Acknowledgments

As always, I must start out thanking my wonderful beta readers, Sarah Engelke, Cindy Wilkinson, and Rue Silver, who had a lot of suggestions for this one (wisely so). I would also like to thank my tireless editor, Shelley Holloway, and the hard workers at Deranged Doctor Design for the cover art and paperback formatting for this series. I hope you enjoy the finished product.

Chapter 1

Sardelle waited in front of the wrought-iron gates to the army fort, the dark stone of the old citadel looming on the far side of the courtyard. One of the corporals standing guard scrutinized the paper she had handed him, an order allowing her access to the complex. She hadn't tried to enter since she had returned from the Magroth Crystal Mines, since Ridge had... disappeared. She refused to accept that he was dead, not until she found his body, not until she knew beyond a doubt.

It bothered her that a week had already passed since the battle where his flier had gone down. She hadn't been able to stay in the mountains and search by herself, no matter how badly she had wanted to. The terrain where he had gone down was too rugged to reach on foot, and all of the soldiers—all of the *pilots*—had been called back to the capital after Morishtomaric's death.

Too bad your new god abandoned you, Jaxi said while the corporal turned over the paper, examining the back side. *Shouldn't a god offer to fly his only high priestess around?*

Bhrava Saruth stayed as long as Phelistoth did. A day. The dragons and the army had only searched for Ridge for a day. It seemed so inadequate. They had found his crash site, then given up, as if there wasn't any chance he had escaped before the flier had landed or that he had somehow beaten the odds. He was a professional at beating the odds. Everyone had given up on him far too soon.

Until those dragons remembered they had that glowing crystal to study. Thus ended their interest in human affairs.

Sardelle was more relieved than disgruntled that the dragons had disappeared, especially Bhrava Saruth. She had tricked him into aiding them, and she had no idea what she would do if he showed up in the city, expecting her to be his high priestess and to help him find worshippers. She hoped he had a short memory and had forgotten the incident. Maybe whatever secrets lay within that repository of knowledge, as the dragons had called it, would preoccupy him for the next century or two.

"It looks all right, ma'am." The corporal handed the paper to her and waved for her to pass through the gate.

"Thank you, Corporal." Sardelle was glad nobody had thought to revoke her clearance, now that General Zirkander no longer occupied an office in the citadel-turned-administration building.

She headed in, her long skirt swishing about her ankles. For once, the ground was dry, the cement walkways clear of puddles. Spring sun beat down upon her shoulders, the air fresh with the scent of the ocean. The warmth and light filled her with hope and determination. If Ridge was alive, she would find him. Even if all she could find was his remains, at least that would allow her to stop wondering. Then she could properly mourn. And wonder if she would ever again find someone who made her laugh and love, whose schemes created danger and excitement in her life such as she had never known. And whose kisses had never stopped making her body sing in response.

Catching a few curious looks from soldiers, Sardelle dashed moisture from her eyes and hustled toward the stone building. She rushed inside, hoping she wouldn't be questioned by any of the officers who worked there. It was after lunch, so with luck, the halls would be empty, everyone tending to their duties behind closed doors.

She half-expected Jaxi to make a joke about some of the unauthorized duties one officer had been engaged in the last time they had been in the building, but Jaxi had been quieter than usual since Ridge's disappearance. Whether because she missed him, too, or if she just respected Sardelle's need to mourn, Sardelle did not know. She knew Jaxi believed that he was dead because neither she nor the dragons had sensed anyone within miles of that crash site. If Ridge had been alive, they *should* have sensed him, no matter how wounded. Even so, Sardelle was not ready to give up.

She made it to the second floor, to the row of offices that looked out over the harbor, and to the office that had most recently been Ridge's. The plaque on the door still held his name. Her throat tightened with emotion, and she had to take several deep breaths before knocking. She wished they could go back in time two weeks and that she could stop him from going on the mission. Then she could be coming to visit him today, alive and well in this office.

"Come in." The deep voice that answered did not belong to Ridge, but she had known it wouldn't.

Inside, she found General Ort gazing out at the harbor instead of sitting at the desk. He looked at her when she entered, then shifted away from the window.

"Sardelle," he said, his voice thick with sympathy as he nodded gravely at her.

The sympathy almost brought tears to her eyes again.

This last week, for the first time in a couple of months, she had been missing her parents again, missing that she no longer had family to turn to, any shoulders to cry upon. She had lost so much before she had even met Ridge, and it had all happened in this last year, at least to her reckoning. She had made other friends in this era, but none that she knew so well that she felt comfortable weeping on their shoulders. She had commiserated with Cas that first night they had returned, but the younger woman missed Ridge as much as she did, and perhaps because Sardelle was older, she had felt the need to be the one to offer the shoulder.

It took a moment before she could return the greeting. "General Ort."

They stared bleakly at each other, neither speaking. She had come for a reason, but her gaze snagged on the desk. Ridge's desk. Even though Ort had occupied this office for years, she had never been in it when it had been his, and she had never known it as anything but Ridge's place.

"It was more organized than I was expecting," Ort said, waving at the desk and the shelves and filing cabinets too. "Honestly, he did a better job than I did at that, despite all his bickering about hating paperwork."

"The first, no, the second time I saw him, he was standing balanced between a desk and a bookcase, dusting."

"His mouth made it easy to forget he was quite good at his job." Ort smiled, taking any sting out of the words. "When he wasn't busy being insubordinate."

"Yes." Sardelle kept herself from imagining Ridge's mouth—and what wonderful things he'd done with it aside from voicing insubordinate comments. This was not the place for that. "General Ort." She took a deep breath, preparing to deliver her request.

"You can call me Vilhem."

"I—thank you. Vilhem, I have a favor to ask."

She thought he might give her a wary look, but he only nodded. "Go ahead."

"I was hoping you could let me borrow Lieutenant Ahn or one of your other pilots and a flier. I'd like to go back and do a more thorough search than we did the day before we left. Since we didn't find his... remains, I feel that we gave up prematurely. I'd like to search until we find—until we're sure. If there's any chance that he could have survived—"

"Sardelle," he said gently. "I saw the crash site. Nobody could have walked away from that."

"Under normal circumstances, I would agree, but we were fighting dragons, and there was magic in use, so you never know. Something extraordinary could have happened."

His gray brows drew together. "Do you have reason to believe someone else was around who could have somehow saved him from experiencing the same fate as his flier?"

"I..."

The dragon Morishtomaric had been the one to knock Ridge's flier out of the sky, and he had died soon after, so he certainly hadn't rescued Ridge. Bhrava Saruth and Phelistoth hadn't been around when Ridge went down. And as far as she knew, she and Tylie had been the only humans in the area capable of wielding magic. Tylie had been with Phelistoth, not anywhere near Ridge, and she... she, too, hadn't been anywhere near Ridge, a decision that she had lain awake every night regretting. By staying in the outpost for the fight, she had been able to save Colonel Therrik's life, but even though she was a healer who should respect all life equally, she would trade Therrik for Ridge in an instant if she had the choice.

I'm not sure if I should say anything and get your hopes up when there's no reason to, but I do remember thinking I sensed Tarshalyn Eversong around right before those three dragons showed up.

Sardelle straightened. She had forgotten about the sorceress. *Jaxi, do you think there's any chance—*

Unfortunately, no. She tried to kill him when the Cofah invaded the capital with their sky fortress, so if anything, he was a pest to her. Even if she was nearby, I'm sure she was focused on trying to get that crystal too. She would have had no reason to help Ridge.

"I'll take that for a no," Ort said quietly.

"I'm not positive. I can't be. That's why I'd like to go check, so we can be positive."

Ort sighed and sat at the desk, waving for her to use one of the leather chairs on the other side if she wished. "Normally, I would say yes without reservation. Even if getting Ridge back wouldn't be a great boon, we owe you a few favors."

"But?" She sensed the *but* hanging in the air.

"The Cofah are back and posing a problem." He pointed toward the window and the harbor, perhaps out to the sea beyond the breakwater. "They know we destroyed two of their airships. The problem is that they think those airships were out over the sea at the time, not hundreds of miles into Iskandian territory. They're claiming that our attacks were unprovoked and that those were simple patrol ships."

"Patrol ships dropping explosives into our heartland."

"Yes, but it *is* possible the rest of the Cofah don't know about that. When we questioned our Cofah captives with Tolemek's truth serum, the men on those airships didn't remember the sorceress and weren't sure how they'd gotten there. In fact, I've been meaning to ask you about that, if you think that Eversong would be capable of controlling the minds of fifty men at the same time. And if so, would they be left confused as to how they got where they were once she let go?"

Sardelle listened to him, though all she wanted to do was rail at the idea that some belligerent Cofah in the area meant he couldn't spare a flier for her.

"For a powerful sorceress from the era she claims to come from, it could be feasible. It would be challenging to manipulate so many at once, but possible for someone who specialized in the mind arts." She frowned, remembering her battle with Eversong. "That said, she didn't try any mind manipulation on me. Her powers seem to lie more in destruction."

"Tolemek brought that point up, that she didn't seem the type to spend years studying people's minds."

"It's hard to know. It might have come easily for her. I can make guesses, but I don't have a true grasp as to the abilities those direct descendants of dragons had. I only know they were far more powerful than any other sorcerers I ever knew."

Maybe Wreltad is the one with the mind skills.

Wreltad. That was her soulblade, right? Sardelle frowned down at the carpet, realizing that Jaxi brought up a good point. A soulblade contained the consciousness of someone entirely different from the handler who wielded it, someone who had once been a human being with passions and skills of his or her own.

Yes. We chatted briefly. As you'll recall, he looked forward to meeting me in noble battle and destroying me.

Did anything in your chat suggest he might have such skills?

He didn't try anything like that on me, but it wouldn't have worked against another soulblade. We don't have brain matter left to manipulate. Just blades and pommels.

Ort stood and came around the desk. "I'm sorry I can't give you anyone right now." He touched her shoulder. "We all miss Ridge, and when the Cofah threat is dealt with, I'll be happy to send Ahn with you to do a more thorough search."

"I understand," Sardelle murmured, but she could not afford to wait. If Ridge *was* alive, it was very likely he was injured, and even in late spring, those mountains were not hospitable.

"I hope you'll stay close, Sardelle." Ort lowered his hand. "I'm saying that partially out of selfishness, of course, since you're amazingly helpful. But we would miss you too. I know Ridge was what brought you here to the army, but I hope you'll stay around for other reasons too. The general population might not be ready to accept magic and sorceresses yet, but we—" he waved toward the army fort, "—and the king certainly appreciate you."

"I understand," she said again. "Thank you for your time, General. Vilhem."

"Sardelle?"

She turned, hoping he had changed his mind. "Yes?"

"I'm riding out to see Fern this evening, if you want to join me. I think she'd like to see you."

A sense of bleakness filled Sardelle. Ridge's mother *had* made her feel like family, but she had also never learned what Sardelle was, of the magic she could wield. Would she *truly* like to see Sardelle? Or without Ridge there, would it be uncomfortable and awkward? General Ort had known Ridge and presumably his mother for years. Sardelle had come into his life so recently and into Fern's life even more recently. Besides, going to see her would be like admitting that Ridge truly was dead. She wasn't ready to do that.

"I'll think about it. Thank you for offering."

Ort smiled sadly at her, and Sardelle turned for the door. She wouldn't abandon the army or Iskandia, but she wasn't going to take the chance that she was leaving a living but wounded Ridge out there somewhere. She would check on him, one way or another.

We're not going on foot, are we? Jaxi shared an image of Sardelle on a horse, a cloak wrapped around her as she tried to find a snow-covered trail that wasn't there up into the treacherous mountains.

I hope not. There's one more person I can ask for this favor.

***

Two guards escorted Tolemek through the castle and toward the big glassed-in patio outside the throne room. Even though he had been invited to meet with the king several times since being placed on the royal payroll, they regarded him warily, fingering their pistols and walking too close to his side for comfort. As usual, he had endured a search that involved poking through his pockets, patting down his arms and legs, making him remove his lab coat, and even lifting his long ropes of hair. Clearly, a man's hair was the natural hiding place for bombs, poisons, and nefarious serums.

Tolemek wagered Zirkander had strolled into the castle unchallenged, the guards not even bothering to remove his sidearm. He frowned at himself as soon as the thought percolated through his mind. Being jealous of a dead man? Not acceptable. Besides, Zirkander had proven himself a hero here for decades. Tolemek would always be an outsider, and his background was far from heroic.

"The king will join you shortly," one of the guards said, pushing open the door that led to the atrium and letting the heady scents of flowers, loamy earth, and citrus fruits escape. "You're to sit at the table and wait. Don't touch anything."

"How can I sit at the table without touching the chair?"

"You're a witch, aren't you? Figure it out."

"I'm a scientist." When had it become common knowledge that he had dragon blood? He hadn't even known for most of his adult life, until Jaxi had told him.

"No kidding," the second man growled, his eyes haunted.

The door shut behind Tolemek and would have bumped him in the butt if he hadn't scurried into the atrium quickly enough. No, his background was not heroic, and neither Iskandia nor Cofahre wanted to let him forget it.

He walked between the potted trees and vining plants, their

limbs stretching toward the glass ceiling, the blue sky visible above. There was already somebody sitting at the wrought-iron table, its surface covered with a forest green tablecloth embellished with leaves stitched in golden thread. His mood lifted immediately.

Caslin "Raptor" Ahn stood as he approached, her uniform pressed, her boots shined, and her short hair flattened from her army cap, which now rested on the table in front of her. She had returned to the military and Wolf Squadron and wore her lieutenant's insignia once more. Her face was somber—she had just started smiling again after Apex's death, but then she lost her commander. Still, she greeted him with a hug.

"I wasn't expecting you." Tolemek glanced toward the trees, suspecting a few more guards stood on the outskirts of the atrium, hidden by fountains and foliage. He gave her a quick kiss before taking a seat next to the one she had claimed at the far end of the table from where the king sat for these meetings.

"I'm not surprised to see you. I was told this was about a new mission. We'll probably need knockout grenades and healing goos."

Tolemek grimaced, fearing his help would be requested not for an enticing new mission but for a very unappealing war. The rumors floating around the capital said that the Cofah were threatening to launch a full-scale invasion to avenge the airships that had been destroyed the week before. The empire might not be Tolemek's home anymore, but his soul ached every time he had to fight against his own people. He'd been a part of the Cofah army once, and whatever orders the emperor issued, the men were just men, no more evil or bad than their Iskandian counterparts.

"You're not pleased by the opportunity to share your goos?" Cas asked.

"I would be tickled to share Healing Salve Number Seven with anyone who wanted it. Somehow, I doubt that's what the king called me here about. He always wants weapons."

"If the Cofah would stop attacking us, maybe he'd want something less dire." Cas sat down again, clasped his hand, and lowered her voice. "I know you don't want to fight your own people. Maybe this will be about something else."

Tolemek grunted dubiously. Cas, known for her marksmanship, wouldn't likely have been invited to this meeting if the king had anything peaceful planned. He was surprised she was the only one from her squadron here. Tolemek would have expected General Ort or whoever had taken over Wolf Squadron after Zirkander had been promoted.

"Were you the only one of your pilot people invited to this meeting?" Tolemek eyed the table. It could seat more than a dozen, but there weren't any place settings or anything to hint as to how many people would be at this meeting. It couldn't just be him and Cas, unless this had something to do with the bounty Emperor Salatak had put on Tolemek's head. But that wouldn't involve a "mission" for Cas.

"Yes. Captains Crash and Blazer seemed envious. I'm not sure if Colonel Madiken was envious. He's hard to read. He got transferred over from Cougar Squadron on the East Coast. I don't know any of those pilots well."

"Is he the one who took over for..." Tolemek spread his hand. He was trying to be circumspect with Cas in regard to Zirkander's death. Besides, he would have found it difficult to be blunt. If he was honest with himself, he would admit that even he missed Zirkander. Aside from Cas and Sardelle, there weren't many people here who went out of their way to talk to him, and Sardelle hadn't been around much since Zirkander's death. Cas had been a more frequent visitor of late, fortunately, but with Tylie still studying with and staying with Sardelle, Tolemek's work days and evenings had been quiet. Lonely even. He ought to go out to visit them, but it felt strange going to see Sardelle without Zirkander around.

"Yes," Cas said. "We didn't have anyone with enough rank to lead the squadron, and nobody ready to promote into the position. At least General Ort didn't think so."

"Ah."

Cas rested her hand on his, running her thumb along his knuckles. "I walked past a house for rent on the way here. It had an upstairs and a downstairs, with bedrooms on each end. We could have guests over, and it would still be... private."

"Oh," Tolemek said neutrally.

He did not want to discourage Cas's interest in making more permanent arrangements with him, since neither her room in the barracks nor the studio the king had arranged for him was ideal for two, especially two who liked to engage in amorous activities in private. When Tylie visited, such activities were effectively squelched. But the idea of committing to a lease or buying a property made him twitch. Even though he adored Cas, he hadn't stopped thinking of Iskandia as temporary. A place to live for now.

He had to admit that he had speculated about taking Cas off to explore the world one day, something he might have brought up during the weeks after she had quit the army if she had been around more then. He eyed her shiny rank pins, accepting that it was less of a possibility now. He couldn't ask her to quit and leave her country for his sake.

"I could show it to you later," she went on, watching his eyes, a hint of wariness in her own. She didn't want to push. "Or we could look for something else together. Only if you're interested, of course."

"How long was the lease?"

"This one required two years, I believe."

With great effort, Tolemek kept his eyes from bulging out of their sockets. Twenty-four months. Did he want to commit to twenty-four months in Iskandia? What if another assassin came looking for him? He would hate to leave Cas to pay for a house by herself. As far as he knew, her wealthy father kept his wealth to himself, so she had only her lieutenant's salary.

"Perhaps we could look for something with a shorter term," he suggested.

She smiled and squeezed his hand. "I would be open to that. It would be nice to have a place that we could make entirely our own, with elements of both of us in it."

"Like artwork on the walls made from used bullets and volumetric flasks?"

She swatted him. He probably deserved it.

A thump sounded, the door opening. Tolemek leaned back to see who would join them next. A single set of boots thudded lightly behind the trees, so it wasn't the king. When he arrived, at least two bodyguards would escort him.

Captain Kaika strolled into view, also wearing her uniform.

"Who's ready for a new mission?" she asked, giving them a cheerful wave before plopping into a chair near the head of the table.

Cas frowned slightly, as if finding the cheer inappropriate. Kaika hadn't known Zirkander that long. His death probably hadn't left a giant hole in her life.

"I wasn't aware that I was someone who was sent on missions." Tolemek waved to indicate his lack of a uniform.

"Please, you've been on almost every mission I've been on this year."

"Captain," Cas said, "do you know what this is about?"

"Yup." She smiled at them.

"Are you going to tell us?"

"Nope." Her smile broadened.

"Because you enjoy being mysterious or because you've been ordered not to?" Tolemek asked.

"It was more of a suggestion than say a royal order, but I can take a hint."

The door thumped open again, and a guard said, "That way, sir."

Sir. Still not the king. Someone who got more respect than Tolemek, but that wasn't unusual.

He, Cas, and Kaika turned to look at the newcomer, another officer in uniform, this one wearing more rank than anyone else in the atrium. A colonel. Tolemek had seen the markings often enough to recognize them. He did not, however, recognize the man or the name on his jacket. Quataldo. The officer appeared to be bald under his uniform cap, or close to it, but he probably wasn't much older than Zirkander had been. Early forties. None of Zirkander's humor showed in his blue eyes. The man had plain features with a saturnine turn to his mouth. There was something akin to a dancer's grace to his movements, even if he appeared hesitant here.

Cas and Kaika stood together and saluted. The colonel returned the gesture. "At ease." He had a soft voice.

Kaika had *been* at ease, with her boots up on the table. Both she and Cas appeared much more at ease than the new fellow, who eyed the birds flapping about in the treetops like a man who had never been here before. He considered the open seats and chose the one next to Kaika. He didn't have pilot wings on his uniform, so he wasn't one of Cas's bosses. Tolemek looked to Kaika, wondering if this might be another elite forces officer, someone the king had selected to lead the mission. Remembering Therrik, Tolemek grimaced. That hadn't gone well.

"You needn't look so morose, sir," Kaika said, flipping a hand toward Quataldo. "You'll like it. I bet you'll find some eggs."

"Eggs?" Tolemek mouthed to Cas.

She shrugged at him.

"You have previous knowledge of this mission, Captain Kaika?" Quataldo tilted his head. "I was told—I was led to believe that nobody had been briefed yet."

"Were you?" She smiled. "Huh."

Tolemek had heard rumors that Kaika had started a relationship with King Angulus. He wasn't much for listening to gossip or assuming anything from it, but he now wondered if it was true. Her boots went back up on the table. She certainly appeared comfortable around the castle.

A throat cleared by the door. "His Royal Highness has arrived."

Chairs scraped on the flagstone patio as everyone scooted them back. Kaika's boots came down from the table. Tolemek stood along with the others, though he never felt certain of what he was supposed to do when Angulus entered. The officers saluted. A civilian or a soldier out of uniform was supposed to genuflect, but that presumed they were subjects. Nobody had yet suggested to Tolemek that he should become a subject, and he was relieved by that. So far, he had been treated well enough by the king, even if his reception by the average Iskandian was lacking, and he had a fantastic laboratory to work in. Still, if not for Cas and the fact that Sardelle was instructing his sister, he doubted he would be on these shores.

Four bodyguards accompanied the king into the atrium, then disappeared into the foliage at a flick of his hand to observe discreetly. Angulus strode to the table, clad in unadorned wool and cotton clothing, nothing like the embellished robes he wore when he addressed the people, but his height and broad soldiers gave him a presence that conveyed his position even in the simple attire.

He walked around Kaika and Quataldo's side of the table, pausing beside her shoulder. He touched a smudge on the tablecloth where her boots had been.

"What is this?" he asked.

Kaika made a show of bending forward to study it. "In the army, we call that dirt, Sire."

"It wasn't on my table this morning."

"No? It probably fell." She lifted her gaze toward the vines tickling the glass ceiling. "From a plant."

"Does that happen often in the army? Dirt falling from plants?"

"You never know what will get knocked off when those dragon fliers are zipping around in the sky."

Angulus grunted and moved to the head of the table. Kaika's grin never faded. Angulus was harder to read, but his eyes had held an amused gleam as they spoke. Perhaps the rumors were right. When Kaika sat down, she did not put her boots back on the table.

"Tolemek," Angulus said as soon as he sat down.

Tolemek, his hands still on the armrests, paused. He had assumed he had been brought in as an adviser and had not expected to be involved in the conversation from the start. "Sire?"

"I understand your emperor has been hiring assassins to kill you."

A throat cleared again, and a servant brought in a tray bearing pastries, glasses of water, and mugs of coffee. While she arranged the treats in front of everyone, Tolemek settled more fully in his chair. He wasn't surprised the king had this information—

after the airship battle, General Ort must have included it in his report.

"That's true, Sire," Tolemek said as the servant departed. He grabbed his freshly delivered coffee mug, feeling the need for a bracing substance.

"Pardon my bluntness," Angulus said, "but I grow less and less patient with small talk as the years pass. I also have more meetings later. One with the Cofah diplomat." His lips thinned. "Absurd title for the man since all he does is deliver threats."

"It's fine, Sire. I don't like small talk either. I also don't consider him *my* emperor anymore."

"No? Good." Angulus threaded his fingers together and rested his hands on the tablecloth. "I have a new plan, and I thought you might be willing to assist, since it could solve both of our problems."

Cas shifted her weight. Unease settled in the pit of Tolemek's stomach. He did not consider himself an imperial subject anymore, but that didn't mean he wanted to join in on some assassination plot.

"Are you targeting the emperor himself, Sire?" Colonel Quataldo asked.

"Is that a mission you'd be keen to take on, Colonel?" Angulus responded.

Quataldo brooded down at his coffee mug. "I would be willing, of course, if you assigned it. To get close to him might take a better operative than me. Since he's not a beloved figure, as I understand it, and he's ruled for nearly twenty years, his security must be impressive."

"Yes, and he rarely leaves his palace, my reports tell me. Except when his youngest daughter is being married off in a foreign land."

"Because he's especially fond of that youngest daughter?" Cas asked. "He has fifteen or twenty legitimate children, doesn't he?"

"Not quite that many," Angulus said, "but to your point, I believe the alliance he wishes is perhaps more important than the marriage itself."

"When is this wedding happening?" Quataldo asked.

"Very soon. I wished our intelligence people had learned of it sooner, but it was fortuitous that they discovered the details at all. I wasn't invited, oddly."

"Imagine," Tolemek murmured.

Angulus looked around the table, holding each person's gaze as he shared his thoughts. "It's not an assassination I have in mind. I know it has not always been the case, but I should like for the history writers of the future to look back and acknowledge that Iskandia maintained... if not the moral high ground, then at least that we acted with honor. I have tried to do that since I took over for my father, but we can no longer simply think of defending ourselves. The Cofah never grow weary of trying to annex us, and this emperor is even more determined than previous ones. I have weapons now that I can launch from our ships that would devastate the Cofah continent." Angulus nodded to Tolemek, who had seen the king's rockets when he had helped move the contents of the secret facility that had created them. "That would be even less honorable, though, as it would destroy far more civilian lives than military or government ones. I have always considered those weapons a last resort."

Tolemek was relieved to hear it. "If you don't intend to assassinate him, then what?"

"I plan to send in a pair of elite forces soldiers—" Angulus spread his hand toward Kaika and Quataldo, "—delivered by some of our best pilots—" his hand shifted toward Cas, "—to kidnap the man while he attends his daughter's wedding."

"Kidnap the emperor?" Tolemek asked. "To what end?"

"Exile. He'll live out his life in a remote prison that only a handful of trusted Iskandians and I know about."

"Will it be a lighthouse?" Kaika asked.

Angulus gave her a sour look. "Something less austere. Definitely less moldy. I want him out of the way and where nobody will find him—that's the only requirement. I'm basing this mission on the assumption—and Tolemek, perhaps as a former imperial subject, you can let me know your opinion on this—that if we're successful in getting away with him and eluding immediate pursuit, his people and his heirs won't try that hard to find him."

"There are seven sons and four daughters," Tolemek said, correcting Cas's count, "with the oldest prince being in his forties. I imagine he's ready for his time to rule, but I don't know what kind of ruler he would be. I never followed the gossip or news about the royal court. I do know he's one of the less conspicuous heirs. He's married with children of his own."

The idea of kidnapping Emperor Salatak seemed crazy and impossible, but it intrigued Tolemek nonetheless. Having the man out of power could get rid of his bounty problem. Also, perhaps the emperor's eldest son would be less aware of Tolemek's past crimes and less likely to want retribution for them.

"I have a full report on the heir," Angulus said. "He's reputed to be a mathematician and an inventor—I've seen some of his designs for scientific apparatuses and was most intrigued by the promise of a non-leaking ballpoint pen." Angulus wryly looked at ink on the tips of his fingers. "While I don't know if he'll be friendly to Iskandia, especially if we kidnap his father, he seems to be a reasonable man overall. Perhaps we'll have better luck negotiating and reaching an accord with a reasonable man. Also, if we succeed here and set a precedent, future emperors may regard us as more formidable and dangerous."

Cas lifted a finger. "Sire, I'm certain you've considered this, but even with elite forces, getting to him will be close to impossible. He won't travel without legions of troops surrounding him."

"No, it won't be easy. This may be the only opportunity we have for some time. I have to believe there *will* be opportunities. His daughter is marrying a shaman who rules over the city of Tildar Dem in Dakrovia. The emperor will have to travel by airship or sea vessel to get there. Such craft are vulnerable to the elements—and our fliers."

"What if the sorceress is with him? Or another one? We don't even know how she came to be in our era yet, right? Couldn't there be more like her? Will Sardelle be coming?"

"I'm going to talk to her this afternoon—she actually requested an appointment with me." Angulus met Tolemek's eyes. "I did have the thought that *Tylie* might go along."

"My sister? On a dangerous kidnapping mission?" Tolemek

gaped at him. "She's not a trained combatant. She's not a trained sorceress yet either. She's—"

"The one who commands Phelistoth."

Tolemek slumped back in his seat. Of course. The king wanted the *dragon* to help.

"She doesn't *command* him, Sire. They're just..." Tolemek groped for a word. He didn't know how to describe that relationship. He wasn't sure he entirely understood it. "Friends."

"Nobody else here has a dragon friend," Angulus said dryly.

"Sardelle talked one into helping us at the outpost." Granted, Tolemek hadn't seen or heard anything about that dragon since they had left the mountains. That might have been a one-time deal. Or maybe Sardelle had told the dragon she didn't want to be his high priestess, and their relationship had ended after that.

"I would be most pleased to send two dragons to kidnap the emperor," Angulus said, "but I'm hoping for one, especially since two of the other gold dragons that showed up at the outpost have since been reported over Cofahre territory. Being nuisances, is what I've heard so far, but the emperor may try to strike a deal with one or both of them. I'd like to attack while we have the dragon advantage, if I may presume that we have it." The wry twist to his lips suggested he wasn't presuming so much as hoping and not with a great deal of conviction. "We're only going to get one chance to take Emperor Salatak by surprise."

"We?" Kaika asked. "Are you coming along?"

Quataldo made a choking sound at her audacity.

"I was using the royal we," Angulus said. "You've seen my grappling skills. I wouldn't qualify to be on your team."

"You grapple better than you think, Sire," Kaika said, a glint in her eyes.

"Colonel Quataldo will lead the mission." Angulus locked eyes with the officer, who nodded firmly. He shifted his gaze to Cas. "I trust I don't need to say that I expect Quataldo to arrive in Dakrovia with the pilots, not to get dumped alongside the road before you leave the country."

Quataldo's eyebrows flew upward.

"Relax, sir," Kaika said. "You're not nearly as unpleasant of a commander as Colonel Therrik. As long as you don't threaten the pilots—or our ex-pirate scientist—they shouldn't have any reason to disgorge you."

"Comforting," he murmured.

Angulus hadn't stopped looking at Cas. He didn't think *she'd* had anything to do with Zirkander's usurpation of that previous mission, did he? Cas didn't break rules or take matters into her own hands. Tolemek opened his mouth, intending to say as much, but she spoke first.

"I wouldn't think to arrange any such thing, Sire," Cas said, "but I'm confused. I'm only a lieutenant. Why am I here representing pilots instead of one of my superior officers?" She looked around, as if expecting other officers to wander out of the foliage.

Tolemek could guess at least part of the reason. Angulus wanted her on the mission to ensure *he* wouldn't be tempted to stray or succumb to threats against his family. Since his parents still lived in the empire, Tolemek admitted that was a valid concern. He wouldn't want them to be harmed as a result of his actions. He hoped he did not end up in a position where he had to choose between them and Cas.

The king's gaze flicked toward him, as if he heard and acknowledged the thoughts, but came back to rest on Cas. "I want your guns on the incursion team," Angulus said, "so you were going to be assigned, regardless, but I will leave choosing the other pilots to you. I'm less familiar with the rest of your Wolf Squadron teammates and your new commander. I asked General Ort what he thought, and he said anyone could fly the elite forces troops over there. I'm not sure he imagined his pilots being a part of the action." Angulus smiled. "I, however, like to plan for the worst. I would have given the job to Zirkander—despite his proclivity for getting rid of mission commanders he's not fond of—but he's obviously not here, and I know he considered you his protégé and would have trusted your decisions in this."

Cas's eyes widened. Tolemek wondered if *she* knew Zirkander had considered her his protégé. She looked down, blinking a few times, and he caught the glint of moisture in her eyes. He rested his hand on her forearm.

"If you pick higher-ranking officers, you'll follow their orders, of course, with Colonel Quataldo at the top of the chain of command, but it's up to you if you want to do that. I understand some of the other lieutenants in your squadron have some unique skills."

"Yes, Sire," Cas said quietly. "Dakrovia, you said? Jungles and swamps, right? Duck would be useful if we need to survive out there. How many people do we need?"

"Pilots to fly Tolemek, Kaika, Quataldo, and Sardelle, if I can talk her into it, and you'll need an open seat for your passenger. And Tylie—"

Tolemek's head came up. "Is not going, Sire. She's too young. She can't go into combat."

"Even with a dragon to protect her?"

"There's no guarantee Phelistoth will go for it. He's a *Cofah* dragon. He doesn't even like Iskandians."

"I suppose Tylie would ride on his back, if they were to go, so she wouldn't require a flier."

Tolemek felt his nostrils flare. Was Angulus planning to talk to her behind his back? That was *not* going to happen.

"Put together your team, Ahn."

"Yes, Sire."

"Tolemek, you will go, won't you?" Angulus asked. "I realize I'm presuming. I can order the soldiers, but you're not under any obligation to obey me. You did sign a contract to deliver healing potions and knockout grenades, but I think your team would be more comfortable if you went along personally."

Quataldo's eyebrows twitched, but he did not object.

"They're salves," Tolemek muttered. "Not potions."

He rubbed his face. Was Angulus truly trying to recruit him at the same time as irking him with this insistence that Tylie go? Maybe there was a reason that he hadn't been able to negotiate a peace with Cofahre.

"I'll go. Tylie won't."

"Of course." Angulus did not appear concerned by his half victory. Maybe because he still planned to talk to Tylie himself.

Tolemek would have to speak with her first, to make sure she didn't volunteer for this, thinking it some grand adventure.

"The wedding is in four days," Angulus said. "You'll leave in the morning."

"Yes, Sire," the officers said while Tolemek gaped. Why were these things always done on such short notice? Did everyone think it was a simple matter to make enough supplies to take along?

"Dismissed," Angulus said.

Cas tugged on Tolemek's hair. He was the last one sitting at the table. Sighing, he stood. They walked out together behind Kaika and Quataldo, and she linked her arm in his.

"You look pleased about all this," he observed as a pair of guards fell in behind them to make sure they headed out instead of wandering around the castle for a private tour.

Cas seemed to have gotten over being stunned about being referred to as Zirkander's protégé and now had a gleam in her eyes.

"Relieved is the word," she said. "When I saw that I was the only pilot in there, I thought he would want me to take the awful sword to wield again. Especially when he started talking about dragons and a shaman fiancé. If all he wants is for me to pick some good people and go along to guard the rear after the kidnapping, I'm relieved."

"Where *is* that sword?" Tolemek asked as they walked out of the building and crossed through the courtyard, where landscapers trimmed the manicured lawn and flowering hedges. "The last I saw of it was at Galmok Mountain."

"Ort left it up there with Therrik, since the sorceress was believed to still be in the mountains and likely up to mischief. Also, he wasn't sure if more dragons would come for different artifacts. Sardelle mentioned that there were others, though now that most of the levels of mines have been collapsed, even a dragon would have a hard time getting at them."

Tolemek grimaced at the idea of Therrik with Kasandral, a sword happy to slay anyone with a smidgen of dragon blood. Still, if Tolemek, Sardelle, and Tylie weren't up in the outpost and the only possible people for Therrik to attack were enemies, he supposed it was in capable hands.

"I'm not positive it's still up there," Cas said, "but I'm hoping it is. I prefer sniper rifles to swords."

"Who doesn't?" He wrapped his arm around her shoulders, some of the tension fading from him as they passed through the castle gate and headed along the cobblestone drive that led down the hill and back into the city—and to his lab.

"It won't take me long to pack and get my people ready. Are you going to be up all night mixing goos? Or shall I stop by?"

"Yes and yes. Mixing *goo* is lonely work."

"I noted that you didn't object to being turned into a pharmacy when the king was doing it," Cas said, "not the way you used to when General Zirkander did it."

"The king *pays* me to be a pharmacy. Or whatever else he needs. And he supplies my lab. Chemicals, books, tools, state-of-the-art equipment."

"It sounds like he's courting you effectively."

Tolemek snorted. "I guess he is. So long as he leaves Tylie out of this."

"You don't think Tylie would like to help get rid of the person who issued the bounty on her brother's head?"

Tolemek halted, not caring that they were in the middle of the street and that a steam carriage was clanking in their direction. "Don't tell me *you* think she should go along."

Cas lifted her hands. "I understand your concerns and agree that she shouldn't be in a combat position, but I also think she's safer on Phelistoth's back than anywhere else in the world. This mission might be more likely to succeed with a dragon's help, especially if..."

"What?"

Cas pulled him to the side of the road so the carriage could pass without rolling over them. "I'm not sure if Sardelle will go. The last time I talked to her, she was very determined to go back to the Ice Blades. I don't think she's going to give up until she finds Zirkander's body."

"But that could wait until we got back."

"Could it? If she thinks he's injured out there somewhere, she'll be worried about delaying."

Tolemek stuffed a hand in his pocket and stared at the ancient cobblestones. "*You* don't think he's alive, do you?"

"No, but I'm not his—" She groped in the air with one hand. "Let's just say that if it was you, I'd want to make sure too."

"Hm." Even though they were musing about his death, he found this proof that she cared, and would perhaps even care to the exclusion of reason, heartening. He wrapped his arm around her shoulders again and steered them back onto the road, this time walking to the side so they were not in danger of being run over. "I'm glad to hear that."

"Does that mean you'll talk to Tylie about coming?"

He grunted. That wasn't what he had been agreeing to at all. "Maybe I'll talk to *Phelistoth* about coming. Tylie could stay home and study."

"Have you spoken with him often?"

"Not... often." As far as he knew, Tylie tended to be everyone's intermediary for the dragon. Oh, Phelistoth spoke from time to time, especially when he was in human form, but he always gave the impression that it was tedious for him to have to do so.

"That should prove interesting," Cas said.

"Yes," he murmured. As they continued into the city, he dwelled upon what sort of bribe he might offer to a dragon to help with a kidnapping.

Chapter 2

THE GUARDS LED SARDELLE INTO the atrium, a part of the castle that usually soothed her nerves, thanks to its gurgling fountains and chirping birds. This time, she wasn't in the mood to be soothed. She twisted her hand in the sash that wrapped her waist, acting as a belt for the elegant blue dress she had chosen for this meeting. She wanted to look professional, even if the king never seemed to require much in the way of ceremony or formality. She planned to return to the Ice Blades one way or another, but it would be much easier to go with a flier.

Or a dragon.

Find me a dragon, and I'll consider that. I haven't even seen Phelistoth since we returned.

No, he's probably cuddling with that crystal. When Bhrava Saruth lets him.

"Sardelle?" came Angulus's voice, almost hesitant. That was unlike him.

She followed the sound to a wide wall fountain that occupied the far corner of the atrium. He sat on the rim, goldfish darting about in the shallows of the pool behind him. She sensed bodyguards in the room, but they were being discreet and stood far enough away to allow a private conversation. Did he have something in mind that he wanted to discuss? When she had sent a message requesting an appointment, she hadn't mentioned what *she* wished to discuss.

"Please sit." Angulus gestured to the ledge.

Sardelle shifted the material of her dress so nothing would dangle in the water and perched beside him, leaving a few feet between them, not wanting to presume any intimacy. She had expected to be led to his office or to the throne room rather than this serene setting.

"I'm glad you're here." He leaned over and rested his hand on the back of hers for a moment. "I'm sorry that Zirk—Ridge—didn't make it."

"Thank you, Sire."

He leaned back, withdrawing his hand. "We have about an hour until the council heads start arriving, and I'll be swamped with attending to their needs—excuse me, listening to their wisdom—for the next week. There's something I'd like to ask you—two things, actually—but tell me what you need first."

"Yes, Sire. I want to go back and do a more thorough search for Ridge. It's possible that he's injured somewhere and that we've all abandoned him. I talked to General Ort, and he said all of the flier squadrons are occupied and that he can't spare anyone. I know you keep a flier or two here, for your personal use. I was wondering if I could borrow one if I could find a suitable pilot." She thought about saying she could figure out how to fly the craft herself, with magic if not with skill, but she wasn't sure that would make him more likely to lend it to her.

Less likely, I should think. You know even less about machines than I do.

That's not true.

You didn't read all those scintillating books in the prison library while you were knocked out for three hundred years.

"Judging by the reports—by what General Ort reported—it's unlikely that he could have survived," Angulus said, his tone gentle.

"Yes, Sire. Unlikely, but not impossible. And then there's the sorceress."

Angulus's eyebrows rose. "Yes?"

"Jaxi sensed her in the area right before the other dragons showed up. We think—"

Oh no, don't include me in this. You think.

"I'm not sure what to think, Sire," Sardelle admitted, "but if Eversong was nearby, she adds an unknown factor to the equation. Also, it might be useful to locate her, get a feel for what she's up to." So long as Sardelle could *survive* locating her.

Their last confrontation had left her devoid of ideas as to how to defeat the woman. In truth, she only mentioned her in the hope that Angulus would be more likely to provide a flier.

"I won't deny that," he said, "but I have had other matters on my mind this week. I was going to ask if you would go with Tolemek, Lieutenant Ahn, and Captain Kaika on a mission to kidnap the Cofah emperor."

Sardelle stared at him, not certain she had heard him correctly. He'd said it so casually, as if emperors were kidnapped all the time. "I—now, Sire?"

"They're leaving in the morning. We have an opportunity to catch him out of the empire, a rare one. We have to act swiftly to exploit it."

Sardelle stared down at the fish darting under the rippling water of the pool. Even without hearing the details, she judged this mission to be something that would take many days, if not weeks. "Sire, I would normally agree to help, but if Ridge is injured somewhere out there, he may have very limited time."

She made herself look up, though she was afraid she would catch a pitying look in his eyes, the same one Cas had given her, the one that said that it was sad that she'd lost the love of her life but that it was misguided of her to believe he might still be alive. And yes, that was exactly the look Angulus gave her. She didn't need to brush his mind with her senses to tell what he was thinking.

"Sire, I chose to stay down in the outpost when they went into the air. I—I didn't factor in the wind and the storm, so I didn't realize how far away the battle would take them. I thought I could protect the fort *and* Ridge and the others at the same time. But by the time I made it over to them, it was too late. If I'd gone up with them, maybe I could have done something. Maybe—" She swallowed and looked down at the fish again. She'd thought she could get through this without falling apart. She wanted him to help her because of reason, not out of pity or because she was weeping into his fountain.

"I know what it's like to make mistakes," Angulus said softly. "Trust me. Though I'm not sure you made one. I think

Ridge would agree that protecting hundreds of people is more important than protecting one."

"Jaxi didn't agree," she muttered.

"Your sword has spoken to me a few times. She seems... young."

Young? What does that mean? Is that an insult? Do I need to incinerate his nose hairs?

"She's six hundred years old, Sire. And passionate."

"Hm." This time, he was the one to gaze down at the fish. He dragged his finger through the water. The fish must have thought that implied feeding time, because a school of them formed and came to the surface, lips pursing eagerly. Angulus snorted and reached over to a shelf beside the fountain. He pulled off a canister, opened it, and tossed in some flakes of seaweed or whatever it was goldfish ate. "I think you could be a great help on this other mission, but I understand that your heart calls you another way. You're not a soldier—or a king—so you're allowed to choose what your heart wants over any duty imposed upon you by others." A wistful smile flashed across his face, the expression gone almost as soon as it formed. "And if you believe Ridge might still be alive, then I can't help but wonder about that too. Losing him is a great blow. Even if I haven't always approved of his methods of doing his duty, there's no doubt that he always *did* do his duty, and that he and his squadron brought down more enemies than anyone else in the country."

Sardelle leaned toward him, hoping this meant he would give her what she wished.

"It would also be useful for me to know where that sorceress is, even if we don't have the means to destroy her currently." Angulus had been dropping pinches of fish food into the fountain, but he paused, his hand dangling. "Actually, we might." He looked at her, his eyes narrowing.

"The sword?" Sardelle guessed. "I can't wield it, Sire."

She almost pointed out that Cas could and that she could be her pilot in this, but if she was heading out on another mission, they would have to find someone else.

"Wait here a moment, please." Angulus returned the canister

to the ledge and stood. "I want to show you something."

High priestess! sounded a cry in her mind.

Sardelle was so startled that she nearly pitched backward into the fountain. Fortunately, Angulus had already disappeared through the potted trees and rosebushes and didn't notice.

Bhrava Saruth? she asked, though she recognized the voice, a voice she hadn't heard since the day the dragon had helped with the search for Ridge.

Bhrava Saruth, the god, yes! I have been looking many places for you. You left your mountain fortress.

Her fortress? Hardly that. *Yes, I live down here most of the time.*

In a castle? Yes, that is fitting for my high priestess. Look at all the people in this city. So many! There were never so many in one place in my time. Do they worship another god? Could we convert them to worship me?

I—uhm. We need to talk about that, Bhrava Saruth. Sardelle looked in the direction the king had gone, wondering how long she had until he returned. This might require a lengthy discussion, and what if she irked the dragon with her admissions? She didn't want to risk bringing down his ire on the castle or the town.

What, you don't think he'll appreciate that you lied to him?

I didn't lie, Jaxi. I just let him think... things. And I did give him what he sought. Sardelle shifted her mind's focus, imagining the dragon, though she wasn't sure where he was. Somewhere in the city? Outside of it? The general populace did not know about dragons yet, so she hoped he wasn't perched on a clock tower somewhere. Wherever he was, he was beyond her range to sense, and she wouldn't have been able to speak to him if he hadn't been reaching out to her. *Were you able to get any useful information out of the crystal, Bhrava Saruth?*

I have learned some things about my kind.

Sardelle waited for him to explain further. He did not.

Apparently, gods don't share all of their secrets with their priestesses, Jaxi said. *Maybe if you suggest that you don't just live in the castle but that you own it and it could be turned into a shrine for him.*

Funny, Jaxi. A fresh idea came to mind. Perhaps she didn't need to borrow a pilot and a flier for her search. The thought of asking the dragon to carry her around was daunting, and she didn't know if she could give what he might ask for in return, but perhaps she could make another deal with him. She just couldn't let him think she would be his servant or mouthpiece—whatever he imagined a high priestess might be. *Bhrava Saruth? I was trained to be a healer. I wasn't raised to be much of a theist either. I'm not qualified to be a priestess, high or otherwise.*

We all must start somewhere. You will be an excellent high priestess. I was not born a god, you know.

Imagine that, Jaxi thought.

Sardelle ignored her. *How did you become one?*

I came into my power and gained many worshippers.

Images jumped into Sardelle's head with such vibrant intensity that she had to grip the edge of her fountain seat with both hands to brace herself, lest she fall over. She saw Bhrava Saruth in dragon form, flying over a huge gathering of yurts and tents stretching along the grasslands of northern Iskandoth, the ocean crashing against the high walls of the fjords in the distance. Then he landed and transformed into a handsome golden-haired man and lounged on a stone throne carved into a huge boulder. Men and women limped, slouched, and hobbled to him, some assisting others or carrying ailing children. They set down gifts such as dried meat, furs, and baskets of fruit, then he stretched out a hand and touched the heads of the injured or sick. When they walked away, they stood straighter and appeared haler.

You healed people? Sardelle asked.

Of course! A god must take care of his worshippers. I healed dragons, too, but humans are so much more appreciative. Adoring.

The next image he showed involved a pair of women showing their adoration in a rather naked manner that left Sardelle blushing fiercely. If the vision was to be believed, Bhrava Saruth had been enthusiastic in returning his worshippers' adoration.

I gathered so many of the clansmen and women in the area that my contemporaries grew jealous. They thought I was trying to amass an army to use against them. I had no interest in war. Only love. The others could not understand. They sought great power and thought every other dragon was the same. Such ignorant fools! They condemned me and imprisoned me in that cavern, as if my actions were criminal.

Do you believe him? Jaxi asked.

I'm not going to forget that Morishtomaric lied to Angulus, Sardelle told her. She could, however, imagine Bhrava Saruth basking in the adoration of worshippers. Whether he had been as benevolent as his vision implied, she could not know.

I am a very good god, the dragon said earnestly. *If you are my priestess, I will treat you well. You will live a long and healthy life. I will bless your offspring, and they will become powerful sorcerers.*

Offspring. Sardelle's throat tightened as Ridge's face filled her mind. He might have been mildly horrified at the idea of powerful sorcerers for children, but he would have found a way to accept them, as he had her. And he would have been a good father, despite his reservations on the subject. Even if he hadn't been able to see it, she had.

That is the one you lost, yes?

Yes, Sardelle thought numbly. *I wish to go back to the mountains, to search and try to find... We never found his body. I am hoping we were mistaken and that he might still live.*

I will take you, Bhrava Saruth said brightly.

You will? She expected him to try to make a deal with her—after all, she had been thinking of making a deal with him.

Of course. You are my only high priestess so far. My only worshipper in this new era. A mournful emotion not unlike a keening sound filled her head. *I must start again, but demands on my godliness are few right now. I can take you wherever you wish.*

Bet you didn't know you were his worshipper already, Jaxi thought.

Ssh. If he's willing to give us a ride, I'll kneel in a temple and light a candle.

Jaxi snorted. *He may expect more than that, given the gifts that his past followers gave him. You better make sure Ridge is truly gone before draping your naked self across a dragon's lap.*

Sardelle's cheeks warmed, and she did her best to push away the memories Bhrava Saruth had shared. Jaxi was right, though, in that she should make sure certain expectations weren't set up.

Unless you want *expectations*, Jaxi said. *Dragons are reputed to be magnificent lovers.*

That's what the romance novels from that time say?
Absolutely. And a romance novel wouldn't lead you astray.
Oh, certainly not. One does wonder how such arrogant creatures—that's the adjective you always use, Jaxi—could be magnificent lovers.
Magic.
What exactly do you expect from a high priestess, Bhrava Saruth? Sardelle found herself curious, even if she had no intention of applying for the job.

I need an intermediary. So many humans flee from a dragon. I need someone to tell them that I won't destroy their villages or slay them. I am benevolent. And magnificent!

You would think his magnificence would be self-evident, Jaxi said.

Your sword is very mouthy, Bhrava Saruth observed.

Sardelle snorted, not surprised he heard everything Jaxi said. Phelistoth had proven himself capable of reading her thoughts, even when she had her mental barriers up, and Morishtomaric had also pried.

I could melt her, and we could find you a different soulblade, the dragon offered. *A respectful one who agrees with your wisdom.*

Jaxi fumed silently, the pommel of her blade heating enough that Sardelle felt it through her clothes. It seemed to smoke in the humid air next to the fountain. Jaxi did not say anything, however, perhaps feeling constrained now that she knew her words weren't as secret as she thought.

I'm fond of her, Bhrava Saruth. Jaxi challenges me and makes me laugh. I would be bored by someone who agreed with everything I said. You don't expect your followers to agree with everything you say, do you?

So long as they love me, they may say whatever they wish. But the most adoring and least mouthy ones get my attention first.

I'll keep that in mind.

But I will always make time for my high priestess. When do you wish to leave for the journey to the mountains?

Sardelle closed her eyes in relief. She didn't know why Bhrava Saruth had bothered seeking her out—surely, he could have found a "priestess" out in the Ice Blades or perhaps among the clansmen who still lived in small communities up north—

but to know that she could leave soon to search for Ridge... She didn't even know how to express her gratitude.

He looked like he enjoyed tongues. Jaxi must have gotten over her silent fuming.

Not quite what I had in mind.

That's good. Do you realize he could be your distant ancestor? If he was as fecund as that vision suggested, half of the Referatu sorcerers who lived in our time could have been his descendants.

If so, he could be your ancestor too.

I'll point that fact out to him the next time he threatens to melt me.

Bhrava Saruth? Sardelle heard someone coming, so she hurried to finish the dialogue. *I need to gather a few things, and I can be ready to go in the morning.* She was tempted to say that they could go that night, but it wouldn't take a dragon long to make that journey, and searching those mountains by starlight would be difficult. She didn't want to risk missing Ridge in the dark, especially since he wouldn't have an aura to sense if he truly had passed on. A new wave of bleakness came over her at the notion that she might simply be going out to search for his remains.

"Sardelle?" Angulus returned to sit beside her, a folder in his hand.

She lifted her head, trying to push aside her grief. As long as there was still hope, it was too soon to mourn. "Yes, Sire?"

"I know this has been hard for you. I'm sorry."

"Thank you."

"Will you forgive me if I assign you another mission?"

She frowned warily at him. She had made it clear she couldn't join the others until she found Ridge—or laid his soul to rest.

"You already hinted that you would be open to it. As long as you're going out there, I would love to have that sorceress killed or removed from my land."

Kings are so needy, Jaxi observed.

"I could certainly try to pinpoint her location, Sire. More than that..." Sardelle paused. If she had Bhrava Saruth with her, then it might be possible to "remove" Eversong, after all. After she found Ridge.

"I thought I could send some help with you," Angulus said.

"Someone who could help track Ridge, too, if there's any chance he's alive."

"Ah, who?" Sardelle doubted a human could find what a dragon couldn't, but it might not hurt to have assistance. As Jaxi had emphasized, Bhrava Saruth might not be telling her the entire truth, and he could have other motivations. Or he could simply be distracted and take off at some point in their journey.

"Colonel Therrik."

Jaxi made a coughing noise in Sardelle's mind at the same time as Sardelle sputtered, "What?"

"General Ort left the dragon-slaying blade up there, so Therrik has it. I understand it works on sorcerers."

"Yes, and he tried to use it on *me*."

Angulus frowned. "The reports I've received, both from him and from General Ort, said he only used it on the dragon."

Because Sardelle and Cas hadn't reported that incident in the artifact room. Therrik had never gotten his hand around the hilt of the sword, but when he'd been in its presence, he had definitely wanted to kill Sardelle. Atop the roof, when he had gripped the weapon, he'd pushed past her and run after the dragons, but she didn't know if that indicated any control or conscious choice on his part. Kasandral may have simply seen the dragons as a greater threat.

"He doesn't care for magic users," Sardelle said. "He's made that clear. I don't believe he would be a reliable traveling partner." She almost sputtered again as she imagined trying to get Therrik to climb on Bhrava Saruth's back for a ride. The man hadn't even been able to stomach flying with Ridge.

"He's a good fighter, he knows how to use a sword, and he used to teach the infantry class on wilderness survival and tracking." Angulus tapped the folder. "If you could keep the sword in the box and then point him in the right direction at the right time, he might be a match for the sorceress."

The sword had been *in* the box when Therrik had thrown his fit. Sardelle did not believe that container provided as much insulation as people believed.

"I don't think he would deign to work with me."

"I could send a royal order."

"I'd be afraid to sleep around him." Not entirely true. Jaxi could always keep watch. Still, why invite an enemy into her camp? "He wants me dead. I think he'd try to make that happen if I ventured into the wilderness with him."

"Perhaps not." Angulus opened the folder to the page on top and held it out to her.

She skimmed the contents. It was a report about the events that had transpired at the outpost, including the dragon attacks, the attempt to kill Morishtomaric by collapsing the mines, and the final battle, including details about Therrik's role in hurting the enemy dragon. This was *his* report, she realized. To his credit, he had not embellished and claimed to have landed any killing blows. He was almost self-effacing, admitting the sword had been in control and also that he had been unconscious for part of that final battle. Unconscious? He had very nearly died. He *would* have died if not for Sardelle. He hadn't mentioned her help in the report, and she didn't know why the king was showing this to her. Then she reached the end, almost a postscript.

Sire, I withdraw my objection to having the witch, Sardelle, working with the army. She was an asset.

"The witch, Sardelle," she murmured. "That's the first time I'm aware of that he's used my name."

"Yes," Angulus said, "he usually refers to you as Zirkander's witch."

She winced at the mention of Ridge's name, then wished she hadn't. She didn't want Angulus or anyone else to feel compelled to tread lightly around her, nor did she want them feeling they had to comfort her all the time.

"I'm sorry," Angulus said. "If it makes you feel better, the entire nation misses him. Someone started a petition to add a national holiday to celebrate his life. It's possible they just want a day off to drink beer."

"Ridge would approve of that then." She managed a smile.

"I wanted to show you the report so you would realize he considers you an asset now."

"I healed him in the courtyard. He would have died otherwise."

"I thought it might have been something like that." He took back the folder and held it up. "Given the source, that was a great compliment."

"I guess I could try working with him." If Bhrava Saruth proved an unreliable traveling companion, it *would* be better to have someone wielding that sword if she had to battle Eversong.

So long as he gets pointed in the right direction, Jaxi said.

We know Kasandral's command words now. That should be doable.

Uh huh. We knew them up on that rooftop, too, but Morishtomaric also knew them, and his voice seemed to carry more weight.

I know. I was there.

Just reminding you. I don't want you to be blindsided.

I know. Sardelle closed her eyes, drained by the idea of a battle with a powerful sorceress. *I just want to find Ridge.*

Jaxi didn't say anything, because Jaxi thought he was dead. Sardelle understood that even if she couldn't accept it herself.

"I can stop by," Sardelle said, "and see if he's willing."

Angulus grunted. "You'll take my royal orders with you, and I assure you he *will* be willing."

"Thank you, Sire."

"As to a pilot—"

"I actually found a solution for that while you were gone."

Angulus looked around, then into the fountain. "Oh?"

"I had a chat with a dragon, and he offered to take me." She waved toward the east and the edge of the city, so he wouldn't worry that Bhrava Saruth was nearby, harassing anyone.

I wouldn't harass anyone, high priestess, entered a mournful comment into her mind. *You must get to know me better.*

And get used to having him monitoring her and speaking into her mind as often as Jaxi did. She held back a grimace. *You're right. I will. I apologize for my words. For my* thoughts. She gave that last word extra emphasis, hoping he would get the hint that she didn't feel she should have to apologize for thoughts.

I accept your apology, he proclaimed.

"A dragon?" Angulus asked. "Phelistoth? I was hoping he might be coerced into going on the mission with Tolemek and the others."

"This is one of the new dragons, the one who stayed at the outpost and kept Cas from falling to her death along with Morishtomaric. I'm—ah. He believes he's a god and thinks I'm going to become his high priestess."

From what Sardelle had seen, Angulus was generally an unflappable man, one who kept his expression closed and hard to read, but his eyebrows launched upward, almost disappearing into his curly hair.

"I see," he said, recovering his equanimity. "Does that mean you won't consider moving into the castle to be a healer here when your teaching and other work doesn't call to you? I had thought to make you that offer again."

"I haven't committed to any job offers yet," she said with a smile. She wasn't ready to figure out what she wanted to do next in her life, and she still had to teach Tylie, but she did appreciate that he was offering. Both he and General Ort had been kind. She had worried that she might not be welcome here by anyone if not for Ridge's influence.

"I hope you'll consider my offer then. I'm not sure I can give you as much as a *god*, but I assure you the pay would be more than fair."

She stood, thinking of the bag she wanted to pack and that she should take Tylie to stay with Fern if she and Tolemek were both going to be out of town. It looked like she would be joining General Ort for the trip to visit Ridge's mother, after all.

Angulus cleared his throat. "Before you go, a question?"

"Of course, Sire."

"My motivations for asking you to be the healer in residence are not selfless."

"One of your people has a problem?" Sardelle had a lot to do but could work in an appointment with someone in the castle if necessary.

"Ah." Angulus stood, glanced toward the walls where the guards stood silently, then turned his back toward them. He faced the fountain and leaned close. "*I* have a problem. A question, rather." Were his cheeks flushed red?

Maybe Bhrava Saruth has been sharing images of his adoring worshippers with him too, Jaxi suggested.

Let's hope not.
A king would be a very high-ranking worshipper.

"What's your question, Sire?" Sardelle asked when he did not continue. "I assure you, I'll keep anything you tell me confidential."

Jaxi sniggered. Since Sardelle did not think she had said anything amusing, she assumed Jaxi was surfing in the top layer of Angulus's thoughts. She did not want to intrude upon her king's privacy, so she did not ask what Jaxi had found.

You're so noble.

"I know you will." Angulus nodded, took a deep breath, and went on. "It's about having children."

She sublimated the thoughts of Ridge and the conversation they had shared on the topic. "Something you're interested in?"

"No. I mean, yes, but not right now. Not, uhm, illegitimately. I'm not sure if that's a problem or not based on my history. Or lack of history, as it were." He wiped his hand down his face. "Neither my first wife nor my second conceived, and we weren't taking any measures to ensure that wouldn't happen. After a while, I assumed the, ah, issue might be me. Of course, my second wife and I weren't that frequent of, uhm." He eyed her uncertainly. "I'm just wondering if as a healer, you can tell if I'm safe insofar as causing women to become pregnant. I don't mind using contraceptives, but I didn't once recently due to, er, irresponsibility, I suppose. And I've been concerned."

Well, this isn't at all an awkward conversation, Jaxi observed.

I've had it numerous times. Not with royalty, necessarily. "I would have to examine Captain Kaika to know if anything happened, but—"

Angulus grimaced. "Zirkander said he couldn't keep any secrets from you."

"Oh. I'm not sure he knew that was a secret. As to the rest, I suggest using the lambskins. I can't tell just by looking at you—" she touched her temple to imply she could *look* with more than her eyes, "—or your swimmers."

He snorted and glanced at the goldfish.

"If at some point in the future, you decide you *do* want

children, I know someone who claims to have healing powers even greater than mine who might be able to help."

Someone? Jaxi asked. *Are you talking about Phelistoth or Bhrava Saruth?*

It's true that I've witnessed Phelistoth's healing powers firsthand, but I would find it easier to ask Bhrava Saruth for assistance with the king's fertility.

Even if it meant signing the king up as a new worshipper?

He might consider it a fair tradeoff if he wants children.

Children with whom? Jaxi asked. *I can't imagine Kaika as a queen.*

We don't know if that will last or what their understanding with each other is. He's young enough to find another wife if he chooses.

"I see," Angulus said, his brow crinkling faintly. "Well, good. I'll keep that in mind. If you want to follow me to my office, I'll write up orders for Therrik."

"Yes, Sire."

As they headed out of the atrium, Jaxi made a diffident throat-clearing noise. *Just so you know, you're young enough too. To find someone else. When you're ready.*

I don't want to find anyone else. She wanted Ridge.

* * *

Ridge Zirkander woke up with a headache so intense that it felt like he had a bullet lodged in his brain. He squinted up at the brown and gray rocks of a cave ceiling, trying to remember where he was and how he had come to be here. He also tried to remember whether it was possible that a bullet *was* lodged in his brain. Despite concentrating so hard that it made his head throb even more, he couldn't recall either detail. Panic burgeoned in his chest as nothing came from swatting at the cobwebs in his mind.

He sat up, a heavy fur falling about his waist. Cold air that smelled of rain and lichen chilled his bare torso. His headache intensified, making him want to collapse back onto the packed earth he had lain upon, but he refused to succumb. He touched bandages that circled his chest. He could breathe without pain from his ribs, but his muscles ached almost as much as his head, reminding him of the time he had crashed his flier in Cofah territory and been captured.

Why could he remember *that* and not how he had come to be lying in a cave? Lying *naked* in a cave? Coarse fur pricked at the bare skin of his legs.

He found a few more bandages—one wrapped around his upper thigh and another around the crown of his head—but he only grew more confused as he continued his examination of himself. Had he crashed again? It had been some time since the Cofah incident, but given his occupation and the occasionally reckless way he pursued it, that was all that made sense to him.

Another cold breeze teased the bare skin of his back, and he turned toward the draft. About ten feet away, the jagged entrance of the cave lay open to the elements. He glimpsed boulders and scree poised on a steep slope in the distance. Was he in some mountain valley? *Whose* mountain valley? Had he crashed in the empire? Or at home in Iskandia? He couldn't imagine why he would have been flying over the mountains of his homeland—his squadron always met threats out along the coast, intercepting enemy airships and naval vessels before troops could make it inland.

"You're awake," came a woman's voice from the shadows in the back of the cave.

Ridge jerked his head around to locate her, wincing at the pain that came with the abrupt movement. He didn't recognize the voice, but he hoped whoever this was had answers.

"Apparently," he croaked, his voice rusty from disuse. How long had he been unconscious? "Who are you?" He could barely see the figure in the cave's depths.

"A friend. Do you know who *you* are?"

Ridge licked his lips and considered whether he should answer. How had she known? Why would she guess that his memories eluded him? He still didn't recognize the voice, and she had a faint accent. A faint *Cofah* accent.

"I'm not sure," he said.

You have nothing to fear from her, came a soothing voice from the back of his mind.

Ridge touched his temple, his puzzlement growing. Was that his own inner voice talking to him? What else could it be? But how would his inner voice know more than *he* knew?

What about from the stiff, crusty bear fur poking my cannonballs? Your what?

Never mind. If that was his inner voice, it seemed a little dull.

"Maybe this is what going mad feels like," he mumbled, pulling the fur over his waist as the figure moved out of the shadows and into the sunlight slanting through the cave entrance.

Blonde hair tumbled about her shoulders in rich waves, and deep brown eyes regarded him from a beautiful face with arched cheekbones and full lips. She wore riding leathers with a wool button-down shirt and a fur cloak that seemed appropriate to a mountain climate. She appeared young, maybe twenty-five, but something about the way she knelt confidently beside him and touched her hand to his chest gave him the sense that she was older than she appeared.

"Does General Ridgewalker Zirkander sound familiar?" she asked, her hand drifting from the bandages on his chest up his throat to his jaw. She ran her fingers along his jaw as she gazed into his eyes, scrutinizing him. Her touch wasn't unpleasant, but he wasn't about to let himself enjoy some strange woman's ministrations when he didn't know if he was in enemy hands or not.

"Uh, *general*? No."

"No?"

"It's colonel," he said, then wondered if he should have even said that much. "Where are we?"

He drew his legs up under the fur, tempted to stand up and walk to the cave entrance so he could see if he recognized the peaks. He was, however, reluctant to leave the covering and stride around naked in front of the woman. Logically, it shouldn't matter, since she had probably been the one to strip off his clothes, wash him, and tend his wounds, but logic wasn't always easy to heed when women were concerned.

"Hm." She rose and walked back into the shadows.

Ridge took the moment to stagger to his feet, his body protesting the movement. He wrapped the fur around his waist like an oversized towel and shuffled to the entrance, rocks prodding his bare feet. He squinted into the sun. Rocky mountains fenced him in, the peaks covered with glaciers. Judging by the stunted foliage, he was at a high elevation. Was it spring? Summer? He had grown up by the coast, and he doubted his ability to identify the seasons based on rocks and lichens. He couldn't see anything blooming from his perch. A stream meandered through the middle of the valley, winding past the cave, with low green plants carpeting the ground to either side.

"We're in the Ice Blades," the woman said, coming to stand beside him. "About a hundred miles east of Hedgewood."

She lifted her brows at the way he clutched the fur about his waist, but he barely noticed. His gaze was riveted to the dirty, rumpled clothing in her hand. She held up a dark blue army officer's jacket with gold bars and braids on the collars, a general's rank. Several rips and stains rendered it unacceptable for duty wear, but did not keep him from reading his name sewn onto the breast pocket tag.

"I don't remember..." Ridge touched his temple, the bandages snug above his eyebrows as they wrapped his head. "The last thing I remember..." It had been summer, General Ort's birthday celebration. He'd invited everyone in Wolf and Tiger Squadrons to his house, where they had grilled sausages and played brisk-ball while trying to get Ort drunk enough to ask the neighbor's grandmother for a date. Had there been a mission assigned after that? He couldn't remember. He *definitely* couldn't remember getting promoted. He had been offered that promotion before, but he had always weaseled his way out of it, not wanting to give up commanding Wolf Squadron or flying. If he was a general now, what had he been doing out where he could crash? He should have been chained to a desk somewhere, pushing papers around. He grimaced, almost as disturbed by that notion as by his faulty memory.

Aware of the woman watching him, he shook his head. Just because she said they were in the Ice Blades did not mean that was true. The tall peaks *could* belong to the rugged range. He would have known for certain if he had been flying above them, but one mountain looked much like another from halfway up the side of it. Besides, the Cofah had a couple of rugged, glacier-capped ranges too. And this woman had an accent.

"You must be wondering who I am," she said, lowering the jacket. *His* jacket. "I'm Mara Trembuckle. I grew up around here. My mother is—was—a mercenary before she fled trouble back home and settled out here."

"Your mother."

"She was from Cofahre." The woman's—Mara's—gaze lowered. "I hope you won't hold that against me. I know you're a hero and usually fight the Cofah."

A hero. He didn't feel like a hero standing there naked and barefoot.

"My mother was an outcast here because of her heritage, but I've never known anything except for these mountains. She's gone now, and I have little left." She gazed sadly out at the valley, her shoulders slumped.

Ridge wasn't certain he believed her—would someone who had grown up here have an accent? Even if her mother had possessed one, would it have influenced her language skills?

You can trust her, the voice in the back of his mind said.

Oh? Can I trust you?

Of course.

Why don't I believe you? Ridge rubbed his temple. Maybe the voice would go away once his head stopped hurting.

She spent much of her youth alone or with only her mother to talk to. She is shy and awkward with people. She doesn't always say the right things, but it's not a sign of dishonesty.

How do you—we—know that? If this was his own voice speaking to him, how could it know things he didn't know?

You don't seem to know much right now.

He snorted. That was the truth.

Mara lifted her gaze and met his eyes, her own eyes imploring. An urge to comfort her trickled through him, an urge to trust her.

"I'm sorry you lost your mother," he said. "I hope you'll forgive me for being self-centered, but I have a duty as an officer—as a general, apparently—to report in as soon as possible. Can you tell me how I came to be here with you? I can't remember."

"You hit your head. You should see the crash site."

Ah, he *knew* there had been a crash.

"You tumbled down a slope and into a river. I thought you were dead, but I was able to reach you, so I checked on you and pulled you out of the water."

Ridge looked down at the stream meandering through the valley. It wasn't large enough for him to have tumbled into without breaking every bone in his body. And how had she hauled him up the slope to this cave? He wasn't the brawniest man in the army, but he was six feet tall and certainly not scrawny.

"Not that stream. A river at the end of this valley that it merges into." Mara pointed downstream, toward a bend.

She *definitely* could not have carried him that far. He opened his mouth to ask, but she continued first.

"I found a couple of trappers, and they helped me carry you up here."

Strange that she'd seemed to guess what he had been wondering. Or maybe it was an obvious question.

"They had their trap routes to attend to, so they left a few days ago." She rested her hand on his forearm and gazed up into his face, smiling. "I've been taking care of you. I never would have thought I'd get to meet the great Ridgewalker Zirkander. It's been an honor to tend your wounds."

Her flattery almost distracted him from the rest of what she had said. Trappers. He had doubted his ability to tell the seasons, but he was positive it wasn't winter—at this altitude, the valley would be smothered with snow if that were true. But didn't trappers work in the winter? When animal fur was thick? Lieutenant Duck would know.

"Uhm." He debated questioning her, questioning her *story*, but maybe he had better keep his mouth shut until he had more of a feel for what had happened. Besides, he was a city boy. What did he truly know about trapping or the ways of mountain folk?

Very little, the voice said agreeably.

Ridge supposed it was reasonable that the voice of his madness would be as sarcastic as he was.

"Mara, thank you for helping me," he said, aware of her watching him. "I'm sure I would have died without you."

She nodded solemnly.

"Would you mind showing me the crash site?" His aching head protested the idea of a tramp across the boulder-littered landscape, but he had to see for himself what had happened. Maybe his memory would come back once he saw his flier. Also, maybe it could be salvaged, and he could get back into the air, return home, and report in.

"I wouldn't mind, but you should rest for another day." Mara lifted the hand she'd had on his arm up to the bandages on his torso, studying them, or maybe studying his chest. She wouldn't be the first woman to do so, and he had the sense that more than medical needs were prompting her to stand close and keep touching him.

"Probably so," he said, stepping back so that her hand dropped, "but I'm not good at following doctors' suggestions. Or anyone's suggestions. I don't suppose my boots came down the river with the rest of me?"

She hesitated, a hint of disappointment in her eyes, then nodded. "I have them back here."

"Good. I appreciate your help," he said, hoping to take the sting away from what she might see as a rejection. Besides, he *did* appreciate her help. Even if he wasn't positive he believed her story yet, if she truly had saved his life, he owed her something. What he could offer, he didn't know, but he would figure it out. Maybe the same time he figured out what he was doing out here.

Chapter 3

Ridge squinted at the distant mountainside, little more than rocks covering the steep slope. "Are you sure?"

"Here." Mara handed him something.

To his surprise, it was an Iskandian military-issue collapsible spyglass. Though she carried only a small pack, she was well outfitted for the mountains. He supposed he shouldn't be surprised if she had grown up in the area. Still, he wondered where she had gotten the spyglass. The majority of Iskandia's military forts lay along the coast. With the exception of the clansmen up north, internal strife was rare within the country. All those Cofah attacks over the centuries had helped his once fragmented people unite, to fight off their common enemy.

"It's about a third of the way up the slope, below that point on the ridge," she added, watching him study the spyglass.

Assuming she had traded something for it along the way, he lifted it and scanned the landscape until he saw what he sought, the wrecked remains of a military flier, one wing torn off and the tail missing. A boulder hid half the fuselage, but he could tell the craft had struck so hard that all form had been smashed out of it.

"I survived that?" he breathed. It did not look like the kind of crash a man walked away from. It didn't even look like the kind of crash a man could be carried away from.

"I saw you come down. You flew out of the cockpit when it struck, slid down the rocks, and fell into that canyon and into the river."

From their vantage point, high on a goat trail on the mountain opposite the one he was looking at, he could not see the river, but he had glimpsed it along the way. It meandered through the canyon until the walls widened into a valley farther downstream. It wasn't that deep. He judged the fall from the lip of the canyon to the bottom to be close to two hundred feet. Water was more yielding than land, but he knew from jumping off cliffs into the sea north of the capital that a fall from even fifty feet could mess up a man if he didn't land well. To have survived a drop from four times that height after having already crashed... It was hard to believe.

Do you not believe in miracles? the voice in the back of his head asked, the tone dry.

Like the kind where gods pluck you from certain death so they can then use you for their own purposes? I've only heard of that happening in legends.

Legends often have a seed of truth about them. Perhaps the gods are once again returning to a more active role in the world.

Uh huh.

This voice that his subconscious had conjured had strange ideas. Ridge couldn't imagine where they were coming from or what they meant. Aside from his impending madness.

Mara was looking at him. Ridge smoothed his face, not wanting her to know he was chatting with himself.

"I didn't have a parachute, did I?" he asked. That might explain things.

To the best of his recollection, the flier parachutes he'd seen and tested were extremely experimental and weren't safe enough to be distributed yet, but he also didn't know how much of his memory was missing. A year? Five years? More? He shuddered. He hadn't seen himself in a mirror—or even a pool of water—yet, and he reached up to touch his hair, afraid he might have gone gray and not even remember the years that had led to it.

"A what?" Mara asked after a puzzled second.

Ridge thought about explaining it, but she would have guessed what he meant if she had seen it. Too bad. That might have solved part of the mystery, or at least convinced him that the landing had been survivable. As it was now, the math didn't add up for him.

Gods, the voice said blandly.

You're not one of these gods, are you? Ridge asked it in jest. He'd never seen anything to make him believe that the gods were real or that, if they were real, they cared overmuch what happened to humanity.

Would you believe me if I said yes?

No.

Then, no.

So, what are you?

An adviser.

An adviser that I, in my encroaching madness, made up for myself?

Perhaps.

I would have preferred it if you were a god.

"It's nothing," Ridge said. Mara was gazing at him with a concerned expression. Whether she was concerned for his health or his sanity, he couldn't tell. He wasn't going to ask—or mention the voice chatting with him. "Where did you pull me out of the river?"

"Down there. Where the canyon opens up."

"The trappers were with you then?"

"I found them later and asked them to help. We carried you to that cave together."

Once again, Ridge's senses twanged, finding implausibility in the story. Was she strong enough to have fished him out of the river and up onto land? And what odd chance had led her to be here to see him crash and fall in?

He studied his young companion, her blonde hair falling about her shoulders, her face and body more what he'd expect from a dancer in a men's club in the capital, not from some mountain woman who led a hard life. He supposed she was young enough that the demands of a rough life wouldn't have taken their toll and affected her beauty yet.

As he returned the spyglass to her, he caught her right hand and rubbed his thumb along her palm to see if she had callouses. He half expected to find soft hands that never did any manual labor, but her palm was indeed calloused, including a ridge of rough skin that ran from her index finger to her thumb. Any tool might have accounted for it, but Ridge's old friend Abagon Mox had belonged to a saber club and dueled in competition. Ridge had shaken his hand often and remembered his callouses, similar ones to these. Odd. He looked down to her waist. She carried a utility knife there, but that was her only weapon, unless she had a pistol in her pack. That was odd too. They were high up in wild country, where big cats, bears, and wolves lived. A lone woman might make an appealing target for a pack of hungry animals.

Realizing she must be wondering why he was fondling her hand, Ridge let her go with a, "Sorry."

He looked at her face warily, worried she would have more reason to think him crazy. He caught her gazing up at him, her lips parted slightly. When he met her eyes, she cleared her throat and looked away, pocketing the collapsible spyglass.

Well, at least if his hair had gone gray, the rest of his face must not have gotten too bad. He'd been the recipient of the dreamy look from women often enough to recognize it. It was surprising, given that he hadn't bathed in a few days, but he'd been told he looked better than average, even with beard stubble and dirt smudged on his face. He didn't want to do anything about her attraction, even if she was a beauty. Too many things didn't make sense, and he had a hard time stowing his suspicion. Now that he'd had a good look at the peaks around them, he did believe they were in the Ice Blades, but he couldn't imagine what he had been doing out here.

"I must thank you again for rescuing me," Ridge said, smiling and trying to keep the suspicion off his face. "Did you see what caused the crash? Was I in a battle?"

As hard as it was to imagine Cofah airships this far into his country, his ego refused to accept that he might have simply been flying across the mountains on some errand and crashed of his own volition. He wished he was close enough to see if the sides of his flier were riddled with bullet holes. He was tempted to try to get over there—if nothing else, he might be able to retrieve the power crystal. General Ort would have his hide for losing one of the valuable energy sources. But the terrain looked inhospitable, if not impossible to traverse. At the least, he would need a climbing harness and tools to get up there. He made a note of the surrounding terrain so he could return someday to retrieve the crystal.

Mara hesitated before answering. "There was a big storm that night. I think you might have been hit by lightning."

Lightning? He supposed that was better than simply crashing because of some stray wind, but what would he have been doing flying into a storm? And for that matter, why would he have been out here in a military craft by himself? If he had been hunting down enemies, he would have taken a couple of his pilots with him, if not his whole squadron.

"Were there any other fliers with me?" Ridge asked.

"Not that I saw."

That, he was inclined to believe. If there had been, they would have looked for him when he went down. They wouldn't have left him for dead. But that brought him back to the question of what he had been doing out here alone in a storm.

"You said it was night? What were *you* doing out here? Especially if there was a storm?" He smiled again, trying to make his questions seem innocent instead of suspicious, but he watched her intently.

Mara shrugged. "There was a lot of lightning and hail too. It was impressive. I've always liked storms."

She pointed toward the goat trail they had come up to find this vantage point, a hike that had left his sore and battered body with more aches. "We should go. You'll want to get out of these mountains, I presume? I can find a path that will eventually lead us to some villages. We can trade for a horse there."

Without waiting for him to respond, she headed down the trail. He let his eyelids droop to half-mast, noting that she hadn't truly answered his question. He walked after her without comment. More questions would only make her warier, but he vowed to pay attention as they traveled.

"I hope you have something to trade," Ridge said. "My wallet must have washed downriver along with my sock."

She had been able to provide him with most of his clothing, but the sock had been missing, as well as his cap, goggles, scarf, and the wallet. More than all of that, he missed his little wooden dragon luck charm. He had checked every pocket six times, hoping to discover it, but he either hadn't had it with him on this flight, or it was hanging in the smashed cockpit he couldn't reach.

She looked back. "I will handle it."

Well, that was vague.

She has furs and many skills she can trade, the voice in the back of his head said.

If it's that crusty bear fur that smells like mildew, I don't think she'll get a horse for that.

She has many skills she can trade, the voice repeated.

Ridge was tempted to ask what they were, but he wasn't coming out ahead in the conversations he was having with himself, so he doubted he should encourage them. He prodded at an itch under the bandage that wrapped his head, hoping the voice would go away once his brain stopped hurting.

As they rounded a bend that would take the crash site from view, he gave it one long look, once again doubting that anyone could have survived that landing.

* * *

Mist hung over the dense green landmass that stretched ahead of and below Cas's flier, the sun setting behind an equally green mountain range that ran northeast to southwest in the distance. No glaciers or snowpacks adorned those peaks. Even with the sea breeze tugging at her scarf, and the sun's intensity fading, Cas sweated beneath her uniform. She had stuffed her flight jacket into her pack earlier in the day, as they had crossed the equator, but she wouldn't have minded stripping off more clothing. The season should be autumn down here, but she doubted that frost ever blanketed the ground in Dakrovia or that the jungle leaves turned color and fell off.

"Reminds me of Owanu Owanus," Tolemek called from the back seat. "Except much bigger."

As they had flown up on Owanu Owanus earlier that spring, the tropical island where they had freed Tylie and discovered Phelistoth, they had been able to see the sea on all sides. According to the maps, the Dakrovian continent was much larger than Iskandia. An entirely different ocean lay on the far side, and they would have had to fly through the night if they wanted to see it. The coordinates the king had provided were on the eastern shore, so that wouldn't be necessary.

"Have you ever been to this continent before?" Cas wiggled in her seat, hoping they landed soon. Her legs and butt ached from sitting for so long. They had left early and flown the entire day to cross the ocean, the entire day and then some, since they had been following the path of the sun.

"I've ordered numerous plants, poisons, and reptile specimens from suppliers in some of the bigger cities down here," Tolemek said.

"So, no."

"No. But I've perused many catalogues and am quite familiar with the flora."

"Good to know." Cas tapped the communication crystal nestled into the grip of her flight stick. "Has *anyone* been here before?"

She had chosen Captain Blazer and Lieutenants Pimples and Duck as the other Wolf Squadron officers for this mission. They were all capable pilots, with Duck and Pimples already knowing about dragons and sorcery. Blazer had more experience than any of them, including an aptitude for mechanical repairs, and nothing seemed to faze her. When Phelistoth had joined them halfway across the ocean, Tylie sitting astride his back and the sun gleaming off his silvery scales, Blazer had merely taken a puff of her cigar and said, "Pretty." It hadn't been clear whether she'd meant Tylie or the dragon, since her tastes ran toward women.

"Colonel Quataldo has," Duck replied. "We've been discussing the animals and plants in the jungle. Apparently, there are giant wolves five times bigger than the ones back home. And black panthers that can turn invisible. Massive vining carnivorous plants. Alligators big enough to swallow a squad of troops whole."

"Is anyone else alarmed that he sounds *excited* by those things?" Captain Blazer asked.

"Not really," Pimples said. "It just means we can volunteer him to go first."

"I've been here," Kaika yelled from Pimples' back seat. "It's exceedingly difficult to find explosives or ingredients to create explosives in the towns. Last time, I had to wander around some jungle hot springs looking for my own sulfur."

"Are there any continents you haven't blown things up on, Captain?" Pimples asked.

"I haven't been to Subarctic Zharr yet."

"We're not going to land and find a wanted poster with your face on it, are we, Captain?" Cas asked.

"Nah, that was a humanitarian mission. I helped them turn aside lava flows on an erupting volcano to save a town. It's too bad we're not going there. I could probably get us some of the vanilla bean alcohol they make here. It's cracking."

"Colonel Quataldo says none of us will be showing our faces anywhere," Duck said. "We're landing twenty miles south of Tildar Dem and walking the rest of the way, so nobody will notice our fliers."

"Walking past the giant wolves and alligators and man-eating plants?" Pimples asked.

"We'll stick to the beach most of the way, so we're less likely to run into hungry predators." Did Duck sound disappointed?

"Haven't seen any airships along the coast," Captain Blazer said. "We just getting lucky or do they not have any here?"

"A lot of merchant ships come down here," Tolemek said, "and a few of the bigger cities have air and naval fleets, but we're on the stormy coast. The villages are smaller and more rustic here."

Cas relayed his words to the others.

"Rustic jungle villages," Pimples said. "Why would the Cofah emperor marry one of his daughters off to somebody from such a place?"

"The king said her fiancé is a shaman," Cas said.

"A lot of the Dakrovian shamans come from this region," Tolemek added, "and if I recall my history, dragons are believed to have originated on this continent."

Cas caught Tolemek looking over at Phelistoth. The dragon was shadowing them, but Tylie did not have a communication crystal, so they had no way to include her in the conversation unless she or Phelistoth spoke telepathically to the group.

"The emperor has a few shamans working with the air military already," Tolemek continued, "as you and your squadron have encountered, so this is likely about firming up a treaty to acquire more. I imagine Salatak is worried now that Iskandia has dragon allies." He glanced at Phelistoth again.

Cas wasn't sure the silver dragon counted as an *ally*. His willingness to stay in Iskandia seemed to have more to do with Tylie's choice to train with Sardelle than any interest in helping the nation.

"Did any of you people who are snuggled up to the king's bosom ever hear where that fireball flinging witch came from?" Captain Blazer asked. She had been among those who had returned in time to battle against the Cofah in their flying fortress, so she had seen firsthand the destructive power of Eversong's fireballs.

"The king doesn't have a bosom, does he?" Pimples asked. "He seems fit for someone who sits on a throne all day."

"You'd have to ask Captain Kaika," Duck said, a smirk in his voice.

After a pause, Pimples said, "She says our intelligence people haven't discovered where the sorceress came from yet, just that Sardelle thought she'd come out of a stasis chamber somewhere, much like our dragon friends. She also says—oh, ma'am, I can't say that."

Cas snorted, imagining some comment about the king's chest or his other manly attributes.

An airship approaches from the southwest, a voice rumbled in her head. Phelistoth.

Cas peered in that direction. Though mists clung to the landmass, the sky was clear over the ocean, and the sun still provided enough light to see for miles. "How far away? I don't see anything."

Belatedly, she realized she was speaking to everyone, thanks to the communication crystal, and she did not know if the dragon's message had been delivered to everyone. She also did not know if he could hear her from his position, about a thousand meters off her right flank.

Forty miles away, Phelistoth responded. *It is following the coast toward us.*

"Our coordinates for landing are another thirty miles down that same coast," Duck said. "That'll be a problem. Even if it's a merchant ship out of another country, we don't want it spotting us. If it's an imperial ship, we *definitely* don't want it spotting us."

As far as Cas had heard, the Cofah did not have radio technology yet, nor did they have anything like the communication crystals that Sardelle had made for the fliers. Still, they could get messages around quickly enough, and being identified at the very beginning of their mission would not be good. The emperor might turn around if he heard Iskandian fliers were in the area.

"Shall we land early?" Cas asked.

"Colonel Quataldo says yes," Duck said. "We'll look for a protected area that appears unpopulated."

In the seat behind him, Quataldo leaned over the side, a spyglass to his eye as he considered the coastline. He tapped Duck's shoulder and pointed.

"Follow me down," Duck said.

"I guess we get forty miles of crocodiles and carnivorous plants instead of twenty." Cas remembered the vile tentacled creature that had tried to drag Tolemek to the bottom of a river on Owanu Owanus. It was hard to shoot at something underwater, and she also didn't care for the idea of vines and tendrils snaking out to wrap around her legs.

"You're not scared, are you, Raptor?" Captain Blazer asked. "I saw you pack your sniper rifle, and with your aim, I'm sure you can shoot anything before it kills you."

"Shooting is problematic when you're sneaking up on a town and trying not to be heard."

"I've seen you take down Cofah warriors with rocks and sticks before too."

"I know which part of a Cofah warrior you aim at. I'm less certain with carnivorous plants."

"The part trying to eat you, I imagine."

"Rocks and sticks?" Tolemek asked as she dipped the nose of the flier downward, following Duck toward a beach far below. "You haven't mentioned that story."

"An early survival training mission on a deserted island that wasn't that deserted. A Cofah ship had wrecked on a reef on the far side."

Gusts of air battered at her wings as they switched from following the air currents to flying against them. The beach Duck angled toward was more rock than sand, with algae-coated boulders rising amid clumps of green vegetation that curled around them. Cas was glad they were flying the two-seaters with their thrusters. Finding a landing strip down there would have been impossible.

A wide river emptied into the ocean, and Duck turned to follow it, cruising low over the water. Cas took the rear, letting Pimples and Blazer go ahead, and she scanned the sky in both directions before descending below the tops of the mangrove trees lining the banks. At the far edge of the horizon, an airship had come into view, the dark shape hovering in an azure sky deepening with the promise of twilight.

When she checked behind her, she twitched in surprise. Phelistoth had been behind her, but he was nowhere to be seen now. Had he already dipped into the trees? Or had he not been paying attention to Quataldo's instructions? If that airship spotted a dragon, it was just as likely to send along a report that might keep the emperor from landing here.

Shaking her head, Cas dipped lower, skimming along the water. She had to trust that the dragon had the sense to stay out of sight—after all, he had been the one to warn them about the approaching craft. Besides, she had her own team to worry about. The buzz of their propellers seemed twice as loud with the noise echoing off the wall of mangroves. She hoped the roar of the ocean would muffle the sound farther out and that the airship was still too distant to hear anything.

Huge birds squawked and flew up from the thickets of exposed roots as the fliers cruised up the river. Though alarmed by the noise, some of those birds were as large as Cas was. Were all the animals down here giants? If so, she had little trouble imagining dragons evolving in this climate.

With the trees and foliage so dense, Duck had to fly a couple of miles inland before finding a spot to park the fliers. Even then, the inlet wasn't ideal, consisting of mud and shallow water choked with reeds rather than hard earth. Cas ended up flying farther upriver while waiting for the others to find landing spots. There wasn't much room for maneuvering in the muddy cove. After a minute, she did a loop, skimming past outstretched branches and flying upside down so she could turn around without rising above the treetops.

"You *are* Zirkander's protégé," Tolemek said.

"I didn't think you got airsick or minded being upside down."

"I almost dropped one of my knockout grenades."

"Isn't your gear buckled down?" Cas glanced over her shoulder as she righted them and cruised back toward the inlet.

"Yes, but I was getting one ready in case fierce predators are waiting for us. You didn't sound that enthused at the idea of shooting up the jungle."

"I think we're still forty miles from the town. It's probably safe to fire a weapon this far out."

"With the airship flying past?"

"Ah, that's true. We don't want them to hear us." Cas turned into the inlet, hoping the land-based wildlife would find the buzz of their propellers as alarming as the birds had and stay away. "Does your noxious smoke work on carnivorous plants?"

"Not likely. I have some of the dragon-blood-eating acid along. That ought to kill just about anything."

Pimples, Duck, and Blazer had landed, though Blazer's craft had sunk in past the tires. She thumped on the dashboard, trying to urge more power from the thrusters, so she could lift and find a more stable spot. Cas flew over her, eyeing the murky water dubiously. Vine-draped branches stretching everywhere did not leave much headroom for maneuvering.

"Looks more like a swamp than a jungle," Tolemek observed.

Cas tipped her wings to avoid a tall stump jutting from the middle of the muddy water and chose the best-looking place she could find, a dense thicket of reeds. Their presence should mean that ground lay only a few inches down. She hoped.

"This landing spot is dragon piss," Blazer announced. "Who picked it?"

"Duck," Pimples said. "Are you going to beat him up?"

"If I don't get hopelessly mired in mud, I might."

"Just don't grab my ears again," Duck said. "That's not fighting fair."

"If a man comes with handles, it's fair to use them."

The thrusters incinerated the reeds as Cas cut the propeller and settled down, leaning out to watch her descent. She would vote for moving their craft to harder ground as soon as the airship had flown past. Weren't swamps full of quicksand? Maybe they should have kept going up the river, in the hope of finding something better. Fortunately, her wheels settled on something solid six inches under the surface.

"We have company," Tolemek said quietly.

Cas lifted her head, her hand going to her rifle. It was secured in the side of the cockpit with fasteners, but she had them unclipped before she spotted what Tolemek was talking about. About fifty meters away, at least a dozen men stood among the trees, looking toward the fliers and holding rifles in their arms. Given the wildness of this place, Cas had expected loincloth-wearing aborigines with spears. These men, an eclectic mix of skin and hair colors making the groups' nationality impossible to pinpoint, wore factory-made cotton shirts, rubber trousers, and boots. Most importantly, they carried lever-action rifles that appeared as deadly as the most recent models of Iskandian firearms.

"Hope you didn't lose your grenade when you were upside down," Cas murmured.

She slid her Mark 500 free, keeping the weapon below the level of her seat. She doubted any of the other pilots had more than pistols close at hand, so it would be good to see what these people wanted before starting a firefight. The lightweight flier hulls were not bulletproof, so ducking and shooting wouldn't necessarily keep them safe. Cas did not like the way the men were darting from tree to tree, fanning out to surround her group.

She glanced toward Duck's flier to see what Colonel Quataldo wanted to do, but his seat was empty. Cas blinked. She hadn't seen him leave. Everyone else was still in their fliers, and Blazer looked more irritated at the mud sucking at her wheels than the men approaching. It was possible she hadn't *noticed* the men approaching.

"Any of you boys speak a civilized tongue?" Captain Kaika asked loudly, her Iskandian accent disappearing and the words coming out in the flat tones of a Cofah subject. She draped her elbow over the edge of her flier, appearing unworried about the weapons the men held.

She probably had a bomb in her hidden hand. In front of her, Pimples was staring intently through his windshield, his hands likely on his machine gun triggers. Not much of a threat. Since the fliers' machine guns had stationary mounts, they were next to useless on the ground unless someone was dumb enough to wander into their line of sight.

A couple of the men spoke to each other. Their words drifted across the marshy land, which lay quiet now that the propellers had stopped, the twilight stillness broken only by distant howls and the occasional scurrying of something through the undergrowth. Cas could hear the words, but she did not understand them.

Kaika leaned forward and murmured something to Pimples.

"The captain says they're croc hunters," Pimples' voice came softly over the crystal, "but they're saying they could get a lot of money for our fliers, or at least the power crystals. They want to shoot all of us, but they don't want to damage the fliers."

"Thoughtful," Duck said.

"We shooting them first?" Cas asked quietly, indignation filling her at the thought of thieves pawing over her flier.

She had already picked out the leader. An older man, he

wasn't one of the two talking, but the others kept glancing at him as they discussed their plans. Cas looked back at Tolemek and tilted her head in the man's direction. He nodded once, holding up two grenades that she recognized, one that contained his knockout gas and another that would spew out a harmless smoke. Unfortunately, it would take a powerful throw to reach the hunters with the grenades. Also, out in the open air, the gases wouldn't be as effective as in a confined space.

"Captain Kaika says we're the invaders here and not at war with Dakrovia," Pimples said, "so don't shoot to kill."

"Can't I be at war with the thugs who want to steal my flier?" Blazer growled.

"No."

Cas understood Kaika's reticence, but agreed with Blazer's sentiment. She was inclined to deal with thieves decisively, no matter what nationality they were, and thought they could end the situation quickly by taking down the leader. Fighting to wound against people fighting to kill rarely went well. Still, she wasn't in charge, and she would obey orders.

"Do you have healing salves along, Tolemek?" she murmured, noting that the hunters had stopped talking. Several had eased further behind trees, finding protected positions from which they could fire. Her finger twitched; it was tempting to shoot before they stationed themselves, to try to get the surprise, but Kaika hadn't given the order. Hells, *Quataldo* should be giving orders. Where had he gone?

"Yes," Tolemek said.

"Kaika says for Tolemek to get ready to lay down some smoke when we get the signal," Pimples said quietly.

"What signal would that be?" Tolemek asked.

Before Cas could relay the question, gunfire broke out in the trees at the hunters' backs.

"I'm guessing that's it," Cas said, vaulting over the side of the flier.

She had already picked the spot she wanted to shoot from. As soon as she landed in the water, mud sucking at her boots, she jumped through some reeds and squatted between a stump and the wheel of her flier, keeping the craft at her back. She trusted Tolemek to find his own position once he threw his grenades. More shots were ringing out, echoing from the mangroves. In the beginning, the noise had come from one area, but now all of the thieves were shooting. Return fire came from her own team.

Cas had intended to shoot the man she had pegged as the leader, but he already lay on the ground, his legs flopping uselessly. The two hunters who had been talking about stealing the fliers had been knocked down, too, and neither moved. Briefly, Cas felt miffed that she had been slower to react than someone else, but she spotted a thief leaning out from behind a tree and targeting Blazer's cockpit. She could have taken him in the forehead but aimed for his exposed shoulder instead. The man shot at the same time as Cas. His bullet glanced off the frame of Blazer's windshield. She must have seen him aiming at her, because she ducked first. Cas's bullet struck true, slamming into his shoulder. The hunter spun away, dropping his rifle.

Smoke rose from four locations around the cove, obscuring the figures of other men who were alternating between firing and ducking behind the trees for cover. Tolemek's work. If his knockout grenades were also out there, spewing gas, she might not need to keep firing.

A bullet clanged off the frame of her flier, and she growled, feeling protective toward her craft. She spotted the thief as he ducked back behind a tree. She held her fire, not wanting to alert him to his danger. After a few seconds, he leaned out from the other side of the tree, aiming at the pilots again. Cas, as still as a stone except for the slight flexing of her finger, fired. Once again, the bullet slammed into her foe's shoulder.

A few more shots fired from the fliers—most of the pilots had stayed in the cockpits, but Kaika was also down in the mud a few meters from Cas, her rifle in hand. When the would-be thieves stopped returning fire, Cas's teammates stopped shooting. Silence fell upon the river, the earlier animal cries now still.

"All clear," came Quataldo's voice, not from anywhere near the fliers but from out in the smoke that hung about the trees. "I'm disarming them and trying not to pass out." He strode into view, his kerchief tied over his mouth and nose, three rifles and two swords in his hands.

Cas realized he must have been the one who had taken out the first three men. She was surprised she hadn't seen him moving about out there. Her eyes were usually sharp.

Kaika jogged out to join him, waving at the haze.

Cas rose from behind her stump and looked up—Tolemek was still in his flier seat. "How many knockout grenades did you throw?"

"Only two. Four smoke grenades." His head dropped down as he rummaged in his pack. "I'll find my healing salve."

The smell of burning tobacco drifted across the water. Captain Blazer had left her flier, and she strode toward Cas, a cigar clenched between her teeth and mud spattering the blonde hair she had tied back. She must have left her cap and goggles in the flier.

"We're going to have a problem," she told Cas.

A painful groan came from the trees.

"Witnesses?"

Blazer nodded. "Not starting a war is good, but not announcing our presence would have been even better. I assume someone's staying here with the fliers to guard them while this kidnapping happens, but what are we going to do with these men? If we let them go, they might come back with reinforcements. Worse, they could tell everyone within a hundred miles that Iskandian soldiers are here. Wedding's not for three days, right? And we don't know when the emperor is scheduled to arrive?"

"You know as much as I do, Captain." Cas had briefed the other pilots when she had chosen them, giving them all the information the king had shared in the meeting.

"Do I? That's troubling."

Tolemek swung down, his long hair swaying about his shoulders.

"I don't suppose you have any formulas that can make a person forget the last few hours," Cas said.

"That would be convenient, but I'm not sure it's possible to make something like that."

"Pimples and Duck," Kaika called from the trees. "Come help us drag these men to a dry spot to tie them up."

"Won't Tolemek's gas make us pass out?" Duck asked.

"You've smelled worse in the barracks. Now get out here."

Duck and Pimples shrugged at each other, then shouldered their rifles and marched through the mud to join in the task. Cas started to walk that way, too, but caught movement in the trees upriver.

Expecting more hunters, she leaned around her flier and raised her rifle. Tylie and Phelistoth walked out of the woods, the dragon in his silver-haired human form. One of the injured thieves groaned, and Tylie looked around, her eyes troubled. As usual, Phelistoth wore a haughty, indifferent expression. The king had wanted him along, but Cas wondered how much help the dragon would truly give them.

"What happened?" Tylie asked, stopping to stare at one of the downed men as he gripped his knee and rolled about. Quataldo had already taken his weapons, so he wasn't likely to be trouble, but Tylie's face crumpled with sympathy. "Do people need a healer? I can do a little. And Phel..." She turned toward the dragon, her eyes imploring.

Judging by the way they gazed silently at each other, they were having a telepathic conversation. With all the time Cas had spent around Sardelle, she should have been used to that, but she still found it disturbing. Tolemek went to meet his sister, and Cas headed the other way. She lacked the brawn to haul a grown man through the mud, but she could lend Kaika a hand.

A man cried out in pain as Pimples and Duck lifted him.

"They might have appreciated us more if we'd killed them," Blazer said, hauling a short fellow by herself in a shoulder carry. She wasn't as tall as Captain Kaika, but she had a sturdy build and boxed for a hobby, sometimes in the ring, sometimes with anyone who irked her on the runway. She plopped her man down unceremoniously with five others on a hard piece of raised earth.

One of the prisoners eyed the rifles stacked ten meters away, and Cas detoured to guard the weapons instead of trying to tote anyone. She glared at the men, her rifle gripped in her hands.

Quataldo deposited a man, then stopped to pull rope out of a pack before going back for more.

Tolemek and Tylie walked over, speaking quietly.

"We'll heal anyone who's not making trouble," Tolemek said.

"None of them will be making trouble in a minute." Quataldo wrestled a man's wrists behind his back and started tying. Many others were barely conscious, whether from their injuries or the knockout gas Cas did not know.

Tylie knelt next to one who wasn't moving while Tolemek unscrewed the cap from his salve and waved for one of the men Cas had shot to take off his shirt. Phelistoth came to stand behind Tylie, his arms folded as he glared down at the thieves.

"You missed the fun," Kaika said to Phelistoth when she came back, dragging the last of their prisoners with her. Her tone was casual, but Cas got the feeling she was wondering where he had gone. Did she, too, believe having Phelistoth with them might not be the boon the king thought?

"Fun?" Phelistoth said, his tone flat.

"You're right. It wasn't much fun. I didn't get to light any explosives. If I had, there would have been arms and legs all over this swamp." Kaika grinned down at a man staring up at her. He must have understood their language, because his face paled and he ducked her gaze, staring down at his bleeding thigh.

"Where were you?" Colonel Quataldo asked the dragon, less subtle than Kaika. "The airship didn't see you, did it?"

The dragon's eyes narrowed. "We went hunting. I require food after flying across an ocean. I assure you, nobody saw me except for my dinner."

Cas was glad Phelistoth's cold amber eyes were not pointed in her direction.

Quataldo returned the gaze without flinching. "We would appreciate it if you would let us know when you're leaving the group."

"I am not here to fight your battles, human."

"Why *are* you here?"

"I asked him to come." Tolemek looked up, some of his greenish salve dangling from his fingers. He shook his head slightly at Quataldo. A warning? "Actually I asked Tylie to ask him. At the king's request."

"If the king didn't want him here to help us with our battles, then what?"

"He did warn us about the airship," Cas said. She had no problem letting Phelistoth come and go as he wished and relying only upon the team. She preferred that, actually.

"And I shall warn you about it again." Phelistoth turned to face downriver, his eyes lifting toward the sky. "It appears they, too, heard your noisy battle and are coming to investigate."

"Dragon spit," Kaika said, "I might as well have thrown some explosives."

"It's coming inland?" Blazer asked. "We need to camo these fliers quick. Raptor, Duck, Pimples, get your nets out."

Cas hustled to obey. "How long do we have?" she asked over her shoulder.

"The bloated craft is slow, but already it turns up the river," Phelistoth said.

Kaika cursed and glared down at their captives. "You couldn't have hunted your crocs ten miles *that* way?" She flung her hand toward the swampy depths, shadows growing deep between the trees as twilight deepened.

One of the men sneered at her, but nobody spoke. Quataldo merely continued to tie the prisoners.

"Is there any way to tell if it's a merchant airship?" Cas dug into the small storage compartment behind the second seat of her flier, tugging out the bundle of netting designed to make what it covered look like a mound of earth. She did not know how effective the brown and green colors would be when draped over mud in a swamp, but there wasn't time to move the fliers, nor was there anywhere to move them to—the trees around the inlet were too densely packed.

"I do not know the difference between your merchant ships and other ships." Phelistoth curled his lip, letting them know that he didn't *care* about the difference. Of course not. A ship full of humans wouldn't have the means to hurt him.

"It's an imperial warship," Tylie said.

"What?" several voices asked at once.

She was still kneeling beside her patient, a hand on the man's chest, but she gazed at the sky, her eyes glassy. "Many cannons, many men, and..." She looked toward Phelistoth.

"A sorcerer," he said. "Yes. A weak one."

Cas did not stop tugging the netting over her flier, but she groaned. Without Sardelle here and with Phelistoth an unreliable ally, what would they do against magic users?

"You think all of the sorcerers in this time are weak," Tylie chided.

She didn't sound nearly as worried as Cas felt. She couldn't *shoot* a sorcerer. All the ones she had encountered had the ability to shield themselves from bullets.

"They are," Phelistoth.

"Not so weak that they won't sense us."

"That is true. My presence may be drawing this one."

"Wonderful." Quataldo frowned at the half-covered fliers. "We may have to abort. We can't take down an airship on our own."

"Aw, sir, where's your sense of arrogance?" Kaika asked. "I brought *plenty* of explosives."

"What are they doing down here? You're sure it's an imperial ship?"

Tylie nodded.

"They may be part of an advance party," Tolemek said, "to ensure it's safe for the emperor to come down."

"I can leave," Phelistoth said. "Then my aura will not be a problem. Tylie can hide the rest of you."

Cas jumped down from her flier. "Hide? How?" She draped a corner of the camo netting artistically across the stump.

"I can't hide us from their eyes," Tylie said, "but when Morishtomaric was looking for us, I learned how to hide our auras, to make him believe we were dead. I believe it could fool a sorcerer."

Quataldo nodded. "Good. Do that now. Everyone under the camo or into the trees." He glanced up. "The branches and leaves should cover these men from the sky, as long as they don't make noise." He glowered at the ones who were awake. "I'll fashion gags. Everyone else, hide any sign that we were here."

Cas finished arranging the netting, staked a couple of corners into the mud, then crawled underneath it. She wanted to be able to look up through the holes and watch the airship, see if it truly was a Cofah craft.

Phelistoth walked into the woods, soon disappearing from sight. The rest of the team hid near the tree trunks, where the thick foliage would hide them from above. Tolemek squirmed under the netting and crouched beside Cas.

"I had a feeling when your king gave us this mission that it wouldn't be as easy as he thought," he murmured.

"I don't know that he thought it would be easy. Maybe he just considered us expendable." Cas bumped her shoulder against his.

"Speak for yourself. His army has ordered five hundred jars of my healing salve, and I haven't been able to fill that order yet. I'm not expendable."

"I'm glad to hear it." Though she kept her rifle in one hand, she clasped his closest hand with her other.

"I hope this display of affection doesn't mean you're sure we're in a dire situation and about to die," he murmured, squeezing her hand back.

"No, it means I'm having a hard time keeping my balance with three inches of mud sucking at my boots, and I need you for support."

He snorted. "Always glad to be support."

"I know." Cas thought about leaning over to kiss him on the cheek, but a strange sensation came over her. She froze, trying to examine it. Some probe from the enemy sorcerer? No, it felt less inimical than that.

"That's Tylie," Tolemek murmured. "I don't know how she's doing it, but I can feel her... laying a blanket on us. Magical camo netting."

Cas started to reply, but shut her mouth when the bow of an airship came into view high above. Her stomach sank down to rest between her boots as she recognized the green and gray Cofah colors. From directly beneath it, she couldn't see weaponry or soldiers stalking the deck, but she knew they were there. Was this a single craft, scouting ahead and reporting to the emperor as Tolemek suspected? Or was it one of many? What if Salatak had sent a whole fleet ahead? If the sorcerer up there had sensed Phelistoth, would the wedding or at least the emperor's attendance of the wedding be called off?

"Tylie says she thinks it's a shaman, not a sorcerer," Tolemek whispered.

"What's the difference?" Cas averted her eyes as the rest of the airship hull came into view, lumbering over their muddy inlet. She worried that the craft wasn't high enough for the lookouts to be fooled by the camo.

"I'm not sure, except that sorcerers come out of Cofahre and Iskandia and have—had—a formal school with a lot of written tests and study. The magic users from this continent have an oral tradition and some different ways. She says we'll also need to look out for animal familiars."

Cas remembered General Zirkander telling the story of battling a shaman and a giant owl familiar and how the outpost had needed Sardelle's help to defeat them. Once again, Cas wished Sardelle had come with them. Tylie might be a better resource than Cas had expected, but she wouldn't be as experienced.

"Maybe that's what Phelistoth hunted down for dinner," Cas murmured.

"That would be nice."

The airship disappeared from sight as it continued upriver. Cas hoped their subterfuge had worked, but even if it had, would it be enough? Her gaze settled on their prisoners, prisoners they couldn't take along but that they couldn't let go, not without further risk of being discovered.

Chapter 4

FLYING ON A DRAGON'S BACK was exhilarating—and terrifying. Sardelle did not feel the wind like she expected, not the way she did when she cruised in Ridge's flier. A comforting cloak of magic wrapped around her, keeping her astride Bhrava Saruth, not dissimilarly to the harness in Ridge's back seat. Except that the "harness" was made of strands of invisible power. She was glad Bhrava Saruth cared enough to put out the effort, because they were zipping along more quickly than a flier, the land below passing by in a blur. The jagged peaks of the Ice Blades grew larger with each passing moment, the dawn sky lightening from pink to blue behind them.

We will arrive soon, high priestess.

Excellent. Thank you. You can call me Sardelle, if you wish. She certainly wished he would, but she didn't want to complain when he was doing this favor for her. She wondered what she could do to pay him back.

Perhaps you can find him a worshipful ingénue or two in the villages down there, Jaxi suggested.

Maybe I can get him some of that cheese that Phelistoth likes.

They passed a flock of ducks, startling the poor creatures into diving for the nearest lake. Despite the magical harness, Sardelle held on tightly as Bhrava Saruth's back tilted and they climbed toward the tops of the mountains. She closed her eyes and rested her face against his cool scales. Tylie had taken to this right away, but Sardelle found it more alarming than riding in Ridge's flier, perhaps because she didn't know if Bhrava Saruth was exactly what he appeared or if he had hidden—and possibly dangerous—depths.

Speaking of dangerous depths, you better make sure the king's orders don't fly out of your pack, Jaxi said. *Therrik may greet you with*

Kasandral in hand, especially if you come in on dragonback.

They're securely fastened. She did intend to have the king's orders in hand as soon as they landed. Just because Therrik had called her an asset in that report did not mean he would be eager to help her.

As they passed the first peaks and headed closer to the spine of the Blades, Sardelle opened her eyes and leaned her head to the side of Bhrava Saruth's neck so she could watch the glaciers and valleys passing below. They weren't to the crash site yet, but if Ridge had walked away and hadn't been able to climb back up to the outpost, he might be searching for a route that would take him out of the mountains. Flying made the peaks seem less daunting, but she remembered from her childhood just how long it took to traverse the Ice Blades and that climbing gear was required in many places.

There are people here and there, Bhrava Saruth informed her, *but I do not believe they are the one you seek.*

She did not know if he could recognize Ridge's aura through her thoughts, but she said, *Thank you for looking.* She would keep searching herself.

I'm looking too, Jaxi said. *I hope I'll be wrong and that he's alive.*
Thank you.

Bhrava Saruth took them over the crash site, the rocky slope still in shadow as the sun rose behind Goat Mountain. She spotted the remains of the flier once again. Nothing had changed, not that she had expected it to. Ridge wouldn't have been able to climb back up to it if he had fallen out and into the river below. That river was even farther below than she remembered, and the pit of her stomach grew heavy. Maybe she *was* being delusional about all this. Maybe there was no way he could have survived.

Do you wish to search further now, high priestess? Or collect your servant in the human fort first?

My, ah, servant? Sardelle was quite positive she hadn't explained Therrik that way.

He will serve you in this matter, yes? My priestess should have as many servants as she needs.

Just don't call him that. Sardelle pointed to the slope. *Do you think it's possible to find a spot to land down there? By the wreckage?*

They had not been able to do that in the fliers. Even the two-seat models with the thrusters required a flat surface for landing.

Yes, of course. Bhrava Saruth tilted his wings and they swooped low.

Even though he had talons and could grasp onto a perch like a bird, she wondered at finding a landing spot down there. It was so steep. If the body of the flier hadn't come to a stop behind a boulder embedded in the earth, it would have fallen all the way down into the canyon below.

Bhrava Saruth slowed himself as he neared the ground by tilting his body upward. His talons came out, and he alighted on the boulder right next to what remained of the battered flier. The big rock shifted, and pebbles bounced down the slope, skipped over the edge, and disappeared into the canyon. Sardelle tightened her grip on Bhrava Saruth's smooth scales as the boulder shifted more, a soft scraping sound coming from below. He adjusted his weight, and it grew still. She told herself that he would simply leap up and flap his wings if it gave away, but she couldn't help but feel as if her life teetered on the edge. From above, she hadn't realized just how steep this slope was. She couldn't imagine that Ridge could have walked away without falling.

Regardless, she looked to either side of the crumpled flier, seeking footprints or skid marks that might indicate someone had disturbed the rocks. From her position near Bhrava Saruth's shoulders, it was hard to read signs on the ground.

Bhrava Saruth bent his head, his long neck allowing him to lower his snout to the earth. He sniffed at the cockpit of the flier, then sniffed at the ground all around it.

Did he say he was a god *or a* dog? Jaxi asked.

Hush. Sardelle did not want to insult him, especially not when he was helping her.

I just thought he might be confused. If it helps, I don't sense Ridge nearby. But as before, my senses are muddled by his divine presence.

Sardelle did not sense much, either, beyond marmots hiding in the rocks.

I detect a faint scent from the cockpit, Bhrava Saruth announced, *but rain has come and washed away most of the signs.*

Sardelle eyed the lifeless power crystal and wondered if that had been the reason Ridge crashed. Had the dragon destroyed it while he was in the air? She looked to the side, spotting the tip of the ammo belt that fed bullets into the machine gun. She thought some of Tolemek's special ammunition might remain, the bullets with his acid in the tips, acid capable of doing damage to dragon scales.

She couldn't get down and fiddle around in the cockpit by hand, but she unfastened the belt with her mind and floated the remaining ammo up to her hand. There weren't more than thirty or forty bullets left, but maybe they would make a difference in the future, or maybe Tolemek could use them as a model to craft more. She carefully tucked them into her pack.

Can you take me over to the edge of the rockslide area? Where it levels out a bit? Sardelle doubted anyone could have walked across the slope and reached the less treacherous ground, but Bhrava Saruth flew her to the area. She slid off and walked around, studying the stark ground as if she knew what she was doing or might find a clue so obvious that even a tracking neophyte might recognize it.

Perhaps this would be the time to get Therrik, Jaxi said.

Sardelle sighed and looked toward the canyon, where she could hear the river flowing past far below. *You're right. At the least, we'd have more eyes on the ground.*

She would have preferred not to need him, but with the king's orders, Therrik shouldn't object too much. She directed Bhrava Saruth to take them back into the air, feeling quite presumptuous every time she made a request. She rarely asked *people* for favors. To ask a dragon to cart her around felt strange indeed.

How are we going to keep the miners from shooting at him—and us? Jaxi asked as they sailed around Goat Mountain and the outpost came into view.

A valid concern. Sardelle knew the cannons and rocket launchers poised on the walls wouldn't get past Bhrava Saruth's defenses, but he might not feel welcome if he was greeted with a barrage of weapons fire.

A distant wailing reached her ears, the alarm being sounded in the valley. She stretched out with her mind, searching for the one person down there who could stop the alarm and the attack that had to be imminent. So what if he happened to be the one person who would least appreciate a sorceress speaking telepathically to him?

Maybe it would be better to land shielded and use your lips with him, Jaxi suggested.

I'm not sure he wants anything to do with my lips either. Sardelle found Therrik's aura among the soldiers on the wall just before he came into sight. Bhrava Saruth had slowed down and was coasting in.

She reached out to the man, sensing his grumpy disposition even before she fully touched his mind. He was so different from Ridge. She braced herself for the discomfort before she sent her words to him. *Colonel Therrik? It's Sardelle. I have orders for you from the king. This is the dragon that helped us defeat Morishtomaric. He and I would appreciate it if you commanded your men not to fire.*

A long pause came, followed by a single word. *Shit.*

I don't think he's changed as much as the king thinks he has, Jaxi said.

Bhrava Saruth, not appearing concerned by the weapons on the towers or the soldiers on the wall banked and descended, heading for the rooftop in the courtyard that the fliers used for landing. Out of habit, Sardelle prepared her own defenses, even though the dragon's would likely protect her. Bellowing came from the parapet. Judging by the gruffness, it originated with Therrik.

She wasn't sure whether he was yelling for his men to fire or not to fire. Bhrava Saruth flexed his wings and floated down to the rooftop. A lot of tense faces followed his flight, but nobody fired. Sardelle let out a slow breath.

Good morning, humans, Bhrava Saruth announced cheerfully. It took Sardelle a moment to realize he wasn't just addressing her. Was he speaking to the entire outpost? *If you are in need of healing or blessings, please come to me. There is no need to be alarmed by the god, Bhrava Saruth, but if you are uncomfortable speaking to me, you may address my high priestess, and she will direct you on my behalf.*

Sardelle felt her mouth dangling open, but she couldn't quite manage to close it. She wasn't sure whether the humans to which he spoke would charge up to see him or would run for the tram cars in the hope of cowering down in the mines.

The first person to appear, climbing the stairs to the roof, was Therrik. Sardelle slid off the dragon's back, her hand already dipping into her satchel so she could retrieve the envelope that held his orders.

"What in all the levels of hell is going on here?" he demanded.

She noted with great relief that he wasn't striding around with Kasandral. "I need the help of a tracker, and King Angulus recommended you." She pulled out the envelope and held it toward him.

He had come up the stairs to greet Sardelle—and the dragon—by himself, with nothing but a rifle in hand, but he seemed reluctant to approach. His jaw worked back and forth as he glanced toward the courtyard, then toward the envelope, and finally toward Bhrava Saruth, whose wings, when spread, extended farther than the sides of the building under them.

He is thinking unkind thoughts toward me, high priestess, Bhrava Saruth said. *I do not believe he would make a good worshipper.*

Perhaps some of the other people here could use your help and would be grateful for it.

Finally, Therrik squared his shoulders and strode toward them. He accepted the envelope, then stepped back, careful not to touch her. Sardelle suspected he was thinking unkind thoughts toward her too.

I get the sense that he thinks unkind thoughts toward everyone, Jaxi said.

"Tracking what?" he asked as he pulled out the page.

"I want to see if there's any chance that Ridge is still alive. Also, the king thought you might like to get out Kasandral and help me find the sorceress."

His gaze jerked up, fastening onto her face for the first time. His nostrils flared, and his eyes burned, alert and intent. Even with Jaxi at her hip and a dragon behind her, Sardelle shifted uneasily, not sure how to read that sudden intensity. Was he imagining that he might get his chance to use the blade to kill her?

Actually, he's getting excited by the idea of killing Eversong and redeeming himself in the king's eyes, Jaxi said.

Oh. He wouldn't mind working with us if he got his chance to do that? One confrontation with the powerful sorceress had been enough for Sardelle. She would be happy to aim Therrik and the dragon-slaying blade in the right direction while standing back to assist.

I doubt you'd want to turn your back to him when he's polishing Kasandral around the campfire at night, but he's not fantasizing about killing you at the moment.

That's an improvement.

I'll say. The man does have a lot of violent urges. One wonders about his childhood.

"The king is tired of Eversong wandering around in his country and causing mischief," Sardelle added, feeling the need to say something since several moments had passed since Therrik had spoken.

He stirred, looking down at the orders again. "I can understand that. All those damned witches ought to be killed."

A deep rumble sounded from behind Sardelle. Was that a growl? Did dragons growl?

Bhrava Saruth's neck stretched past Sardelle's shoulder, his sleek golden head huge next to hers. He glared at Therrik with cold, green reptilian eyes as his tail twitched, then curled about to rest on the ground between Therrik and Sardelle. She blinked a few times in surprise, realizing he was protecting her. It was strange but a little exhilarating too. Was that what Tylie felt when Phelistoth protected her? She wondered why Bhrava Saruth would bother. She wasn't a Receiver and hadn't spent years sharing a mind link with him, the way Tylie had with Phelistoth.

You're his only high priestess right now, Jaxi said dryly.

Therrik looked up, fear flashing in his dark eyes as he realized that growl had been for him. He quickly turned the emotion into a sneer of defiance, or perhaps contempt. "Oh, not her. She's Angulus's witch. I mean the ones that make trouble."

Ah, he's promoted you from Zirkander's witch to the king's witch, Jaxi said. *Your career is advancing nicely.*

Sardelle knew it was a joke, but it filled her with bleakness. She had no interest in being anyone's "witch" except for Ridge's.

"We have to track Zirkander first?" Therrik had taken a few more steps back from Bhrava Saruth to finish reading the note. "I thought they were positive he was dead."

"We found his crashed flier, but we never found him."

"Huh. You think the witch has him?"

Sardelle started to say no, but her lips froze before the word fully formed, the thought leaping into her mind again. Was it possible? If Jaxi had sensed Eversong nearby and she had been on the way to the outpost, might she have diverted when she saw the dragon battle? What if she had gotten to him first?

We discussed this, Jaxi said. *Why would she bother? I assume it was the crystal or something else in the old Referatu stronghold that drew her here, the same as the dragons. Why divert to get a crashed pilot instead?*

I'm not saying it's likely, just that it's possible. Ridge was the second-highest-ranking military man in the area then, and he knows all about the outpost. He probably knows a lot of military secrets too—how defenses are laid out here and back at home in the capital. She could have wanted him to... She trailed off, grimacing as her mind finished the sentence. Imagining Eversong dragging him off to torture him for information was almost as bad as imagining him dead.

Therrik was staring at her, waiting for an answer.

"I don't know," Sardelle said, "but I want to start with him. If he *is* out there, he may not have much time. Angulus said you were a good tracker." She smiled, hoping he might be more amenable to working with her if she proved herself pleasant. She wouldn't flatter him unduly, but Angulus *had* said Therrik had survival skills.

Instead of looking pleased, he scowled. "You're on a first-name basis with him, are you?"

What? *Everyone* called him Angulus. Granted, they usually prefaced it with King, but even the newspapers referred to him by first name.

She shrugged and said, "He's asked me to work in the castle as a healer." Maybe that would explain the familiarity to Therrik's satisfaction.

All he did was grumble and turn his back. "Twenty years I've served him, blood and soul, and who does he trust? Some strange witch woman who's been here for three months and climbed into his bed." He stalked away as he spoke, disappearing down the stairs.

"That's hardly accurate," Sardelle said.

No, we've been here six months now.

He is surly, Bhrava Saruth observed. *I don't believe he will be bringing me an offering.*

He's getting the sword, Jaxi said a few minutes later.

Not to use on us, I trust, Sardelle said.

Probably not. He's stuffing underwear into a pack too. It appears he's getting ready for a trip.

Good. Sardelle gazed toward Goat Mountain and the white-capped peaks looming behind it. *We're coming, Ridge.*

* * *

After clunking his knee against three stumps and a rock, Tolemek found Cas standing guard beside a tree overlooking the river. If not for his growing ability to sense people the way Sardelle did, he might have stumbled into the water before finding her, assuming she hadn't said anything. Between the layers of thick foliage and the clouds that had rolled in, blotting out the stars, the night was darker than the inside of a dragon's stomach.

"Are you looking for me?" Cas murmured. "Or for a private place to relieve yourself?"

"I wouldn't have come this far for that."

"We're only ten meters from camp." *Camp* was an ambitious term for what they had, which was the camouflaged fliers parked in the mud and people hunkered on the lumpy mangrove roots, the only dry things around, aside from the patch of land they had turned into their prison.

"What's your point?"

Tolemek couldn't see Cas crinkle her nose, but when she said, "Men are gross," he had no trouble imagining it.

"Does that mean you're not interested in cuddling?"

"Probably not when I'm standing watch. You're supposed to be sleeping so you can leave before dawn. Colonel Quataldo said you, he, and Kaika have to get an early start."

"I heard. I suppose you, Blazer, Duck, and Pimples get to sleep in."

Tolemek understood why the pilots would be staying behind, since they had to be able to swoop in and pick up the kidnappers once they had collected the emperor, but he wasn't tickled at the idea of going in without Cas. He would have preferred to stay behind and let the two elite forces soldiers handle sneaking in on their own, but Colonel Quataldo wanted him—and his collection of grenades and salves—along. Tolemek did not know whether he should feel honored or not. He had a hunch the colonel also wanted to ensure Tylie—and Phelistoth—would stay nearby, something that might be more likely if he went.

An ominous growl, followed by a loud splash came from fifteen or twenty meters downstream, and Tolemek jumped.

"Oh, I don't think we'll be sleeping in," Cas said. "Not with prisoners to guard and a swamp full of creatures that want to eat them. And us."

Tolemek also did not like the idea of leaving Cas and the others to keep watch over twelve men who would spend the next three days trying to escape or otherwise make trouble. The pilots had to worry about the imperial airship patrolling the coast too.

"It would be better for you if there weren't prisoners to guard," Tolemek said.

"We can't let them go, and I don't think anyone is going to agree to a mass throat slitting."

"I wasn't suggesting *that*, but I have an idea. One that relies upon my dreadful reputation, assuming it's made it to this continent." He wouldn't know if it had until he saw how the men reacted.

"What is it? Have you run it by the colonel?"

"Not yet. I need to see if Captain Kaika will help, since she can speak the language here. But first, I need you to know that I have something of yours."

"Oh?"

"Actually, it's from Duck's flier." Tolemek opened his hand where she would see it. A warm yellow glow escaped from his palm.

"You were able to get it out? I thought your fancy blood might be useful."

"Yes, my fancy blood and a screwdriver." Tolemek closed his fist on the communication crystal, cutting out the light. "It's smaller than I realized. I'll need to fasten it to something so I don't lose it, but we'll be able to keep in touch with your group and let you know when we need company."

"Good. I don't think smoke signals would be effective here."

"Not across forty miles." Tolemek grimaced at the march they had ahead of them. Even if they followed the beach, it would take all day and into the night, and he didn't know if they would be able to stick to the beach, not if enemy airships cruised by regularly. They probably couldn't risk flying closer, either, lest they be spotted. "Let me see if I can get anything to come of my idea."

He started to move away, but Cas caught his arm.

"Be careful out there," she urged. "I wish I was going with you."

"I wish you were too." He bent his head and found her cheek with his lips.

"Just so you know," Cas said, her voice so soft he had to lean closer to hear her, "Wolf Squadron's orders are to protect the flier that's carrying the emperor at all costs. Right now, the plan is for Blazer to get him. The rest of us may have to stay behind, deal with pursuit so they can get away."

"So the rest of us are expendable?" he asked dryly.

"It would seem so. I hope you left the recipe for your healing salve behind."

He snorted. "It takes magic as well as ingredients. Nobody would be able to duplicate it."

Cas brushed his hair away from his face. "Then we should try to make sure you return home too."

"Let's all return home."

"I'm amenable to that."

"Good." The second time, he kissed her on the lips, not pulling away until she lowered her head and murmured something about being on watch.

Not liking the way that kiss had felt like a goodbye, Tolemek hugged her and returned to the camp. He washed his hands thoroughly, a challenge in the muddy environment, then dug a lantern out of his pack, along with a scalpel, a spool of suture, and a few chips of calcite that would be harmless under the skin. To be on the safe side, he doused the chips with his healing salve, which should keep an infection from taking root.

"Captain Kaika?" he murmured, picking his way through the mud to where she slept on a knot of roots.

"Yeah?"

"Can I borrow you for translation purposes?"

"That's not the usual proposition men give me in the middle of the night."

"It's not the middle of the night," Tolemek said. "Only a couple of hours past dusk."

"I guess that changes things." She pushed herself to her feet with a soft splash as her boots landed in the mud. "What do you need?"

"I want to perform surgery on our prisoners and for you to tell them what I'm doing. What I say I'm doing."

Kaika paused a moment, either to rub sleep out of her eyes or to regard him like he was a crazy man. "Does Cas ever tell you that you're odd?"

"No," he said.

"Huh. You should keep her then." Kaika grabbed her rifle, having no trouble finding it in the dark. "Lead on, surgeon."

Tolemek turned his lantern up to full strength, swinging it at his side as he approached the prison. He whistled to himself to draw attention. A few open eyes watched him, the light glinting off them. Tylie had healed everybody to the best of her ability, with his salve helping, so the men were not in pain now. This ploy might have worked better if they *hadn't* healed the men, but he hadn't thought of it until he had lain down to rest.

"Which one first?" he asked Kaika.

She gave him a quick what-are-you-doing look, then nudged one with her boot. "This one tried to shoot me earlier. I think he was one of the ringleaders."

"He should be punished then."

"Of course."

"Translate, please. Oh, and tell them my name, will you? My pirate name. In case they haven't already guessed."

Kaika nudged the closest man again and said a few words. He hoped one of them was Deathmaker.

A few of the men shifted on the ground and glanced toward the trees. One's shoulders hunched as he tried to pull his tied wrists free. Tolemek found the reaction promising, at least for the purposes of this exercise.

"Will you assist me and hold the lantern, Captain?" Tolemek held up the vial of flakes and shook them. They tinked softly against the glass. "I plan to insert these devices under the skin of each prisoner before we free them. They will allow me to track them, and they will also allow me to kill them from a distance, should I deem it necessary. Such as if they attempt to inform anyone that they saw us."

One of the prisoners cursed under his breath, leading Tolemek to assume at least a few of the people understood their language.

"Oh?" Kaika squinted at the vial. "For the rest of their lives or for a limited time?"

"For the rest of their lives. Translate, please."

Kaika spoke in a casual tone to the men, as if she were discussing meal preferences. From the way some of the thieves' eyes grew round, he trusted she was doing more than that.

Tolemek grew aware of someone behind them, and he glanced back to find Colonel Quataldo standing in the shadows, his arms folded over his chest. He did not say anything, but his lips were thin with displeasure. Perhaps Tolemek should have run this by him first.

He shrugged. He would perform the surgery. It would be up to the colonel if he wanted to let the men go. Tolemek just wanted to leave Cas with as few problems as possible back here.

"Nobody's volunteering to be first," Kaika said.

"No? A pity. The procedure is quite painless. Let's do that one." He pointed to the man she had nudged.

The thief rolled away from him. He bumped into one of his comrades and did not get far.

"Colonel," Tolemek said. "Will you assist me by holding the subject?"

Quataldo walked over wordlessly. He shot Tolemek a narrow-eyed look, but that was his only objection. With ease that suggested more strength than it seemed his lean, wiry form should possess, he hauled the big thief to his feet.

"Where do you want him?"

"Close enough to the light that I can see what I'm doing." Tolemek pointed to roots protruding from the water nearby. "Drape his arm across those and push his sleeve up."

Quataldo did so while crouching behind the man with a knee in his back. He was very effective at making it so that his prisoner could not struggle. Tolemek remembered the way he had dropped three of the thieves before Cas had even started shooting. In Angulus's atrium, he had seemed an unassuming enough man, but Tolemek had since decided Quataldo wasn't anyone he wanted for an enemy.

Tolemek set about his work quickly, slicing a slender line in the man's forearm. The prisoner gasped and tried to pull away, but Quataldo held him fast. The shallow wound should not hurt much, but it was good that the thief was worried about this. He would be less likely to doubt Tolemek's words, less likely to tattle on the Iskandians. All they needed was three days of silence. Then his team would either be gone or captured. Or dead.

Tolemek inserted one of his flakes into the wound, digging in to make sure it would be embedded deeply enough that his prisoner could not easily scrape it out. The man gasped again. Considering the thieves had been trying to kill his group, Tolemek did not feel too badly about causing a little pain.

"If you try to take it out," Tolemek said as he finished up, now stitching the cut closed, "it will send poison into your bloodstream that will travel to your heart."

Kaika, who stood nearby while holding the light, translated.

"Your heart will stop within three minutes." He held the man's eyes as Kaika translated, making his face as grim as possible. Sometime after he had started working in his lab in Iskandia, he had tucked his pirate attire into a cabinet, shaved his goatee, and donned clothing typical of the locals. He'd left his hair long, though, the ropy locks tangled and wild, since he believed it made him look fiercer, less like someone people would want to chance irritating. He tried to summon all of that fierceness now as he held the thief's eyes.

The man only held his gaze for a second, then whispered something to Kaika.

"He says he's sorry," she said. "They shouldn't have been greedy. He has a family, two small girls, and he sends the money he earns from crocodile skins and meat home to them, so they can get by. The fliers were too good to pass up. It could have sent his girls to school." Kaika snorted. "I don't believe his story."

"It doesn't matter," Tolemek said, keeping his tone hard so the man would find him more daunting. "So long as he knows he won't make it back to that family if he betrays our position. Make sure he understands." He gripped the man's forearm, his thumb pressing on the fresh sutures. "Do you understand?"

The thief's head bobbed up and down.

"Get me the next one," Tolemek said.

"Do you want them retied?" Quataldo asked, the quirk to his lips suggesting he found it odd that he, the mission commander, was asking *Tolemek* what he wanted done.

"I'll leave that up to you, Colonel, as to whether you want to release them or not before we go."

Quataldo tied the thief's hands behind his back again. Probably not a bad idea since that would keep him from scratching at the sutures even more effectively than Tolemek's threat. "We'll decide in the morning."

In a slow parade, Quataldo fetched him thieves, bringing each one over and holding the man while he received a supposedly magical tracking flake.

Tolemek was tired by the time he finished, but he walked away from the lantern and the eyes of the thieves before cracking a yawn. A sleepy Deathmaker wouldn't be as frightening of a man, he suspected.

"Do you think they'll believe it?" Cas asked quietly from behind him. She must have been relieved from her watch by one of the others.

He wondered how long she had been observing. He grimaced, wishing she hadn't witnessed him being cruel. It might save the group trouble, so it was worth it, but it bothered him that his reputation still worked so well, all these thousands of miles from where he and the Roaming Curse pirates had worked.

"Would you want to risk it?" Tolemek asked.

"Probably not. And we don't need them to believe it forever."

"If your colonel agrees, you can set them free in the morning. Letting them go back to wherever they came from will mean you don't have to worry about feeding them either."

Cas nodded. "We'll likely move the camp so they wouldn't be able to find us again, if they decide to risk telling someone. Make sure to keep the communication crystal close, so we can let you know where we go. We'll try to get closer to the city, as originally planned."

"I understand."

Tolie? Tylie whispered into his mind.

He looked toward the woods, where she slept against Phelistoth's side. He couldn't see them from here, but his senses told him the dragon was back in his usual form, the swamp creatures going nowhere near him. Tylie was in the safest place on the continent.

Yes? He hoped she wouldn't censure him for playing the role of deranged scientist. She had such a gentle soul. Being a healer would be a good career for her.

Phel senses something, she told him.

Another airship?

Another dragon.

Chapter 5

Since Ridge had already been sore when he and Mara started their trek out of the mountains, he did not know how many of the aches, pains, and blisters he could blame on the walking and climbing, not to mention the unwise command decision he had made to slide down a steep slope on a sled improvised from a large piece of bark. The infantry soldiers back home would laugh at him if he admitted to finding the trek difficult, so he would never speak of it, but pilots weren't meant to use their feet so much. Especially when one of those feet was missing a sock.

When the smoke of a campfire or perhaps a hearth came into view, Ridge doubted they had gone more than twenty miles as the dragon flier flew, but they must have covered two or three times as much ground to get there, winding around mountains and through irritatingly indirect valleys.

"There's a settlement ahead," Mara said.

For the first time, they followed a hard-packed, man-made trail with branches cut back along either side. Unlike the animal paths they had used for much of the journey, the trail was also wide enough for them to walk side by side. Instead of leading, as she had been doing for most of the trip, she dropped back to walk at his shoulder.

"That's good to know. I worried some bears might be up ahead, making a bonfire in anticipation of a succulent Ridge Roast tonight." In truth, they hadn't had any trouble with animals, to his surprise. At times, growls had sounded in the foliage nearby, and coyotes had cried to each other from the sides of the trail, but Mara had glared defiantly into the woods, her hand on her knife, and nothing had come out to bother them.

Mara gave him a curious look. That was her usual response

to his comments, as if she couldn't quite understand him. As if *he* was the mysterious one.

She disappeared into the woods often and did not talk much when she *was* with him. She never shared anything about herself unless he quizzed her directly. Even then, she often avoided answering his questions by jogging ahead "to scout" or going into the woods "to hunt." She always came back with food, some animal or fish that they could cook, with no explanation as to how she had caught the game. All she had was that knife, and there were never any marks on the animals to explain their deaths. Every time Ridge opened his mouth to ask about her methods, the voice in the back of his head chided him lightly, suggesting it would be impertinent to question the woman keeping him alive. Oddly, that voice didn't seem to know that he and impertinence were old friends.

Oh, I know, it whispered into the back of his mind. *This is an interesting place.*

This? The inside of my head?

Yes. You're not quite like other people, are you?

Uhm. Ridge didn't necessarily disagree, but he had the feeling that his attention was being diverted from Mara's eccentricities. It wasn't the first time. Assuming that his subconscious was responsible for the separate voice manifesting itself in his head, why would it do that?

Perhaps to protect you, it suggested.

Do I need protection? From Mara? He hadn't had the sense that she was dangerous, but it was possible he was being naive. There was that unexplained accent, the callouses, and other clues about her that made him question her story.

I am simply observing that nosy people are sometimes punished by the gods for their nosiness. This sounded like a threat, but for some reason, Ridge couldn't bring himself to worry.

Mara smiled over at him.

"I'll go ahead and see if I can trade for a horse," she said. "There are decent trails the rest of the way out of the mountains, so a horse could handle them."

"You'll go ahead? Why don't I go ahead with you? Maybe

someone in that settlement will recognize me and feel kindly toward pilots. Kindly enough to lend a horse. Or perhaps two horses."

She kept mentioning *a* horse, but they would make better time with two, if two could be found. Besides, he was skeptical about riding double with her. She had been sleeping close at night, offering to share her single blanket with him, and giving him smiles that mixed between shy and flirtatious.

"I'll take care of it." Mara started to jog ahead.

"I'll come with you. In addition to a horse, I wouldn't mind seeing if someone has a razor I can borrow." He rubbed his jaw, then wrinkled his nose as he caught a whiff of his armpit. "Some soap, too, perhaps."

She paused, frowning back at him. "You should wait outside of the village. Someone might see your injuries and try to take advantage of you."

See his injuries? Aside from the sore muscles, he had amazingly few after that crash. He had removed the bandages and found scars beneath them rather than fresh scabs, making him wonder how many days he had lost being unconscious.

"I'll take the risk," Ridge said firmly. "I don't think I look so sickly and anemic as to be wolf bait."

If anything, people would see Mara, who stood more than half a foot shorter than him and appeared much more innocent, as a target, but he had visited enough small villages in his life to know that the residents were usually hospitable.

"I don't think it's a good idea." Mara looked up the trail and toward the trees, almost like a doe poised to flee. Maybe she thought that if she disappeared, he couldn't find the village on his own? Even if finding things from the air was easier, nobody had ever had reason to mock his sense of direction.

"I'll come anyway." He pointed at the collar of his uniform jacket. Though it was decorated with dirt, grass stains, and a couple of rips, the rank tabs had survived. "Officers are supposed to be in charge of things, you know. Especially generals." His mind still boggled at the notion that sometime since he'd lost his memories, he had let someone promote him.

"Officers are in charge of soldiers. I'm not a soldier."

"Well, at least let me be in charge of myself, eh?"

Her face took on a mulish cast, but he kept walking down the trail, his step determined. And his ongoing suspicions about her returned—why didn't she want him to contact other people? A part of him almost doubted his belief that he was truly in the Ice Blades. What if he was in Cofahre somewhere, and he was about to find out? The stars had been the same when he'd gazed into the clear sky the night before, but that didn't prove much. Parts of the empire were at the same latitude as Iskandia. Still, the peaks seemed familiar, even to a city boy who hadn't spent much time in the mountains. The Ice Blades were visible from the capital, after all.

"I'm sorry." Mara had let him pass by but she hurried to catch up and walk beside him. "I'm afraid you won't need me anymore once we're with other people." She clasped his hand.

"Ah." Ridge debated whether to extract himself from her grip or not. If that was her fear, it was a true enough one. He hadn't enjoyed having to depend on someone else, and he looked forward to returning to the city and his squadron. He hoped that seeing his comrades would punt his memory into working again. If nothing else, a doctor should have some ideas. "I'll always be grateful that you helped me."

"But you *are* planning to leave," she said sadly. "I thought you might take me with you to the capital. That's where you work, isn't it? I've never seen a big city." She smiled up at him, her eyes bright.

The words were believable—he could understand that a rural woman might see him as a way to a more exciting life—but there was calculation in those eyes. She was trying to manipulate him. Over the years, he'd had numerous women try to ensnare him, thinking they could use him as a way to a better life. It bemused him somewhat, since army officers didn't make piles of money. Anyone who saw his house on base could tell he wasn't rich, but he supposed they imagined his days to be glorious and interesting. He'd managed to avoid entrapments thus far and had learned to been careful with his dalliances. He hated it when he ended up feeling like a callous ass because he couldn't be what women wanted.

"It's not nearly as peaceful in the city as it is out here," Ridge said.

Mara's face fell, and there he was, feeling like an ass again. She *had* saved his life.

"I can take you back and show you around," he found himself saying, and it was as if the words were being pulled out of his mouth by someone else. Strange.

"Oh? Wonderful." She gripped his hand tighter, swinging it as they walked. "Are you married, Ridge?"

"Uh, what?" Sweat beaded on his forehead, and it had nothing to do with the exertion of the walk. "I mean, no. I shouldn't be."

He couldn't imagine it. Given the way his first forty years had gone, he seemed destined for bachelorhood. He grimaced as he thought of his fortieth birthday when Captain Crash had tried to set him up with a woman he might like, an artist like his mom. Except she had been nothing like his mom. She'd made those pots with human hair incorporated in them. And she'd had that collection of used butcher knives as wall art in her dark warehouse apartment. She had been so delighted when those mousetraps had snapped while he'd been there. He hadn't stuck around long enough to ask if she incorporated the captured creatures into her art as well.

Missing memories or not, Ridge was certain that he was not married.

"Ridge?"

"I'm sorry, what?"

Had she said something else? He had been too busy remembering and shuddering. Sure, things like *that* he could recall.

"I asked if you had any lady friends you were involved with." She still wore her smile, her arm swinging casually as she held his hand, but her eyes were intent. Intensely intent.

"No. I don't think so."

"Good."

"Not according to my mother," he said, struggling for a dry, nonchalant tone. And a way to divert this conversation to another topic. He'd liked it better when Mara hadn't been speaking.

"She'd like you to marry?"

"Oh yes. And to have children. Lots of them."

"Do you want children?"

"I don't think so."

"I don't either."

"No?"

"I just like to have a good time. It's lonely out here in the mountains."

"I imagine it would be."

She stopped on the trail, and since their hands were linked, he perforce stopped too. "I'm sure this has been an unpleasant experience for you, but I've enjoyed your company."

She had? He hadn't been very witty or charming. Of course, that was her fault, for being on the odd side and disappearing whenever he asked questions.

"Good," he said, because she was gazing up at him and seemed to expect him to say something.

"You meant what you said?" Mara asked. "You'll take me with you to the capital?"

"Sure." He did not know what he had been thinking, other than that he owed her a debt, but he wouldn't go back on his word.

"Can we see the king?"

Ridge shifted uneasily, once again getting that feeling that she was trying to manipulate him into something. "If you're there when he does one of his speeches, anyone can see him."

"Will you take me to see one of his speeches?" she asked shyly, easing closer to him, her free hand coming to rest on his waist.

"Sure," he said again, mostly because he was relieved she hadn't asked for more, like a private audience. As he'd said, anyone could attend the speeches. Angulus was well guarded for those, so it wasn't as if taking her would present a security risk.

"Thank you," she said earnestly. "I can't wait to see the city. And to be there with you."

"Uh." He was on the verge of stepping back and trying to

extricate his hand from hers when she leaned forward, rising on her tiptoes to kiss him.

It wasn't the chaste kiss of some innocent mountain girl who'd had little experience with men. It was the raw, hungry, and demanding kiss of someone used to getting her way, claiming whomever she wished for her own, and it took him by surprise. At first, he merely stood there with his mouth open. His body started to react as she pressed against him, his thoughts of suspicion and wariness scattering in the face of her naked desire, but he found the wherewithal to step back, lifting a hand to keep her from following.

She blinked, a puzzled expression crossing her face. Well, that made two of them feeling puzzled.

"Maybe we should head into the village now," Ridge said, nodding toward the path. "So we don't surprise anyone by coming in late at night."

Her face still crinkled in confusion, Mara headed down the trail, taking the lead again.

A chuckle sounded in Ridge's head. Seven gods, was that the voice of his subconscious again? Cackling now? He'd hoped that voice would disappear once his headaches faded, but if anything, it was developing even more of a personality.

You're not what she expected, it said.

Clearly. Ridge waited until Mara was a dozen steps ahead before following.

Do you not find her attractive? The voice sounded curious.

Oh, she's a beauty. This situation is a little strange, though, don't you think?

Certainly. Strange situations rarely keep men from sleeping with her if she wishes it.

She finds a lot of men out in the mountains, does she? Ridge asked. *Those trappers, perhaps?*

The chuckle returned. *Perhaps.*

Not for the first time, Ridge wondered why the voice in his head seemed to know more about his companion than he did. He would never admit aloud his concern that he was going mad, but that gnawed at him. Did his head injury have something to do with it? What if... what if the doctors back home couldn't figure out what was wrong with him? What if he couldn't hide the fact that a voice was talking to him? He would be taken off active duty if they found something wrong with him, something that couldn't be cured. That would mean no more flying, no more working with his teammates, leading them against the nation's enemies. He stared bleakly toward the sky.

I'm sorry, the voice said quietly.

Ridge didn't want it to be sorry. He wanted it to go away.

Whether it heard his wishes or not, it fell silent for the rest of the walk.

A sense of relief came over him when they reached the outskirts of the village. Dealing with new people would be welcome, whether they gave him a horse or not.

Mara fell back to walk beside him when they came upon the first villagers, two women tossing scraps to pigs in a pen on the outskirts of town. He lifted a hand to the pair, guessing them mother and daughter, and offered a friendly smile, hoping to stave off any natural suspicions of strangers. His uniform, however bedraggled, ought to help. In his experience, most people knew how hard soldiers worked to keep the Cofah from taking over the country again and thought well of them. He just hoped that well-thinking would inspire horse loans.

"Good evening," the older woman said over the clucks of chickens behind them. "Are you looking for someone? We don't have an inn in town, but Brenna and Shuron sometimes put up travelers."

Ridge had only been thinking of horses, but the shadows were already deepening in the valley, and a night in a bed did sound fabulous.

"Hello, ma'am. I'm afraid I don't have money for a room." He didn't know if Mara had any, but he was already beholden to her enough. "My flier crashed in the mountains about fifty miles that way, and I'm lucky to be alive. This young woman found me and has been helping me, but I need to get back to the capital and report in. We saw your smoke, and I thought I'd come by and see if anyone here might be able to lend a horse or two so I can get back sooner." He eyed the pigs, thinking he wouldn't mind the loan of a ham too. As much as he appreciated Mara's foraging abilities, a man could only live so long on rabbit and pheasant. "I can send payment when I get back to my unit. Name's Ridge, by the way."

He waited, hoping they wouldn't simply shoo him away for wanting to freeload. At the least, his name usually started conversations. He was fairly certain his father was the only one in the country who had thought it would be delightful to name his son Ridgewalker, in the hope that they would climb peaks together someday. After tramping through mountains for the last few days, Ridge was glad he had chosen a career of flying *above* them instead of dangling *from* them.

The younger woman, who probably wasn't older than twenty, tugged at her mother's sleeve, her gaze on his nametag. That was promising. Maybe they got a newspaper out here now and then and had heard of him.

"Ridgewalker Zirkander?" the mother asked. She too was staring at his nametag now, either that or his chest was looking particularly fetching. Probably not, given the dirt smudging it, and the fresh-from-the-woods aroma lingering about him. It was a wonder Mara had wanted to be close enough to kiss. "Colonel? The pilot?"

"Yes, ma'am." He thought about correcting the rank, but he didn't even remember receiving that rank. It must have been fairly recent.

"I bet he was fighting the dragon," the young woman whispered.

Ridge nearly fell over. The *what?*

He kept himself from saying the words out loud, because he wasn't sure he should announce the hole in his memory to everyone he met, but he looked at Mara. Had she left something out of her story? Maybe they were referring to some new Cofah airship designed to look like a dragon? She shrugged back at him.

"Was the, ah, dragon a problem here?" Ridge asked.

"It killed Shari and One-eyed Gurth and burned down

several of our barns." The mother waved toward the opposite side of their one-street town. "I'll show you and take you to see Shuron. He's our mayor." She handed the bucket of scraps to her daughter.

"I could show him, Ma," the daughter said and smiled shyly at Ridge.

Ridge made his return smile brief and platonic. He might not be that chaste, but he drew the line at women who were younger than his lieutenants. Besides, he caught Mara glaring at the daughter and didn't want to start any trouble. He hadn't forgotten the sword callouses on his guide's hand or the unexplained peculiarities about her.

"Finish with the hogs," the mother said firmly. "This way, sir."

"You can call me Ridge, ma'am." He walked beside her, curious to see these damaged barns. More than that, he burned to ask for details about this dragon. It couldn't have been a *real* dragon, could it? After a thousand years without a sighting?

"No, sir. I don't think my husband would care for that." She led them down the main street, an even gravel road kept filled in and level, with a few businesses but mostly houses lining the sides, the frames a mix of log and planks, the steeply pitched roofs attesting to the amount of snow that fell in the winters. "He teases our friend Mirath mercilessly because his wife has one of your newspaper clippings hanging in the kitchen. Framed." She quirked an eyebrow at him.

She was closer to his age—at least what he remembered his age to be—but still an attractive woman, so he could see why the husband might grow jealous if she showed familiarity to other men.

"Is it one of the ones with my flier in the background?" Ridge asked. "It's a handsome craft. I'd frame a picture of it too."

"Yes, of course. The *machine* is the reason she hung up the photo." She snorted and pointed. "There's one of the barns, what's left of it."

In a pasture behind a smith's shop stood the charred remains of a structure, a single half-burned support post and the foundation. He wouldn't have known what it had been if she hadn't told him. What weapon did the Cofah have that would have done that? Some bomb? If so, why would they have dropped it on an insignificant mountain village?

"Did you see the... dragon?" Ridge asked.

"Yes. Scariest thing that's ever descended from the mountains. Huge with gold scales and fangs bigger than the pickets on that fence there. Claws longer than pitchforks. Cold eyes, like those of a snake, but intelligent. It wasn't just an animal hunting. It was tormenting us, scaring us. It knew exactly what it was doing, and it was enjoying itself."

As she spoke, all Ridge could do was stare at the charred remains of the building. This was no Cofah airship she was describing, and he had absolutely no memory of any of this.

"I don't suppose you killed it when you were up there?" the woman asked.

"I really don't know."

Ridge grimaced. His amnesia had been a problem for him before, but now he worried that it—and his absence—might be a problem for a lot more people. Was he missing out on some big battle that was going on? A battle with *dragons*?

He rubbed his forehead. More than ever, he needed to get back to civilization and figure out how to get his brain functioning on all thrusters again.

* * *

Cas stood guard as Pimples cut the last of the prisoners free. As with the others, the man raced into the swamp, glancing at the stitched wound on his arm as he ran. He never looked back.

"I hope that wasn't a mistake," Pimples said.

Cas lowered her rifle when it became clear that none of their captives planned to return for revenge, at least not immediately. She and the others had kept their weapons, so the thieves shouldn't be a problem, at least until they could resupply. If Tolemek's threat worked, they wouldn't try to gather reinforcements and return. Cas was more concerned about the dragon Phelistoth had sensed. Quataldo, Kaika, and Tolemek had still left, carrying on with the plan. The colonel had said it was possible the dragon had nothing to do with them. Cas doubted they would be that lucky.

"I don't think there's time for it to become a mistake. One way or another, we should be done with this mission and in the air in three days—more like two, now." Cas nodded toward the darkening sky, visible over the river. "Besides, we would have run out of food if we'd had to feed all of them."

"Aw," Duck said from a stump he had claimed as his own. "I could have found something to feed them. I've been tempted to go hunting, see if I can find some of those giant critters."

"It's been my experience that giant critters aren't easily taken down by standard military rifles," Cas said.

"Didn't say it would be easy." Duck winked.

"Better watch out," Captain Blazer said from under the camo for her flyer. "Might be some of those critters are eyeing us from the trees and thinking about hunting *you*."

"I can handle them."

"Predators don't always fight fair, you know. An alligator might do more than use those ears for handles."

Duck scowled and touched a mud-crusted lobe. "That's not funny, Captain."

"No? Why am I giggling into my tobacco tin?"

Blazer had been rolling a fresh cigar for the last hour, working toward precision, apparently. Assignments like this didn't keep the team that busy, and they had already done their best to clean and check their aircraft, a challenge thanks to the pervasive mud. Against logic—and gravity—Cas had found the dark sludge all over her propeller blades and crusted in the casing for the power crystal, so she'd had to spend an hour wiping everything out. If General Zirkander had been here, he would have led the group in some physical training, but nobody had responded enthusiastically when Cas had brought up the idea of calisthenics. They were planning to move the camp in the morning, so that would give them something to do.

A splash sounded in the river. Critters, as Duck called them, giant and otherwise, seemed to find the waterway an excellent place to drink and hunt. At dawn, as Cas had been watching Tolemek, Kaika, Tylie, Phelistoth, and Quataldo depart, she had spotted a twenty-foot alligator swimming across the river. The animal activity had increased throughout the day, and she wondered if the dragon's presence had kept it to a minimum the night before. Sardelle and Tolemek had said they could sense his powerful aura, even when Phelistoth was in human form, and Cas wouldn't be surprised if animals could too.

She had been patrolling their camp before Blazer had decided they should let the prisoners go, so she returned to the task. She had barely gone a half a circuit when the swamp grew silent, abruptly and noticeably. Frogs ceased croaking, the fish in the river stopped jumping, and the birds in the treetops halted their squawking and chirping. Her comrades looked toward the trees. Duck hopped to his feet, his rifle in hand.

Cas continued to the river so she would have a view to either side of their reed-choked inlet. She stepped lightly, not wanting to break the silence or draw attention to herself. Something was out there.

On the muddy bank, she climbed onto the roots of a large mangrove and crouched where she could see the camp and the waterway in both directions. She kept the rough bark of the tree at her back and grew still, scarcely breathing as she blended with her surroundings.

Nothing stirred on the river. The trees cast deep shadows along the banks. Overhead, heavy clouds suggested it would rain that night, and the air felt close and thick, with the scents of vegetation denser than they had been when the team had first landed. The faint roar of the ocean drifted up the river, but the swamp remained quiet and still.

Out over the ocean, the dark bow of an imperial airship came into view. It was more than two miles away and flying parallel with the coast, so it shouldn't be looking for the Iskandian fliers, but Cas leaned her back harder into the tree, nonetheless, as if she could disappear into it. She caught Pimples looking in her direction, and she pointed to her own eyes, toward the airship, and then toward their camouflaged fliers. The others wouldn't be able to see the craft from their positions.

Pimples whispered to Blazer and Duck, and they ducked under the camo netting of the nearest flier. Cas remained on her perch, trusting the branches and the distance to hide her.

The airship continued up the coast, the rest of its body coming into view, and then the bow disappeared behind the trees. This one had a darker hull than the one from the day before, and gold and silver paint embellished the sides.

Cas tugged out a collapsible spyglass, hoping to glimpse the name on the side. Only a handful of Cofah military craft were notorious enough for her to know them by name, but maybe...

"The Sprinting Eagle," she read, the gold letters passing before the lens of her spyglass as the airship continued onward.

The emperor did not travel out of Cofahre often and, as far as she knew, did not have a designated aircraft, but the *Eagle* belonged to the royal family and ferried his offspring and important dignitaries around. It rarely flew away from the mainland where Iskandian fliers might chance across it, but everybody was briefed on what the royal ships looked like. This one might be taking the princess to meet her groom. Unless she was already in Tildar Dem. Then this could be the emperor's ship.

When it disappeared from sight, Cas rose from her crouch, intending to hop into one of the cockpits so she could contact Tolemek. Thus far, the crystals had remained silent with no communication from the other group. There hadn't likely been anything to report, but this was important, and she needed to warn them.

Even as she lifted her foot to hop down from the roots, something else flew into view out over the ocean. Cas froze. A dragon. A *gold* dragon.

Phelistoth had been right. This had to be one of the ones that had been freed from the cavern. Cas didn't think it looked like Bhrava Saruth, the dragon that had saved her from dying, but there were two others she had never seen. This one was *huge*, as large as the airship it was following.

Its head swung to the side, looking up the river. From two miles away, Cas couldn't see the eyes, but dread made her freeze, her foot dangling in the air. She felt certain that its sight was keen enough to see *her*.

As the airship had before it, the dragon soon passed out of sight, disappearing behind the trees. For several long seconds, Cas remained unmoving, her thoughts whirring. What did the dragon's presence behind the airship mean? That it was working with the empire? With the *emperor*?

Before she was conscious of making a decision, Cas found herself leaping from her perch. She splashed through the mud of the inlet, water tugging at her thighs and mud sucking at her boots. She barely noticed. She pushed her way out of the murk on the far side and ran toward the beach.

"Back shortly," she said as she ran.

"Raptor!" Blazer barked after her. "Where are you going?"

Afraid to yell, afraid the dragon would hear them, Cas continued her sprint without responding. Ducking between trees and leaping puddles and rocks, she ran as fast as she could, following the river toward the beach. Would she make it in time to spot the dragon and the airship? Would seeing them tell her anything more than what she already suspected?

Birds flapped out of the reeds as she ran, dodging trees. She glimpsed movement out of the corner of her eye and ducked when her instincts screamed for her to do so. A giant snake hissed, its long tongue darting out, and his head moving toward her. Thanks to her timely duck, it missed her, but she forced herself to slow down, to watch her route more carefully before plowing forward.

By the time she reached the beach, she had run past three snakes, a giant black panther that sprang away, and something that had growled at her from a bamboo thicket. Her breaths came in pants, and her legs felt like lead. She paused between two trees instead of running into the open, and turned her eyes down the coastline. It was lighter out here than in the swamp, and she could still pick out figures against the clouds. Large figures.

Flying low, barely higher than the treetops, the airship had drifted a couple of miles down the coast. She didn't have any better a view of it than before, but what she saw told her much. The dragon flew lazily about the craft, circling it, coasting, and definitely not attacking. Had a battle been going on, she would have heard the booms of cannons and seen the flash of gunpowder being ignited.

With sweaty fingers, she dug out the spyglass again. She had to wipe her palms before she could manage to open it and growled in irritation at the delay. Finally, she got it pointed at the airship in the cloudy sky.

As she had suspected, the shaven-headed Cofah soldiers were not preparing for battle. Many of them had tense postures as they watched the dragon circle, but nobody had a weapon raised.

"Correction," she mumbled, halting her perusal of the deck when she chanced upon two queues of soldiers, pistols and swords in hand. They weren't aiming at anything, but were ready to defend themselves—and the person standing between them, a bald man with loose flowing purple garments trimmed in gold.

Cas had never seen Emperor Salatak, but those were the colors of royalty in Cofahre.

He leaned his hands against the railing, looking out toward the dragon. Cas couldn't see his face or the dragon from this point of view. The soldiers and the hull, railing, and deck structures on the airship were in the way. Cas clambered atop a rock, no longer worrying about being seen as she tried to get a better view. Was he talking to the dragon? Communicating with it? Judging by his stance, he did not appear concerned.

"Not good," Cas mumbled.

The dirigible turned a few degrees, following the coast as it continued south, and she lost sight of the emperor. She lowered her spyglass. It didn't matter. She had seen enough. She needed to warn Tolemek and the others. Since Tylie and Phelistoth were with them, the group might be in more danger than if Tolemek, Kaika, and Quataldo had gone in alone. It seemed likely that if Phelistoth had sensed this dragon, it would be able to sense him right back.

At only a slightly slower pace than before, Cas ran back up the river. More snakes hissed and animals growled as she passed through, but luck was either with her, or their hunting instincts were subdued in the wake of the dragon's passing. She made it back to the camp without running into trouble.

Once again panting, she came to a stop as soon as the others spotted her. Pimples had rolled back the camo netting from the front of his flier and sat in the cockpit.

"You need to contact Tolemek," Cas blurted without preamble.

"I'd ask if General Zirkander let you go haring off on your own," Blazer said, her cigar lit and tucked in the corner of her mouth, "but I know he didn't. Next time, ask permission, *Lieutenant*."

Blazer didn't usually pull rank, but even in the dark, her irritation was evident. Cas resisted the urge to bristle—they had probably been worried about her and wondered if they had been spotted.

"Yes, ma'am," she said. "Pimples?" He hadn't activated the communication crystal yet, and she bounced on her feet, tempted to clamber up into her own cockpit. "The emperor's airship just went past, along with a gold dragon, a gold dragon that appears to either be allied with him or in the process of forming an alliance. The others need to know."

Duck spat. "What's a dragon want with that curmudgeon of an old stick?"

"I don't know, but—" Cas pointed at the cockpit. Why wasn't Pimples obeying? "Pimples?"

He glanced at Blazer before meeting her eyes again and sighing. "We already tried to contact the others."

The dread Cas had felt earlier returned, settling heavily in her stomach. "And?"

"They're not answering."

Chapter 6

SARDELLE PACED ABOUT ON THE rocky bank of the river, her senses reaching up and down the valley as she hoped to catch a glimpse of Ridge's aura. Bhrava Saruth flew overhead, searching from the sky. Colonel Therrik was walking along the water's edge, his gaze toward the ground.

It had been an hour since Bhrava Saruth deposited them in the canyon, and Therrik had finally recovered some of his color. His face had been paler than chalk after riding with Sardelle on the dragon's back, and he had thrown up behind a boulder as soon as they had landed. Sardelle was relieved he hadn't done that in the sky. She couldn't imagine what she would say to Bhrava Saruth as she cleaned his scales; somehow vomiting on a dragon seemed a far greater crime than doing so in the back seat of a flier.

Even I'll agree with that, Jaxi said. *Though it would be moderately amusing to see you polishing a god's scales. He probably likes his high priestesses to attend him so.*

Have you seen any sign of Ridge? Sardelle asked, ignoring the teasing.

No, but I'm not the one with the tracking skills.

I do not sense anyone, high priestess, Bhrava Saruth announced.

How far can your senses extend?

Many miles. Forty? Fifty? Dragons do not use such measurements, but I can sense humans and settlements in the mountains. I have not found the one you seek.

Forty or fifty miles? It had been more than a week since the crash, so it was possible Ridge could have walked out of that range, but was it likely? If he was injured? Was she deluding herself and wasting everyone's time in being out here?

"This terrain can lick dragon ass," Therrik announced, his

fists on his hips as he scowled down at the rocks. Kasandral hung diagonally across his back in its scabbard, and it glowed occasionally, the sickly green seeping out around the hilt.

"You haven't found anything," Sardelle said, another layer of defeat draping itself over her shoulders.

"Do not question me, woman," Therrik growled, glaring over his shoulder at her. Kasandral's glow intensified. Therrik turned, taking a step toward her.

"*Meriyash keeno*," Sardelle said, directing the ancient words at the sword, the phrase that told it to stand down.

She wished Therrik had kept the blade in its box instead of wearing it openly, but he seemed proud and eager to be carrying it. She rested her hand on Jaxi's pommel.

The green glow faded, and Therrik stopped before drawing close to her. His glare grew less intense, and an exasperated expression twisted his face.

"How do I tell it to make me pissed at the right targets?" he demanded.

"I'm not sure it's necessary for you to be... *pissed* at any targets," Sardelle said. "Wouldn't you prefer to be calm and in control when you go into battle?"

"I'm always in control." He glanced at the sword hilt poking above his shoulder. "I *was* always in control."

"But not calm?" She smiled, trying to lighten the mood. She could feel the tension radiating from him, crackling in the air between them.

"I'm not a calm person."

"No, you seem quite strained. I don't know if that's because of me, or you're always like that. As a healer, I could recommend some adaptogenic herbs that might help you modulate your stress levels. I could even make a tea that would relax you. You'd wake up feeling well rested and perky."

Do we really want to see a perky version of Colonel Therrik? Jaxi asked.

Therrik was looking at Sardelle as if she had three heads. "Tea? Is that what you give Zirkander?"

"No, he never seems that tense or stressed."

Therrik snorted. "He just makes other people feel that way."

Sardelle frowned, not wanting Therrik speaking ill of Ridge, especially if he was—

"He came out here," Therrik said, pointing to the riverbank.

"What?" She gaped.

"I should say *someone* was dragged out of the water here," Therrik amended. "There's no way to prove it was him, but who else would be idiotic enough to throw himself into this remote river?"

Sardelle walked toward him, pushing aside her irritation at the insult. If Ridge was alive, what did it matter what Therrik called him?

"What do you see?" she asked, looking at the damp rocks.

Therrik's eyes narrowed as she came close to him, and she thought she might have to order the sword to stand down again, but he simply crouched to touch a rock, then another. "These have been disturbed. That one's been flipped over."

Sardelle couldn't see the difference between one rock and the next, and it seemed scant proof of someone's passing, but she wanted to believe so badly that she found herself nodding eagerly.

"Someone was dragged out here." Therrik pointed.

"Dragged," she murmured, tamping down some of her hope. That didn't mean he had been alive when it had happened.

"Impossible to track them or see steps in this." He waved at the rocks. Unlike dirt or mud, they held no prints. "But I looked around, and there's no sign of horse or donkey droppings. Whoever pulled him out probably didn't go far, not if they were carrying his cloud-humping ass."

Sardelle found the news promising, though Therrik's delivery could use some work. "Shouldn't you call him general, since he outranks you and it's possible he's alive?"

"General Cloud-humping Ass?"

Was that humor gleaming in the man's eyes? He needed far more than tea.

"I'll keep looking." Therrik gazed at the slopes to either side of the river. "See if I can find a cave or sheltered area where he might have been taken."

"Thank you."

Dare I hope, Jaxi? Sardelle asked.

That Therrik will start calling Ridge something flattering? Probably not.

That's not what I was asking.

There's nothing wrong with hope, Sardelle. This probably happened a week ago though. He must have been pulled out of the river during the storm, before we came looking.

Meaning he could be outside of Bhrava Saruth's range by now. Still, a cave would be a starting place. If they found evidence that he had been there, evidence that he was alive, that would be more than she had dared hope twenty minutes ago. And if he was alive, he might already be making his way home. She might be reunited with him soon.

I've been thinking about that, Jaxi said.

Our joyous reunion?

Not exactly. Assuming he is alive, then why didn't we sense him when we searched that morning? He must have been wounded, and it doesn't sound like anyone could have carried him far. Was someone hiding him from us?

The sorceress? Sardelle wondered.

I still don't know why she would want him, but if it was *she, maybe it's possible that she has a skill like Tylie does and that she could hide herself and Ridge from our senses.*

Sardelle didn't know what to say to that. She wanted Ridge to be alive, but she didn't want him to be in the clutches of their enemy. *If that's the case, then we'll need Therrik's tracking skills more than I realized. We'll have to hope she left physical signs of their passing.*

Better make him some tea then, if we're going to remain in his company for a while.

You think some calming herbs will make him a better tracker? Or help him keep a leash on Kasandral?

Perhaps. Something to calm his libido too. He has an interesting mix of feelings toward you these days.

Define interesting, she said, a desolate feeling coming over her as she watched Therrik's back.

Do you really want me to?

Perhaps not. She would be careful around Therrik and hope that they could find Ridge soon. She lifted her gaze, spotting the dragon soaring among the peaks. *Bhrava Saruth? Would you mind also looking for nearby caves?*

Certainly, high priestess. Will we return to the outpost tonight? I am disappointed that I did not get time to heal and bless the people there. They seemed rough and lost souls, in need of the guidance of a god.

I don't doubt that. I don't know if we'll go back tonight, but I'll be happy to return with you later if you want to heal people. Sardelle remembered the miner who had died trying to rescue her, the one who had possessed dragon blood. When there was time, she wanted to return to the outpost and figure out if there were any other criminals there with dragon blood, people who might have been condemned because of that blood rather than because they had committed true crimes.

I will help you search for them, Bhrava Saruth said. *You could teach them of their heritage, and they could become my worshippers.*

Yes, of course. For now, I need to find Ridge and a Cofah sorceress that may hold him prisoner.

Cofah! Those moose molesters.

Almost my exact thoughts.

Did you know Phelistoth is a Cofah dragon? Bhrava Saruth shot her the telepathic equivalent of a suspicious squint. *I almost let him touch my crystal.*

Yes, but we're trying to woo him to our side. Perhaps you should let him touch your crystal.

He cannot be trusted.

Since Sardelle could not be certain about Phelistoth's allegiance, she did not argue the point.

I see a cave, Bhrava Saruth announced. He had disappeared from sight. *Around that bend. Up here. This way.*

His directions leave something to be desired, Sardelle told Jaxi.

If he's a god, maybe you're supposed to follow him by his divine glow.

I don't know about divinity, but I can sense him by his dragonly aura. I suppose that will do.

"Therrik?" she called. "There's a cave around that bend. It may be what we're looking for."

He had been studying the ground. He lifted his head and frowned over at her. "How do you know?"

"The dragon told me."

He looked toward the bend, back at the ground, then toward her again. "You're a strange woman."

As if it was her fault Bhrava Saruth chatted with her.

You were the one who originally opened up communications with him. Jaxi sounded amused.

That was a dire situation.

I'm not sure that invalidates Therrik's statement.

You think I'm strange?

Yes, but so am I. We're practically sisters.

Therrik's forehead wrinkled. "Are you talking to it now?"

"The dragon? No." Sardelle thought about stopping there, lest he have more reasons to find her strange, but what did it matter what he thought? She gave him an edged smile. "Now I'm talking to my sword."

Jaxi offered a soft hum, so she must have approved.

"I'm going to investigate the cave," Sardelle announced and headed off to find Bhrava Saruth.

* * *

Tolemek did not have much of a belly, but he sucked it in as a keelboat glided closer, its arrow-shaped prow parting the murky water. The evening shadows and the stout tree in front of him should hide him, but Kaika shared his tree, and he worried that one of their rifles or some of their gear might stick out and give them away. The men striding along the sides of the keelboat, maneuvering it through the swamp via poles that pushed off the bottom, had eyes that were far too alert as they regarded the banks.

Their presence should indicate that the city lay nearby. It was hard to imagine, given the water stretching everywhere and the dense canopy of vines, branches, and leaves that blocked out the sky, but this was the third boat that had gone by in the last half hour. One of them, a steam-powered paddleboat, had carried a crew of at least ten with twice as many passengers, men and women who had prowled the deck with rifles as they looked toward the branches. A pole had stuck up diagonally from the prow with a slab of meat tied to the end. Bait, Tolemek assumed, though for what he did not know. He didn't *want* to know.

Creatures that sounded more like bats than birds kept making noise up in the treetops, but he had not seen what they were yet. They sounded much larger than bats. He much preferred it when they had been walking along the beach, an area mostly devoid of predators, but Colonel Quataldo had moved them inland for the last couple of miles to avoid the notice of the numerous fishing boats that had been coming in from deeper waters, angling for a delta farther up the beach. Of course, Quataldo had disappeared soon after that, as seemed to be his way. Scouting, he'd said.

Tolemek didn't need a scout to be certain the animals here were more dangerous than anyone they were likely to run into in a fishing boat. Thus far, they had passed venomous bats and vipers, fanged spiders the size of his head, and they had run from two alligators intent on making them dinner. He was relieved that Phelistoth had gone off "to hunt" with Tylie, taking her up above the canopy and hopefully to a safer area, but he felt uneasy down here with only Captain Kaika at his side. He had never considered himself timid or cowardly, but in addition to the real dangers, the growls, squawks, hisses, and roars kept a man on edge.

Someone on the keelboat cried out, and a rifle fired. Tolemek's instinct was to lean out and see if he could help, but Kaika gripped his forearm. She held a finger to her lips.

Wood crunched. More shots fired, someone cursed, and another man cried out, this time in pain. The hair on the back of his neck pricked up, and he felt certain someone was using magic. The thrashing of something hitting the water repeatedly drowned out everything else. For several long seconds, it continued. Finally, the noise stilled. Grunts, pants, and a loud scrape-thump sounded next, followed by chatter in a language Tolemek could not understand. It sounded oddly cheerful.

He contained his curiosity for another ten seconds, but then he had to poke his head around the tree and look. The keelboat had continued onward, and the pushers' backs were to him, so he felt safe. The sight of a huge alligator—seven gods, did that alligator have wings?—draped over the cabin roof made his jaw fall open. A bite had been taken out of the rear of the keelboat, a *large* bite.

"Hunting's good today, it seems," Kaika murmured.

"Is that what these boats are out for? Seems suicidal."

"Someone has to gather specimens for scientists from distant lands." The boat disappeared behind a copse of trees leaning out over the water, and Kaika waved that they could continue on. "Don't you pay handsomely for your powders and potions?"

"Chemicals, formulas, and ingredients," he grumbled.

She raised her eyebrows.

"And yes, I do pay well for the imported ones." He had, however, never ordered an ingredient derived from a *winged* alligator, at least insofar as he knew.

Shaking his head, Tolemek followed her as they continued skirting the swamp toward a pair of posts that marked the first of the legendary rope bridges he'd always heard associated with Tildar Dem. The rope-linked wooden slats extended for as far as he could see, crossing water of indeterminate depth. Occasional pairs of posts kept the boards from slumping to the surface, though no part of the bridge was more than a couple of feet above it. Given the willingness of the local fauna to eat through wood, he found the frailness of the route alarming. The openness was also discouraging. Even with the deepening gloom of twilight, they would have trouble hiding if more boats came along.

"Are we crossing here?" Tolemek asked when Kaika halted at the entrance. Trees loomed on either side, with support cables from the bridge wrapped around their bases.

"Yes, but we should wait for—"

A hiss sounded inches from Tolemek's ear, his only warning. He resisted the urge to look, instead dropping to the ground and rolling away. His elbow clunked against the bridge, sending a stab of pain up his arm, as he yanked out his pistol. From his back, his hair dangling in the water, he aimed at—

Colonel Quataldo stood where he had been a second before, one hand wrapped around the throat of the viper that had hissed in Tolemek's ear. It struggled in his grip, but he calmly lifted his other hand and snapped its spine.

"Avert your firearm, please," Quataldo said.

Tolemek had already lowered it, but he waited to be positive the snake wouldn't move again before holstering the weapon. He kept himself from glowering at the colonel—he wished he could have handled the snake by himself. He was hardly some damsel in need of rescue, no matter what the mud dripping from his hair implied.

"Been anywhere exciting, sir?" Kaika asked. She looked like she might yawn. She hadn't moved from her spot at the start of the bridge.

Tolemek pushed himself to his feet, wondered if he could say anything to appear more manly and less in need of saving, and decided he couldn't.

"Scouting." Quataldo let go of the snake, leaving it dangling from the tree. A rare smile crossed his face. "I also found an unfertilized egg."

"What?" Tolemek asked.

Kaika did not appear surprised. "Alligator?"

Quataldo carefully removed a large, dark green egg. "It looks like an emu egg, but this isn't the right habitat for emus."

"So you don't know what it is?" Tolemek frowned at it. He was familiar with a wide variety of reptiles and birds, but this wasn't his native continent, and he couldn't have said for certain what type of egg it was either. "Is it wise to take it along? How can you tell if it's been fertilized or not without breaking it open?"

"I can tell."

Tolemek shook his head. The man was either a loon, or maybe a few drops of dragon blood lurked in his veins. He would ask

Sardelle, if they all survived this mission. Would she be enthused or intimidated by teaching a soldier who specialized in killing how to access his power?

"What are you going to do with it?" Tolemek asked.

"Carve it, of course."

Quataldo tucked the egg back into his pouch, the insides insulated, then shrugged off his pack. He drew a small wooden box from a side pocket and unlatched it to reveal a padded inside, as well as tiny carving tools tucked under the lid. A yellow egg lay nestled inside, part of the shell carved away. Tolemek leaned close, trying to tell more about the design—was that some large bird standing on one leg? The poor light made it difficult.

"When you're in the elite forces," Kaika said, "you spend a lot of time sitting, standing, perching, and crouching while waiting for your enemies to do something. The colonel carves eggs while he waits."

"A unique hobby," Tolemek said, not seeing the point of making something that was purely decorative.

"He sells them for hundreds of nucros, if not thousands, right, sir?"

Quataldo inclined his head. "I don't sell all of them, but I'm saving money so my children can afford to continue with their educations and follow their passions. My daughter is almost ready for the university."

"Doesn't your officer's pay provide enough for that?" Tolemek asked.

"Well. I have a wife."

Kaika grinned. "She likes to shop."

"Ah." Tolemek tried to imagine Cas shopping for something besides military supplies. Perhaps he should be relieved she lacked an interest in clothing and baubles.

"It's getting dark." Quataldo carefully stored his eggs as he spoke. "We should be able to risk traversing the bridge, since night will hide us, but be careful. The boats come out to hunt at twilight but will return to the city soon. Being caught outside after dark is not wise. The number of predators active at night can grow unmanageable."

Tolemek shifted his weight. "Just around the city, or are Cas and the others in danger?"

"I am certain they can take care of themselves, but my reports say this area is more dangerous. Some of the unnatural predators covet human flesh over that of animals and fish, and they know that many tens of thousands live in the city." Quataldo shouldered his pack and stepped onto the bridge. The ropes creaked softly.

"Nothing like being coveted," Tolemek muttered, following when Kaika waved for him to go second. "Unnatural. Does that mean descendants of dragon pairings?"

"That's one of the explanations I've heard," Quataldo said. "Others say that shaman scientists in the area used to do experiments, and that some of those experiments changed the ground in places, affecting animals born in proximity to those areas."

"Scientists, always making trouble."

He'd meant it as a joke, but the long look Quataldo leveled over his shoulder suggested agreement.

Kaika brought up the rear, her rifle crooked in her arms. Tolemek left his own rifle strapped to his pack, instead keeping his pistol in one hand and a knockout grenade in the other.

They walked along the bridge for what seemed like miles, the night closing in about them. Now and then, they came to a small island rising up from the murky water, but the bridge would simply continue on the other side. Sometimes, other bridges branched off, heading perpendicular to the main route. Quataldo kept going straight.

The paddleboat and the keelboats returned, gliding along more quickly than the group was walking. Each time a boat passed, Tolemek, Quataldo, and Kaika laid on their stomachs on the bridges, not moving until the craft passed. Tolemek wondered if they might have sneaked aboard the bigger boat and gotten a ride to the city, but it never steered close enough to the bridge to truly consider that. He certainly wasn't going to suggest going for a swim. It had been a while since he had seen an alligator, but water snakes wriggled through the murky swamp more than once.

"We'll reach the lights soon," Quataldo said. "There will

be more bridges then, and we may encounter guards on the outskirts of the city. Tolemek, if you will provide us some of your smoke and knockout grenades, we would appreciate it."

"Are you going into Tildar Dem without me?"

"You'll come with us into the city, but we'll be leaving you at the Mysora Malosh, an inn that has Iskandian connections and where you should be safe. You have the communication crystal, so we will go out and explore and then come back to you. If anything happens to us, the innkeeper should hear about it and inform you. You can tell the others and decide if the mission might be salvaged or if it must be abandoned."

"It won't need to be salvaged or abandoned," Kaika said firmly, almost fiercely.

Quataldo gave her a long look over his shoulder, but did not comment.

"I have the grenades, and I can give you some of my compound that can eat through walls too," Tolemek said.

He had no trouble being left behind in an inn while these two skulked about. That should keep him from having to attack his own people—his own emperor. *Former* emperor, he reminded himself. He wondered why he still had a hard time thinking of the man that way. He had never even met Emperor Salatak. He'd spent far more time talking to King Angulus. Yet, when he had been a young officer in the Cofah army, he'd sworn an oath to defend the emperor and the empire. Even years later, it was hard to forget that.

"Excellent," Quataldo said.

Tolemek dipped his hand into his pocket, checking to ensure the communication crystal remained there. He had embedded it into a piece of wood so that it would not be easy to lose. He drew it out, its faint glow comforting in the dreary swamp. Since he had nothing to report yet, he fastened it in again, buttoning the pocket flap.

Tolie?

Tylie? Are you staying close?

Fairly close. Phel has been hunting again. He seems to get hungry a lot here.

Tolemek wondered if the dragon was truly hungry or if he just didn't want to stick around and help with the Iskandian kidnapping scheme. He was still surprised Phelistoth had so readily agreed to come along. He had almost seemed eager at the prospect, if a dragon could be eager. Maybe he was simply staying away now because he didn't want to be sensed by the other dragon. Tolemek could not object to that.

We saw the city from above as it was getting dark. It's beautiful. All these lights stretching out into the swamp. The mountains are beautiful too. Phel takes me there to hunt. It's so wonderful seeing the world this way. Tylie's contented sigh whispered into his mind. *I want to paint everything I see.*

I'm sure you'll have time to do that when we get home. Are you and Phelistoth going to come into the city with us?

Phel is looking at some ruins buried under the trees and vines now, Tylie said. *Bhrava Saruth did not let him look at that crystal library for very long or up close, and he's still seeking clues about his missing kind.*

So that means you're not joining us? Tolemek did not mind leaving his sister out of the danger—and he could only surmise that the city would explode with gunfire once the emperor was taken—but Phelistoth could have been a useful ally.

Do you want us to join you? The other dragon is nearby.

Nearby where you are? Tolemek asked. *Or nearby where we are?*

Where you *are.*

Tolemek grimaced toward the dark canopy overhead. Flying alligators might be the least of their problems.

"Look out," Kaika barked, a hand landing on his shoulder and jolting him back to awareness.

Tolemek crouched down as a loud splash came from their right. Even in the shadows, he could see the dark shape of something springing out of the water, something big.

A winged form sailed toward them, arching over the bridge. Water droplets spattered Tolemek in the face, and powerful jaws snapped at the air. If not for Kaika's warning, the creature might have taken his head off.

"Don't shoot," Quataldo ordered as the creature splashed into the water on the other side of the bridge. "We're too close to the city borders. We'll alert guards."

Tolemek had been pulling his rifle off his pack, but he dipped into his pocket for one of the tiny ceramic jars of dragon-blood-eating acid instead. Neither smoke nor knockout gas would be reliable against an animal—or whatever that had been. He'd no sooner than wrapped his fingers around the vial than the boards under his feet were bumped upward. The jolt almost knocked him off the bridge, but he squatted low, finding his balance. More water splashed.

"I suppose explosives are out then," Kaika said.

"Yes."

"Shall we run?"

"You two go ahead." Quataldo crouched, a knife in hand. "Get to the next spot of land and wait for me."

A second splash sounded, farther out than the first. Was the creature moving? Or was there another one out there?

Kaika hesitated, but then pushed Tolemek ahead of her. "Go."

Quataldo eased aside to let them pass. There wasn't much room on the bridge, especially with the lack of ropes or railing to grab.

"Down," Quataldo warned.

Tolemek dropped to his hands and knees, careful to protect the ceramic vial he'd pulled out. This time, the creature landed on the bridge. The wooden boards heaved. Tolemek gripped the edge with one hand, lest he be flung into the water, which was churning not five feet away as something else approached.

"Could use some light," Tolemek muttered and dipped into another pocket where he kept matches he'd created that burned for several minutes. He lit one, dropping it onto the bridge.

A mix between a squawk and a roar sounded from behind him. He turned, his thumb on the cork of his vial. Quataldo grappled with some animal—one of the alligators. Wings beat at the air. The creature was long, its back half off the bridge, its tail thrashing in the water.

The animal snarled, and Quataldo gasped in pain. Something akin to a pig's squeal came from the creature's throat. Whatever it was, it wasn't entirely an alligator.

As Tolemek edged closer, hoping for an opportunity to dump acid on it, something batted him in the face. Hard. He tumbled backward into Kaika.

"Hells," Kaika growled, pushing past him.

Were there two alligators attacking them? Or one? Tolemek glanced around, trying to see what had struck him. Something flying past?

Ignoring orders, Kaika fired her rifle. The gunshot sounded, ringing out across the swamp. For an instant, the creature grappling with the colonel froze. Tolemek lunged in, brushing against a wet, scaly hide as he dumped acid on it. It cried out, its tail lashing the water and creating waves. Quataldo came down atop the alligator, driving his knife into its spine. It squealed again, a dying squeal, Tolemek hoped.

The alligator shuddered, then lay still.

"Get to land," Quataldo said, jumping up. "Hurry."

Knowing he did not dare spill any of the acid on himself or either of them, Tolemek took the time to cap his vial. Splashes sounded all around them, the water churning on either side of the bridge, as if dozens of sharks closed upon their position.

Tolemek jumped to his feet and ran after Kaika and Quataldo. The bridge quaked, partially from their boots pounding it, but partially from creatures bumping it.

In the darkness ahead, the shadowy forms of trees came into view. Tolemek ran faster. The tiny island might not offer sanctuary, but at least it would be easier for them to make a stand there.

He was no more than twenty meters away when a splash came from ahead of them, and the bridge heaved. An alligator's powerful jaws snapped down on the wood boards. It jerked its head from side to side, while its wings beat at the water. Wood cracked, and the bridge shuddered.

Kaika paused to fire. The bullet might have struck but it did nothing to stop the alligator. While she reloaded, Tolemek brushed past Quataldo and ran ahead of her. The effort of maintaining his balance on the roiling bridge left him flailing, but he managed to keep hold of his vial. He sprang for the alligator, dumping the concoction on its head at the same time as it finished destroying the bridge.

The wooden boards sank, and Tolemek sank with them. Cursing and sputtering as cold water swallowed him, he lost all interest in attacking the creature. He simply tried to get by it, so he could swim to the island. The entire bridge was sinking now and useless, and the water was too deep for him to touch the bottom. His pack weighed him down, but he wouldn't contemplate leaving all of his formulas and salves.

Something hard slammed into his chest—the alligator's tail? He didn't stop to analyze it. He kept paddling toward land.

Gunfire sounded, several shots. Kaika shouted from somewhere behind him. Tolemek hesitated. Though every instinct cried for him to get to land, he didn't want to leave the others to their deaths. He pulled out his knife, lamenting that it was the only weapon he could reach that might do anything now—the gunpowder in his pistol and rifle would be soaked.

Sharp teeth grazed Tolemek's arm as a maw snapped down right next to him. He could barely see the creature, but he jabbed with his knife. It sliced into a rubbery hide. A squeal sounded, and Tolemek slashed with the knife, trying to keep it back as much as hurt it. It cried out again and disappeared beneath the surface. It wasn't fleeing. The animal bumped his leg. He kicked, a useless gesture with the water slowing his limbs, and flung the empty vial toward the churning water that signified the alligator was underneath. It wouldn't do anything, but he couldn't think of a better tactic. He paddled backward wildly to put space between him and it.

A huge fiery explosion came out of nowhere, and flames leaped into the night. They created enough light that Tolemek could see countless alligator heads in the water, and some other creatures that looked like giant frogs swimming around on the surface. He could also see someone swimming away from the explosion and toward him at top speed. Captain Kaika.

Something grabbed Tolemek's pack from behind, and he yelped, imagining alligator jaws clamping down on it. But the water had grown still in the wake of the explosion, with only

Kaika's arms disturbing it as she swam toward land. Tolemek realized Quataldo was the one dragging him back. His heel bumped against something. The shore. He could finally touch the bottom. Needing no further urging, he spun and ran.

He and Quataldo reached the island together. Though Tolemek wanted to hug and kiss the closest tree, he turned back toward the water to make sure Kaika did not need help. The explosion had died out, but bits of burning bridge floated in the swamp, providing the light he had longed for earlier. The water was still behind her, no sign of the alligator heads or any other creatures, except for two that floated belly up, wings lying limply on the surface.

Kaika clambered up the muddy beach, sloughing water. She leaned against one of the posts that supported all that remained of the bridge, a few boards extending into the water before the rest disappeared beneath the surface.

"Sorry, sir," she said. "Something was trying to take a chomp out of my leg. I had to discourage it."

"Loudly." Quataldo sighed.

"I haven't had much luck finding quiet bombs yet. Maybe Tolemek can make me something." She thumped him on the arm.

"As it is," Tolemek said, inhaling deep breaths and trying to slow his heart, "I wish I'd known… about the dangers of the swamp before. Could have had time… to design more effective weapons."

"That one critter sure hated whatever you dumped on it," she said.

"Quiet," Quataldo whispered, raising a hand, his head turned toward the opposite end of their small island.

Tolemek grimaced, expecting the approach of more hungry predators.

Instead, men with lanterns were striding toward them along the next stretch of bridge. They wore uniforms and carried rifles as well as nets, and they had the look of soldiers or perhaps city guards. Tolemek counted ten people and thought there might be more behind them without lanterns. A pungent scent reached his nose—something burning in the lanterns besides oil? Maybe the aroma deterred the swamp creatures. It would certainly deter him from approaching the men.

"Any chance they're here to show us to that inn?" Kaika asked.

Quataldo sighed again.

Tolemek did not know whether they could expect a helpful escort or one that would imprison them, but he figured he had better warn Cas what was going on in case they were arrested. He slipped his hand into the soggy pocket that held the communication crystal, the pocket that *should* have held it.

With dawning horror, he poked into all of the nooks, hoping it was there and he'd just missed it. But his pocket was empty. Even though he distinctly remembered keeping it in that one—he'd even chosen the one with a button flap so he couldn't possibly lose it—he checked all of the others, hoping his memory was faulty. Some of his vials and grenades had fallen out too. He cursed. Why had he flailed around so much in the water? He should have just yelled at Kaika to blow up the swamp two minutes earlier, Quataldo's order for silence be damned. He looked behind them, hoping to find the faint glow of the crystal coming from one of the bits of wood floating on the water. But uninterrupted darkness had reclaimed the swamp in that direction. He tried to extend the senses Sardelle kept promising him he had, but apparently, they were only good for detecting something as large and magical as a dragon.

"Problem?" Kaika asked quietly.

Tolemek responded equally quietly, since the first of the soldiers had reached the island. "I lost the communication crystal."

"So our pilots won't know when to come pick us up?"

Tolemek shook his head. Too bad, since it was now starting to look like a good time for some fliers to dive down and rescue them. As soon as the lead soldiers came off the bridge, they spread through the trees, surrounding Tolemek and Kaika, rifles pointed at their chests.

Kaika lifted empty hands and said something in their language. She sounded polite, and she even winked at one of them. The words they snapped back at her sounded less polite.

Tolemek glanced behind him, wondering if Quataldo thought they should go along peacefully, not that there was much choice when they were so outnumbered. Quataldo wasn't there.

"Don't draw attention to him," Kaika whispered. "They might not have seen him."

One of the soldiers snapped at her. She raised her eyebrows innocently and touched her chest.

The man jerked his rifle toward the bridge. The meaning was clear, but Tolemek whispered to Kaika again as he walked in the indicated direction.

"What are they saying? Blowing up the wildlife in self-defense can't be a crime, can it?"

"They're taking us into custody because we're suspicious. Sane and normal people don't wander the bridges at night. Also..." One of the soldiers was frowning at her, so she finished with, "I'll explain the rest later."

As they were herded onto the bridge, Tolemek realized she had been speaking with a Cofah accent instead of an Iskandian one, even when she had been addressing him.

Tylie? He tried stretching out with his mind, even though his range for telepathy was as limited as that of a mundane person's. Still, she hoped his sister might be monitoring him, that she and Phelistoth might be close. A rescue from a dragon would be timely now.

Tylie did not respond.

Instead, another voice spoke into his mind, one he had never heard before, but one that resonated with great power.

Who are you? it asked.

As the soldiers pushed him along the bridge, Tolemek decided it would be best not to answer.

Chapter 7

THERRIK HELD UP A HEAVY fur, his back to Sardelle and Bhrava Saruth, who crouched on a boulder just outside the cave entrance, his long neck craned so he could peer inside. Sardelle also watched Therrik from the entrance. She wanted to run in and look around herself, but she did not want to risk trampling upon evidence that would identify the occupants. The rough floor was mostly quartz and granite, but dirt rested in the crevices, so perhaps Therrik could find some footprints. Unfortunately, none of the items left in the cave contained any magic, and her senses could only tell her about life in the area now, not life that had been here days ago.

The marmots and chipmunks that scurried for cover when Bhrava Saruth approached were amusing but not exactly what we're looking for, Jaxi said.

"There were two beds." Therrik tossed the fur to the floor, where he had found it. "Here, and one in the back." He pointed toward more furs in the shadows along the far wall. "They would have had easy access to water from that stream outside. There aren't any food tins or other garbage, but there are some bones over there." He waved to a side wall, then crouched to examine the floor, touching some of the packed dirt. He frowned toward Sardelle, or maybe Bhrava Saruth. "Could you tell your dragon that his big head is blocking all the light?"

Sardelle turned toward Bhrava Saruth at the same time as his head rotated toward her. It was easy to think of him as benign, even friendly, when he chattered amiably into her head, but it was impossible not to notice the length of his fangs, the size of his powerful jaw, and the alienness of those slitted pupils when he was so close.

I do not think this one will ever make a suitable worshipper, high priestess, he said with a mournful quality to the words, apparently oblivious to the fact that those fangs made her want to step back.

Would you want him for a worshipper? Sardelle asked. *He's rather crusty.*

Crusty is too innocuous of a word, Jaxi said.

This is true, Bhrava Saruth thought agreeably. *I much prefer the humans who are adoring and adorable, though sometimes one feels triumph at adding a challenging worshipper to one's following.*

Sardelle was pondering, with some concern, whether he considered her adoring and adorable when Therrik scowled over at them and snapped, "My light? It's getting dark out there. Do you want me to identify the occupants or not?"

Bhrava Saruth's eyes narrowed and locked onto Therrik for a long, cool moment, then he tilted his snout toward the ceiling, and his jaw parted. The feeling of magic being called upon battered at Sardelle's senses, so she had some warning, but she was still surprised when flames shot out of the dragon's mouth.

For a stunned second, she thought Bhrava Saruth had grown tired of Therrik and decided to incinerate him. But Therrik shouted in alarm and ran to the side of the cave, pressing his back against it. The flames were not searing the air where he had stood; rather, they bathed the ceiling of the cave, emitting intense heat but intense light as well.

Sardelle almost laughed, both at the dragon's solution and at the pure alarm contorting Therrik's face.

Jaxi *did* laugh, the peals echoing in Sardelle's mind.

Against my better judgment, I may be starting to like him, Jaxi admitted.

Shall I ask him if he's ever been worshipped by a soulblade?

I don't like him that *much.*

"I believe your light is being provided," Sardelle said above the soft roar of the flames. Therrik's eyes were darting around in his head while the rest of his body remained frozen against the wall. "You may want to take advantage of it before Bhrava Saruth runs out of air."

Therrik blinked a few times, eyed the flames dancing on the ceiling, then managed to peel his back from the wall. He walked in a hunch as he returned to the spot he had been examining, clearly aware of the fire roiling above his head.

"You may want to thank him, too. He's being quite nice about providing for you." Sardelle wiped sweat from her brow. The temperature inside the cave must have risen thirty degrees already.

Therrik glared balefully at her. "I'm doing this for *you*."

For the king, more like, Jaxi said.

"So I should thank Bhrava Saruth on your behalf?" Sardelle asked.

"Do whatever you want." Therrik crouched, two fingers touching the ground lightly.

As I said, some humans are more challenging to win over, Bhrava Saruth said.

Indeed.

Therrik worked quickly, leaving drops of sweat all over the rocky floor as he did so. He rose a couple of minutes later and waved toward the entrance. "I'm done. You can turn the lights off."

The flames disappeared. If dragons could smirk, Bhrava Saruth did so, revealing a few more inches of fang than usual. One might easily mistake it for a sneer.

"Any conclusions?" Sardelle asked, keeping her voice calm, though hope danced in her heart. She was ready to run forward and throttle Therrik if he didn't share his findings quickly enough.

"There were definitely two people here. Zirkander might have been one of them. I found this." Therrik presented his open palm, revealing a dusty, scratched brass button with crossed swords stamped on it in addition to the letters IA. Iskandian Army.

Even though she recognized the button immediately, Sardelle's gaze lurched to Therrik's chest, to verify. Yes, several matching buttons ran down the front of his military jacket, his polished and less battered.

Sardelle reached out and took the small disk, almost reverently. She had unbuttoned Ridge's jacket numerous times, and even though every officer in the army had similar buttons on their jackets, she felt certain this was his.

You sure? Jaxi asked. *It looks old and battered.*

Crashing and being laundered in the river can't be good for maintaining the quality of clothing. Besides, what other soldiers would have been out here?

If we go back as far as those buttons have been standard on military uniform jackets, there could have been many. Perhaps someone went mad guarding those prisoners and fled into the mountains.

Sardelle sighed at the argument but reluctantly admitted that a button wasn't the indelible proof she sought that Ridge had been here. It also didn't prove he was alive.

"I also found a toy in the rocks on the way up to the cave." Therrik sounded puzzled and fiddled with something in his other hand.

"A toy?"

He held it out, and Sardelle's breath caught. It was the small wooden dragon charm Ridge kept in his pocket or dangling in his flier, so that he could rub it for luck whenever he needed it. She took it from Therrik and blinked away tears that wanted to form in her eyes.

"This is his," she whispered.

"He carries toys around?"

"It's a luck charm."

Therrik grunted.

"Is there any way to tell how long ago he was here?" Sardelle asked.

"There's no dust in the furs, no sign that animals have been in this cave. The people who were here didn't leave that long ago."

Sardelle nodded, finding the report promising. "Thank you."

"One more thing," Therrik said. "Judging by the footprint sizes, one person was a man and the other a woman."

The sorceress? Sardelle closed her eyes, not wanting to give voice to fears that came to mind at the thought. If Eversong had Ridge, who knew what she might be doing with him? *To* him.

"*If* the man was Zirkander," Therrik said, giving the charm a skeptical look, "and if he was wounded as badly as we believe he must have been, he wouldn't have walked up here from the river by himself."

She nodded again. "You said he was dragged out."

"We're almost three miles from where he was pulled out. It's highly unlikely that a woman carried him up here."

"Unless she had magic," Sardelle said slowly, hating that their suppositions were pointing more and more toward the sorceress.

"That's your arena. I'll try to pick up the trail." He shrugged and walked outside, lifting his chin and making a shooing motion as he passed by Bhrava Saruth, as if his bravery now could make up for the fact that he'd nearly wet himself when the flames had entered the cave.

Nah, he didn't do that, Jaxi said. *I definitely would have pointed that out.*

I'm sure you would have. Sardelle regarded the dragon again. He retracted his head from the cave to watch Therrik study the ground. She felt that twinge of guilt again for keeping him here when he probably had more important things to do, a following to develop or a crystal repository to investigate. Remembering that neither she nor Therrik *had* thanked him, she did so now. *I appreciate your help, Bhrava Saruth.*

Excellent! His neck curled toward her, and she thought he might put his head on her shoulder. Unintentionally, she stepped back. He paused and gazed at her. Even with those strange reptilian eyes, he managed to convey a sad expression. *You are alarmed by my largeness.*

No, she blurted. The realization that she couldn't lie to a mind reader prompted her to shrug apologetically and add, *A little. I'm sorry. It will take me some time to get used to you.*

And his fangs, Jaxi said. *They're bigger than I am.*

Perhaps this will be easier for my high priestess? Bhrava Saruth backed away a couple of steps, then his form wavered, scales changing color and turning to skin as he shrank in size. Soon, a handsome young man with bronze skin and golden hair stood before her. Unlike when Phelistoth took human form and showed off his flowing silver locks, Bhrava Saruth's hair was shorter and mussier, flopping into his eyes in a way that made her want to reach out and tidy it. He had also forgotten—

Clothes. Jaxi smirked into her mind. *His largeness is still notable. No wonder all those young females were so eager to worship him.*

Jaxi!

Yes?

Stop looking. Sardelle had seen nudity aplenty as a healer, but she cleared her throat and shifted her attention to the stream. Perhaps because the dragon had shared with her visions of some of his shape-shifted sexual exploits, she felt more discomfited by this form than the last.

Did I do something wrong? Bhrava Saruth asked.

No, but you don't need to change for me. Or for anyone. We'll learn to be comfortable around you, eventually. She eyed Therrik, who had moved down to the stream, his gaze toward the ground. *Maybe not all of us, but enough of us. I'm sure you'll be able to find many friends.* She couldn't bring herself to promise him followers.

Perhaps, but let me try one more time. I do not wish my only high priestess to feel uncomfortable around me.

Sardelle eyed him warily out of the corner of her eye, afraid of what he might come up with next. A cat? A parrot? A tail-wagging hound?

Bhrava Saruth did not shift into an animal, but into another human form, one that made her step back, the tears she had held back earlier springing to her eyes. She tightened her fingers around the dragon figurine and brought her fist to her mouth, unable to speak or even think. The dragon had changed into a perfect replica of Ridge, right down to the twinkling eyes and boyish smile.

Well, Jaxi said, sounding stunned herself. *At least he's wearing clothes this time.*

Sardelle dashed away the moisture in her eyes and looked away, even though a big part of her wanted to stare, to touch, to drink him in and pretend it was really him again.

"Did I get it right?" Bhrava Saruth asked, looking down at himself and smoothing his uniform.

"No. Yes." Sardelle shook her head. "Just choose another form. Anything. Please."

Bhrava Saruth tilted his head, the puzzled expression so human, so *Ridge*, that it drove a dagger into Sardelle's soul. He stepped forward and touched her arm. "I thought this form would please you."

Sardelle shook her head again and stumbled away. She raced down the slope toward Therrik, hardly noticing when she slipped on the loose rocks. She understood that Bhrava Saruth, for whatever reason, wanted to help her, but she couldn't look at him without her heart hurting, not when he looked like that. Her jumble of emotions made it hard to even find words to explain the problem to him.

Therrik heard her stumbling over the rocks and looked back. His eyes widened when his gaze shifted past her, toward where she had left Bhrava Saruth.

"What the—" His jaw drooped, the rest of the words forgotten.

Maybe the dragon was changing form again. Sardelle did not check. She did not want to risk looking at Ridge's face again, not when an enemy sorceress had him and was doing who knew what to him. She didn't even know for sure that Ridge was still alive. What if Eversong had sucked all of the information from his mind and then thrown his body into the river?

Sardelle's fist tightened, the wooden charm digging into her palm.

Wait, Bhrava Saruth called.

Sardelle stopped, more because she had reached Therrik and didn't know where to go from there than because of the plea. Still, the way Therrik's gaze shifted to something on the ground made her realize it might be safe to look. She turned just as an animal ran up her leg. It happened too quickly for her to react, and soon a blond—or perhaps golden was the better word—ferret sat on her shoulder. It chittered at her in a squeaky voice.

That's you, right? Sardelle asked, though she was fairly certain neither polecats nor domesticated ferrets, which he appeared to be, were native to the Ice Blades.

Of course! I sometimes assumed this form so children would not be afraid of me. It was difficult to convince them to worship me like this though. They thought I was a pet.

I can see where that would be problematic.

"Angulus better promote me after this." Therrik was staring back and forth between Sardelle and her new shoulder warmer. "This is officially the strangest assignment I've ever had."

"It's not typical of my usual day either," Sardelle said.

"I don't believe you. You must be amazing in bed."

"Uh, what?" She stared, startled by the abrupt topic change.

"For Zirkander to put up with your entourage." Therrik's wave included the sword at her waist as well as the "ferret" on her shoulder. "Trail's this way. Come on."

It took a moment for Sardelle to recover enough to say, "Actually, he hasn't met Bhrava Saruth yet."

"Lucky him," Therrik said without looking back.

The proper response, Jaxi said, *would have been, Yes, I am amazing in bed.*

I don't want him imagining me between the sheets.

Too late. Fortunately for you, Kasandral is still oozing hatred for you and the dragon into him, so he's fantasizing about killing you more often than about rutting with you.

Fortunate. That's me.

* * *

The sound of a rifle firing woke Cas from sleep. She jerked alert, finding her own rifle in the dark of her cockpit. She had chosen to sleep up here, rather than trying to find a dry spot in the swamp.

"What is it?" Pimples asked from the flier nearest to hers.

"Animals," Blazer said. It sounded like she had climbed into the back of his flier. "Some kind of swimming hogs, I think. They came out of the dark and chased me off my stump where I was standing watch."

"So you decided to hide behind Pimples?" Cas squinted into the gloom. There weren't any lanterns lit, but she could hear shuffling and grunting noises, along with a splash here and there.

"Yes, I was drawn by his manliness," Blazer said.

"Captain, you teasing us again?" Duck asked, then cursed. "I think there's one trying to eat my wheel." A thump sounded as he tried to scare it away instead of shooting. Cas couldn't see the details in the night gloom.

"I wasn't teasing *you*, Duck," Blazer said, "but if you'd like to volunteer for the Pimples treatment, I can include you in later comments."

"Nobody wants the Pimples treatment."

"Thanks," Pimples said dryly.

A howl came out of the trees across the river, raising the hair on Cas's arms. She wondered if she had stirred up the predators in her twilight run to and from the beach. Or maybe, as she had surmised earlier, the animals weren't being cautious now that Phelistoth and his fearsome dragon aura had left.

A splash sounded, followed by moist chewing sounds. Duck cursed and thumped the side of his flier again.

"Anyone else entertaining the notion of moving the camp *tonight?*" Captain Blazer asked.

"You're in charge, ma'am," Pimples said.

Blazer grunted. "If only that were true."

Duck lit a lantern and dangled it from his cockpit by a rope. Cas caught a glimpse of tusks, a bristly snout, and a stocky, mud-spattered body before the four-legged creature scampered back into the darkness.

"If I were in charge—" Blazer inhaled, the red tip of a cigar burning in the darkness, "—I would have flown us to the city, landed at their docks, and gone in under the pretext of needing a break from a long flight. Stayed at a nice hotel with feather beds, enjoyed some shopping from the exotic southern markets, ordered in some grilled tuna steaks—"

Growls came from below her, as one of the pigs thumped against Pimples' flier, maybe trying to bite the tires again.

"Or grilled pig," she growled, leaning over the side and shooting.

The creature squealed and ran away. Cas glimpsed it and could have fired a shot, one that would have killed it, but she did not want a pile of carcasses to draw more predators to their camp. She didn't know if Blazer shared the same mindset.

"That would have been suspicious." Pimples, apparently not worried about pigs eating his flier, was sketching in his notebook by the tiny glow of his communication crystal. "If they would have let us land at all. We might have been shot upon approach. Our fliers clearly mark us as Iskandians, and if the city is in the middle of cementing an alliance with the empire..."

"You're awfully logical for a lieutenant, Pimples. Not all women appreciate that, you know. They want a man to console and commiserate, not point out the reasons why staying in a feather bed is a bad idea."

"They also want him to have a name more manly than Pimples," Duck said.

"As manly as Duck?" Blazer asked.

"Ducks can be manly. The males are tough."

"Don't the males gang up on the females and attack them?" Pimples asked.

"Only some species. And only during mating season."

"Very manly."

"Don't you have a pimple to pop?" Duck grumbled.

"Not lately. I stopped eating that slop in the mess hall, and it's helped. Raptor, what do you think about male ducks attacking females?"

Cas was never sure whether to feel pleased or not when they included her in their silly conversations. It was good to be a part of the group and be able to talk about something besides death and battle, but she would rather have spoken with Tolemek. It worried her that they hadn't been able to get in touch. She'd tried using the crystals in the other cockpits in case something had failed. He hadn't responded on any of them. It was possible he had gone out of range, but she'd been told that the crystals could reach fifty miles, and the city was closer than that.

"I think we should move our camp tonight," Cas said. "It's dark as pitch out there, and if it's as misty along the beach as it is along this river, we could get within five miles of the city without anyone seeing or hearing our approach. The roar of the ocean should drown out our propellers."

"The problem is then finding a place where we can land and hide that close to the city," Blazer said.

"True," Pimples said. "Tildar Dem is supposed to have a population of fifty thousand. Even if the marsh is kissing the borders, I bet there's development outside of the core area. I would like to see it." He wished wistfully. "I heard that there are a lot of tree houses."

"You're not planning to design one of those next, are you?" Cas waved to his notebook.

"I might."

Something growled from a branch near the river. Blazer took her cigar from her mouth and growled back.

"This place could make you crazy," she said. "Raptor, you want a scouting mission?"

"You want me to look for a closer place where we could land?"

"Yeah, you and Duck. No, take Pimples. I need Duck to drag whatever it is I shot down there out into the river, so it doesn't attract whatever's growling in the trees."

"Me?" Duck protested. "Why me?"

"You're the wilderness kid. Raptor, you two go ahead and see if there's a good place to land. If there is, you can sneak into the city and try to locate the others, find out if they're in trouble. Two of us better stay back here, since we're not able to communicate with Quataldo. He might be irked if he kidnaps the emperor, drags him all the way back here, and we're gone."

"Agreed," Cas said, though she was not enthused about taking Pimples as a partner for skulking around in a city, especially if they ended up needing to mount a rescue. Maybe she would leave him to guard the fliers and go in alone. She couldn't help but think of the Cofah volcano lab mission where the elite forces soldiers had gone in by themselves, and one of them hadn't come out.

"If you can't find a landing spot, just come back," Blazer said. "You don't want us to get lonesome. Or for Duck to join in with a bunch of bachelor drakes and start pummeling females."

"Ha ha," Duck said. "Is this because I teased Pimples?"

"If it is," Pimples said, "I approve."

The hogs must have gotten tired of being targets. When Blazer hopped down into the mud, nothing ran forward and bothered her. She did not linger. She made her way to her own flier and scrambled up into the cockpit.

Cas hit the starter on her dashboard, and the power crystal flared to life. "Let's go, Pimples. I won't tease you."

"That's because you're a *good* teammate."

"You might want to reserve judgment on that until you see if I get us lost." Cas also hadn't forgotten that there was a dragon lurking out there somewhere. She planned to be extremely careful as they approached the city. Full darkness had fallen some time ago, but she had no idea if dragons slept at night—or at all.

Muddy water rippled as she ignited her thrusters. As her craft rose, the stick responded sluggishly. She doubted the humidity—and the nap in the mud—could be good for the fliers, and she hoped they would not have any trouble before they got back home. Blazer had been a mechanic before going into flight school, but they had limited tools out here and were a long way from their hangar back home.

"My engine sounds like there's a dying lizard in it," Pimples announced as they rose out of the water and turned down the river.

"I wouldn't be surprised if there was," Cas said.

"Keep us in the loop, you two," Blazer said over the communication crystal.

"On lizards?" Pimples asked.

"On your progress, you lout."

Curtains of mist thickened the air, and Cas wished they could fly slowly, but as soon as they transitioned from thrusters to propellers, they had to maintain the minimum flier speed to stay aloft. The mist cleared somewhat as they reached the mouth of the river, a stiff sea breeze pushing it inland, but clouds hung low up and down the coast. That was good. Cas did not want to be visible to anyone who might be out late. It was less good that scouting and finding landing spots would be difficult in the gloom.

"Wing to wing?" Pimples asked.

"Yes, we don't want to lose each other in the dark."

Cas kept her goggles resting on her forehead since the thick sea air left droplets on them, and visibility was already poor. She led Pimples out over the water, so their propellers should not be audible to anyone on land, not that the dark depths of the marshes suggested anyone lived on this section of coast.

She and Pimples traveled at least twenty miles before that changed. After that, the occasional lamp burned, and she spotted the outlines of houses here and there. The coast did not appear as marshy in this area.

"I don't see any tree houses," Pimples said. "Those appear boringly normal."

"Maybe the tree houses are inland," Cas said. "Look for a stream or bay, or maybe some nice cliffs full of caves large enough to hide fliers."

"That would be convenient."

Unfortunately, cliffs did not appear to be a feature here. The land remained relatively flat, offering few interesting topographical features—and few hiding places.

The houses disappeared as the shoreline grew wild and swampy again. Cas started to wonder if they had flown past the city without realizing it, but then a huge delta came into view. As they passed it, they could see clumps of lights burning all along the bank of a wide river, as well as along platforms and bridges on either side.

"Those don't look like natural flames," Pimples said. "At least not all of them."

Many of the lanterns had a bluish cast, and Cas instinctively nudged her craft farther out to sea—if there were magic lamps, there could be shamans here, people who might sense intruders. "I guess they don't share the Cofah and Iskandian fears of magic."

"Or maybe the citizens don't ask too many questions when someone shows up with practical tools, much like our power crystals."

"Could be." Cas continued flying past the delta. "There's no way we can land in there without being noticed."

"No, and I didn't see any likely spots along the way. Should we fly a few more miles and see if we find something farther up?"

"Yes. The other option is to circle around the city and try to land inland somewhere."

"Inland looks extra swampy."

"There might be tree houses."

As they continued up the shoreline, Cas tapped her fingers on her flight stick, wondering if this scouting mission would be for naught. Unless there was a lake inland, she did not know where they might find a spot to land, not with the trees a solid mass from the beach to the distant mountains. Whatever the denizens of this city did for their livelihoods, clearing land and farming wasn't it.

"Is that a bay?" Pimples asked.

Up ahead, the beach turned inland. Cas followed the shoreline, staying low as she had been for most of the trip. Because of this, she flew around the trees instead of over them, and she twitched in surprise when the lights of multiple airships came into view. She veered away immediately, heading back out to sea, but she craned her neck for a view. Pimples was right behind her and doing the same thing.

"Guess we know where the emperor's ships are parked," he said, the dryness in his tone not quite hiding his alarm.

There were five huge airships anchored in the bay, lines attaching them to thick trees. Numerous naval ships occupied the quiet inlet too. A few docks thrust out from the shore behind them, with fishing boats moored there, but Cas only had eyes for the Cofah craft. Enough lights burned on the decks that she had no trouble verifying that those were imperial ships. Her shoulder blades itched as they flew away, and she worried that alert soldiers on watch might have spotted her and Pimples. She did not hear any alarms or gunshots, but that did not mean much. Seeing an Iskandian flier would be enough to put those people on guard, and that was the last thing her team wanted.

After they passed out of sight of the bay, Cas reluctantly tapped the communication crystal. "Captain? We found where the imperial ships went—there are seven naval warships in addition to five sky-cruise class airships, and they're moored in a bay approximately a mile south of the city."

"Did anyone see you?" Blazer asked.

"Unknown. We were flying close to the waves, and it's dark, so I'm hoping not, but it's possible." Cas hated admitting that. They had needed to stay low so they could look for hiding places in the dark, but now she wished they had flown up high for an initial pass before dropping low. Then they would have seen the bay from miles away and known to avoid it. Zirkander wouldn't have made such a foolish mistake.

"Find a place to put down yet?" Blazer asked.

"No."

"All the good bays are taken," Pimples added.

"See any dragons?"

"No, but I wasn't looking for any either."

"I'm tempted to tell you to come back," Blazer said.

"What if Tolemek and the captain and colonel ran into trouble and need help?" Cas asked.

"I'm not sure two lieutenants are supposed to be the backup forces."

"We can't leave our people behind..."

"Cas," Pimples blurted. "Up ahead."

She spotted it as soon as Pimples alerted her—the form of a dragon flying along the coast.

"Inland," she said, though she had no idea whether they would be more likely to avoid it over the marsh than over the sea. She thumped her fist on her thigh, annoyed that they hadn't stayed put and given the other team another couple of days before worrying.

Wait, a voice said in her head. *It's Tylie.*

And Phelistoth? Cas resisted the urge to ask if the dragon was done hunting. She'd never seen such a scarce ally.

I talked him into bringing me here, even though he wanted to avoid the female. Tolie is in trouble.

The female?

"Raptor?" Pimples asked.

Though she had ordered him to head inland, she hadn't

followed. Tylie had started talking to her. "That's Phelistoth. I'm speaking to Tylie."

"Ah." Pimples did not sound that comforted.

The female gold dragon, Tylie explained.

That's the dragon I saw communicating with the emperor's ship this evening, I presume?

Likely so. I wasn't there. If you follow us, Phel will lead you to a place to land.

A safe *place*? Cas looked back in the direction of the bay, half-expecting to see someone back there, following them. The airships would not have their fliers' speed, but she hadn't forgotten that the Cofah had fliers of their own now. She hadn't seen any in the bay, but there could have been some on the decks of those airships.

The swamps are not safe, Tylie said, *but Phel will protect us.*

"Goody," Pimples muttered.

Cas did not feel much better about the situation, but they would never find a place to land on their own, not in the dark, with the mist cloaking the marshes.

I understand, she responded to Tylie. *We're following.*

CHAPTER 8

THERRIK LED THEM ALONG THE river and out of the valley at a brisk pace, pausing occasionally to crouch and study some sign on the ground. Once it became clear that the two people who had left the cave had followed the waterway, he didn't check as often. Sardelle had been following at a distance, not wanting to be too close to anyone whose sword was fantasizing about killing her. They passed several streams that dumped into the river, and he always paused to check the trail on the other side before assuming the two people had continued this way.

About five miles into their trek, Sardelle trailed Therrik into a narrow canyon with high walls. Had the river been higher, they wouldn't have been able to enter it at all. As it was, only a couple of feet of dry rock lay exposed on either side of the waterway, and deposits on the walls showed the heights the water could reach during heavy rains or periods of great snow melts.

As soon as Sardelle stepped into the area, something jangled her senses. Magic.

Bhrava Saruth? she asked, prodding him gently. He was still in ferret form and had fallen asleep draped across her shoulder.

She stopped, backing toward the entrance. *Therrik*, she called, using telepathy because she did not want to shout. He was nearly two hundred meters ahead of her. Might the sorceress be somewhere nearby? Waiting to ambush them? The memory of the woman's deadly fireballs flashed into Sardelle's mind.

The ferret stirred and jumped to the ground. In an instant, Bhrava Saruth changed back into a dragon, his massive form filling the tight canyon. He would not be able to spread his wings without backing out of the passage.

I sense it, Bhrava Saruth said. *Some residual magic in the rocks.*

Is it possible the sorceress is here? Sardelle already had her senses out, trying to locate another person. The rocks above the canyon walls teemed with wildlife, including a prowling mountain lion, but she hadn't detected any humans.

Not unless she's hiding her presence from me.

Sardelle frowned, because she already suspected that the sorceress might be able to do that when she wished. How else would she have found Ridge and hidden him in that cave when Sardelle and the others had been searching for him?

It is possible she could hide from me, Bhrava Saruth admitted. *If not her, her soulblade may have the ability to mask their presence. I encountered that sometimes when I went into battle with human riders.*

Was that before or after he became a god? Jaxi asked. *I think she may have set a trap, not that you asked for* my *opinion.*

I didn't know I had to ask for your opinions. You usually give them to me whether I want them or not. Sardelle waved to Therrik, wanting him to return to the canyon entrance with her. They might risk losing the trail if they avoided the canyon, but perhaps Bhrava Saruth could fly them to the other end and they could pick it up there.

I will search for signs of a trap while he returns. Bhrava Saruth backed out of the canyon so he could spread his wings. *Stay safe, high priestess.*

Sardelle eyed the walls, imagining rocks tumbling down to crush her. *Therrik,* she said his name again, since he had stopped but wasn't walking back toward her. Instead, he had crouched down to check something. *I sense what might be a trap. Let's look for another way around.*

His head came up, and he frowned in her direction, then he considered the cliff walls to either side of him. He picked up something nestled in a crevice, stood up, and headed toward her.

I have discovered a trap, Bhrava Saruth announced.

Before Sardelle could respond, a cacophony of noise arose from the far end of the canyon. Rocks sloughed from either side of the rock wall, the top edges crumbling down, boulders crashing into the river. White dust filled the air, blotting out the view.

It was at least a half a mile from where Therrik stood, so Sardelle relaxed. He jogged toward her while tossing glances over his shoulder, but he didn't appear too concerned.

I have triggered a trap, Bhrava Saruth said, his voice dry and perhaps abashed.

Didn't mean to? Sardelle asked.

No, I—wait! There's another.

Therrik must have heard the message, too, because he froze. He was still forty or fifty meters from Sardelle. A crack sounded in the rock wall beside him.

Instinctively, Sardelle lifted her hand and summoned the energy to create a protective barrier around him. The instant she drew upon her magic, something snapped in her mind, and she had the sense of stepping on a twig and alerting someone to her presence. A feeling of disorientation washed over her, and she stumbled to the side, her foot landing in the river.

Before she could recover her mental and physical balance, the ground heaved beneath her.

High priestess! came a cry in her mind at the same time as the rock walls tumbled down from above.

Jaxi formed a barrier above her, a half second before Sardelle recovered her wits and added her own energy to the effort. Boulders slammed down, striking their invisible barrier and landing two feet above her head. She swallowed and gathered more energy, carefully adding layers to the shield as more rubble crashed down, trying to bury her alive.

And here you thought you had to be down in a mine for this to happen, Jaxi said.

Even though the rocks continued to fall, blocking out the daylight as they surrounded the shield, Sardelle felt confident that nothing would get through. *Apparently, nowhere inside, atop, or next to a mountain is safe. Thank you for your fast reflexes.*

You're welcome.

The rockfall ended, and Sardelle stretched upward with her senses, checking how much of a pile had landed on her. Fortunately, only about five feet of rock had settled directly on her barrier, and only a few were large boulders.

It would have been enough to kill a person without power to draw upon, Jaxi noted. *It looks like our sorceress didn't want people following her.*

Agreed on both counts. Sardelle shoved some of the smaller rocks aside with her mind. *A few minutes, and we should see some light.*

Several of the large boulders flew away, slamming into what remained of one of the cliff walls with enough force that Sardelle had no problem hearing the rock shattering from within her prison.

That wasn't me, Jaxi said.

Light spilled in, and another huge boulder flew away.

Ah, Bhrava Saruth landed on top of the cliff up there. You can have a seat while he does the hard work.

Scrapes sounded, and a figure came into sight, silhouetted by the blue sky above. Therrik. He held Kasandral in one hand, and the tip brushed against her barrier. A backlash of power struck her like a rubber band shot to the eye, and her shield disappeared.

Most of the big rocks had been removed, but smaller ones tumbled down, and she gasped, raising her arms to protect herself. Jaxi growled into her mind.

Not certain about Therrik's intentions—had that been an accident or an attack?—Sardelle worried more about him than the rubble. He was leaning in, and she tried to push him back with her mind, but with Kasandral in his grip, she could do nothing to him.

He loomed in close and wrapped his free hand around her forearm. He started to pull, but something slammed into him like one of those boulders. As he disappeared from her view, she glimpsed golden scales flashing past.

Sardelle clawed her way out of the rubble, coughing on dust and dashing grit out of her eyes with her sleeve. She stumbled into the water before she found her feet.

"I was *helping* her," Therrik shouted.

He and Bhrava Saruth stood just outside of the canyon entrance—had the dragon's attack thrown him that far? They faced each other like boxing combatants about to clash. Therrik held the sword and stared defiantly at Bhrava Saruth, who towered over him in his full dragon form.

You tried to stab her with that vile sword, Bhrava Saruth shouted into their minds with so much power that Sardelle winced in pain.

He's worse than the rocks, Jaxi said.

"I was just holding it," Therrik responded. "I thought that sorceress might be around."

You tried to hit her.

"I did not." Therrik truly sounded indignant. "I don't *try* to hit people; if I want to hit them, I hit them."

Though she felt battered and tired after the incident, Sardelle forced her feet into motion. She didn't know what would happen if these two engaged in a real fight, and she did not want to find out.

"Bhrava Saruth?" She waved to get his attention as she approached. They were both so intent on each other, circling now, their bodies coiled for action, that she didn't know if they would hear her. "I'm fine. It was an accident. Let's not fight each other. We have a common enemy."

It was not *an accident,* Bhrava Saruth insisted. *That sword wants both of us dead. It whispers into his mind all the time.*

"It doesn't whisper—it growls. And I tell it to shut its metal yap."

He does, actually, Jaxi said.

Sardelle had reached the would-be combatants. Though she did not know how wise it was, she jogged out and stepped between them. She was tempted to draw Jaxi, since Kasandral glowed green and appeared ready for a fight, but she spread her arms instead. She *did* face Therrik and that sword, trusting Bhrava Saruth at her back far more than him.

Bhrava Saruth made a contented noise in her mind.

"If anyone's suspicious, it's *him*." Therrik pointed the sword over Sardelle's head, toward the dragon's golden snout. "Why did he leave you when you thought there was a trap?"

I was triggering the more obvious trap, Bhrava Saruth said. *They were well laid. I barely noticed them. This sorceress is skilled.*

"More skilled than a dragon?" Therrik asked.

Of course not. I could make excellent traps, if I wished, but I have no desire to harm people. Even you, sword-wielder, unless you try to hurt my high priestess.

Bhrava Saruth settled onto his haunches and no longer appeared ready to spring into battle. Therrik still breathed heavily, the tendons in his neck standing out under his skin. His glare shifted from the dragon to the sword, and Sardelle took a couple of steps back, sensing that he was battling with *it* now.

Kasandral doesn't want to be put back in his doghouse, Jaxi said.

I wish there was a way to teach him who his enemies are—and who they aren't. Sardelle focused on the blade and whispered the calming control words with her mind.

Therrik growled and jerked his arm down. He sheathed Kasandral, and the green glow diminished. He looked sourly at Sardelle and Bhrava Saruth.

If he requests light again, I am prepared to give it to him, Bhrava Saruth said, his voice quieter this time, just for her mind.

I don't think he'll make that mistake again.

Therrik looked into the canyon, where two rock piles now blocked the way. They could travel over them, but Sardelle liked her earlier idea of asking Bhrava Saruth to fly them to the other side, so long as Kasandral had calmed down enough to endure such close proximity to the dragon again.

"She set those traps to go off if someone was following her trail, right? She's not in the area?" Therrik sounded disappointed. Kasandral wasn't the only one dreaming of eviscerating a sorceress.

"I don't think she's here," Sardelle said.

"But she was."

"Yes."

"So was he." Therrik dug into his pocket and withdrew something. He spread his palm. A second button. That must have been what he was picking up down there.

Sardelle swallowed and accepted it, placing it in her pocket with the dragon figurine and the other button.

* * *

Cas finished draping the camo netting over her flier, then joined Pimples and Tylie on the ground. Phelistoth stood several paces away, now in human form, gazing up toward the trees. The boughs shifted. At first, Cas thought it was the wind, but trunks all around their little clearing groaned and tilted.

"Uh?" Pimples lifted his rifle, but he didn't seem to know where to aim.

Cas waved for him to lower it as the branches closed in above them. A trunk that had been leaning away from her flier returned to a straight position, halting less than a foot from the wing.

"I think he moved the trees to make a spot for us to land," Cas said as the trunks settled, all returning to an upright position. When they'd landed, she hadn't realized they had all been leaning away to form a clearing.

"Yes, he did," Tylie said brightly. "I want to learn how to talk to the trees the way he does. I'm already learning about mammals. And insects. And birds. And Tolie's snakes." She grinned, as if chatting with snakes was quite delightful. "But trees don't have brains. I'm still trying to figure out how he talks to them."

Cas was more concerned than impressed by the idea of talking to trees, especially since their fliers were effectively trapped now. She did not think they could escape without Phelistoth's help, and that made her uncomfortable.

Pimples stepped close, bumping her elbow with his. "Are you thinking what I'm thinking?"

Cas sighed. "Yes."

Phelistoth looked over at them. "I risk much to be here, helping you."

"We appreciate your help," Cas made herself say.

However dubious this landing spot, they were only a couple of miles from the city now—they had flown over it on the way here, the lamp-lit bridges stretching out like spider webs on either side of the river, where the majority of the population seemed centered. If this location put them closer to Tolemek and the others, that was a good thing. If she had to, she would steal saws and cut their fliers free.

"Good," Phelistoth said. "If Yisharnesh senses me, she will attack. It is not breeding season. She has no need for a male, and it is likely she has claimed this as her territory."

"This?" Pimples looked at the gloom all around them. "The city? The river?"

"The continent."

"Oh, is that all?"

"There are few dragons remaining in the world. There are continents enough for all the golds." It was too dark to see facial expressions, but his tone conveyed his displeasure at that idea, or maybe at the idea that there was not a continent for a silver dragon?

Cas had no idea about dragon politics, other than that silvers were weaker than golds. She did know Angulus wouldn't be happy to hear that a dragon had "claimed" his continent. Which dragon would that be? Bhrava Saruth? The one who thought himself a god?

"Will she sense you here when she's this close?" Cas asked. "And do you know if she's working with the Cofah emperor? I saw them talking. I assume that's what they were doing."

"What?" Phelistoth asked sharply.

"It—uhm, *she* was flying alongside the emperor's airship, circling it, and they seemed to be communicating with each other. You didn't know?"

"I do not know why she is here. Tylie is using her power to hide my aura from Yisharnesh."

"She can do that?" Pimples asked, looking at Tylie, who was crouching near the trunk of a tree. The darkness made it hard to tell, but she appeared to be stroking its bark.

"She has many gifts." Phelistoth turned toward her.

She looked back at him, and they stared at each other. Having some private conversation?

"Phel wishes to spy upon the emperor and see what's going

on between him and the female dragon," Tylie said.

"Spy?" Cas frowned. A second ago, Phelistoth hadn't wanted anything to do with the female dragon. What had changed? Just the information Cas had shared about the meeting.

"Yes, but I've asked him to take us into the city first, to find Tolie."

Cas did not know how far to trust the dragon, but she nodded and said, "Good. I want to find him too. Do you know where he is?"

"Captured," Tylie said, her shoulders drooping.

Cas had been afraid of that. What if his captors—imperial soldiers or local guards?—had taken the crystal from him and someone recognized it and knew it was an Iskandian military item? Worse, what if Tolemek himself was in danger? The emperor had tried to hire her father to assassinate him. If he found out Tolemek was right here in town, he was sure to send men down to finish the job.

"Are Kaika and Quataldo with him?" Cas asked.

"I'm not sure. Phel?"

Phelistoth was frowning, gazing into the distance, and did not answer. Something hooted from across water that spread out to one side, but the marsh had been nearly silent since they'd landed. Cas suspected that had more to do with his presence than with the noise from the fliers.

Tylie walked over and touched his arm. "Phel?"

"A woman is alone in the marsh," he said. "An oddity."

A dangerous oddity, given all the deadly animals here. Even with her marksmanship skills, Cas would not have felt comfortable walking around out here at night alone.

"Can you take us to her?" she asked. "Maybe she can give us some information on how best to get into the city."

"Yes," Pimples said. "Maybe we can rescue her."

Cas arched her eyebrows. "Rescue her? Because she's a woman alone, you automatically assume she needs rescuing?"

"Er, no. But, come on. This place is scary. Would you wander around here alone? Even with your sniper rifle?"

"What if she's a shaman?"

Pimples blinked a few times.

"Let's go find out." Tylie smiled. "I would love to meet more magic users. I miss Sardelle. And Jaxi." She and Phelistoth headed into the trees, the decision made.

"I just want a guide," Cas mumbled, shouldering her pack. Her experience with shamans was limited, but they always seemed to come to Iskandia in the company of aggressive Cofah, so she was predisposed not to like them. She would keep her rifle ready.

Cas and Pimples let Phelistoth lead. Cas was content to follow him since he was going in the direction of the city, and after a murmured request from Tylie, he conjured a small silver sphere of light that hung in the air over his shoulder. Pimples trotted ahead and peered around him whenever they came to a turn or the top of a hill. He was either looking for tree houses, or he was excited by the idea of rescuing some maiden.

Phelistoth stopped at the edge of a pool that disappeared into the mist in all directions. A rope and wood bridge stretched away from the bank.

He bent low, considering the construction. "So frail. A dragon could snap this by accident with a tail flick."

"You could fly us across the swamp if you're worried about it," Tylie said.

Phelistoth gazed past her shoulder to Cas and Pimples, peering disdainfully down his nose at them. "We will walk."

"I think we've been rejected as unworthy to fly on a dragon's back," Pimples murmured to Cas as they followed Phelistoth and Tylie onto the bridge, the ropes creaking ominously.

"Fine with me," Cas said. "I prefer my flier."

At first, the bridge stretched across the water in darkness broken only by Phelistoth's light, but after they came to a small island with other bridges stretching away from it, the support posts started to carry lanterns. Strange lanterns that glowed with soft blue flames that could not be natural.

"The woman comes this way," Phelistoth said when they came to a second island, this one having a few fishing dinghies tied on a beach, as well as two more bridges that disappeared into the darkness to the sides.

Pimples pointed upward toward a hut perched in the branches of a species of tree that Cas did not recognize. It had big, sturdy branches that easily supported the structure. Several of the floorboards were missing, and a jagged hole opened up on one wall. A window? Or evidence of an attack? It looked like a cannonball had gone through it.

"Not the most impressive architecture," Cas commented.

"No," Pimples agreed, but he scampered to the side and climbed wooden slats nailed to the trunk in the guise of a ladder. He stuck his head inside. With Phelistoth and his magical light continuing along the bridge, Pimples couldn't have seen much, but he said, "It's empty," his voice echoing hollowly. "There are some supplies up here. Food and a bucket of water. Kind of odd. Aren't we only a mile or so out from the city?"

"I don't know, but our dragon is leaving. Come on." Cas jogged to catch up with Phelistoth and Tylie.

As she reached them, a shot rang out from ahead. Cas jerked her rifle up, though she couldn't see anything yet. The lighting was too intermittent to drive the shadows far from the bridges, and the mist hanging in the air further muted the illumination.

"It's the woman, isn't it?" Tylie gripped Phelistoth's arm. "Is she all right?"

Phelistoth merely tilted his head, perhaps studying the darkness ahead with his magic.

Another shot rang out, and an animal screeched. The bridge trembled as Pimples ran to catch up with them, his boots hammering the wooden planks. Phelistoth had stopped—maybe he didn't know about rescuing maidens—so Cas pushed past him.

"We'll go ahead," she said. She had intended to lead, but Pimples thundered past her, nearly knocking her from the bridge.

Cas jogged after him, feeling more cautious as she wondered at the possibility of traps. She also wondered if Pimples would be so quick to race ahead if Phelistoth had proclaimed a *man* was wandering the bridges alone.

When he stopped abruptly and lifted his rifle, Cas frowned,

unable to see around him. At her height, her nose was even with his shoulder blades. Pimples fired at something. His target roared, and the bridge rocked, water lapping onto the boards.

"Kneel," Cas ordered, wanting to see and be able to shoot if necessary.

Pimples dropped to one knee as he cranked the lever on his rifle to load another round. More shadows than light lay ahead, but Cas could see enough. A cloaked figure crouched in the center of the wood planks, firing at something huge leaping over the bridge and snapping at her with a giant maw. As Cas lifted her rifle, the long creature surged out of the water again. The woman dropped to her belly, avoiding being knocked off the bridge—barely.

Cas fired, pegging the creature in the side as it soared over its target, narrowly missing. Pimples fired at the same time. Cas was certain of her aim and thought Pimples' bullet had hit, too, but when the predator splashed into the water, it immediately swam in a curve, coming back to launch itself again.

Pimples sprang from his crouch and ran toward the cloaked figure. She had rolled onto her side and was aiming her rifle toward the churning water. Cas had only taken a few steps when the creature surged above the surface again. This time, it didn't leap over its target. It slammed into the bridge. The woman got a shot off as wood snapped and shattered, but was then hurled into the water on the other side. Pimples yelled and jumped in after her.

Cas fired three times in rapid succession, aiming at the creature's big head. It had grown tangled in the bridge, its jaw caught around boards. It shook its head, trying to extract its fangs from the wood. The bridge bucked and heaved, and Cas worried she would be in the water next to Pimples in a second.

Her bullets found the creature's head—it looked like one of the giant alligators, though the shadows still made it hard to pick out details, and those were definitely wings flailing at the water. It broke free from the bridge and dropped below the surface of the water. Cas did not know if it was hurt and would flee, or if it meant to swim under the bridge so it could reach Pimples and the woman.

She sprinted forward, her rifle still to the crook of her shoulder as she hoped the bridge would hold. Splashes sounded to either side of her, and she had the sense of more creatures swimming toward the battle. More alligators? She grimaced. Her bullets hadn't done noticeable damage to the first.

The water in front of the woman stirred, and she flailed, scrambling backward. "It's coming!"

A part of Cas's brain registered that she understood the words and that they had been uttered with a Cofah accent at the same time as she took aim and fired again. The winged alligator had come up between the bridge and Pimples. He pushed the woman further back, trying to keep her safe while he traded his rifle for a dagger. He plunged down at the head arrowing toward them. Cas wanted to shoot at it, the most immediate threat for them, but she could see what Pimples couldn't, that two more alligators were coming in from farther out in the water, heading straight for him and the woman.

Cas fired at each of them as Pimples grappled with the first one—its maw opened wide, fangs looming only inches from Pimples' face. He jammed his knife into the top of the alligator's mouth. One of the creatures Cas had struck jerked its head about and paused in its attack. The second kept swimming toward the woman.

"Dragon," she barked, not daring to look away to see if Phelistoth was anywhere close. "We could use some help."

She had no sooner than uttered the words then a giant shape flew past her, the air stirred by its wings almost enough to knock Cas from the bridge. Phelistoth, back in dragon form, reached the battle and plucked the charging alligator from the water as if it weighed no more than a fish. Bone crunched as his long neck whipped up and his jaw crushed the creature. He snapped his head and let go. The alligator sailed twenty-five meters before splashing down on the other side of the bridge.

Pimples, in the middle of wrestling with the first alligator, disappeared under the surface. His adversary was under the water now, too, and Cas had nothing to aim at. Feeling useless, she sprinted as close as she could to where boards had been torn from the rope framework of the bridge. The water churned around where Pimples had been. She pointed her rifle, waiting for a target, the right target. All she needed was a split second.

The woman was still fighting, treading water and turning in a circle, bashing the butt of her rifle down whenever she saw—or thought she saw—something. Maybe the alligator was bumping her with its tail. Whatever it was doing, it didn't come back to the surface. Sweat dripped down the sides of Cas's face. She was aware of Phelistoth killing another alligator in the distance, but she didn't take her eyes from the water next to the woman. It crossed her mind to jump in and try to find Pimples down there, but what could she do in a grappling match with an alligator that weighed five times as much as she did?

The water grew still, aside from ripples flowing away from the woman as she bobbed up and down, treading water. Fear crept into Cas, her limbs growing heavy with dread. Had it killed Pimples? Dragged him away for some underwater meal?

"Get on the bridge," she told the woman. She could have extended her rifle to help, but she kept hoping that the alligator would come up, that she would get a chance to shoot it.

The woman seemed to notice her for the first time. She hesitated, then paddled awkwardly for the bridge, not letting go of her rifle. Cas did lower one hand to help her pull herself up. Tylie appeared behind her and lent further help. The woman gasped, clearly exhausted as she collapsed across the boards.

Farther out in the water, Phelistoth had finished with the other alligators. He turned toward them, half of his silvery body under the surface. He flexed his wings and rivers of water fell from them.

"Dragon," Cas said, "can you help Pimples? Can you tell if—"

Phelistoth, he growled into her mind.

She glowered at him. He was worried about *names* right now?

"I sense him," Tylie whispered. "He's—"

The water broke, a dark shape surging to the surface. Expecting the alligator, Cas almost shot, but she lifted her rifle, shifting her finger from the trigger. It was Pimples, his hair matted to his head, water streaming into his eyes as he gulped in air. He coughed and nearly choked.

"Here." Cas extended her rifle.

He dashed water from his eyes, spotted it, and gripped the barrel.

"What happened?" she asked as she pulled him in.

"It had my pack." Pimples glanced over his shoulder. "It *still* has my pack. It was crunching down on my canteen and all my rations, and I think it thought it had me. I couldn't get away. It was dragging me somewhere. I had to cut the straps off, but I was all tangled up, and I thought I was going to drown." He hauled himself onto the bridge. "Then it let go and just disappeared."

You are welcome, Phelistoth said into Cas's mind. Into all of their minds, most likely, because the woman looked in his direction and gaped at him.

"Thank you, Phelistoth," Cas said, though she wished he hadn't hesitated and had jumped in earlier.

"It's true," the woman whispered, still staring at Phelistoth's sleek silver form. "I'd heard they were back in the world."

"Heroic soldiers who leap to the assistance of women under attack?" Pimples asked. "Yes, we're back in the world."

Seven gods, was he trying to flirt? *Now?* Had Cas been closer and had he looked haler, she would have jabbed an elbow into his ribs.

The woman glanced at him, her brow wrinkled, but her gaze was soon drawn back to the dragon. Riveted to him. Phelistoth had recreated his sphere of light, and he directed it over the bridge as he waded closer, shaking his wings off with a disdainful sneer for the water, or perhaps the entire marsh.

Cas had an opportunity to study the woman while she stared at him. She was younger than she had guessed at first, not much older than Tylie. Maybe twenty? Cas would call her cute rather than beautiful, with olive skin, dark brown eyes, and black hair. She wore practical travel clothes, trousers and a long-sleeve shirt full of pockets. Cas would have assumed her a local if she hadn't spoken with a Cofah accent. What would a Cofah woman be doing down here? Their military was all male, so she shouldn't have come from any of those ships. She looked too young to be some world explorer, and she had nearly lost her life tonight.

Phelistoth sprang out of the water, droplets flying everywhere. Cas lifted an arm to block them, and by the time the bridge shuddered, signifying someone landing on it, the dragon had shifted back to human form. Tylie grinned and hugged him. Phelistoth did not return the hug, but he also did not object to it.

"Amazing," the woman breathed, coming to her feet. "I'd read that dragons could assume many forms and that some of the unnatural creatures remaining in the world were a result of dragon-animal breeding in eras past, but I had no idea if the texts could be trusted or if someone back then had a fanciful imagination."

"Unnatural." Phelistoth sniffed. "Really."

Pimples sighed softly, and Cas looked at him.

"Is it all right to be jealous that the dragon is getting all of her attention?" he whispered.

"Probably."

Pimples looked past the dragon and back toward the island. "I bet I know why that hut has supplies now, and why there's a long ladder you have to climb to get into it. You're probably supposed to sprint to it if you hear alligators coming and hide out until dawn."

The woman finally tore her gaze from Phelistoth and looked at Pimples. "Actually, based on my reading, the winged 'gators are crepuscular. I believed I was leaving the city late enough to avoid them." She pushed her tangled, wet hair over her shoulder and with a wry smile said, "Apparently, you can't believe everything you read in books. They clearly have a longer hunting period than the dawn and dusk hours."

"Clearly." Cas stuck out her hand, then lowered it, remembering the Cofah did not have handshakes as part of their traditional greetings. "I'm Cas. That's Tylie, Phelistoth, and Pimples."

Pimples stood and bowed.

"Phelistoth?" The woman looked at the dragon again, scarcely noticing Pimples. "You're not one of the ones I heard about."

Pimples frowned at Cas and whispered, "Next time, say my name *before* the dragon's. And for the sake of all the gods in the pantheon, call me Farris, *please*."

"You can tell her to call you whatever you like." Cas dug into her ammo pouches to reload. She was careful to wipe her hands, aware of all the moisture around. The last thing she needed was for the powder in her shells to get wet.

"I'm sorry," the woman said. "I didn't mean to stare and ignore you. My name is... You can call me Zia."

"Zia?" Cas lifted her eyebrows, suspecting that was a fake name.

"It's my childhood nickname. I always liked it." She smiled at Cas and also at Pimples, who beamed in response and stood rigidly straight, as if he had been called to attention by General Ort.

"My name is Farris," Pimples told the woman—Zia. "Are you injured at all? We have first-aid kits." He jerked a thumb over his shoulder, then seemed to remember his pack had been torn off, and flushed, as if losing it to an alligator's maw was a cause for massive embarrassment.

Cas plucked a wet, limp reed off his jacket. "I have a kit if you need it. Either of you." She eyed Pimples' and Zia's soggy forms.

Zia looked at a cut on the back of her hand that dripped blood, but shook her head. "I wasn't seriously injured. But he, ah, Pimples, was it?"

Pimples opened his mouth, no doubt to correct her on the name, but she continued on.

"He was pulled under." She looked him up and down.

"I'm fine." His cheeks were still flushed.

Cas supposed she should be glad Pimples' romantic interests were not turned toward her anymore. "Miss Zia, we were on our way into the city. Can we take you back somewhere? I'm sure you want to change clothes. We were also hoping you might direct us to a safe place to stay." A safe place where Cas could leave Pimples while she went to scour the city jails for sign of Tolemek and the others.

"Back?" Zia's eyebrows rose, and she looked over her shoulder, scrutinizing the distant lights burning in the mist. "No, I can't go back. In fact, uhm." She pointed past Tylie and Phelistoth. "I appreciate your help, but I need to keep going." She picked up her rifle from the bridge—amazing that she hadn't lost it in the chaos. "That way."

"Uh." Pimples scratched his jaw. "We just came from that direction. There's nothing there."

"Except more alligators," Tylie put in. "They won't bother us now that they know Phel is around, but you should probably stay with us."

Zia's expression had been admirably cheerful, considering the circumstances under which they had found her, but she bit her lip and eyed them with concern now. Her gaze locked on Phelistoth, less out of interest in his dragonness now, Cas sensed, and more because he was blocking her path.

"We won't force you to stay with us," Cas said, guessing as to why she would be concerned. "But we also don't think you should continue into the swamp alone."

"I'm not going far."

Cas couldn't imagine what was out here that wasn't "far." Then, with a jolt, she realized where the young woman must be headed. Cofah accent. Cofah ships.

"Are you going out to the bay?" Cas asked. "Where the Cofah ships are anchored?"

Zia's eyes widened. "I—"

A distant clank sounded from the direction of the city, then a clatter as someone dropped something and cursed. Cas didn't recognize the language.

Zia cursed. Cas had no trouble recognizing *her* words, a disparaging remark about the dragon god's testicles.

"I have to go," she whispered, pushing past Tylie as she spoke. "Thank you for the help. Uhm, if you could delay them, that would also be appreciated. Thank you."

She tried to push past Phelistoth, too, but he frowned down at her and did not move. She bounced off his chest.

Zia glanced over her shoulder again. Cas could not yet see who was coming, but a pair of lanterns had come into view from the direction of the city.

"Kindly let me pass, please, dragon." Zia's tone remained polite, but it had developed an edge.

"Let her go, Phelistoth," Cas whispered. "Please. And we should go too." She made a shooing motion toward Tylie and Phelistoth. Whoever was coming from the city, she guessed they would be guards or police and doubted they would direct Iskandian invaders to the nearest inn.

"The hut," Pimples whispered, following Cas.

They didn't make it far. Phelistoth still hadn't moved. He was gazing down at Zia and wearing a frown. His legs were spread, his stance saying he wasn't letting anyone by.

The men with the lanterns spoke again, their voices closer. The mist stirred, their figures coming into view.

"Phel?" Tylie asked.

Without a word, he sprang into the air, transforming into a dragon. Cas smacked her forehead. *Here?* He was going to show himself off *here*, where those guards might see?

Zia did not question the dragon's transformation. She simply hustled past once the bridge was clear. She did not, however, make it far. After flapping his powerful wings a few times, causing ripples in the water on either side of the bridge, he snatched Zia up with his talons. She squawked in surprise, dropping her rifle for the first time.

Cas jerked her own weapon up, but paused halfway. What was she supposed to do? Shoot their ally? While she stood there, gawking, Phelistoth flew back in the direction of the fliers.

A shout came from behind. The guards must have heard that squawk.

"Go," Cas whispered, charging toward the island and waving for Tylie to run ahead of her. Pimples snatched up Zia's rifle and followed after them.

Cries of halt—Cas assumed that was what, *"Noos, noos!"* meant—rang out behind them.

Cas did not halt. Even if she hadn't wanted to avoid the local authorities, she would have chased after Phelistoth. What in all the levels of all the hells was he thinking?

When they reached the island, Pimples brushed past Cas to take the lead.

"Watch it," she grunted reflexively when he jostled her.

"That dragon just kidnapped my—our—girl!"

"Just so you know," Cas responded, her breaths starting to come in gasps as they sped along the next bridge, "we weren't going to keep her."

"She still doesn't know my name," he moaned.

Cas forced herself to slow down. She had passed Tylie and she was falling behind. Instead of practical boots, she wore sandals, and she slipped several times as they navigated the wet boards. The guards hadn't given up the chase, and they were gaining on her group. A few more cries of, "Noos, noos!" pierced the mist, followed by a gunshot.

Cas trusted it was a warning shot, but her shoulder blades itched nonetheless. She picked up her speed, wishing she could heft Tylie over her shoulder and carry her. There were times when she envied men their size and strength. She thought about turning and shooting back to discourage their pursuers, but the second island came into view and a new idea came to mind.

When they reached it, she traded her rifle for her utility knife. Cutting the ropes fastening the bridge to the posts wasn't as easy as she would have wished, and she had to saw like a lumberjack hounded by a whip-cracking overseer, but just as the men raced into view, she cut through the last rope. The bridge sagged immediately.

She didn't know if her work would be enough to send it to the bottom of the swamp, but the men clearly felt the give, for they cried out in alarm and faltered.

She sprinted after Pimples and Tylie who had kept running while Cas had been sawing. In a few minutes, they reached the end of the last bridge. There was no sign of Phelistoth or his prisoner.

Shouts came from the direction of the island. There were more than two voices now. The broken bridge must not have deterred the pursuers that much. Whoever that woman was, it didn't seem the guards were going to let her go easily.

"Which way?" Pimples panted softly, eyes straining as he peered into the trees. "We can't lead them back to our fliers."

No, and they couldn't take off until Phelistoth showed up

to move those trees again. Cas growled. She gripped her knife, wondering if she should cut the ropes on this bridge too.

"Tylie," she whispered, "do you know—"

"He went that way." Tylie pointed along the shoreline, fortunately not in the direction of the fliers.

Cas let her lead, relieved when she took off at a run. "Do you know why he took that girl?"

"No."

"Of course not," Cas grumbled.

Tylie smiled back at her. "I do know who she is now."

"Who?"

"A Cofah princess."

Cas tripped over a root.

"*What?*" Pimples whispered.

"Emperor Salatak's youngest daughter," Tylie said.

"The one who's here to marry someone important from the city?" Cas asked.

"I believe so, yes."

Cas slapped her forehead for the second time that night. Did that damned dragon know he had kidnapped the *wrong* member of the imperial family?

Chapter 9

The clip-clop of the shoed horses turning onto the road was a beautiful sound. Not a mud road or a gravel road or a weed-choked path barely discernible amid the trees and foliage, but a well-maintained stone and cement road with runoffs for rain on either side. It wasn't one of the imperial highways that crossed the nation, but chances were that it eventually led to one. Ridge imagined he could see the capital, the king's castle, and the butte that held his beloved hangars full of fliers in the distance.

That was, of course, premature—all he could see were more trees, and the mountains still loomed above the road to the right—but a sign promised they were only five miles to Aspen Creek, the town the mayor in the last village had suggested he visit. Apparently, an ex-pilot lived there and had acquired an old flier that he rolled out for barnstorming shows during the summer holidays. If the man would let Ridge borrow it, he could be home by morning, maybe even tonight. A journey that would take days on horseback could be over in hours. Then he could find someone to fix his head and tell him how there had come to be a dragon attacking villages.

Your head doesn't need to be fixed, the ever-present voice said.

If General Ort finds out I'm having conversations with myself, he'll worry I'm not fit to command troops. He might take me out of the sky. Ridge's stomach churned at the thought.

Who would fight the dragons?

Puppies. No, that wasn't fair. His young officers were good and certainly qualified to fight for the country. He just couldn't imagine them doing it without him.

I could speak to your general in his head too.

I see. Would sharing my insanity with him make him more or less likely to think fondly of me?

You'll have to answer that. I don't know him that well.

Don't you? Ridge rubbed his head. The only explanation for this voice that he could imagine was that he had subconsciously created it somehow, perhaps because of his head injury. But it should know everything he knew, if that were the case.

It would be foolish of him to remove you from the defensive team of this nation.

He started to respond with a thank-you for the rare compliment, but then realized he would be thanking himself, if his hypothesis was correct.

If nothing else, it will be good to get back to town, so General Ort can fill me in on what I've been missing, Ridge thought. And maybe there would be no need to mention the voice...

His mother might know something, too, depending on when he had last visited her. Having a gaping hole in his memory would still be uncomfortable, but it could be worse. What if he didn't even remember who he was?

This flier you seek, will it have room for two?

Uhm. Ridge eyed Mara out of the corner of his eye. She had led the way since leaving the last village, but she rode at his side now, the afternoon sun gleaming on her blonde hair. He hadn't forgotten that he'd promised to take her to the capital with him, even if he *had* forgotten how exactly he'd allowed himself to agree to that. *I didn't ask.*

She wishes to go with you.

I know.

I feel I should warn you, when men break their word to her, it doesn't usually go well for them.

What did *that* mean? *I wasn't planning to break my word. We'll figure something out. If she wants to see the capital, that's fine. I owe her that much.*

You owe her... less than you think.

Pardon?

Forgive me. She would not wish me to speak so bluntly to you.

What? Why? What is she to you?

The voice did not respond. Ridge wished he could figure

out a way to shoo it out of his head. If not for its presence, he might have believed he had fully healed from his injuries, aside from the troubling memory gap, but he continued to worry that having his subconscious split into another personality indicated that his head might not be the quick fix he hoped.

Mara shifted in her saddle, her gaze turning toward the woods on the left side of the road. Her leg brushed his leg again, either inadvertently or not. She had been riding close and giving him speculative looks often. She hadn't tried to kiss him again—he had asked for separate rooms for them last night and been thankful for their hosts' generosity. The mayor and his wife had lent them the two horses as well as the two rooms. Someone had, however, knocked on his door after the lights in the house had been out. He couldn't know if it had been Mara, but he had feigned sleep and the person had gone away.

"Someone is watching us," Mara announced.

"Oh?" Ridge hadn't heard anything other than birds alongside the road, but he was no woodsman.

"I also believe someone may have been sent ahead to warn the other village that we're coming," Mara said. "Earlier, I sensed a runner on a trail that seemed like it might be a shortcut to this road."

"You sensed?"

That was a curious way to say it. Did that mean she had heard someone?

"Yes." Mara touched her ear. "Do you have any reason to believe anyone in that village may have mistrusted you or wanted harm to come to you?"

"No. I don't think you usually lend horses to people you mistrust."

"Perhaps they wished harm to come to me," Mara said, her voice dropping to a whisper.

"I doubt it. You barely said three words to anyone."

Mara eased her horse closer and handed the reins to him. "Watch this animal for me. I'm going to investigate."

Before he could decide if he wanted to object, she slid off and trotted into the woods.

"I believe her name is Maloof," Ridge called after her. His was a feisty mare named Petty that gave the other one a suspicious side-eyed look whenever it came too close. Such as now. She bared her teeth, and Maloof shifted as far away as she could while Ridge held the reins. "Females," he muttered with a sigh.

He watched the woods while waiting for Mara to return. It crossed his mind that she might not return before he reached the village and that he might be able to slip away in the flier before she caught up. But no, he had promised to take her, and he did not want some vengeful mountain woman stalking him to the city to make his life strange. Stranger.

Wise choice, the voice said. *Besides, she believes a dragon might be following us. You are unarmed and without a means to fly away. You would be an easy meal for a dragon.*

A dragon? Even though he had seen the burned barn and heard the stories of the villagers, Ridge still wasn't positive he believed that some dragon from the olden days had appeared to raze the land. *I didn't think she knew anything about the dragon.*

She never said that.

Didn't she? Ridge tried to remember.

The horses rounded a bend, and several riders came into view, bearded men in simple clothing, with hunting rifles or bows thrusting from carriers on their saddles. There were six of them, and even though they stood about, chatting and apparently having some meeting, they were blocking the road. They also had a toughness about them, with thick arms and broad shoulders. Ridge kept riding forward, but the reminder that he didn't have any weapons of his own came to mind. They looked like a group out for a hunt, but they could be bandits, too, or men who might take the opportunity to *become* bandits when presented with unarmed prey. Not that he had anything to steal. Except the horses.

Several faces swiveled toward him. He lifted a hand and offered a friendly wave.

"It's him," one cried, a toothy grin splitting his beard. He waved back so fiercely, he was in danger of falling from his horse.

Ridge decided to find that encouraging.

"Hello," he said as he drew nearer. Petty nickered and seemed uncomfortable at approaching strange horses, but the other one tried to surge ahead, as if she thought the men might be carrying apples in their pockets.

"General Zirkander," one of the older men said, lifting his fur cap in greeting and revealing brown hair shot with gray. "We heard you were coming. Colonel Mayford sent us out to welcome you and bring you to our humble town."

"I appreciate that." Ridge maneuvered Petty close enough to clasp the man's wrist. He'd never worked with a Colonel Mayford, but from the mayor's description of a wild white-haired man with a cane, he suspected Mayford may have retired before Ridge had been old enough to enter flight school.

"We heard you were fighting the dragon," a younger man blurted, his blue eyes gleaming above a blond beard.

"Yeah, I've heard that too."

"Will you share some stories tonight? The colonel—he's a retired pilot, you know—has got his wife and granddaughters planning a feast."

"Always happy to share stories." So long as Ridge didn't have to talk about dragons he'd never seen. He hoped he could get away with sharing some battles about pirates and Cofah invaders. "Especially if there's a feast to be enjoyed."

"We have a brewery too. Known all through the foothills for our black bear stouts."

"That's the best news I've heard all week." True, Ridge would rather jump straight into the flier and head home—even though he liked a beer as much as the next man—but he could manage a few hours with the locals if they were willing to lend him a flier.

"And, ah, your traveling companion is welcome to come too." The leader pointed past Ridge's shoulder.

Mara was walking toward them, her chin up, her face difficult to read. Maybe she knew he had been contemplating leaving her behind.

"Though my little sister will be disappointed if you show up with a woman," the blond man said with a laugh.

Mara vaulted onto her horse without using the stirrup and

accepted the reins, clasping his hand for a moment and smiling at him. No, he wasn't going to get away with leaving her behind.

"This way," the leader said and nudged his horse into a trot.

Ridge and Mara followed the group down the road for another mile and then onto a dirt lane that meandered along a stream lined with aspens. The smell of yeast lingered in the air, promising the brewery was in use.

When they reached the village, which was three or four times larger than the last one, claiming *two* main streets rather than one, it seemed that the entire populace was out in a field in front of a barn, milling around tables and a bonfire. A cheer went up and people waved enthusiastically.

Mara gave Ridge an incredulous look. "Is it like this everywhere you go?"

"Not in the capital, but I think people in small towns have fewer entertainment options and like an excuse to have festivities." As much as Ridge appreciated the townsfolk's enthusiasm, his gaze was drawn to the barn doors. They stood open, and he thought he caught a glint of metal inside. The flier? His heart sped up and not just at the thought that he could go home. It was silly, but he missed flying, even if it had only been a week or two weeks—he still didn't know how long he had been unconscious—since his last flight.

One would think you would be terrified to go up in one of those contraptions again, the voice in his head said, the tone somewhere between dry, incredulous, and admiring.

Ridge stiffened in his saddle, fixating on the words rather than the tone. One of *those* contraptions? How odd that his subconscious would call a flier such an ignoble thing. He looked over at Mara, as if she might have an explanation—he wasn't sure why, since he hadn't mentioned the voice to her.

She was too busy glowering down at a flock of women and children running to greet the riders. A boy of nine or ten ran up to Ridge's horse, offering to take the reins.

He handed them over and slid down, giving the boy a pat on the shoulder while searching the crowd for a white-haired man with a cane. He spotted the fellow sitting in a chair by the barn door, his cane hooked on one of the armrests. Ridge responded to greetings and gave waves and handshakes but made his way to the man.

Mayford stood up and offered his hand.

"Good to meet you, Colonel," Ridge said, resisting the urge to crane his neck and peer into the barn. He wondered what model of flier it was. He'd flown some of the old ones, including the museum pieces, and knew he could handle anything. It would even be fun to pilot a relic.

"General," Mayford said. "That's my beauty in there. I reckon you'll want to take a look at her. I flew her in Frog Squadron forty years ago, though I've heard Frog is no more."

"I think they just renamed it, sir," Ridge said. "Someone decided we should have fiercer names to drive fear into the hearts of our enemies."

"Back then, we were lucky if our fliers could hop over puddles without needing to land for repairs." Mayford grinned.

A young woman came up and foisted a mug of beer into Ridge's hand. Mayford took him into the barn for a tour, patting the flier, which appeared to have been meticulously maintained—not an iota of dust besmirched the fuselage.

To his surprise, old Rawlens machine guns were mounted above the simple controls. If he remembered his history, they had been the first ones with an interrupter gear to keep the bullets from hitting the propeller blades. Before that, shooting from the cockpit had been a gamble, from what he'd heard.

Grinning, Ridge ran a hand along the nose. "I can't believe they let you keep the guns."

"Why not? They were outdated by the time I retired. I've even got some ammo left if you think you might run into dragons on the way back." Mayford gave the flier another loving pat. "The real challenge was walking away with a power crystal. Even though I paid a hefty price for it, I had to blackmail my old C.O. for it. It helped that I'd saved the king's life a few years earlier. The old king. Angulus's daddy."

"There is only one seat," Mara said coolly, making Ridge jump.

He hadn't realized she had followed him into the barn.

"Yup, she's one of the originals." Mayford gave Mara a friendly smile, but she was too busy frowning at Ridge to notice. "Miss, you can stay here with us for a while, if you like. We can always use an extra hand in the orchards."

Mara's eyebrows flew upward. "Orchards?"

"Yes, miss. Rows of trees that grow fruit. You might have seen them before."

Ridge snorted. The sarcastic streak must have been cultivated in pilots from the flier squadrons' earliest days.

"I told her I'd take her back to the capital with me for a visit," Ridge admitted. "I suppose I could fly home and bring a couple of pilots and fliers back. We'd need to return your craft, anyway, and I could pick you up then, Mara."

"I will go with you," she said.

"She's small enough, maybe you could fly with her in your lap," Mayford suggested.

"That sounds... distracting," Ridge said.

Mayford looked Mara up and down, his expression just short of a leer. He winked at Ridge. "I'd think so, yes."

Mara either didn't notice or didn't mind the leer. Her expression softened, and she linked her arm with Ridge's. "Yes, I will fly to the capital in your lap with you. I can't wait to meet the king."

"Meet?"

That hadn't been her original request. Ridge frowned, looking toward Mayford, as if he might offer support. But the lap idea had been his, and all he did was wink at Ridge again, give him a swat on the back, and say, "Enjoy the festivities, General."

* * *

Tolemek stood still as the guards searched him, doing his best not to seethe as his vials, canisters, and jars were removed from his pockets and tossed onto a table without enough care. If something broke open and ate through the table, the wood floor, the platforms underneath their elevated building, and finally to the swampy water below, he would do nothing to help. The two men patting him down were less casual when they removed the grenades from their loops on his utility belt. Apparently, those looked enough like weapons to warrant care.

Kaika, who had already been searched and placed in a cell behind him, had left a pile of weapons, explosives, fuses, and detonators even higher than his pile. Quataldo had not been captured, and the guards hadn't indicated that they had noticed him, so Tolemek held some hope of being rescued before the night was out, but he couldn't help but feel they had bungled the mission to the point of being unsalvageable. How were they supposed to sneak in and kidnap the emperor now? Even if they escaped, the city would be on high alert. Already, he could hear people running past on the elevated boardwalks outside the police headquarters. Distant shouts sounded. He couldn't understand the words.

After the guards finished removing his gear and weapons, they pushed Tolemek past the tree trunk that rose through the center of the room and into the same cell as Kaika. She barely acknowledged him. Her ear was tilted toward a small open window. It was too high on the wall for Tolemek to see anything more than leaves rustling in the treetop that held this building, but maybe she could understand the shouts outside. Not that Tolemek thought he needed a translation. He suspected everyone was yelling about intruders in the city and increasing the guards on patrol.

One guard remained once the search was done, and Kaika and Tolemek were secured behind bars. Tolemek could have eaten through those bars with one of the formulas on the table, but it lay more than ten feet away.

Tolemek leaned his back to the gate. "Any chance you can seduce that fellow?" he whispered.

One of Kaika's eyebrows rose. "Is that what you think elite forces troops do?"

Tolemek thought of Colonel Quataldo and couldn't imagine

the man seducing his own wife. "I thought it was what *you* do."

"Were you talking to Zirkander about me at some point?"

"No. Your reputation precedes you. From numerous fronts."

"How flattering." Kaika rolled up the sleeves of her jacket and buttoned them above her elbows. She, too, leaned against the bars, her back to the guard. "Before we worry about our company, let me fill you in on the conversation they didn't bother hiding from me."

"Yes?"

He watched her hands as their conversation continued. Either from her sleeve or from somewhere under it, she produced a small hook with a curved tip.

"They think we're *Cofah* insurgents here to do something to upset the wedding."

"Because of your fake accent?"

"And your face. I'm not too pale to pass for a Cofah, but you're too tan to look like an Iskandian. Plus you have the big Cofah nose." She extricated a second pin, this time with a straight tip, from the other sleeve. "I can't believe they didn't bother stripping us."

"Big nose? My nose is perfectly normal for my face."

"For a Cofah face. Move your butt over." Kaika nudged Tolemek with a hip when he did not ease to the side of the gate quickly enough.

"You're a very physical woman, aren't you?" Tolemek asked, aware of the guard watching them. He assumed she wanted to pick the lock. Maybe if they kept talking, the guard wouldn't pay much attention to her hands. He did not know if the man understood their language, but he would keep his voice low and assume he might.

"I am indeed," Kaika said, shoving him to claim another inch of space. Elbow room so she could work, he guessed. Naturally, the lock hole faced the guard rather than the inside of the cell.

"Careful, I'll tell Cas you were touching me in inappropriate places," he said.

"Oh? Would she get jealous if I fondled your ass?"

"I'd be disappointed if she didn't. Wouldn't Angulus get

jealous if I fondled yours?"

"Not if it was mission critical."

"Mission-critical fondling. You live in an interesting world."

Kaika grinned and draped her hands so they appeared to hang over the lock hole, doing nothing, just hanging. "Just the way I like it."

"You Cofah talk too much," the guard said, his words so accented, Tolemek struggled to understand them. Still, the man could probably catch the gist of the conversation. Tolemek was glad he had said Angulus's name softly.

"This is how we engage in foreplay," Kaika told the guard. "We're going to have sex soon, if you want to join in."

Tolemek gaped at her, more alarmed by her bluntness than that she would make the invitation. He assumed her thoughts were to clobber the guard if he was foolish enough to wander over.

Kaika shrugged at him. "I thought you wanted me to seduce him."

"I wasn't imagining myself being involved."

"No? You just like to watch?"

"Be quiet," the guard growled, tapping the side of his rifle. "Or say something useful."

"Such as?" Tolemek immediately asked, sensing an opening.

The guard drummed his fingers on the rifle as he considered them, then walked to the door. He opened it, looked out, then closed it. He pointed the muzzle of his rifle at Tolemek's pile of jars and vials.

"Tell me what these things are and if any of them are valuable."

"They're extremely valuable. I'm a chemist."

"A what?" The guard's forehead wrinkled. He must not have known the term.

"Scientist," Tolemek said, resisting the urge to look down at Kaika's hands, though he would occasionally notice her fingers moving slightly. "That little ceramic jar there contains a compound that can burn through iron and stone."

"This little jar?" The guard pointed at the correct one with his rifle. "How much iron and stone?"

"Bring it here, and I'll demonstrate on the bars."

The guard snorted. He leaned his rifle against the table and bent low, studying the jar, his back mostly to the bars.

Tolemek glanced at Kaika's hands, then met her eyes. "How long?" he mouthed.

"One minute," she mouthed back.

"Be very careful if you remove the lid," Tolemek advised. "It can burn through human skin even more easily than iron."

"I must see a demonstration."

"Who are you going to sell it to?" Tolemek asked. "That jar contains such a small amount that the earnings potential might not be great, but perhaps we could form a partnership. Were I free of these bars, I could gather the components to make more. I could sell it to you, and you could sell it to your contact for a mark up."

The guard grunted. "Of course, I will let you go, so we can do that." Despite his dismissal, his gaze remained fastened on the jar.

"As far as I know, we're not being held for any crime," Tolemek said.

"You blew up a bridge."

"Only because it was covered with winged alligators."

"You're suspected of being here to interfere with Chief Razthar's wedding."

"Just because your superiors suspect something doesn't mean it's true. There's absolutely no proof to indicate we have anything to do with that wedding. I'm a scientist, looking for new markets to sell my formulas in and also for new ingredients with which to experiment."

Kaika tapped a finger on the gate and wriggled her eyebrows at Tolemek. He hadn't heard the click of a lock, but trusted she knew what she was doing.

"I want to try this," the guard said, gingerly reaching out and tapping the jar a couple of times before committing to touching it for longer.

Tolemek rolled his eyes. They hadn't worried about touching any of his containers when they had been removing them from his pockets and flinging them on the table.

The guard decided to risk unscrewing the lid. He found the applicator brush fastened to the bottom and poked it into the cream. He looked at the dollop, then pressed it to an iron support post in the corner of the room. The dab started smoking.

"You spoke the truth," the guard said, staring in wonder. His back was fully to them now.

Kaika eased the gate open and slipped across the room without making a sound. The guard must have spotted her shadow on the wall, because he whirled as she reached for him, but she was too quick. She unleashed a barrage of punches, kneed him, and spun him around, finally locking her arms around his throat. Seeing that she didn't need his help, Tolemek strode for the table and returned his gear to his pockets. He grabbed his rifle from a rack it had been stuffed into with several local firearms. By the time he finished, the guard lay unconscious on the floor. Kaika found some rope, tied him and gagged him, and dragged him into the cell, where she locked him in.

Voices came from outside, so Tolemek did not know how long it would be before someone walked in and discovered the man, but if they could escape the building, they might disappear into the maze of walkways, rope bridges, and boardwalks that connected the different layers of the city.

While Kaika donned her gear, he stepped to the door and eased it open for a look. He closed it immediately.

"Six more guards outside," he whispered. "They look like they're waiting for someone. The man in charge of our interrogation, perhaps."

Kaika snorted. "I don't think blowing up a bridge is likely to bring a godly ordained inquisitor to our cell."

Tolemek had no idea if that was an actual position in the city or if she was making it up, but he didn't ask. He climbed onto the table to look out the window he had been studying earlier. It was too small for them to squeeze out, but it offered a view of the back side of the building. Unfortunately, there wasn't a walkway or platform below it, so they couldn't sneak out that way. Tolemek considered the tree trunk in the center of the room. Less than two inches remained open around its girth, but he would widen that with his compound.

"Down?" he asked.

"Can we do up?" Kaika looked toward the ceiling around the trunk. "I have a hunch."

Someone shouted outside. Did one shout when an ordained inquisitor headed over? Though Tolemek thought down would be better, so that they could disappear into the lower levels of the city, it might take the guards longer to look up and spot their exit hole, especially if their prisoner remained unconscious and didn't see which direction they went.

"You just want to see if I can climb," he muttered, grasping the tree trunk. All of the limbs within the building had been cut, removing the easy handholds.

"Yes, and to gauge whether fondling your butt would be worth dealing with Lieutenant Ahn's ire."

Tolemek almost said he doubted it, but that might reflect poorly on his physique. He scrambled up the trunk as gracefully as he could, his jacket clanking with its contents. Kaika stood below, her rifle pointed toward the door. With his legs and one arm wrapped around the trunk near the ceiling, Tolemek had to apply his stone-eating concoction with great care. He tried to make his hole look artful, like a couple of boards had simply rotted away. They were thinner than expected, and the first of those boards broke away before he had finished dabbing the others. It dropped and smacked Kaika on the shoulder.

"Sorry," he said.

She caught it before it hit the ground and made noise. "Your revenge for me making you climb?"

"Inadvertent, but yes. More are coming down. I don't have a hand free to grab them."

Kaika caught the three other board ends, looked around for someplace to hide them, and settled for the bottom drawer of a filing cabinet in the corner. While she climbed up after him, Tolemek eased his head through the hole he had made. Disappointment smothered him when he found a pair of boots and the tip of a rifle waiting for him. What was one of the guards doing up on the roof of the police building?

The man's back was to him. Maybe he could scramble up and overpower him before the guard reacted.

Before he'd lifted even his shoulders out of the hole, the boots shifted, the rifle swinging toward him. He started to yank his head down, but realized that rifle was exactly like the ones he and Kaika carried. He looked up into Colonel Quataldo's surprised eyes, his head nearly hidden by branches. He was squatting to avoid them.

"That will make my rescue easier," he murmured.

Tolemek climbed out, keeping his grunts to a minimum since he could hear someone addressing the men on the platform below. He eased to the side, making room for Kaika to crawl out after him. Quataldo squatted down, peered through the hole briefly, then nodded at them.

"I've obtained some information."

A loud voice spoke from below, as if to rouse the men to action. Several sentences came out, with Quataldo and Kaika both listening intently. A bang followed, then the thunder of boots on wood. The guards Tolemek had seen took off down one of two rope bridges extending from the platform that held the police building.

"Had I known they were leaving, I could have saved myself a climb," Tolemek muttered. He also could have saved his valuable compound.

"Most of the city has been called to help with a search," Quataldo said, not bothering to whisper. Everyone had left the platform.

"A search for you?" Tolemek guessed.

"No, I don't believe they're aware of my existence. They're searching for Zilandria Hallistan."

"As in Emperor Salatak Hallistan's youngest daughter, Zilandria?" Tolemek asked. "The one who's down here to get married?"

"From what I heard, she disappeared a couple of hours ago. City guards claimed to have spotted her heading out into the swamp and followed her, but that someone helped her get away.

That's the story the police are circulating. I've also heard that a faction that doesn't want the alliance between the city and the emperor kidnapped her. Another rumor suggests Chief Razthar found her an unwilling bride and fed her to the alligators."

Tolemek blinked. "Does he have a reputation that would support that?"

"He's a shaman. Shamans aren't always adored, even here where magic is more accepted."

"Yet they elect them as city leaders?"

"Leadership is taken by power, financial or magical, down here."

"The wedding hasn't occurred yet, so how could she have been an unwilling bride?" Tolemek asked.

"The custom down here is for men and women to try each other out before a final commitment," Kaika said. "It's supposed to be to the benefit of both parties, but only the men are allowed to run a comparison with other women at the same time. Both sides, however, can agree to break off the marriage before the ceremony. I assume that's why she came down ahead of her father and his escort."

"In this case, she probably doesn't have the power to break off anything," Tolemek mused, "as the emperor is responsible for the marriage of all of his kin. It's a longstanding tradition to use them to cement alliances."

"Right, so she might have found her groom wanting and decided to run away," Kaika said. "I'm more inclined to put faith in the story the police are claiming."

"As am I," Quataldo said.

"What are we going to do about it?" Tolemek shifted his weight, more than ready to get off this roof.

"Take advantage of the chaos," Quataldo said.

"To do what?" Tolemek asked, thinking of the young woman roaming the swamps out there. Even if he wasn't a loyal Cofah subject anymore, he couldn't help but feel he should do something to keep one of the princesses from being eaten by alligators.

"Our mission."

Kaika nodded. "If the emperor sends troops out to help

search, the ships will be more lightly guarded. It could be our chance to get to him."

"My exact thoughts." Quataldo pointed toward one of the rope bridges. "I've learned where the emperor's ships are, naval and air. I can take us out of the city. We might even be able to sneak in before dawn. Tolemek, you're with us?"

Nerves teased his stomach, but he nodded. This was why he had come along, for his chance to remove the man who'd placed a bounty on his head from power, and perhaps to see a wiser person sitting on the Cofah throne. He would have to hope that the princess knew what she was doing and could take care of herself.

Chapter 10

It took an hour to catch up with Phelistoth. Tired, sweaty, and grumpy, Cas struggled not to curse at him when they spotted him. He was still in dragon form, perched on a hillock surrounded by trees and water with his prisoner sitting on a log in front of him. Phelistoth's sphere of light floated over the hillock, but the darkness might have been preferable, given the frosty glare that Zia leveled at Cas, Pimples, and Tylie as they walked out of the marsh. The princess might have been pleasant enough to deal with after they had pulled her out of the water, but any feelings of gratitude she'd had were surely gone now. Though she wasn't bound, at least not physically, Cas wouldn't be surprised if she was being restrained by magic.

Pimples shrank under the young woman's glare.

"It's not our fault," Cas whispered to him as a reminder.

"Yes, but *she* doesn't know that."

"Phelistoth." Cas shrugged off her pack and let it drop to the ground. Her shoulders ached after slogging through the marsh with it, especially since they'd had to run for much of that slog. It had taken forty-five minutes to elude their pursuers, and Cas wasn't positive the guards wouldn't continue to track them, especially now that she knew who they had. "What are you doing?"

Phelistoth ignored Cas and shared a long look with Tylie, the kind that usually meant they were communicating secretly with each other.

"What do you people want?" Zia asked. *She* wasn't ignoring Cas.

Cas looked at Pimples, wishing they had brought Captain Blazer. Someone with more rank. Someone who knew what to do with a princess, not that Cas knew if Phelistoth would even let them touch Zia. What could he possibly want with her?

"I honestly don't know," Pimples told Zia.

"Who are you?" she asked.

"I'm Farris," Pimples said. "Like I told you. This is Cas."

Zia's eyes closed to slits. "I thought you were from the city at first, until I realized you're speaking the wrong language. You're too pale to be Cofah."

"But intriguingly and attractively pale, right?" Pimples asked.

Cas elbowed him. This was not the time for flirting.

To her surprise, Zia snorted. It wasn't exactly a sign of true amusement, but she didn't glare at him the way she was glaring at Cas.

"You must be Iskandians," Zia said.

Cas was surprised that she'd had to work it out, that she hadn't guessed right away from the accent. But she supposed an imperial princess would lead a sheltered life most of the time, until trussed up and sent off to marry a foreign man in a foreign country. Maybe she had only read about Iskandians in books, much like winged alligators.

"Are you travelers?" Zia's gaze lowered to Cas's and Pimples' rifles. "Hunters?"

"Travelers," Cas said, amazed the young woman hadn't guessed they were soldiers. They weren't wearing their uniforms, since they had come to skulk around uninvited in a foreign country, but she thought they had a military mien about them, even without the clothing. She *was* wearing her army boots.

"Travelers with a dragon?" Zia shot a glare over her shoulder. Phelistoth and Tylie still seemed to be communicating. Tylie's frown spoke of rare disapproval.

Cas suspected she wouldn't like whatever Phelistoth eventually told them. She was very aware that the night was passing and that they were farther from the city and from checking on Tolemek and the others rather than closer.

"The dragon is inexplicable," Pimples said when Cas didn't answer.

I will go now, Phelistoth announced into Cas's mind. *You will stay. Guard the prisoner.*

"Uhm, what?" Cas asked.

Zia stood up, only to be shoved back down onto the log again by some invisible hand.

"Phel." Tylie crossed her arms. "We're not going to guard your *prisoner* for you."

Phelistoth transformed into his human form. He strode over to Tylie, though he slowed his pace when he drew close. He put an arm around her shoulder. At first, she merely continued her frown and stood with her feet planted. He bent his head low, murmured a few words, then walked toward the edge of the water. She let herself be guided along.

Pimples looked at Cas. She shrugged, but let her lips thin to show her displeasure. She didn't know what was going on, but she didn't like that a dragon seemed to think he was in charge of this portion of the operation.

After speaking for a couple of moments, more telepathically than out loud, Tylie lowered her arms. Phelistoth transformed into a dragon again and crouched at the edge of the water, spreading his wings.

"We'll be back before dawn," Tylie said.

"We?" Cas asked. "You're going too? Where are you going?"

Tylie hesitated. "To talk to someone."

Phelistoth gazed at her, his big dragon head above hers, his eyes far more reptilian than human. She shook her head and did not say anything else. The idea that he might be controlling, or at least manipulating her, crossed Cas's mind, and it made her uncomfortable. She didn't know what she could do about it. Once again, she wished Sardelle was here to advise them. She would even settle for Sardelle's sarcastic sword.

Tylie climbed onto Phelistoth's back, scrambling up his smooth, scaled side and making it look easy.

"Uh, we're not going to keep your prisoner here against her will," Pimples said.

She will stay. You will guard her from predators. Phelistoth leaped into the air and flew out over the water, staying low to avoid branches. He and Tylie soon disappeared from sight.

Pimples spun toward Cas. "Are we taking orders from a dragon?"

Cas sighed. While she admitted it might not hurt to have the emperor's daughter as a bargaining chip—was it possible they could trade her for him?—she felt as affronted by all of this as Pimples.

"No." Cas nodded to Zia. "We won't keep you here."

"That would mean more to me if I could step away from this log."

"You mean you can't even get up?" Pimples asked.

Zia tried to stand, as she had earlier, but it was as if something forced her back down.

Confused, Cas stepped closer. She had seen Sardelle use the air or wind to move things around and even levitate objects, but as far as Cas knew, she couldn't do anything that might be permanent.

Pimples waved his rifle through the air above Zia's head. It didn't encounter anything. He tried swiping through the air to either side of her. Cas did not know if magic could be tested with logic. She looked toward the water lapping at the reed-choked beach and hoped the alligators had gone to bed. They had barely driven the last batch off and might not have without Phelistoth's help. She didn't want to be stuck in one place, trying to defend Zia. She also didn't care to be stuck here because a dragon had ordered it. They needed to find Tolemek and Quataldo. She should also report in to Captain Blazer with this rather significant new development.

"Maybe it's tied to the log itself," Pimples mused, lowering his rifle to rest the butt on the ground. "Can you scoot up and down it?"

Zia had been watching him test the air, her expression somewhere between amusement and exasperation. She answered his question by scooting her butt along the log to one end and then the other.

"Maybe we just need to carry the log along with her on it or next to it, and then we can take her with us," Pimples told Cas.

"We?" Long sleeves hid Cas's slender arms, but she pretended to flex a biceps to remind him that she wasn't the brawniest person on the squadron. Pimples wasn't that muscular, either, a few inches shy of six feet and lean of limb. The idea of them carrying a log was laughable.

"Take me where?" Zia frowned at them. "I was heading to a certain place when I ran into you and your dragon. If I could escape this strange prison—" she thumped her knuckles on the mossy bark, "—I would continue on to my destination."

"The Cofah ships in the bay?" Cas asked. "Wouldn't the soldiers just return you to the city to marry your new beau?"

Zia's face froze in a concerned expression. Tylie had whispered that she was the princess, Zia presumably being a nickname. Maybe Cas shouldn't have revealed that she knew, but she had no interest in playing games with the young woman.

Zia looked back and forth from Cas to Pimples, as if their faces might give her crucial information she needed. Cas would have thought she appeared less intimidating than he, at least to someone who didn't know her reputation for marksmanship, but it was after gazing at Pimples for a moment that she confessed.

"I planned to sneak aboard one of the ships," Zia said, her focus dropping to the dirt at her feet. "I assumed they would eventually get tired of looking for me, or assume I'd been eaten by something in the swamp. The wedding would be called off, and the ship would return home. From there... I hadn't decided yet fully. If I return to the palace, it's likely my father would simply arrange everything all over again. I've been considering the ramifications of *not* returning to the palace. Of disappearing."

"I assume you didn't agree to the marriage in the first place," Cas said.

"I said I'd give it a try, because—well, I'm not good at confronting authority figures, especially my father. It's a weakness, I fully admit that. I'm much more comfortable writing down my objections to something, where I can take my time and outline my arguments, come up with supporting evidence." She cleared her throat and shrugged self-consciously. "Let's just say that my father isn't interested in reading my notes. I'm his eleventh child from his third wife, so I've never been a huge priority for him. That was always fine with me. I didn't have that many responsibilities or expectations either. This came out of nowhere. As far as I'd heard, my father wasn't even planning to marry me off to anyone. We have enough alliances to last ten generations. But all of a sudden, since the Iskandians found some dragons, he's sure we need shamans to come to the empire and teach a new generation of sorcerers."

Cas rubbed her chin. As much as she had objected to this diversion, they were getting free intelligence from the woman. Either Zia still hadn't figured out that Cas and Pimples were soldiers or she was only worried about her own fate and didn't care.

Pimples sat next to her on the log, a sympathetic expression on his face. He looked like he wanted to take her hand, but he clasped his hands in his lap instead. Cas tried to decide if he was hoping to gain her trust and get more information from her or if he was hoping she might run away and have babies with him. Knowing him and his romantic notions, the latter was probably more likely.

"I knew it would be a mistake," Zia went on, unprompted, though she did look at Pimples before continuing. "Everything I'd read about this place—it's an oral tradition, you know. They didn't have a written language until recently, and that's largely used for accounting. They don't have *books*." Her voice grew anguished at this statement. "What am I supposed to do if I want to learn something? Or if I need to escape from my own loveless marriage by exploring some fanciful adventure of fiction? Ask someone to tell me a story?"

"No books at all?" Pimples asked. "That would be distressing."

"You ran away because there wasn't a library?" Cas didn't quite manage to keep the incredulous tone out of her voice. "Not because you object to your fiancé?"

"Oh, he's loathsome," Zia said, "but I'd been told often growing up that I could expect an arranged marriage, so the idea of being betrothed to some old wart is something I've had time to accept. I admit I wasn't expecting an old wart who is also a shaman." Her lips reared back in distaste. "On the night we met, he thought it would be amusing to remove my clothing. With his mind. I found it creepy."

"That's *horrible*," Pimples said. "I'd find it creepy too. Not that a shaman is likely to want to remove my clothing, but I can imagine how uncomfortable that would be."

"There are female shamans," Zia pointed out.

"What?"

"An old wart of a female shaman might want to remove your clothes."

Cas almost laughed at the flustered expression that twisted Pimples' face.

"You are kind of cute," Zia added.

Pimples perked up. "I am? I mean, thank you. You're cute too."

Cas dropped her face into her palm. Duck. She should have brought Duck along. He would have been too busy practicing his hunting skills to flirt with a princess.

"What if you came back with us instead of returning to Cofahre?" Pimples asked.

Cas lowered her hand and shook her head vigorously, trying to catch his eye. Captain Blazer's empty seat was for the emperor, not his daughter. Unless Pimples could talk Phelistoth into carrying two people across the ocean on his back, they didn't have room for her. And Phelistoth seemed to have his own plans for the young woman. Besides, even if Zia *wanted* to run away with them, the rest of the world would see it as kidnapping. King Angulus might be willing to suffer the consequences of making off with the emperor, but if they stole his daughter while not being able to kidnap him, leaving him here and furious, Cofahre would probably throw everything it had at Iskandia in retaliation.

"With you?" Zia asked. "To Iskandia? Is that where the dragon wants to take me? The silver *is* the Iskandian dragon, isn't he? My understanding is that the two golds that left your country aren't loyal to anyone."

"Uhm, Iskandia, yes." Pimples watched her face, probably worried his hope of whisking her off for romance would be dashed once she knew they were soldiers.

"Phelistoth is technically a Cofah dragon," Cas said, though she wasn't sure if she should volunteer the information. Mostly she wanted to disabuse the princess of the notion that Phelistoth was linked to them, to Cas and Pimples anyway. "We've been trying to convince him that Iskandia would be a better place for him, and you'd think he would listen since your scientists were draining him of his blood and experimenting on it when we found him." Cas shrugged. "But dragons are stubborn."

"Oh, I thought he was loyal to your people. I don't know anything about the experiments."

No, why would she? It didn't sound like she played a role in her government.

"What are you two here for?" Zia asked, meeting Pimples' eyes again. "Something to do with the wedding? I trust you weren't invited. If Iskandia has some plan to muck things up with the empire so the alliance wouldn't be made..." She snorted softly. "It's terribly selfish of me, but I confess that I wouldn't object."

"We're just pilots," Pimples said.

Cas grimaced. Iskandian pilots were the most loathed soldiers in the army, at least from the Cofah perspective.

Zia didn't draw back at the revelation. Instead, she leaned closer to Pimples. "You get to *fly*? I've always wondered what that would be like. My father doesn't let any of his daughters travel by airship. He says it's too dangerous. I had to come all the way down here by *boat*."

"Flying is cracking," Pimples said, pumping his arm with enthusiasm.

He launched into the story of his first time going up, and Cas let the back of her head thud against a tree. Something splashed out in the marsh, and Pimples stopped talking, his hand going to his rifle.

"Maybe that's a sign that we should leave," Cas said. "Pimples, has your big math brain formulated a way to move our new friend yet?"

"Math brain?" Zia mouthed.

Pimples flushed. "Uhm, I was thinking about rolling the log down to the water, making a raft, and floating her back to our fliers. I think there's water the whole way, and if she's right about the crocodiles being crepuscular, we might have a few hours where we won't be attacked." He chewed on his lip and looked in the direction that the splash had come from.

Cas wouldn't bet much on them not being attacked, but she was pleased that Pimples had at least been thinking of solutions. Building a raft was a more labor-intensive solution than she would have hoped for, but she would rather do something than stand here and wait. Besides, it would please her if Phelistoth returned to find his captive—and his log—missing. He would find them easily enough, she had no doubt, but he deserved extra work after foisting Cas and Pimples with this duty.

"If Zia is amenable to a raft ride, let's try," Cas said. "We need to check in with Captain Blazer." She wished she could check in with Colonel Quataldo. She wanted someone a lot higher ranking than she to know that they had the Cofah princess. It seemed like something that could be turned to their advantage, but she wasn't sure she had a twisty enough mind to see how. If not Quataldo, she would settle for talking with Tolemek. There was nothing wrong with *his* mind.

"How do we move the log?" Zia switched to straddling it, though she still couldn't stand up straight, and she tried to rock it back and forth. It didn't budge.

"We find a lever of course." Pimples trotted over the hill and eyed a couple of trees.

"A lever? A big branch?"

Pimples returned holding such a branch aloft. It qualified as a small log in its own right. "Yes, my lady. We Iskandian soldiers make do with what we can find."

Cas managed to keep from rolling her eyes, though it was obvious from the way Pimples was toting that branch around that he was trying to impress Zia. She shouldered her rifle and walked over to help, bracing herself for what was sure to be a long night for more reasons than one.

* * *

Flames from the bonfire leaped and crackled, the villagers standing around them, warming their hands and chattering happily as they shared mugs of beer. Ridge sat in a relaxing wooden chair with a reclining back, fighting off yawns. People had finally stopped plying him for stories. He'd had to pull out his best yarns to distract them from the dragon battles they wanted to hear about, and that sense of deception made him uncomfortable, as did hiding his missing memories. Uncomfortable and tired.

Thanks to three or four mugs of the infamous local stout, which he'd been unable to keep the villagers from foisting on him, his head was muzzy too. He definitely wouldn't be flying until the morning. Maybe Mara was drinking somewhere, too, and wouldn't wake up in time to leave with him. He had little interest in piloting home with her in his lap. It would be hard enough explaining his arrival in a fifty-year-old flier made mostly of twine and cloth. He could easily imagine the indignant look General Ort would give him if he landed with a civilian woman in his lap. Besides, he *would* need to return Mayford's craft. There was no reason he couldn't do as he had suggested, bringing out a couple of pilots and fliers with back seats. Landing in a lumpy field behind a barn would be good practice for some of the younger officers. A worried lurch went through him at the idea that he might have acquired some new lieutenants in the last year, and that he wouldn't have any memory of them. He wouldn't be able to hide the hole in his brain if that was the case. Once again, the fear that his disability would come out made him worry that he would be removed from duty for his own good.

"Are you all right, General?" a woman asked, approaching with yet another mug of beer.

She was one of Mayford's granddaughters—he had introduced his family earlier in the evening, an all-female clan that included a wife, four daughters, and three granddaughters, two of whom had yet to marry. This one, Chora, he recalled, was one of the unmarried ones, and she had been giving him sweet smiles all night. Mara had snapped at her a couple of times, but she was off at one of the tables now, chatting with a couple of young men. Maybe one of them would lure her off behind the barn for a good time. It might be easier to sneak away in the morning if she was entangled with some sturdy young farm lad.

Once again, I would not recommend trying to leave without her, the voice in his head warned.

I would come back later the same day or the next at the latest, Ridge replied.

She does not wish to risk letting you out of her sight.

Why not? I'm not that valuable. Really.

You can make her mission simpler.

What mission is that, exactly? Ridge asked. *Meeting the king?*

The voice hesitated and almost sounded sad when it agreed with him. *Meeting your king. Yes.*

My king? He's not your king too?

It's possible that fewer people will be... inconvenienced if she enters the capital at your side.

Ridge thought that word *inconvenienced* sounded like a euphemism. He also noted that the voice had not answered his question. *What exactly do you mean by* inconvenienced? *What do you know that I don't know?*

Much, the voice said, a hint of sadness in its tone again. *But little that's relevant in this age.*

Realizing the young woman was looking down at him with concern and waiting for an answer, Ridge smiled up at her. "Sorry, I'm fine. Just tired and lost in thought." Or just lost. "I'm eager to see home again."

"I suppose our town must seem terribly provincial and boring after the capital."

"It's a fine town, and I appreciate your hospitality." He should not be too friendly with Mayford's granddaughters, especially if he didn't want the flier loan rescinded, but he found himself waving to a recently vacated chair nearby, in case she wanted to pull it up and join him. Having only Mara for company for the last few days had been lonely, especially since he never felt he could trust her. He wished he could feel more grateful for her assistance, but she was so... odd.

"We don't get many national heroes ambling through." Chora pulled over the empty chair and sat next to him. "It's cause for celebration."

"Sounds like your grandfather was a national hero in his day."

Her nose wrinkled. "His stories are old and boring. We've all heard them a thousand times."

Ridge wondered what it would be like for him when people started to find his stories old and boring and no longer sought out his company. Maybe he wouldn't live that long. Retired pilots were a rarity back home.

"What do you do when you're not flying, General?" She leaned on the armrest closest to him and smiled, the firelight highlighting delicate features, freckles, and warm blue eyes. Inviting eyes. They reminded him of someone, but he couldn't quite place it.

"Work keeps me busy," Ridge said, "when I'm not crashing in the mountains."

He *let* work keep him busy, since there wasn't anyone waiting back home for him. Evenings could be lonely, and he'd had fewer people of late to go out with, since his colleagues had all married, one by one, and started spending time with their families instead of with the boys. He'd never considered himself marriage material, but there were times when he wondered what he was missing.

"Will you be busy tonight?"

"I suspect your grandfather would prefer it if I were." Maybe it was the beer, but the notion of irking Mayford was bothering him less than it had earlier. He decided Chora wasn't as young as he'd thought when the colonel had introduced her. Old enough to know her mind and make her own decisions, surely. Would it be so bad if for tonight, that decision was him? She had family here, so she wasn't likely to latch onto him, try to manipulate him into taking her somewhere.

"I think he went to bed already." Her eyes crinkled.

"Did he?" Ridge asked.

"And I'm not so young that he gets to choose who I spend time with." She leaned closer, her hand resting on his arm, a smile flirting on her lips.

"That's good to know," he murmured, leaning forward to meet her halfway, to meet her lips halfway.

It was a sweet kiss, full of wonder and hope, nothing like the demanding, possessive one Mara had surprised him with. She ran her fingers along his jaw, her touch light, hinting of awe. That sense of hero-worship made him a little uncomfortable, but not enough to break the kiss. Tonight, at least, he need not feel lonely.

"Ridge," Mara said, her voice icy and far closer than he would have expected.

Ridge jerked back from Chora, unable to resist rolling his eyes. Must he have a damned jealous keeper?

Mara smiled as she stopped beside his chair, though the gesture lacked any warmth. Chora had much friendlier eyes.

"What is it?" Ridge asked, while he groped for a way to shoo her away.

"Miss Mara," Chora said, "I thought you were enjoying spending time with the Bracken brothers."

Mara rested a hand on Ridge's shoulder. "They were enjoying spending time with me, I'm sure."

Chora frowned. "How nice of you to delight them with your presence."

"Yes." Mara dragged her fingernails up the side of Ridge's neck and pushed them through his hair.

He leaned forward, intending to stand up and put some distance between them. Unfortunately, it appeared his life would be simpler if he slept by himself tonight.

Something bit him in the back of the neck. Startled, he jerked his hand back to slap away the mosquito or whatever it was. His fingers bumped Mara's. For a second, he wondered if *she* had jabbed something into his neck. But that was ridiculous—if she wanted him to fly them to the capital in the morning, she wouldn't be drugging him. Besides, where would she have gotten drugs out in the mountains?

He eased away from her as he stood up. He needed to talk to her about her possessiveness, but it would probably be better done when his mind wasn't fuzzed with alcohol.

"Ladies," he said, "I'm going to—"

"Escort me to the barn, will you?" Mara asked. "I want to see if there's truly room in that flier for the both of us."

"I was thinking more of the nice bed Colonel Mayford offered me in the field hands' bunkhouse. I believe you were offered a room in someone's cottage, weren't you?"

"It's early for that. Show me the barn." She leaned into him, resting her hand on his chest.

He found himself aware of her touch, aware of her body pressed against his. Even if he couldn't say that he liked her, she *was* attractive. Beautiful even.

"It's dark in there. There's nothing to see." Ridge's voice sounded odd as it came out, almost slurred. He looked down at the beer mug sitting on the arm of the chair. He hadn't had *that* much to drink.

"Show me anyway."

Ridge shook his head slowly, but for some reason, his feet didn't move in the direction he wanted them to, toward that bunkhouse. Instead, Mara steered him toward the barn. Sadly, Chora vacated her seat and walked away.

You're truly resorting to drugging him? It was the voice in the back of his head, and it was full if indignation. Ridge frowned in confusion. Usually it spoke to him, but the question didn't make any sense. *There is no honor in this, and it's not necessary. He plans to take you with him.*

After he sleeps with every farmer's daughter here? That sounded like a woman's voice. What was a woman's voice doing in his head? The worry that he was going insane returned, though his body felt too numb to grow too concerned about it. Numb and relaxed. There was nothing to worry about here, not tonight.

What does that matter? The voice that Ridge had been thinking was a part of his own subconscious sounded exasperated. *He'll*

get you into the castle, as we planned. I thought that was all you wanted.
Not... all.

Mara's fingernails dug through the material of his shirt as they walked toward the dark entrance of the barn, scraping Ridge's chest. He'd left his jacket draped over the back of that chair. He ought to go back for it. Despite the thought, all his legs wanted to do was to head in the direction Mara was leading him.

You weren't this libidinous over any of the emperor's soldiers, the male voice remarked. *They would have been willing playthings.*

They were bald and thugly. I don't know when the trend toward shaved heads came into existence, but I don't approve of it. Mara pushed the hand that wasn't busy rubbing Ridge's chest up to the back of his head and through his hair. Some very distant part of his mind had started jumping up and down and telling him to do something when the voice mentioned the emperor's soldiers. But it was so far away that he could barely hear it. Instead, he found himself enjoying Mara's touch. They'd entered the barn, the darkness wrapping around them, the voices of the villagers growing distant. She guided him toward the side where bales of hay were stacked along the wall. *He's far more handsome*, the female voice added. *And not as easy as I'd expected he would be.*

So you had to drug him? Tarshalyn, I forbid this. There is no honor in treating a man so.

You forbid it? You are not my commander. You are my sword.

Her sword? What was going on? And who was Tarshalyn? This couldn't be Mara's voice, could it?

I do not belong to you. I am a sorcerer, the same as you are. You would not have him here, if I hadn't shielded him as his flying contraption smashed into that mountainside.

Sorcerer? Ridge stumbled, but Mara's arms around him kept him from falling.

Yes, you never did explain what motivated you to do that. I'm perfectly willing to use him to get into the castle more easily, but we didn't need him. And it's been irritating playing the role of docile mountain woman. The woman's voice turned dry. *You didn't want him for yourself, did you? I assumed your tastes ran toward women, but we've never had that discussion, I suppose.*

Don't be ridiculous.

You've shape-shifted before.

Not to have sex! You saw that battle. He deserved to live after risking his people and himself and helping to defeat a dragon, especially when he has no magic. What he doesn't deserve is to be mauled by you. Let him go. I insist.

You insist. Please. Is there a reason you're sharing our conversation with him?

The male voice hesitated, as if he hadn't expected that question—or to be discovered? *He won't remember it.*

See to it that he doesn't. And see to it that you mind your own business tonight. Mara stopped, drew her knife, and walked to the doorway. She thrust the blade into the ground outside of the barn. It flashed an angry crimson at her.

Ridge stared at it. What in all the hells was going on?

She turned her back on the weapon, shut the barn door, and strode back to him. Before she reached him, she paused again, and the air crackled, as if they were about to be struck by electricity. Her face twisted into a rictus of concentration. An audible snap sounded in Ridge's mind, and then silence filled his head. The voices were gone, both of them, and his skull felt strangely empty. Was it permanent?

He had the sense that he might escape now, while Mara was distracted. He headed for the door, but she reached out to catch his arm. Normally, he could have jumped back and evaded her, but his feet were leaden, and he barely twitched away. She caught him easily, reached up and stroked his cheek. The conversation he had just heard drifted from his memory like tendrils of smoke on the breeze, and he couldn't remember why he was objecting to her touch. Wouldn't it be silly to avoid the embrace of such an attractive woman?

Mara planted a hand on his chest and pushed him toward the wall stacked with hay bales. The back of his thigh bumped against the edge of one, and she slid her hands under his shirt.

"Sit down, my handsome Iskandian hero," she purred, her lips brushing his. "There'll be no more interruptions for us tonight."

He hesitated as some memory tried to surface, to warn him

to run, to put as much distance between him and this woman as possible. Whatever she was, she was more than some mountain girl. She was dangerous. But his body wasn't paying attention to his memories, and he found himself obeying her, sitting down on the hay and pulling her down with him.

"Good boy," she said with a chuckle, like someone crooning over a hound.

Ridge wanted to protest this—he wanted to protest everything, but his body did not belong to him. When she sat in his lap and kissed him, he kissed her back.

Chapter 11

Tolemek crouched behind the high, gnarled roots of a mangrove, one of the last trees before the marsh opened up into the seawater inlet that held seven imperial navy ships. Five airships floated in the air above, anchored to trees on the other side of the bay. Tolemek never would have felt safe coming this close during daylight hours. He didn't feel safe being this close at night, either, especially when he estimated they only had an hour until the sky started lightening.

He'd heard the footsteps and voices of soldiers on patrol as he, Kaika, and Quataldo had crept through the trees to this viewpoint, and he guessed that an entire company was out in the woods, watching for intruders. The two elite forces officers hadn't seemed daunted by the idea of sneaking in here for a look, but then, Tolemek hadn't noticed that anything daunted Kaika. Quataldo seemed built from the same mold, if a less chatty, barb-slinging version of it.

Tolemek rubbed his thumb over the textured surface of one of his knockout grenades. He'd been carrying it since they left the city, anticipating he would need it. So far, Quataldo had warned them when to duck, hide, or drop to their bellies, with some intuition that seemed as powerful as Sardelle's magical senses, but as they crouched behind the trees, Tolemek's own senses alerted him that they had more to worry about than being stumbled upon by soldiers. He closed his eyes and reached out with his mind, trying to pinpoint the source of the uneasy feeling, the uncomfortable prickle at the back of his neck that he had learned to associate with the presence of something very powerful.

He touched Kaika's back. She was sharing this mangrove while Quataldo, as usual, was off scouting or maybe hiding halfway up a tree so he wouldn't be noticed if Tolemek and Kaika were captured again.

"It's lower," Kaika whispered.

"What?"

"My butt. I thought you wanted to resume our discussion of butt fondling."

"Not at this time. There's a dragon out here somewhere. I think it's in the trees over on that side, under that airship." He leaned around the mangrove to point to the spot. Clouds and mist hugged the shoreline, making it hard to pick out objects in the sky, but he could see the hint of its oblong hull. The airship seemed larger than the others, and he wondered if it was the emperor's craft. He also wondered how Kaika and Quataldo planned to get up to it, if it was his.

"Let's hope that we're insignificant to him," Kaika whispered. "Just some more humans wandering around in the trees out here."

"*Her.*" Tolemek remembered the voice that had spoken into his mind as they had approached the city earlier in the night. Unfortunately, he didn't seem insignificant to the dragon. She had picked him out to question, presumably because of his blood. Maybe something else, too, since dragon blood alone wasn't all that rare. He couldn't imagine what, though, unless she had recognized him from the outpost. That seemed unlikely, since Tolemek and the Iskandian dirigible had been crashing when those other dragons had flown through the area. Maybe the *emperor* had mentioned him to her. "She spoke to me earlier."

It was too dark for him to see Kaika, but he could tell from her voice that she'd turned to look at him. "You didn't think that was worth mentioning at the time?" she asked.

"All she did was ask who I was. I didn't answer."

"Can you tell if it—she—is allied with the emperor's troops?" Kaika asked.

"Her presence here suggests it. It's unlikely that the soldiers are unaware of a dragon sleeping on the bank over there, and nobody seems worried." A few lanterns burned on the ships, and soldiers patrolled the decks, but not nearly as many as would have been out if they believed an attack was impending.

"That complicates matters."

"More than they already are?" Tolemek didn't see how they were going to get close enough to reach the emperor's airship.

"I don't know. We had a plan before, but since we've lost the communication crystal and can't tell Ahn and the others to come get us, the escape part of it was already going to be problematic."

"Are you thinking of aborting?" Tolemek asked.

"No chance of that," Quataldo said from behind him, resting a hand on Tolemek's shoulder. "Please put away your grenade. I'm going to tie your hands behind your back."

Tolemek tensed. "What? Why?"

"For verisimilitude. Captain Kaika, are you ready? I've located the soldiers guarding a hot air balloon that the Cofah are using to ferry soldiers up and down from the airships, when necessary. There are only four there currently. We may be able to simply overpower them and take Tolemek up without subterfuge."

"Subterfuge?" Tolemek asked, forcing calmness into his voice, though his gut twisted as it dawned on him what Quataldo's plan might be. He did not put away the grenade, as requested. "Such as pretending I'm a prisoner you want to turn over to the emperor?"

"You do have that big bounty on your head." Kaika thumped him on the shoulder. "It's just to get us on the ship."

"Nice of you to mention that plan to me."

"We were afraid you wouldn't agree to come skulking through the swamps with us if we told you ahead of time," Kaika said.

"Was this Angulus's idea?" Tolemek had assumed the king wanted him along because he might be useful, but now he wondered.

"No, the colonel's."

"Will you cooperate and come along with us for the ruse?" Quataldo asked, his hand still on Tolemek's shoulder, the gesture not nearly as friendly as it had first seemed. "We won't disarm you, and we have no intention of leaving you behind, once we have the emperor."

No intention. Tolemek judged that to mean the plan was to

take him along, but if the plan splattered like an egg hurled to the rocks, then getting the emperor would be their priority. He rubbed his thumb along the surface of the grenade. Kaika and Quataldo would expect it if he dropped it; they would probably get away from the gas before it affected them. He did not think his odds would be good against Quataldo in a physical fight, not from what he had seen of the man.

"What about the dragon?" Tolemek asked.

"We'll hope she's not paying attention to us," Kaika said.

"She may be able to read our thoughts, relay them to the emperor."

"We'll do our best to avoid any dragons." Quataldo's grip tightened on Tolemek's shoulder. "Come. This way."

Tolemek walked with him because he didn't have much of a choice, but he had no intention of letting himself be trussed up and handed to the emperor. His fear of being offered a deal that would force him to betray someone he cared about returned to mind. Of course, the emperor might simply have him shot. That was also unappealing.

Tolemek? came a soft whisper in his mind.

Tylie? Where are you? He tripped over a root, and a pained grunt escaped.

"Ssh." Quataldo lowered his hand to grip Tolemek's arm, probably as much for support as to keep him in place as a prisoner.

Tolemek resented the idea that he *needed* support, but it was hard to concentrate on navigating through the trees in the dark while talking to his sister.

In the woods near you, Tylie said. *I'm trying to catch up.*

What? Tolemek halted. *You're not with Phelistoth?*

His willingness to bring Tylie along had been predicated on the idea that she would stick with the dragon and be safe. What was she doing wandering around by herself?

We had a fight, she admitted, sadness clinging to her words.

What? Why? He left you?

I insisted on being left. He's going to try to barter with the emperor.

"Tolemek," Quataldo said, pushing him. "We don't have much

time before daybreak. The odds of all of us getting off that airship alive are much better in the dark."

Tolemek wanted to snap at him to shut up, to say talking to Tylie was more important, but he couldn't truly make that argument when all of their lives were at stake. He continued walking, but reached out to his sister again.

Can you explain that?

He didn't tell me before, not until I questioned him about the princess, but he's wanted to try to make a deal with the emperor all along. That's why he agreed to come on this mission. And Tolie? It's my fault. He wants to offer his services to the emperor as a trade. For me. He knows I've missed Mother and my friends from back home, and even though I told him it wouldn't be the same if I went back, he thinks he can make it work. He'd rather serve Cofahre than live in Iskandia, too, but I know a big part of this is because of me. Tylie's words tumbled into his mind rapidly, like a waterfall filling a bucket. It sounded like a confession, and Tolemek wondered how long she'd had a sense that Phelistoth felt this way. Maybe it was an old argument between them.

Tolemek focused on the part that didn't make sense to him. *What does the princess have to do with it?*

He captured her. With Cas and Pimples' help. They didn't exactly know they were helping. He has them guarding her a couple of miles from the city.

Cas is here? Tolemek asked, a mix of emotions filling him, concern that she was so close when there were dragons around—including an ally who wanted to betray them—but also anticipation that she might be close enough to help. Quataldo's plan might get them onto the airship, but getting off with the emperor—or even without the emperor—seemed an impossible task without fliers to come pick them up. Even then, he couldn't guess how they could avoid being shot down without a sorceress to protect them from bullets. He pushed a hand through his hair. How had he allowed himself—and his sister—to get caught up in all of this? *Are Cas's and Pimples' fliers here too?*

Cas and Pimples were a couple of miles from them when Phelistoth and I left, but they are near the city, yes. Blazer and Duck are back at the original landing place.

Can you talk to Cas telepathically?

Not from here. I'm close to the bay, where I made Phelistoth put me down. I came to look for you. She's too far away for me to reach.

Tolemek's mind whirled. He wished it was as easy as sending Tylie back to talk to the others, but she couldn't walk through the swamp alone. She had no way to defend herself from winged alligators and the other dangers that filled the waters. He growled under his breath, almost as annoyed at Phelistoth for leaving her alone in a dangerous place as he was at the dragon for wanting to double-cross the Iskandians. He could understand choosing one's homeland over what one had always considered the enemy nation. He *couldn't* understand leaving a girl alone in this hells-kissed wilderness.

Kaika stopped and raised a hand. "Cofah ahead," she whispered.

"We've reached the hot air balloon," Quataldo whispered back.

"Change of plan." Tolemek had put his knockout grenade away, but he slipped it out of the pouch on his belt again.

"What?" Quataldo's hand tightened on his arm.

"Just listen for a moment, and stop manhandling me, Colonel."

Quataldo growled but let him go.

"My sister is nearby—Phelistoth dropped her off out here, so he could go talk to the emperor."

"*What?*" Kaika and Quataldo whispered in unison.

"I'm just learning about this. Cas and Farris are within a couple of miles of the city with their fliers. They have the princess, though I'm not sure yet if that helps us or makes us more of a target. Either way, if Tylie can get back to those two and let them know what we plan, they may be able to fly in and pick us up at an opportune moment."

"Such as immediately after we kidnap the emperor and before his highly trained imperial guards shoot us?" Kaika asked.

"That does sound opportune."

"Is your sister on her way to tell them now?" Quataldo asked.

"She's on her way *here*," Tolemek said. "Someone needs to escort her back. The swamp is too dangerous for her to navigate alone."

"Not you. We need you."

"As bait, I know." Tolemek rubbed the grenade in his hand. He had no intention of being bait, but he did need to go along. He had the tools to knock out swaths of soldiers without making a sound. Even the deadly Colonel Quataldo wouldn't be as efficient as his grenades. "Quataldo, if you go back with her, I'd feel secure knowing she would be protected. If Kaika and I get in a heap of trouble up there, I'd also be reassured knowing that you were going to be riding in the back of one of those fliers to jump down and get us."

"Just you and Kaika to kidnap the emperor?" Quataldo asked skeptically. "Even if you get aboard his ship, he'll be heavily guarded."

Kaika nudged Tolemek. "Should we be offended that he thought that wasn't a problem when he was coming along but is certain we can't handle it by ourselves?"

"I'm not *certain* of that," Quataldo grumbled. "Just concerned. I'm familiar with your work, and we need the emperor kidnapped rather than blown up."

"Technically, I think both possibilities would give Iskandia a ruler to deal with that's less of an ass."

Quataldo hesitated. Tolemek frowned. He was willing to kidnap the emperor, but he hadn't come to be an assassin, and it bothered him that Kaika had that notion in mind.

"Angulus wants him kidnapped, not assassinated," Quataldo said.

"I do hate disappointing him," Kaika said. "We'll do our best to stick to the original plan. I think Tylie is coming. She needs her escort."

Tolemek sensed Tylie walking straight toward him, having no trouble finding him in the dark. He spread his arms, and she hugged him fiercely. He didn't need magic to sense that she blamed herself for some of the trouble.

"It's all right," he whispered.

"I miss Mother," she said into his chest, "but I didn't want—I don't want to go home. I know it wouldn't be as I remember it, and that they wouldn't approve of me studying magic. Father...

you know how Father is. I want to go back and keep studying with Sardelle and Jaxi. And I want to find out if General Ridge is alive. And I want to see if the squirrels out back had babies. I was feeding them seeds and nuts. Did you know? Phel wouldn't listen. He said he knew what was best for me."

"We'll figure it out," Tolemek said. "We—"

A roar sounded from the direction of the bay, loud and reverberating with power. The combined effect raised the hairs up and down Tolemek's arms.

"What was that?" Quataldo whispered.

Tolemek barely heard him over the raised voices up ahead—the guards around the hot air balloon had obviously heard the noise too.

"The female dragon," Tylie said. "She sensed Phelistoth coming. She's warning him to stay away."

"Will he listen?" Tolemek asked.

"If he's smart."

"Was that a yes or a no?" Kaika asked dryly.

"He *is* smart," Tylie said, "but he's determined too. He wants an audience with the emperor. He'll probably try something crafty to get the female out of the area for a while."

Another roar echoed from the skies, this one deeper and coming from farther north, in the direction of the city. Phelistoth.

"The soldiers will be distracted," Quataldo said. "This is the ideal time for us to go in."

"For *us* to go in." Tolemek waved at Kaika. "You're taking Tylie to find the others, remember? Then coming back in the fliers." Another time, he might have felt presumptuous giving an Iskandian colonel orders on an Iskandian mission, but he knew he was right and that they didn't have much time, not if they wanted to take advantage of the darkness and the dragons challenging each other.

"Very well," Quataldo said. "Don't make me regret this." He stared straight at Tolemek. What, did he think Tolemek had some betrayal in mind?

The lack of trust frustrated him, but Kaika patted him on the back and said, "Let's go."

At least she wasn't hesitating to head into the Cofah camp alone with him. Tolemek would have to win the Iskandians over, one person at a time. If Phelistoth didn't ruin everything for him.

He hugged Tylie and whispered, "Be careful," before letting Kaika lead him away.

I'll be careful, Tylie spoke into his mind as they left, *but you're the one going to visit enemies. You should be even more careful.*

I see my little sister has grown wise as well as accomplished in the ways of magic.

I wish I was accomplished. Then I could be more help.

One day, Tylie. One day.

Tolemek did not share that he hoped this mission would be successful and result in a world in which they didn't constantly have to fling themselves into danger, one where Tylie could finish growing up and study whatever she wished without having to worry about becoming a tool for one nation or another.

* * *

"It's a fine raft, Farris," Zia said from her cross-legged perch on precisely the fourth log from the right, the one that continued to bind her to it.

"Thank you." It was too dark to see Pimples' smile, but Cas could tell from his tone that it was there.

Cas did not say anything but admitted that he had put together an admirably sound raft, given the awkwardness of working around Zia and the limited time and resources they'd had. Now, he and Cas stood on the edges, poling it through the water and staying close to the shoreline while Zia rode in the middle.

So far, nothing inimical had disturbed them. The swamp was much quieter than it had been earlier, with only the occasional squeak of a bat or hoot of an owl. Cas did not know if the stillness had to do with the late hour or if Phelistoth might be nearby. She kept glancing skyward, expecting him to catch up with them and grow angry that they had presumed to move his prisoner.

"I'm sure you'll build a fine house someday," Zia added.

Cas held back a snort. During the hour they had been poling their way toward the part of the marsh where they had left the fliers, Pimples had been chattering about his plans for constructing his dream house. He had also regaled her with stories from his academy days and some of their missions against pirates—either by accident or design, he hadn't recounted any tales that had involved attacking the Cofah. Cas had heard the stories before and had not spoken much, but to her surprise, Zia responded enthusiastically, also sharing a few tales of her school days and explaining her interest in science and history. She wanted to be a researcher at a university and maybe a teacher, but she found the idea of standing in front of rows of students intimidating. Pimples had promised her that she would be good at it, based on the fact that he had known her for almost three hours. Cas poled along silently, letting them bond. It could only help if a Cofah princess thought fondly of them, or fondly of Pimples rather.

"Take us to the right, Pimples," Cas said. "I think the fliers are up that hill. That little beach may be as close as we can get." She *hoped* the fliers were up that hill. All of the trees, waterways, and hills looked the same, especially at night. Usually, she prided herself on her sense of direction, but she wouldn't be shocked if they pushed their raft into a river and out to sea instead of finding the fliers.

"Pushing," Pimples said, shifting to the back of the raft and shoving them off the bottom in the desired direction.

"Why does she call you Pimples, Farris?" Zia asked.

Pimples managed a dramatic sigh while pushing on his pole with both hands. "It's the horrible nickname my squadron gave me. Most of the pilots get names that embarrass them. I'm told it's a rite of passage."

"What's her nickname?"

"Raptor."

"That doesn't sound embarrassing."

"She's special."

Zia frowned at Cas, as if this were her fault.

"Lieutenant Cas," came an unexpected whisper from the trees.

"Is that Tylie?" Cas lifted her gaze, assuming Phelistoth would be nearby.

"Yes, and I'm with Colonel Abram."

"Is that Quataldo?" Pimples whispered.

"I assume so." Cas had noticed that Tylie rarely used people's surnames.

Tylie stood beside a tree and waved at their raft. Cas did not see Quataldo, but trusted he was there. But *why* was he there? And where was Tolemek?

Cas poled harder, pushing them the final few meters to the bank. The raft snagged on something under the water, and she had to jump off early. If Zia weren't stuck on the log, they could have let their little craft go, but she assumed the princess did not want to float away. Pimples jumped in and helped Cas tug the raft to shore.

"Where's Phelistoth?" Cas asked, walking up the bank with Tylie so they would be out of earshot from Zia.

"I didn't agree with what he was doing, so I told him to leave me."

"What he's doing?"

"We can explain it on the way," Quataldo said quietly, stepping out of the shadows. "We need to get the fliers in the air, so we can pick up Tolemek and Kaika in the bay to the south of here. With luck, we'll be picking up the emperor too. Can you communicate with Blazer and get her and Duck up here too? We'll need all of the seats." He gave Tylie a troubled look. If she wasn't able to ride back with Phelistoth, they were actually a seat short.

"Even with all of them, there's not room for Zia," Pimples said, still standing in the water next to the raft where she had to remain, thanks to Phelistoth's magic.

"Our next stop will be Iskandia," Quataldo said. "I'm sure she would prefer to stay with her people. Ahn, go rub a crystal."

"Yes, sir." Cas started toward the fliers, leaving the others to figure out what to do with their guest. Her heart pounded as she imagined Tolemek and Kaika trying to infiltrate the Cofah fleet by themselves. She also hadn't forgotten that Phelistoth had bent some trees to make room for her and Pimples to land, trees that wouldn't likely bend again without him here.

She found the fliers under their camo netting, undisturbed. She wriggled up into the cockpit before bothering to peel back the netting and thumbed the communication crystal.

"Captain Blazer?"

An impressive yawn answered her.

"I'll take that for a yes. Are you and Duck ready to fly, ma'am?"

"Always ready to fly. Do they have the emperor already? Where's the pickup? The city?"

"I'm not sure what the status is on the emperor, but our team is making their incursion now." Did two people count as an incursion? "Kaika and Tolemek, at least. Quataldo is with us approximately two miles west of the city. Pimples and I have to do some work to free our fliers. You should fly within a couple of miles of the city, staying out of sight of the bay and the imperial airships, then circle until one of us contacts you. We'll want to go in together, in and out as quickly as possible."

"No argument from me. We'll be up there faster than Duck can skin a 'gator."

"Does anyone have an axe in their tool kit?" Cas pushed the camo netting away from her cockpit, frowning at a tree that was too close for her to take off without mangling her wing.

"I have a nail file," Pimples said.

"So you can work on your cuticles while you fly?" Cas cursed and jumped down. She had a small survival axe for chopping branches for firewood, but it would take days to hack down the trees around them with it.

"I lost my screwdriver, and the supply sergeant wouldn't give me a new one. The file does in a pinch."

"I don't think it will work to saw down a tree."

"You need the trees moved?" Tylie asked, touching the thick trunk Cas had been glowering at earlier.

"Just that one, and probably those two by Pimples' flier. We'll risk crashing through a few branches to get out of here."

"I think I can do it now. I watched Phel and then asked him about how he talks to the nature." Tylie lowered her chin to her chest and leaned her forehead against the trunk.

"Talks to the nature?" Cas mouthed.

Pimples came up beside her, his own netting already rolled and folded. "You sure you don't want my file?"

A distant roar floated through the marsh. A frog that had been croaking in the reeds halted abruptly.

"What was that?" Cas asked.

"The dragons were posturing at each other as we left," Quataldo said.

"*Dragons?* More than one?"

"I'll explain that en route too. Did you reach Blazer?"

"Yes, sir," Cas said. "She and Duck are coming."

"Tylie insists on going along to help her brother," Pimples said.

Cas shoved her camo netting into its compartment with more muscle than the job required. Tolemek would be devastated if they left his sister to be eaten by alligators, but was taking her into battle any better? What if something happened to her? Tolemek had been hurt enough in his life, and he had so few people in the world who cared about him and whom he cared about. He needed Tylie, perhaps even more than he realized. Cas shuddered at the idea of being responsible for losing her.

"Zia thinks she'll be fine by herself. She said she'd pole the raft back to the city where she'll be safe." Pimples grimaced, his displeasure at leaving her alone obvious, but they didn't have many other options. The princess hadn't been afraid to shoot and had kept her head against those alligators, but that didn't mean she had been effective against them. None of them had, aside from Phelistoth. "I'm hoping we can finish quickly and that I can come back for her," he said.

"She's not coming to Iskandia with us," Cas said. "There's no room in the fliers, and that could start a war."

Pimples' chin came up. "Like kidnapping the emperor won't?"

"He's a crotchety old ass who has successors coveting his throne. How many people will risk themselves to save him? She, on the other hand, is young, pretty, and nice."

"Yes," Pimples said with a dreamy sigh. "She is."

"The entire empire might rally to retrieve her."

A soft moan came from behind them. It wasn't a human or animal noise; it sounded more like wood sighing. The tree Tylie stood next to now leaned away from the flier, as it had when Cas first landed.

Tylie held up her hand, as if she were commanding it to stay, then jogged toward the second tree blocking them in.

"Huh," Cas said. "Maybe she can do more than we think."

Quataldo strode over to join them. "We ready to go?"

"As soon as those two trees over there sigh," Pimples said.

"Get the fliers ready. I'll come with you, Lieutenant Ahn."

"Yes, sir."

"Pimples, you'll take Tylie. At some point, she'll have to transfer back to Phelistoth, so we have room for the emperor." Quataldo frowned, and Cas wondered at the logistics of mid-air transfers. It might be better to leave Tylie with Zia, but then, she was the only one who could communicate with Tolemek and Kaika, since they had lost the other communication crystal. "Let's hope they can reconcile long enough for a flight home."

"Yes, sir," Pimples said. He started for his cockpit, but then sprinted back toward the water.

He splashed into it and leaned onto the raft to whisper a couple of words to Zia. He touched a hand to her arm, then leaned back to go. She reached out and caught him, whispered something back, then took his face in her hands and kissed him.

At first, Cas could only gawk. Then she looked at Quataldo, afraid he would be irritated at the delay—even though Tylie had one more tree to move. The colonel merely looked stunned.

He turned his confused gaze to Cas, as if she could explain. "That's the Cofah princess, isn't it?"

"Yes, sir."

"And that's Lieutenant Pimples, isn't it?" He truly sounded like he wasn't sure.

"Yes, sir. Apparently, she finds his stories more endearing than his squadron mates do."

"I guess so."

Pimples finished his kiss and sprinted out of the water with his knees and head high. He seemed to float up into his cockpit, barely using his hands to make the jump. Cas scrambled up into her own. The third tree had been moved. She flipped the switch, and the power crystal flared to life.

"We're coming for you, Tolemek," she murmured.

Another roar sounded in the distance. She hoped they would be in time.

Chapter 12

As dawn brightened the mountains behind them, Sardelle caught the scent of a campfire. Or maybe a hearth? She, Therrik, and Bhrava Saruth had not run into any other people since leaving the mining outpost, and she had started to long for company. She especially longed for a bath. After being pummeled with those rocks, she was the dirtiest member of their little group, outdoing even Therrik, who was often on his knees, squinting and poking at dirt. She had to take his word for it that they were still on the trail, since they had not encountered any more buttons.

Wouldn't you be concerned if we had? Two is already alarming. Either he's being very rough on his clothing, or she's tearing his jacket off every night, also roughly.

Sardelle stumbled. *Jaxi!*

What? It hadn't crossed your mind?

Why would *it? I've been more worried that she's dragging him along on a leash and torturing him every night.*

I suppose torture could account for missing buttons.

Sardelle rubbed her face, exasperated with Jaxi for putting new ideas in her head. But surely Ridge having sex with the enemy sorceress was the last thing she needed to worry about. She was more concerned that Eversong wanted to use him for some nefarious purpose and was forcing him to trail along with her until they reached the capital. Maybe she was sifting through his brain for military secrets. Or maybe she thought Angulus or someone else would pay a ransom for Ridge. Sardelle certainly would if it meant getting him back, though she preferred her current plan of thrusting Therrik and his hateful sword at her.

Hoping to get her mind off thoughts of what Ridge might be enduring, she stretched ahead with her senses, trying to tell if they approached a nomadic camp or a village.

A village, Jaxi said. *And I'm sorry I made the joke about the buttons. You're right. I don't think women who try to burn his flier down with fireballs appeal to him.*

Certainly not.

Bhrava Saruth? Sardelle called out with her mind. She could sense him a couple of miles in the distance. *Are you still hunting? You may want to stay away a little longer. We're going into a village.*

A village? With potential worshippers?

Uhm. We're just planning to pass through. I don't think there will be time to get them used to the idea of a friendly dragon.

A divine dragon.

That too.

Bhrava Saruth did not comment again, and she hoped she hadn't bothered him by brushing off his hopes and dreams, such as they were. Once she had Ridge back safe, she would go with him to remote villages and try to explain him if he wished.

That should prove interesting, Jaxi said. *High priestess.*

I said I'd try to explain him, not recruit for him.

I don't think there's an explanation for him that makes sense.

The trail they were on turned into a dirt road. Therrik stepped out onto it, looked in both directions, and sighed. The village lay to the left, no more than thirty houses and barns. The road traversed a clearing in the opposite direction before heading back up into tree-laden foothills. Hoofmarks, horse droppings, and wagon wheel ruts adorned the area around Therrik's feet, and Sardelle guessed his problem. Tracking would be harder on such a trafficked surface.

"It's all right," she said, stopping at the edge of the road. "We can check in the town. If anybody's seen them—" She stopped, not wanting to admit that she and Jaxi could sift through people's thoughts if necessary. "Ridge is memorable. Unless she has him chained in the back of a wagon, people will have seen him."

"No, he's been walking along with her. I can't see any sign that he's been forcibly coerced." Therrik scratched his head. "This is the woman who was helping bomb the capital, right?"

"We believe so."

Her mind boggled at the idea that some *other* sorceress might have pulled Ridge from the river and be wandering the wilderness with him. Who else could set magical traps to crush people following them?

Therrik grunted and headed for the village. Sardelle hesitated, then followed him more closely than she had been, concerned it would look odd if they strolled into town at the same time, but with ten meters separating them. She had been staying back, not trusting Kasandral not to misbehave, but they hadn't had trouble since the canyon. There *had* been two more traps, but they hadn't posed a problem. Bhrava Saruth had insisted Sardelle remain well back while he went forward and triggered them.

Kasandral may not be the only problem here, Jaxi said.

What? The village appeared innocuous enough. Despite the early hour, men already worked out in fields, readying the land for whatever crops could thrive in the short mountain springs and summers. Behind the houses, women and children tended gardens and fed livestock.

There's a man working in that smithy who has dragon blood. Jaxi offered a mental shrug. *It may mean nothing, but he may be able to sense that I'm not an ordinary sword, and if Bhrava Saruth comes close...*

I'll ask him to keep hunting deer and wait until the next village to seek friends.

Followers.

"Mama," a boy cried from the garden behind a house. "Another soldier."

Sardelle sucked in a breath. *Another?*

She quickened her pace, forgetting her wariness of Therrik. She passed him and led the way into the village, almost crashing into a chubby freckled woman who stepped out of the house the boy had been working behind. She wore an apron dusted by floury handprints.

"Hello," Sardelle blurted, almost clasping her hands in her eagerness to ask about Ridge.

The woman smiled, but Sardelle restrained herself nonetheless. When she had been a girl, growing up in a village not dissimilar to this, strangers had always been regarded with wariness, thanks to bandits that had occasionally worked the roads.

"Can I help you?" She looked past Sardelle to Therrik.

He was nearly as dirty as she, but his uniform made it clear he wasn't the average stranger—or a bandit.

"Colonel Vann Therrik, ma'am," he said, his voice less gruff and surly than usual. Or at least than it usually was when he spoke to Sardelle.

"Did you crash too?" the woman asked.

"No. We're looking for—"

"General Zirkander!" a boy cried from the doorway of the house, the same boy who had been in the garden. He moved quickly. "He was fighting the dragon. Did you see the dragon?"

"Uhm." Sardelle's first thought was that they had spotted Bhrava Saruth somehow, but maybe Morishtomaric had been here before his final battle. "Was Ridge—General Zirkander here, by chance?"

"He came in the day before yesterday."

"We don't actually know that he fought the dragon," the woman said, making a shushing motion to the boy. "He'd been injured. He seemed nice, but a little confused. Like he didn't know about the dragon, and everybody knows about the dragon around here. We just assumed everyone in the country had heard."

Sardelle had clasped her hands together, almost leaping in excitement at this verification that Ridge was alive, but the talk of an injury and confusion worried her. What did *that* mean?

Interesting, Jaxi said at the same time as Therrik spoke.

"We didn't crash, ma'am," he said. "The king sent us to find Zirkander and take him home."

What's interesting, Jaxi?

Ridge was here with a woman, but she doesn't look anything like the sorceress we fought in the fortress.

Sardelle went from clasping her hands to wringing them. *But the traps... are we dealing with* another *magic user?*

"Home? Are you a pilot too?" the woman asked.

"Did you bring a flier?" the boy blurted, apparently forgetting his shushing.

"No." A hint of irritation entered Therrik's voice, but perhaps not so much that a stranger would notice it. "I'm an elite forcers officer and a tracker. I've been following him since locating his crash site."

It's hard to tell, Jaxi said. *I'm browsing through the woman's surface thoughts when she thinks of him—them. Maybe it was a disguise. Eversong has certainly been able to hide her presence from us.*

"He's not here now, is he?" Sardelle asked. Could they be that lucky?

"They left yesterday morning, him and the woman he was with."

Even though Sardelle knew about "the woman," her hackles went up. "Heading east? Toward the capital?"

"We sent them on to Aspen Creek. There's a retired colonel there with a rickety old flier. My husband thought he might lend it to the general to get him home."

Therrik expelled a noisy grunt and leveled a flat stare at Sardelle. "You and the king have had me tracking him through the mountains for days, when he's already found his own way home?"

"Yes, but—" Sardelle glanced at the woman, smiled and held up a finger, then gripped Therrik's arm and pulled him back a few paces. "This woman he's with, it must be the sorceress."

"She doesn't seem to be impeding him."

"She might want him to take her home, to the capital, where she could have free rein of the military installation as Ridge's... guest." Sardelle grimaced, thinking of the way *she* had been allowed access to the fort, as Ridge's guest. Not easily, but he'd had enough sway to get that letter drawn up for her. Jaxi's words about buttons drifted back to her. What if the sorceress wasn't so much torturing him as she was *seducing* him?

"Guest." Therrik grunted. "What, afraid she'll take your spot at his side?"

"Of course not," Sardelle said, though she had been thinking that exact thing. "But if she did, she could have access to all of your military installations."

"Much as you had?" Therrik scowled at her, as if still affronted by this.

Sardelle kept her voice calm when she responded, though it

made her sad and disgruntled that Therrik still saw her as an outsider, someone who annoyed him. "*I'm* Iskandian. And loyal to this country. She is not."

Jaxi, this other woman she looks like—

I'm thinking she might be able to shape change, Jaxi said with enthusiasm, *like a dragon. I'd heard that some powerful sorcerers in the old days could, but I was never certain.*

Yes, perhaps we can discuss it with her later. What does the woman look like now?

Oh, she's gorgeous. Young, thick blonde hair, perfect body, eyes that aren't quite as innocent as they appear...

Sardelle rocked back on her heels, suddenly finding the seduction scenario plausible. But Ridge wouldn't let himself be seduced, surely. Not when he was—when *they* were together.

Depends on just how confused he is, Jaxi said.

"An enemy sorceress controlling Zirkander *could* cause all manner of trouble," Therrik said.

Controlling? Was that more likely than seduction?

"I'm sure there are numerous military secrets floating around in his mouthy, dense head," Therrik went on, "especially since he's one of Angulus's favorites now." A quick sneer crossed his face. "And if she was walking around with Ridge, she'd have access to other high-ranking officers. He could even take her to the castle to get to Angulus, I imagine. And whatever fancy diplomats are at the castle this week."

Sardelle lifted her fist to her mouth, remembering her meeting with Angulus. "Not diplomats. The council heads. The king said they would all be here this week, presumably to discuss the escalation of matters with the Cofah." She lowered her fist and met his hard eyes. "If she or someone else attacked while they're there..."

"She could wipe out the majority of our government leaders with one wave of her hand." Therrik grumbled something else under his breath, something about using Kasandral on everyone in the world with magical blood.

Sardelle chose to ignore the comment. It was possible she hadn't heard him correctly.

Sure, it is. The blacksmith is coming.

The aproned woman had been waiting quietly while Sardelle and Therrik spoke, but a second person walked up the street now to join her. A muscular man in his thirties, he looked curiously at Therrik, frowned at Sardelle, then scanned the trees beyond the gardens behind the houses.

"Which way to this Aspen Creek?" Therrik asked, raising his voice so the townswoman would hear. "And how far?"

Yes, they needed to know the distance. If Ridge and the sorceress were walking or riding on horseback, and Bhrava Saruth could fly Sardelle and Therrik, maybe they could catch up. Flying hadn't been an option when they had been tracking, but now that they knew where they had gone, they might be able to reach the next village in less than an hour. So long as Bhrava Saruth was willing to—

A chittering noise came from the grass, and Sardelle almost groaned aloud. Even though Bhrava Saruth hadn't shape-changed again since they'd dealt with the traps, she recognized that sound.

"Thirty miles," the woman replied to Therrik. "Follow that road for twenty, then head west on the paved highway."

The blacksmith jumped when the furry ferret raced out of the grass and ran to Sardelle. It leaped up, and she reflexively caught the animal. He scurried up her arm to rest on her shoulder.

The blacksmith's eyes grew rounder than saucers.

"A pet," Sardelle said, though she worried the man already sensed that the ferret was more than that.

A pet? High priestess, really.

"We should probably go now," Sardelle murmured to Therrik, who was glowering distastefully at Bhrava Saruth.

Is there no one here who needs my healing assistance? the dragon-turned-ferret asked. *That man glaring at us looks particularly dyspeptic. Perhaps he has colitis.*

I don't think that's his problem. Sardelle took a step back.

The blacksmith whispered something to the woman, his expression quite agitated.

"Therrik," Sardelle said, "my pet and I will wait for you up the road a ways." She would have preferred to heal people and get to know the villagers, so they would consider her an ally rather than a suspicious stranger, but they didn't have time for that, and she didn't know if it would be possible under any circumstances.

Therrik turned his frown on her—he didn't seem to grasp what was going on—and started to speak.

"Colonel," the blacksmith said, gripping the aproned woman's arm. "Be careful. We believe that you're traveling with a witch and her familiar."

Familiar! Bhrava Saruth stood up on his hind legs and hissed in the man's direction. *That's even worse than being called a pet.*

Stop reacting, please. Sardelle wanted to defend herself, but nothing could be gained by doing so. She turned her back on the village and headed up the road.

"A witch and her familiar," Therrik said dryly. "Imagine that."

Sardelle ignored the urge to scowl over her shoulder at him.

"She could be controlling you," the blacksmith blurted, sounding confused that Therrik wasn't taking his admonition seriously.

"Probably not. She only bothers controlling men more handsome than I." Damn that bastard—Therrik truly sounded delighted.

"I'm getting my rifle," the blacksmith told the woman and jogged away.

This is intolerable, Bhrava Saruth announced. *I will not allow my high priestess to be denigrated so.* He sprang from her shoulder, heading back toward Therrik and the woman.

Bhrava Saruth, Sardelle cried in his mind, having an image of him running up and biting the blacksmith on the ankles. *Stop. Don't bother them. Please.*

Ankle biting wasn't what the dragon had in mind. Once he reached Therrik, he turned into his usual form, his very large, very intimidating dragon form. He towered over the villagers and flexed his wings, spreading them so that they stretched over the buildings to either side of the road. He glared down at the woman, who was gaping up at him, too shocked to move.

I am not a familiar, he announced, speaking into everyone's minds in the area. *I am the god, Bhrava Saruth, and that is my high priestess. You will treat her with respect.*

Therrik growled and backed away from the dragon, his hand going to Kasandral's scabbard.

He won't hurt anyone, Therrik, Sardelle rushed to speak into his mind. *Come join me, please. Let's leave. Ridge and the sorceress are our priority, remember?*

Screams came from down the street. Several of the people out in the fields grabbed shovels and axes and raced toward the town.

Sardelle wanted to cover her face with her hands. How had this gone so badly so quickly?

Bhrava Saruth, Sardelle said. *Nothing can be gained from this. Please, let's go.* Why wouldn't either of these males listen to her?

They will learn to respect my high priestess. Moving more quickly than a cat and far more quickly than his size would have implied possible, he sprang down the street. He caught the blacksmith by the back of his shirt before the man could lunge into his shop.

Someone else had managed to find a rifle. A shot rang out.

Sardelle paused in her retreat. Bhrava Saruth ought to be able to protect himself, but if Therrik was standing nearby when people were shooting, he might be in danger. She might not be able to wrap a shield around him when he carried Kasandral, but she could make a barrier in front of him.

Except that Therrik wasn't standing still, waiting to see what happened. He'd yanked Kasandral from his scabbard and was running toward Bhrava Saruth. Meanwhile, the dragon had lifted the smith up to the roof of a two-story building and dropped him there, perhaps intending to have a chat with him when he couldn't easily escape.

Watch out, Sardelle warned him, not certain he was aware of Therrik bearing down on him.

Bhrava Saruth sprang into the air, wings flapping, as Therrik swung the sword at his backside.

The smith shouted, "Get him, get him!" from the rooftop. Half of the villagers were running into the street with weapons, real and improvised, while the other half were sprinting out back doors and racing for the trees.

Sardelle did not know whether Therrik was acting of his own volition, because he thought the smith in danger, or if Kasandral had taken the moment to rear his obstinate head again. Either way, Sardelle could do nothing to stop Therrik as he leaped, trying to reach Bhrava Saruth with his sword.

Seeing the dragon distracted, the smith raced for the back of the roof. Bhrava Saruth roared in irritation, more at Therrik than at the smith, but the startled man glanced back just as he reached the edge. He stumbled and lost his footing. Instead of jumping or climbing down from the roof as he must have planned, he tumbled the two stories and landed hard. Judging by the way he hit, and the way he cried out, he had sprained his ankle if not broken a bone or two.

Jaxi, Sardelle growled in frustration, as if her soulblade could do something to rectify this situation.

I'm not his high priestess. He's not going to listen to me.

He's not listening to me either. Sardelle ran for the smith, who was writhing on the ground, grasping his lower leg. *And as long as Therrik is holding Kasandral, I can't do anything to him.*

Neither can I.

I know. I'm just—this is ridiculous. We're hurting people, however inadvertently, and this doesn't get us any closer to Ridge.

I'm *not hurting anyone.*

With most of the villagers focused on the dragon and Therrik, Sardelle was able to approach the smith without anyone running over to intercept her. She wanted to stop Therrik and Bhrava Saruth from squabbling, mostly because she worried the dragon would grow weary of being swatted at and decide to drop a building on Therrik, but she also wanted to help the poor man. As if being manhandled by a dragon wasn't bad enough, to tumble off a building wouldn't leave him with fond memories of "witches."

Bhrava Saruth, Sardelle tried one more time as she dropped down beside the smith. *Can you fly out of the village, please? Therrik will calm down if you're out of sight.*

And will these people also allow you to heal that man if they're not focused on me?

Possibly not. She wasn't even sure if the smith would allow her to heal him. His eyes widened as soon as she touched his shoulder, and he realized she was there. He tried to jerk away.

"Witch!"

She remembered the soldier who'd shot himself, rather than accepting her treatment, and uncertainty made her freeze.

He's not armed, Jaxi said. *I'll sit on him so he can't object very strenuously.*

Sardelle nodded. *Yes. Thank you.*

Jaxi sat on him by pushing on him with a blanket of air. Sardelle rested her hand on his ankle, identifying the problem as quickly as possible. A sprain and a fractured bone. She set about knitting the bone back together first, though the commotion from the other side of the building made it hard to focus.

"Don't hurt me," the smith whispered, his eyes creased with pain. "I didn't mean—I was worried for—"

"Relax, my friend," Sardelle said as she worked. "I'm a healer, not a witch. And you have the blood to become one, too, if you ever wish."

Is this the time for recruiting? Jaxi asked. *While I'm smooshing him with air?*

There may not be time afterward. Sardelle smiled into the man's eyes as she commanded his body to heal itself, lending her strength to accelerate the process.

"What're you talking about?" he whispered, appearing more horrified than intrigued.

"You had a dragon for a very distant ancestor. It's why you were able to sense that I also have power."

"Also?" The man's eyes rolled back in his head, and all of the tension drained from his body.

I'm sure his dragon ancestor would have been so impressed to see him faint.

More gunshots fired in the street. The thought of these people shooting at Bhrava Saruth saddened Sardelle, but she could understand why they had misconstrued his appearance as an attack.

"The witch is back here," a boy yelled, peering around the

corner of the building at her. As soon as he spoke, he darted out of sight.

Sardelle sighed, afraid she would have more company soon. She had nearly finished knitting the man's bone back together, but would have preferred to do more, to leave him completely free of pain.

A shadow crossed over the sun. Bhrava Saruth alighted on the ground next to Sardelle and the smith.

I will finish healing him, Bhrava Saruth announced. *I am very fast!*

Gun-wielding villagers sprinted out from between the two buildings. They didn't hesitate to shoot, and Sardelle sprang to her feet, creating a barrier around herself.

She needn't have bothered because Bhrava Saruth had created a larger bubble around both of them, as well as the smith. The bullets bounced off, and when the men with axes tried to run close to hack at him, they were also repelled, striking the invisible shield and stumbling backward.

White light flashed, and a surge of power flowed into the smith. What it would have taken Sardelle another half hour to finish, Bhrava Saruth completed instantly. Not only did he leave the smith without any injuries, but the man almost glowed with vitality, much as when Phelistoth had healed the miners in the outpost. The smith's eyes flew open.

Who else wishes to be healed and saved from disease by my power? Bhrava Saruth asked to the crowd.

Three people shot at him.

Therrik ran around the side of the building, that sword still in his hand.

Bhrava Saruth, Sardelle started to warn.

The dragon sighed into her mind and lowered to the ground like a dog coming to rest. *Yes, I see him. Climb on my back. With him playing the role of scale rot on my hide, we'll never convince these people to join us as followers.*

Relieved the dragon saw the wisdom in leaving, Sardelle rushed to obey. It wasn't until she had scrambled onto his back and Bhrava Saruth leaped into the air with her, leaving everyone gaping and gasping, that she realized how it might look to them. Would they think she had commanded him to appear? To grab the blacksmith?

As Bhrava Saruth sped into the air, Sardelle pressed her face against his cool scales, lamenting that all the work she had done to help the king and his soldiers might be forgotten if rumors of her as some madwoman commanding dragons to attack escaped the mountains.

I don't think Angulus will put any credence into that, Jaxi said. *We simply won't be invited back here again. You'll have to look elsewhere for followers for Bhrava Saruth.*

Assuming Angulus survives the week, Sardelle thought grimly, their guesses about Eversong's intentions returning to mind.

I'm sure we still have time to catch them.

Sardelle was less sure. If Ridge had found access to a flier, he might already be back in the capital.

Bhrava Saruth did not go far before gliding back down to the ground. He stopped a half mile farther up the road from the village. In order to let Therrik catch up with them? Sardelle was surprised he would bother after being the recipient of Kasandral's attack. For the second time, Therrik had been ready to kill him.

Sardelle wasn't certain they *should* wait for the colonel, now that she knew where Ridge was and what was at stake. Still, she took the moment to slide down from Bhrava Saruth's back. Abandoning Therrik out here seemed poor thanks for the help he had given, however grudgingly, in locating this village. If they hadn't been able to track him here, she wouldn't now know where Ridge had gone.

Can you tell Therrik that we're waiting for him, Jaxi? Sardelle's range didn't reach back to the village.

Assuming his pointy friend lets my message through, I can.

Bhrava Saruth's long neck snaked around, his head coming down level with Sardelle's. As alien as his eyes were, she found she could still get a sense of his emotions in them. Or maybe it was the uncharacteristic slump to his spine.

They fear us so much that they won't let themselves understand, he said, sorrow weighing down his words. *We could have helped. There were some who were sick and infirm in that village. I could have healed them, as I did the smith.*

The world has changed since you last flew over this land, Sardelle explained, having no trouble understanding his sorrow and frustration, since she felt it herself every time someone shunned her or let fear keep them from accepting her help. *It's not truly my world, either, and I'm not certain how we can change everybody's opinions of you. Of us.*

No? His head tilted as he considered her.

He must never have dug into her thoughts and gotten her story from her. As nosy as he was, he didn't seem to be as quick to intrude into human minds as Morishtomaric and Phelistoth had been. Since they had a few minutes to wait, she closed her eyes and shared some of her memories with him. She carefully selected what she wanted to share, and it wasn't as intimate as the times she had exchanged memories with Ridge, but she sensed that Bhrava Saruth understood and even empathized. After her dealings with the other dragons, she wouldn't have guessed their kind had the ability to see a human as a being worth empathizing with.

This time is strange, he told her. *In my era, everyone knew to fear dragons, but humans also knew that dragons could be benevolent gods. Allies, even. I do not understand why they would greet us with those noisy fire-making sticks when it is clear we are not harming them.*

Sardelle wasn't sure that had been clear to the smith when Bhrava Saruth had hoisted him up by the scruff of the neck, but she kept the thought to herself.

It is lonely in this era, high priestess. Bhrava Saruth settled his entire body to the ground, as if to lie down for a nap. His tail curled around his torso, but his eyes remained open, regarding her. Forlorn. When had she started to see such emotion in his face?

When he's lying in that position, his fangs aren't hanging out, Jaxi observed. *That helps.*

I agree, Sardelle told the dragon. *It's a lonely era for those with magic. All we can try to do is change people's perceptions of us, one human at a time. There are some who are willing to accept us.* She withdrew Ridge's dragon figurine and stroked the time-worn wood.

I used to have five thousand followers, Bhrava Saruth said.

Dragons are long-lived. You could gather that many friends again, in time.

Hmmph.

Why do you call them friends? Jaxi asked. *He wants legions of people to worship him. He's not looking for someone to play brisk-ball with.*

What he says he wants and what he wants may not be exactly the same thing. Sardelle smiled, walked forward, and rested her hand on Bhrava Saruth's head. *As he admitted, he's lonely. That's understandable.*

You have me to keep you company. You shouldn't be lonely.

Of course not. Sardelle's smile grew a touch wistful. *But he doesn't even have a soulblade.*

That is a tragedy. Therrik is coming.

He's not leading an army full of villagers with pitchforks, is he? Sardelle reached down the road with her senses.

He's alone. And you weren't being observant if you didn't see that these villagers prefer rifles and axes to pitchforks.

It amounts to the same.

Bhrava Saruth rose to his feet. *I will take you to find your mate, but I am disinterested in carrying your servant farther.*

My, ah, servant wants to kill the sorceress who has been troubling us.

He wants to kill everyone.

If he kills the sorceress, and if we help, the king would be quite pleased. He might be willing to issue a mandate that the great gold dragon Bhrava Saruth isn't to be greeted with rifles.

We're back to flattery, are we? Jaxi asked.

It's called persuasion.

Persuasion through flattery?

The great gold god *Bhrava Saruth,* the dragon corrected. He shook dew droplets from his belly and wings, flexed his powerful legs, and turned toward the road. Therrik strode around a bend and into sight.

Did that correction mean he's agreeing to give Therrik a ride or not? Jaxi asked.

I'm not sure. Perhaps we can levitate him along behind the dragon. He'll love that.

Sardelle expected a fierce scowl from Therrik as he approached, especially for the great gold god standing at the side of the road, but all he did was shoot them an exasperated expression.

"Zirkander must love trying to take you out to dinner," he added, then pointed up the road. "The next town is that way."

"We're flying, not walking, and Ridge and I have gone out to dinner several times without trouble."

Therrik's mouth curved into a scowl at the word *flying*. "Was that before or after your *familiar* came into your life?"

Sardelle sighed and looked toward Bhrava Saruth. She wouldn't blame him if he refused to carry Therrik.

A lonely era, the dragon said into her mind, matching her sigh. He lowered his body to the ground again. *Get on.*

Both of us?

Both. But if your servant touches the hilt of that demon sword, I'll arrange for him to fall off. Rapidly.

Therrik's scowl darkened. "Did that dragon just call me your servant?"

"You called him my familiar. I think you're even."

Therrik looked like a cow chewing cud as he mulled on this. Finally, he strode toward Bhrava Saruth, his hands well away from Kasandral's hilt.

As with the previous time they had flown, Sardelle let him go up first, and she took the position behind him. She couldn't imagine having him and Kasandral at her back for the duration of the journey. She was impressed that Bhrava Saruth was willing to allow it.

The sword would not be able to keep him from falling, Bhrava Saruth thought. He sounded like he wouldn't mind at all if Therrik gave him a reason to let him tumble a few thousand feet.

As they took off, Therrik's fingers digging into the dragon's scales, his shoulders bunched to his ears, Therrik gave her a long look over his shoulder. Sardelle waited, expecting him to say something, but he shook his head and looked forward again.

Jaxi snorted into her mind. *He was thinking of asking if you could make his stomach less queasy when he flies.*

Ah. Tolemek might be the better person to ask for that. If nothing else, he could formulate a knockout potion that would keep him from experiencing the trip.

He's also having what I would almost consider a feeling of sympathy.

Toward Bhrava Saruth?

Toward you. He got cheered by the villagers for driving the dragon away. He thinks that's idiotic, since he didn't do anything and since the dragon wasn't really doing anything either. He also had the thought that it was idiotic that they picked on you.

Is it really sympathy when he's thinking people are idiots? Sardelle asked.

It's Therrik. You better take what you can get.

Sardelle would, but she found Bhrava Saruth's words echoing in her mind, that this was a lonely era for those who didn't fit in. Maybe it always had been.

Chapter 13

Tolemek rolled his knockout grenade across the lumpy ground toward the hot air balloon. Four soldiers stood around the basket, which was tied to a stump, ready to lift off at any time. With the men staring toward the dark sky over the harbor instead of watching their surroundings, Tolemek and Kaika might have walked up and clobbered them over the head with their rifles. Instead, they crouched in the shadows, waiting for the grenade to do its work.

A sea breeze gusted, batting at the balloon, and Tolemek worried the knockout gas might dissipate before it affected the soldiers. When one slumped against the basket, his firearm clunking to the ground, he exhaled with relief.

"Corporal?" another asked, stepping toward the man losing consciousness.

"Sarge? I feel—" The man collapsed.

The sergeant took three steps, then joined his comrade on the ground. The remaining two men must not have inhaled as much of the gas. They spun toward the trees, their rifles coming up.

Tolemek dropped to his belly. He held his pistol, but he didn't want to fire and alert all the soldiers on the ships of his presence. He glanced toward where Kaika had crouched beside him, but she had disappeared. Circling the soldiers to attack from behind, he hoped.

A dragon roared again, this time from farther inland than before. Tolemek guessed Phelistoth was leading the female dragon away from the harbor. To what end, he didn't know, but those roars were distracting the soldiers, and that was a good thing for his tiny team of two.

One of the men stiffened, then collapsed. This time, it had

nothing to do with the gas. The last soldier standing whirled toward his fallen comrade's back, and Tolemek leaped to his feet. He ran toward the man, intending to help Kaika, but the Cofah was knocked to the ground with the others before he got there.

"Your basket awaits, Prisoner Tolemek." Kaika gestured grandly at the hot air balloon.

"Should I feel emasculated by the fact that you're doing all of the grunt work?"

"Probably, but I won't tell anyone if you use your magic scientist skills to make me some special grenades someday."

"Anything in particular you're looking for?"

"I've been wondering for a long time if underwater explosives could be made." She gazed thoughtfully toward the ships floating in the bay. Imagining them going up in blazing infernos? "But any improvements to the weapons that mundane technology can currently put into my arsenal would be excellent. I'd settle for bigger booms."

He snorted. "I'll see what I can come up with if we make it home."

"Did you just call Iskandia home?" She thumped him on the shoulder.

"I—uh." *Had* he called it home? When had he started to think of Iskandia that way? When Cas had started talking about house hunting? "I like the lab the king gave me."

"That's good to hear."

Tolemek rested a hand on the lip of the balloon basket and gave the device a cursory examination. It was comprised mostly of lightweight wicker woven inside a crisscrossing framework of slender metal bars. Hooks clipped to the bars held ballast weights for landing the craft. Tolemek started unhooking them.

"Do you know how to fly a hot air balloon?" he asked.

"I assumed you did. There's gas in it. You're handy with gas."

"There's gas in the airships. These things get their lift from the heated air. I'll do my best to steer us to the right ship, if you agree not to use me as bait."

"How else will we get close to the emperor?"

"With stealth and ingenuity," Tolemek said. "Look, I don't

want to risk becoming his prisoner. My parents still live in Cofahre, and he could use me to hurt them. Or he could use them to manipulate me. I don't want to betray Iskandia, but I don't want to betray my family either. You might be able to walk away after selling me to him or whatever your plan is, but I won't be able to escape from all of his imperial bodyguards, not when the first thing they'll do will be to remove all of my gear." He patted his vials and grenades. "Let's sneak in and grab him without alerting them to our presence."

"That might be hard if we're going up in their hot air balloon."

"We just have to overpower the guards at the top and throw them overboard." Tolemek gauged the distance between the airships and the bay. It wouldn't be a *fun* drop for the soldiers, but it should be survivable.

"And have them swim to one of the naval ships to raise the alarm? This isn't the plan Colonel Quataldo had in mind."

"He's not here."

"No, because you sent him off to babysit your sister."

"Kaika..." Tolemek extended a hand toward her, groping for an argument that would work. "We can do this. I'll make you some underwater explosives if we both survive."

"You think that's possible?"

"Of course. It would just be a matter of creating a waterproof shell to protect the components from moisture."

Kaika sighed. "Stealth and ingenuity, you say?"

"That's the plan." Tolemek threw a leg over the side of the basket. "Do we need to tie up those soldiers and stuff them somewhere?"

"I don't think so." Kaika hopped into the basket with him. "By the time they wake up, we'll either be done... or we won't."

Right, they would have either found the emperor—or they would be dead.

Tolemek cut the rope and fired up the burner. He had flown models of these as a kid but did not know if that would give him enough experience to get them up to the appropriate airship. As far as he knew, there were no steering controls, and one had to simply hope the wind was blowing in the right direction.

He needn't have worried. The balloon lifted diagonally, attached to a slender cable he hadn't noticed in the dark. It was almost like the tram cars in the mining outpost. His shoulders slumped in chagrin when he saw that the cable wasn't taking them to the right ship. He also spotted two soldiers leaning over the railing up there and looking down at them, the sides of their faces highlighted by a nearby lantern. They appeared alert and curious. Wondering why the balloon was making an unexpected trip up?

"I believe the big one is the emperor's craft." Kaika pointed to the airship *next* to the one they were heading toward. "They're anchored close to each other, at least. I have some rope in my pack and a collapsible grappling hook. We might be able to shimmy across."

"We have to deal with those soldiers first." Tolemek dipped into another pocket, debating between knockout gas and smoke. He grabbed both.

"Can you throw them up something to think about?"

"Maybe."

The huge balloon blocked part of his view, and it would be hard to loft the grenades up and over the railing without them bouncing off the balloon or the hull of the ship. If Cas were here, she would make the throw look easy.

"I don't like maybe. Give me a yes or no. If it's no, I'll do something to distract them. Take my shirt off perhaps."

"Does that work?"

"Of course. Would you shoot a woman wiggling her bosom at you?"

"It depends on if she's wiggling grenades at me at the same time." Tolemek leaned out of the basket, lining up his throw, eyeing the narrow gap between the balloon and the railing. It only grew smaller as they continued to float higher, guided by the cable.

"Monarch butterfly," one of the Cofah called down.

"Passcode," Kaika whispered.

Having no response for it, Tolemek tossed his first grenade. He threw the second before it landed. The first sailed upward and over the railing, clunking onto the deck behind the two men. Smoke spewed forth, and one turned toward it. The other lifted a rifle, pointing it at Tolemek. He ducked into the basket as the second grenade landed, this one bouncing off the top of the railing and almost hitting the soldier in the face. He jerked his rifle up, deflecting it. He clipped it, and it ricocheted onto the ship instead of falling over the side. Good.

Crouched in the basket, Tolemek waited for shouts to arise from above. It always took twenty or thirty seconds for the knockout grenades to work, even in ideal conditions, and with the sea breeze stirring the air, this was less than ideal.

"Climb out," Kaika whispered.

"What?"

They were less than ten feet from the railing, with the hull of the ship blocking most of their view now. The deck would be in sight in seconds.

"That was too easy," she whispered and slithered over the back side of the basket with a dagger in her mouth. She hung from the lip, then lowered herself further by gripping the metal framework.

Tolemek hesitated, then slung himself over the side as well. His foot slipped as he tried to find a grip that would allow him to hang on the outside, using the basket to block the soldiers' view. He looked down, the water of the bay appearing black in the weak pre-dawn light. The warships looked like toys. He gulped. Had he truly intended to toss the guards over the railing? A drop from this height would not be good for one's health.

Kaika hung on the basket beside him, her head below the level of the lip. "I think we're past stealth and ingenuity. Do we make a ruckus here, or go back to the barter-you-as-bait plan?" She spoke around the dagger in her mouth, her teeth clenched on the back of the blade.

"We threw grenades at them. You don't think we're past bartering?"

"They weren't *deadly* grenades."

"Dragon!" came a cry from the deck above them, from the front of the airship.

"So?" someone much closer to the balloon responded. "It's our ally. The emperor made a deal with it."

"This is a *different* dragon. A silver one."

The basket bumped as it made contact with the railing.

"Now, while they're distracted," Kaika whispered, then disappeared around the side of the basket, crawling as easily as if she were a spider.

Tolemek wasn't sure the soldiers would be *that* distracted, but his arms and legs were already tired from holding his body weight from his fingers.

"Where are they?" someone by the railing asked. "The basket is empty."

"*Someone* threw that grenade. Hawibbs is knocked out."

With more daylight, the men would have easily seen Tolemek's fingers, which gripped the lip of the basket. He poked his head around the corner opposite the one Kaika had gone around, thinking he might be able to clamber over to the railing and pull himself onto the ship before someone noticed. But a row of soldiers waited at the railing.

"There," someone cried.

Tolemek ducked back as a soldier fired. The hells with that plan. He lowered himself, his forearms aching from the effort. He had to let his legs dangle as he maneuvered under the basket, gripping the metal bars with shaking fingers. This was idiotic. Why hadn't he let Kaika use him as bait? They might have gotten all the way to the emperor before being shot at.

He found Kaika dangling from the bottom of the basket already.

"We have a problem," she whispered. "There are eight of them up there."

Rifles fired, and the basket splintered above them, bullets slamming into the wicker. The soldiers thought they were still hanging from the back side. Sooner or later, they would figure out that Tolemek and Kaika dangled from the bottom instead. Not that it mattered. Their arms would give out whether the soldiers started shooting lower or not. Unless...

Tolemek eyed the side of the ship. Were they below the level of the deck? Maybe.

He made sure he had an excellent grip with his left hand, then let his right go long enough to dip into one of his trouser pockets for the corrosive compound he had used in the jail. In a move he could never replicate in a less desperate moment, he used his teeth to unscrew the lid.

"Got a hand free?" he whispered.

"Possibly for up to twenty seconds," Kaika whispered back.

"I need a bunch of that—" Tolemek jerked his chin toward the jar, "—smeared on that." The second chin jerk went toward the hull. "There's a brush attached to the bottom of the jar. Make sure not to touch the substance inside with your hands."

More gunshots sounded right above them.

"As if a burn is the largest of my problems right now," she muttered.

He did not tell her that it would do more than burn, that it would eat all the way through to the bone and into it. He didn't want to alarm her further. Their positions were already cause for plenty of alarm.

"Did we get them?" an eager soldier asked. He sounded like he was leaning over the railing.

"I didn't see anyone fall."

"It's too smoky up here to see anything. Someone kick that grenade over the side."

Kaika maneuvered herself close to the hull and let go with one hand to find the applicator brush for his compound. It was a good thing she had long arms. She swabbed the brush in the jar and reached for the hull, barely touching it with the end, but she did manage to spread a circle of it. Not as large of a circle as Tolemek would have liked, but he thought they could make it work.

"Is that enough?" she whispered.

"The dragon's landing on the emperor's ship," someone called. "Do we shoot it? Or let them deal with it?"

"Is it attacking? Maybe this one wants to make a deal too?"

Tolemek winced at the idea of Phelistoth making a *deal* with the emperor. "Can you put the lid back on and—"

Kaika's hand, the one gripping the bottom of the basket,

slipped. As her fingers fell away, Tolemek dropped the jar and reached for her, horrified as he imagined her plummeting all the way to the bay below. She surprised him by grasping onto his legs before she had fallen more than a couple of feet.

The extra weight startled him, and he nearly lost *his* grip. He jerked his other hand up, barely catching a bar. His already weary arms trembled under the additional burden, and only sheer terror gave him the strength to hold on. Between Kaika and her pack full of gear and explosives, that had to be close to two hundred pounds hanging from him.

"Sorry," Kaika whispered, even as she climbed up him, trying to get to the basket again. "My natural instincts are to grab on."

"I've heard that," he panted. "Try to knock out the hole." Sweat slithered down the sides of his face. If his hands grew damp, there would be no way he could keep holding both of them up.

More gunshots came from above. Tolemek didn't think the soldiers were shooting at them this time—the bullets didn't snap into the basket.

Kaika kicked toward the hull of the ship. Her boot connected with a thump that should have made Tolemek wince, but he was too worried about not falling to care if the soldiers heard them. His formula had burned a hole, and the wood fell inward after Kaika's third kick. When she let go of him, it was such a relief to his shaking arms that it took him a moment to check to see if she'd fallen or found her way inside the ship.

Sweat stung his eyes, and he squinted through the hole and into the gloom of the interior. Kaika leaned out, waving at him. Tolemek reached for a new handhold closer to the edge.

"The emperor is ordering the dragon shot," someone yelled as cannons or other big guns fired in the distance.

"Come help me with this basket," a soldier growled from right above Tolemek. "Get back here, you idiots."

Tolemek swung his legs toward the hole, his heart lurching when his fingers slipped. His hips made it as far as the hull, but his upper body fell too soon. He flailed with his legs, trying to find something to hook them around. Hands gripped his thighs as his butt smacked the bottom of the hole, and his torso fell free.

He might have tumbled out if not for Kaika.

"I'm not strong enough to pull you in. Figure something out," she ordered, her voice strained.

Tolemek peered up at the basket, the balloon, the railing, and the hole. He wriggled his hips, trying to ease himself in. He managed to get a hand up to grab the edge of the hole. Inside, Kaika had her legs planted on either side of the opening, bracing herself as she held onto him. With a heave, he hauled himself the rest of the way inside. They tumbled to the deck together.

Had there been guards waiting inside, they both would have been shot. Tolemek's body refused to do anything but lie there and pant.

"Guess we should thank Phelistoth for being a distraction." Kaika rolled to her hands and knees, pushing Tolemek's leg off her.

"Given his reason for being there, I'm not sure that's necessary."

Tolemek struggled to stand, using a bulkhead for support. Oddly, his legs were quivering as much as his arms.

They were in some officer's cabin, an officer who was on duty, apparently. The bunk was neatly made with boots tucked into a cubby underneath the thin mattress. The built-in wooden furnishings and the gray and blue painted walls made Tolemek pause as memories slammed into him. He had once occupied a cabin very similar to this as a lieutenant aboard a military airship. Later, he had risen in rank to captain, but that command had lasted less than three weeks before Zirkander's Wolf Squadron pilots had annihilated his ship. What a strange twist that he considered Iskandia home now.

"Come on." Kaika waved from the door. "We have less time than before to find a way to the emperor's ship, and it won't take them long to figure out where we went."

Tolemek dashed sweat out of his eyes. "Agreed."

Kaika peeked out the door, then eased out. Tolemek hurried after her. The passageway lay empty, but the pounding of boots sounded above their heads as soldiers ran to stations.

"You dropped that jar, didn't you?" Kaika asked.

"Unfortunately, yes. I valued my life slightly more than it."

"Only slightly?"

"It's one of my best compounds."

"I can see why. We'll have to go up to the deck. Too bad. I wouldn't have minded burning a hole on the other side and trying to throw my grappling hook from there." She headed for weak light filtering down from the end of the passageway.

A ship's ladder led upward, dark treads visible on its steep steps. Dawn was brightening the sky more and more with each minute, and it would be hard to sneak across the deck. Tolemek patted himself down, hoping he hadn't lost more than the jar. He was still lamenting the loss of that communication crystal. Fortunately, most of his pockets had buttons, and fasteners secured his belt pouches. He unclasped one and fished out two smoke grenades.

"Let me go first," he whispered when they reached the base of the ladder.

An eardrum-shaking roar came from outside. Phelistoth? More cannons fired in the distance, but this sounded much closer.

Tolemek scurried up the ladder and poked his head outside in time to see a dragon flying across the front of the airship, its wings almost touching the railing. It was a gold dragon, not a silver. A huge gold dragon. The female.

Judging by her direction, she had come from inland. She streaked toward the emperor's airship. And toward Phelistoth. He flapped away as she approached. She turned to follow him. They flew out of sight, above the envelope of the airship, but screeches and roars drowned out the shouts of soldiers.

Kaika swatted him on the back of the knee. "Get moving. There's our diversion."

"Right." For good measure, Tolemek armed his smoke grenades and rolled them out onto the deck. The soldiers he could see were riveted to the dragon fight, but even so, they might notice two strangers skulking behind their backs.

Tolemek darted through the smoke toward the railing closest to the emperor's ship. When Kaika joined him a couple of seconds later, she already had her rope and grappling hook out. She started swinging it immediately.

The smoke fuzzed the air around them, but the breeze had not abated—if anything, it was stronger up here. Tolemek worried that a soldier who glanced in their direction would be certain to see them. He pulled out his pistol, since he'd lost his rifle in the basket-climbing fiasco, and he watched Kaika's back as she worked.

Her hook sailed toward the other ship, but came just shy of hitting the railing. Tolemek winced, aware of the soldiers on the deck over there. Most of them were looking toward the dragon fight, too, and Kaika was aiming for the rear of the ship, but there had to be forty men near the railings over there. Someone was bound to glimpse movement and spot them.

The alarmed cry came from their own ship, not the other one. A soldier saw them through the smoke. He was in his undershirt, with his boots untied, and he didn't have a rifle. That didn't keep him from shouting for his comrades to help.

Tolemek hated to make noise, but he fired.

He hoped the roaring dragons would drown out the sound, but that was a vain hope. Phelistoth and the female had moved off and were fighting over the trees now, their tails occasionally visible as they flew about each other. Phelistoth looked like he was trying to run away.

Several soldiers turned toward Tolemek and Kaika.

"Here," she barked, shoving the end of the rope into his hands. "Tie this."

As he accepted it, she armed a grenade and hurled it at the men running toward or aiming at them. A bullet glanced off the deck at Tolemek's feet.

He forced himself to stay put, even though his instincts shouted for him to run. Where would he run to up here that was safe? There was nowhere.

Kaika had hooked the rope to the emperor's ship, and it seemed a secure hold. Tolemek tied their end to the railing as fast as his fingers could work. Another bullet slammed into the ship next to him, glancing off the railing two inches from his hand. The smoke might be marring the soldiers' aim, but that wouldn't last for long. Boots thundered toward them.

"Start climbing," Kaika ordered.

"What? We'll be targets for—"

An explosion rattled the deck, hurling smoke and shrapnel as it blew up in front of the soldiers.

Tolemek? Tylie spoke into his mind. *Are you all right?*

No! We're targets right now. Where are you?

"Go, go," Kaika barked. "They all know we're here now."

Wishing he was wearing armor, Tolemek grasped onto the rope, then swung down, hooking his legs over it, and pulling himself along underneath. He felt extremely vulnerable.

Very close. Lieutenant Cas was wondering if you wanted us to swing in and attack, or if the dragons are doing enough.

Attack! Tolemek cried before he could fully gauge the situation. Did they want the fliers coming in now? Before he and Kaika were anywhere close to the emperor? Yes, they needed all the distractions they could get. Otherwise they would never get *close* to the emperor. *Attack*, he said again.

The sound of machine guns firing reached his ears.

"That Raptor and the others?" Kaika asked. She, too, was crawling along under the rope, boots hooked over it as she pulled herself along with her hands.

Flames and smoke smothered part of the deck where she had thrown the explosive, but other soldiers had escaped the carnage and were racing toward the railing that Tolemek and Kaika had just left. Even moving as quickly as he could, Tolemek knew he had a long way to reach the other ship. One shot was all it would take to drop him a hundred feet or more into the water. Or onto that warship just below, the one firing up at the dragons. Dear gods, he was vulnerable from all sides. He couldn't even see the emperor's ship from his position. What if soldiers were already lined up at the railing over there, ready to fire at him and Kaika?

The buzz of a propeller sounded nearby. The familiar bronze body of a flier came into view, cruising past overhead. The pilot glanced down and waved. Cap and goggles hid the face, but he knew from her size that it was Cas. Quataldo sat behind her, a rifle raised as he picked out targets on the airships.

Tolemek nodded toward them, though he dared not lift a hand from the rope.

Her flier passed over him quickly, banked, and buzzed toward the emperor's airship. Risking cannon and gunfire, Cas strafed the deck. Quataldo lobbed a smoke grenade.

Tylie? Are you still with me? Tolemek asked.

Yes. I'm flying with Lieutenant Farris, she responded. *We're right behind Cas. The other two pilots are almost here, and they're going to join in too.*

Good, but I was hoping you could talk to Phelistoth. It looks like whatever deal he was trying to make with the emperor didn't work out. Any chance he'd help us out? If he can get away from the other dragon?

Tolemek doubted the odds were good of Phelistoth being able to do anything with that female after him, but he had to ask. He didn't know if the fliers would be enough against a dozen ships. As good as Wolf Squadron was, the Cofah had ridiculous amounts of firepower to throw at them.

I'll talk to him. Tylie didn't sound that hopeful.

Tolemek's knuckles bashed against something, startling him. The railing. He had reached the other ship. There was no sign of the soldiers he had feared would be lined up to shoot. As he pulled himself over the railing, he glimpsed some men hiding against the cabin walls, seeking shelter from a second flier coming in, slamming bullets into the deck. Other more determined soldiers risked the fire to stay at their guns. One man raced to the bow of the ship and hurled a grenade as Cas's flier zipped in for a second attack. Quataldo shot the Cofah soldier in the forehead, but that did not stop the airborne projectile.

Cas pulled up, disappearing above the balloon as the grenade exploded. Tolemek hoped she had gotten high enough quickly enough that her flier hadn't been damaged. With his gaze riveted to the spot, he clumsily helped Kaika onto the ship.

"This way," she said as soon as her boots hit the deck. She grabbed him and led him toward a hatch in the back. The cargo hold.

"The emperor will have quarters in the forecastle," Tolemek said.

"Maybe so, but we're not ready to visit him."

He raced after her. Booms came from the bay below, and explosions sounded all around the airship, soldiers aiming to take out the fliers. Even though he was on it, Tolemek hoped they aimed too close and took out the emperor's craft.

Kaika flung herself at a soldier who ran around a corner and nearly crashed into her. They went down in a snarl of limbs. For the first time that night, Kaika met a better fighter than she, and after a couple of seconds, he'd gained the upper hand.

Tolemek ran up and clubbed him on the back of the head with his pistol. It wasn't enough to knock him out, but it startled the man enough that Kaika got a knee into his groin, then slammed the heel of her palm into his nose. As he rolled away, Tolemek clubbed him again. There was no finesse to his attack, but it worked. This time, he slumped there without moving.

Kaika grabbed his rifle and tossed it to Tolemek. Not bothering to rise to her feet, she scrambled onto the cargo hold doors in the deck. She unlocked one side and flung it open. Without so much as a glance backward at him, she slipped into the dark hold. Shots were firing all around Tolemek, and he couldn't help but think he would be hit any moment. He threw himself after her without hesitating, hoping the ship's interior would be less chaotic.

He landed on sacks of something. Flour? Grain? He didn't know and didn't care. He rolled away. A good choice, because a soldier stuck his shaven head through the opening and fired at the spot where he had landed. Kaika shot from the floor of the hold. Her bullet caught the soldier between the eyes, and he flopped down, half hanging through the opening.

Tolemek hated the bloodshed, but accepted it as inevitable at this point. Once again, he berated himself, wishing he had agreed to the bait plan. Maybe it wouldn't have worked any better, but they might have gotten so much closer before the chaos and the killing began.

"Hurry, Tolemek," Kaika called, having already found a door leading out of the cargo hold.

Shaking his head, he raced after her, glad she knew the ship better than he did. She probably had the specifications for every Cofah ship in the fleet memorized.

Instead of turning down the passageway toward the front of the ship and the forecastle, Kaika ran in the other direction.

"Boiler room?" Tolemek guessed, starting to realize what her plan might be.

"Boiler room," she agreed without looking back.

They didn't run into anyone until they reached it. Kaika and Tolemek slipped through the door without making a noise. Two soot-stained firemen worked inside, wearing coveralls instead of uniforms as they shoveled coal into one of the big furnaces.

"Two minutes," came a voice from a horn on the wall, the speaker somewhere above decks. "We are departing in two minutes. Engines had better be at full capacity or the emperor will have your heads."

The firemen grumbled and shoveled faster. Kaika started toward them, her pistol in hand, her face grim. Tolemek stopped her with a hand and pulled out a knockout grenade. He was running low on them, but it was worth it if he could keep from killing two men who might not even be soldiers.

She flung her hand toward the boiler, but paused to let him go first. He rolled the grenade across the deck. With the booms and gunfire roaring outside of the ship, the men had no chance of hearing its approach. Tolemek wiggled a finger and tilted his head toward the door. Kaika slipped outside with him, though she bounced from foot to foot, clearly irritated at the delay.

"I'm planning to blow that room into the skies anyway," she whispered.

"I know, but I'd prefer to give them a chance to survive."

"Whoever gave you the name Deathmaker?"

"A pirate."

"Did he not know about your soft, squishy side?"

"Soft and squishy? Are you talking about my ass again?" It was perhaps not the best time to trade quips, but they had to wait for the knockout gas to work—and he had to keep Kaika from charging in prematurely.

"*That*, I trust, is firm. Surely even Ahn has standards." Kaika twitched her chin toward the door. "Will they be out yet?"

Tolemek counted a few more seconds in his head, then nodded. "They should be now. The gas will be lingering. Hold your breath, if you can."

He led the way in. The firemen were indeed lying on the floor, one by the furnace and the other halfway to the door. Kaika jumped over that one, running straight for the boiler. Tolemek grabbed the closest man and dragged him into the passageway. He didn't so much as moan. Tolemek had no idea if leaving the man out here instead of in the boiler room would save his life, but it made him feel better to try. He took a breath before heading back in to grab the other one.

Kaika ran past him, her explosive already set. She was so single-minded and determined that he thought she might leave him, sprinting straight for the emperor's quarters, but she waited, holding the door while he dragged the second man out.

"Boiler room," the voice on the horn spoke, "are you ready for departure? Engines engaging in fifteen seconds."

"Something will be engaging," Kaika said with a snort. "Hurry. That's going to make a mess when it blows."

She raced down the passageway. Tolemek left the firemen behind and sprinted after her.

"How long do we have?"

Before she could answer, something crashed into the side of the ship. Tolemek was hurled into the bulkhead, his boots slipping out from under him as wood splintered and cracked. Kaika's explosive? No, that had been something from outside. Realizing he still had to worry about the bomb, he scrambled to his feet. Another crash threatened to send him down again. A beam snapped in the passageway ahead, one end falling to the deck.

Phelistoth is helping, Tylie spoke brightly into his mind.

Some help. That was Tolemek's last thought before Kaika's bomb exploded behind them. Something slammed into the back of his head, and he pitched to the ground again, the world going black.

Chapter 14

Early morning light slanted in through the open barn doors when Ridge woke up. Scratchy hay poked him in his legs and back—his *naked* legs and back. His head throbbed, and something on the back of his neck itched. He lay on the ground, a woman's limbs wrapped around him, a canvas tarp draped over them. He blinked in confusion, trying to remember how he'd gotten here—and how he'd thought a barn floor was a good place for a union with a woman. His first thought was that he had unwisely inveigled Mayford's granddaughter into joining him, but then he recognized the blonde hair draped across his chest, the smug smile on the woman's face, the possessive way her fingers curled around his shoulder. Mara.

Memories of the previous night slammed into him like a tidal wave, leaving his heart and his mind racing. He couldn't remember all of the details of his actual union with her, but the moments before it had started were vivid. She was a witch. And she'd had a conversation in his head, one he apparently wasn't supposed to remember but did. A conversation with... what? What was the voice that he'd been hearing for days? Not his subconscious. A familiar? Wasn't that what witches had?

A sigh sounded in his mind. *I'm a soulblade, a former sorcerer in my own right, though long dead now.* An image flashed into his mind, Mara's knife as it truly was, an intricately wrought sword she wore at her hip, one that had magical powers independent of hers. *My name is Wreltad.*

Ridge remained utterly still, trying to process the information and also scared of what would happen if he stirred and woke Mara. Tarshalyn. Whoever she was.

I regret that I was not able to intervene last night, the voice continued. *She is more powerful than I am, and my mind manipulation techniques do not work on her. I thought to clear the drug from your bloodstream, but considered that your experience might be less... unpleasant with it there.* Uncertainty mingled with the words, as if the voice—the *sorcerer?*—wasn't sure he had made the right choice.

What did Wreltad care about right choices when it came to Iskandians? Did it matter if it—*he*—was Mara's ally?

You're Cofah, Ridge thought, having had that suspicion about her all along.

Yes. You and I are enemies.

Why did she—no, it was you, wasn't it?—save me? Ridge's mind, which was much clearer this morning, answered the question on its own. Because they wanted to use him to get to the king.

That was what I told her to justify it. In truth, I simply saw the opportunity to keep you from dying and acted upon it. We saw most of the fight. It was a noble battle, with the dragon defeated in the end. There was no need for you to die for defending humanity against a dragon.

If you're Cofah, what do you care about the humanity in Iskandia? Or me?

We are here because there's an opportunity to add this land to the empire, but that doesn't mean we must be monsters. There is no reason to be inhumane or to act without honor. The voice sighed again. *At least, I do not feel there is.*

If there was some disagreement or schism between his two enemies—Mara and this sentient sword—then it seemed Ridge might exploit it somehow, but he had no idea how to do that right now. He didn't even understand fully what he was dealing with. Before this, he'd barely believed that magic existed. He had no knowledge of dealing with witches. Or soulblades—whatever they were.

Not true, the voice said. *You just don't remember it.*

How helpful.

Can you give me my memories back? Ridge's brain locked on two of the words the sword had used earlier: mind manipulation. *Are you the one who took them in the first place?*

I... cannot return them, not now. That would not serve us. I swore to work with Tarshalyn three thousand years before you were born. I can argue for your life, but I cannot betray her. We are—she is all that I have left of my time, of my world.

Ridge would have felt frustrated or exasperated, but he was too confused. Thousands of years? What was it talking about?

What he *did* realize, confusion notwithstanding, was that he wasn't going to get help. He needed to figure his own way out of this situation. Maybe he could knock Mara out somehow and escape without her, though the thought of leaving an angry witch in a village full of innocent people chilled his heart. It might be better to take her with him and try to figure out something to do between here and the capital.

I suggest you simply take her where she wants to go and then leave. If you stay out of her way, I believe she will let you live.

Ridge closed his eyes. *Staying out of the way isn't an option for a soldier. Will you tell me why she wants to see Angulus?*

I cannot.

To blackmail him? To kill him?

Wreltad did not answer.

That in itself was telling. If her intentions had been innocuous, Wreltad probably would have explained that. Ridge had to assume that Mara meant to kill Angulus. If she wanted Iskandia for the empire, getting rid of the regime currently in power would be a logical starting point.

Ridge turned his head, searching for ideas while being careful not to wake up Mara. The colonel's old flier stood in full view, its bronze rivets gleaming in the pinkish morning light, the machine guns just visible. He wondered if the colonel had loaded the ammunition he had offered. Not that it would be much good unless he was in the air and could maneuver the flier around to aim them.

Would a bullet even kill a witch? How did one go about doing that? Or at least disabling her? He wasn't sure he could bring himself to kill someone who had been helping him, even if she had been doing it as part of some scheme against his country. Besides, as far as he knew, the worst crime she had committed so far was drugging him and taking him to bed. He might be personally affronted by that, but he couldn't kill her over it. Assassinating Angulus would be a far greater crime, but he didn't have any true proof that she meant to do that or that she had the ability to go through with it. Could one punish someone for a crime before it had been committed? Not righteously so, surely, but if she succeeded in committing it, later he would have to live with the guilt of knowing he hadn't tried to stop her when he could have.

Ridge was tempted to ask Wreltad if Mara had done anything criminal since arriving in Iskandia, but he doubted he would get an honest answer. He was her ally; he'd said it plainly enough. And he was remaining silent while Ridge wrestled with this.

He spotted Mara's clothes in a heap in the hay next to his and wondered if she had any more of whatever drug she had used on him. Might it dull a witch's powers? He had certainly been a mindless idiot under the influence of it. And it had lasted hours, having worn off some time while he slept. Could he give her enough to get her back to the capital and then hand her over to the king? Or maybe General Ort? Ridge didn't know if either of them would have a clue about how to restrain a witch, but they had to know more than he did on the matter.

Ridge eased to the side, trying to escape her embrace without waking her.

Her hand tightened on his shoulder. He froze.

Mara lifted her head and rested her chin on his chest. Her eyes weren't exactly adoring. Triumphant was the word that came to mind.

"It's light," Ridge said, pretending he hadn't just been contemplating drugging her, "my head only throbs moderately, and if I knew where my clothes were, we could leave for the capital. I suppose clothes technically aren't required, but the harness pinches if you're in the cockpit nude. Long story as to why I know that." He was babbling nervously, but he couldn't stop. Wreltad had proven that he could read his mind. Might she have that ability too?

She patted his cheek. "You're fun. I'm glad I let you live."

"Glad I didn't disappoint," he murmured.

Her eyelids drooped, and she rubbed the inside of her thigh against him while regarding him with an inviting smile. It crossed his mind that he might be able to reach her clothes and search the pockets while distracting her with sex, but knowing what he knew now, he doubted his performance would be very convincing.

Instead, he shifted her to the side and rolled away. "We don't want to delay, do we? You were eager to see the capital. It looks like it's going to be a sunny day. That's not that common along the shore, so we had better take advantage of it."

As he spoke, he casually went to his clothing. He reached for his shirt, eyeing her garments while he did so. She studied him like a hawk watching a titmouse, but with rather more sexual interest. It made him especially aware of and uncomfortable in his nakedness, but he supposed it was better to have her thinking about that than noticing the way he bumped her garments, trying to knock things out of the pockets while he donned his own clothing.

"I only made one dose, hero," Mara said, "but I am flattered that you would rather drug me than kill me."

Ridge focused on buttoning his uniform jacket and keeping the panic off his face. "Are we done with pretenses now?" he asked, trying to sound casual. Hawks probably went for the most worried titmice first.

"Since my sword has taken to sharing confidences with you, I believe so." She stretched languidly, then rolled to her feet. She sashayed over to him, patted his ass, and grabbed her shirt.

He didn't give in to irritation that often, especially when dealing with women, but he considered knocking her away. He had a half a foot and a lot of muscle on her; he ought to be able to keep her from manhandling him.

Don't try, Wreltad said. *Trust me.*

Her slitted eyes seemed to hold a challenge in them, as if she *wanted* him to try something. She might enjoy flattening him to the ground with some magical power.

As she was aware of his every thought, she smirked. With her shirt hanging open, she reached up toward him. He started to step back, but some force held him in place. As surely as if he were drugged again, he couldn't move away from her, nor could he lift a hand to block her when she gripped him by the back of the neck and pulled him down for a kiss. At least he could keep from responding this time.

She didn't seem to care. She got what she wanted, then released him with another degrading pat on the cheek. "Finish dressing and turn on your machine. I'm ready to go."

He had no choice but to obey.

* * *

Cas did not know whether to be relieved or horrified when Phelistoth landed on the railing of the emperor's airship and drove his head down into the deck like a steam hammer. It looked like it hurt, but he must have magical protection. Wood smashed and boards flew. Soldiers fired at him, but the bullets bounced off. Phelistoth didn't seem to notice he was being attacked. Some unexplained fury drove him, and he smashed his head into the ship again, this time into the hull below the railing.

If Tolemek hadn't been somewhere in the bowels of the craft, Cas would have cheered for the dragon's frenzy, but he and Kaika had disappeared into the cargo hold a few minutes before. Cas had been watching as she flew around the airship, trying to be a supreme pest to the Cofah to buy her teammates the time they needed to find and kidnap the emperor. She had no idea if that was still feasible. What had been planned as a stealth mission had turned into such a ruckus that everyone on the continent must know about the battle.

Another shot fired from the seat behind her. Colonel Quataldo had such deadly accuracy that Cas was surprised she hadn't run into him out on the range before. He must practice religiously. She welcomed the help now, since it meant she could concentrate on flying and wreaking havoc with her machine guns while he focused on picking out officers on the deck. A couple of times, when they flew close, she caught him leaning over the side, looking like he might jump out so that he could join Kaika and Tolemek's incursion, but he hadn't yet ordered her to get him in close enough for that. They were probably doing more damage from the air than a single man on foot could do.

Naval vessels fired from the waters below, giant shells arching into the air and exploding. Cas and Pimples were careful to stay near the emperor's craft, flying beside it or above it. Neither the other airships nor the warships in the water would dare risk shooting too close to the vessel holding their supreme political and military commander.

"We're coming in to help," Blazer said over the crystal.

Cas glimpsed the captain's flier cruising toward them from the direction of the city. Duck was right behind her. He didn't have a crystal, since that was the one Tolemek had removed, but he waved as they approached.

"Watch out, Raptor," Pimples said.

The massive gold dragon was circling, trying to attack Phelistoth without damaging the emperor's ship—at least, Cas assumed that was why she hadn't unleashed as much power as she possessed. However, seeing Phelistoth tearing into the hull and deck must have incensed her. She dove for him, talons outstretched. Before she touched him physically, some force struck him, flinging him from the railing and to the deck. He rolled in an ungainly somersault, his tail smashing into people and cabins. The female landed atop him, fangs snapping for his throat.

By now, Cas knew well that her bullets would not do any damage, but she flew in, anyway, hoping she might distract the dragon. She wished she still had some of the special ceramic bullets Tolemek had made to fight Morishtomaric. But nobody had expected dragon battles over here. It frustrated her to think that this female had flown right over here, seeking out an alliance with the emperor when Angulus, the one who had ultimately been responsible for freeing all of those dragons from that cavern, couldn't even get Phelistoth to stay loyal to him. Oh, the silver dragon might be fighting against the emperor now, but from what Tylie had hinted at, it was only because the emperor had rejected his deal—or maybe because the female had already claimed the emperor and the empire for her own. Cas couldn't begin to guess how dragon politics worked.

Briefly, the female was on top, and Cas had a good view of her back. She fired several short bursts.

Surprisingly, they struck the scales. Maybe the dragon couldn't keep her magical defenses up when she was fighting Phelistoth. Cas could not tell if her bullets burrowed through the scales or did any serious damage, but the female's head jerked up as Cas flew past. She leaped away from Phelistoth, knocking soldiers aside as she raced for the railing, her head ducked to keep from hitting the bottom of the balloon. She sprang into the air and chased after Cas.

"Lieutenant," Quataldo warned. "There's a—"

"I see her," she said, taking her flier out of there at top speed.

The dragon followed them, pouring fire from her maw.

Cas dipped toward the trees on the north side of the bay. Flames crackled in the air above her head. Her tail smoked, but she had evaded the brunt of the attack. Booms erupted from the ships in the water, and a cannonball sailed by less than a meter off her port side. Now that she had moved away from the emperor's ship, the rest of the vessels were opening fire on her.

Gunshots came from behind her. As good as Quataldo's aim was, Cas doubted it would do any good.

The dragon continued after them, gaining ground, far more agile in the air than a flier. Cas expected another burst of fire. Instead, a wave of power slammed into her. Her tail flipped over her nose, and the harness dug into her shoulders as gravity tried to dump her out of the flier. Trees blurred past, then the sky, then trees again. The flier frame groaned under the abuse. Cas managed to right herself. Her first thought was to pull up and put a safety margin between her and the trees that skimmed past, almost brushing her belly. But the dragon was still behind her. Instead, she made her wings wobble, then bucked, hoping the dragon would believe the craft was damaged so severely that a crash was inevitable. She dove between a couple of trees, twisting her wings to avoid striking the branches.

"Lieutenant," Quataldo said again. "This is a ruse, right?" A note of concern had entered his generally calm voice.

She was too focused on flying to answer. She dove under branches and between trees, searching for a landing spot. When she had dropped fully below the canopy, she switched the power from her propeller to her thrusters, trying to slow herself. She would surely crash if she tried to navigate between the densely packed trees at full speed. As quickly as she could, she settled on some fern-like plants under a tree. She cut her power and spun in her seat, looking past Quataldo's head. Had the dragon fallen for it?

His face pale, he also looked back, his gaze riveted. Cas couldn't see anything through the canopy, but nothing parted the leaves and came crashing through the branches to chomp on her.

"Raptor?" Pimples asked over the crystal, uncertainty tinging his voice.

"We're all right. Did the dragon stop chasing us?"

"Yes, she's heading back here again. Phelistoth has been hurling imperial soldiers over the sides of the airship railings, but she's charging in to stop him again."

Cas turned her thrusters back on. "Coming."

"You might want to hurry." Even though Pimples now knew she was all right, the concerned tone hadn't left his voice. "Kaika blew up the boiler in the emperor's airship, and it's going down. Also, Tylie says the emperor has Tolemek."

Cas cursed. What could she do to help with all *that*? "Can you relay a message to Tylie?"

"Yes," Pimples said.

"Tell her to tell Phelistoth to do something *useful*. Like getting Kaika and Tolemek."

Chapter 15

SARDELLE PACED BACK AND FORTH while Bhrava Saruth lay in the grass on the side of the road. He'd had to change out of his dragon form three times while they had been waiting for Therrik to return from checking on this new village. Even though it was still early, and they were more than a half mile outside of town, they had come down from the Ice Blades and into more populated areas now. This road saw much more foot and horse traffic than any of the others in their journey.

An irreverent part of her—perhaps a part she had developed after meeting Ridge—wanted to tell Bhrava Saruth to remain in dragon form as people passed by, and she would simply lean an elbow against his side and nod and say good morning, as if wayside dragons were perfectly normal.

Yes, I'm sure these farmers and ranchers will simply nod back, Jaxi said.

Sardelle stretched out with her senses for the fifth or sixth time, checking to see if Therrik was on his way up the road yet. With her greater reach, Jaxi had already informed her that Ridge wasn't in the village. Sardelle had almost asked Bhrava Saruth to continue on, to head straight back to the capital, but she didn't want to assume anything and risk missing him. What if the person with the flier hadn't let him borrow it and Ridge had proceeded on foot? Or what if something had happened and he hadn't made it to the village?

Like what? Jaxi asked. *A sorceress was standing on the side of the road with a dragon, and it ate him?*

Bhrava Saruth yawned, flopped over on his side, and stretched on his back in the grass.

It would have had to be a more bloodthirsty dragon than this one, Sardelle said.

Back when I had followers, Bhrava Saruth said, looking at Sardelle from an upside down position, *some of them used to rub my belly.*

For luck? Sardelle touched the pocket that held Ridge's dragon charm, and she smiled, wondering what he would think of rubbing an actual dragon before flying into battle.

Because their god thought it felt good.

Oh.

Somehow, even with his head upside down, Bhrava Saruth managed to look hopeful.

I believe that look is for you. Jaxi smirked into her mind. *Swords aren't good at rubbing things.*

In the light of all the favors he could ask for in exchange for his help, this is an innocuous one.

Sardelle walked over to the supine dragon, hesitated while she debated where to rub, then simply went for a convenient spot. He could correct her if he wanted something else. Bhrava Saruth laid his head back on the grass, crooked his forelegs, and rested there contentedly. The tip of his tail twitched now and then.

Did your romance novels ever mention that dragons liked belly rubs, Jaxi?

No. I think you found yourself a unique dragon.

Unique. That is one word for him.

Sardelle did not find the experience quite as soothing as patting one of Fern's cats or the friendly dog her brother had kept, perhaps because the scales were cool, with a stone-like feel. Not quite as appealing to touch as fur.

He would probably turn into a ferret—or a dog or a cat—if you asked. Or if it got him more belly rubs.

Hm. Since the dragon was more relaxed than she had seen him, unless she counted the time he had slept on her shoulder in ferret form, Sardelle decided to ask something she had wondered about since his reappearance. *Bhrava Saruth? What happened to the crystal we pulled out of the mountain? You all wanted it so badly that I assumed it had invaluable information in it, but you made it sound like you didn't learn much at all.*

I hid it.

He had been uncharacteristically terse when she'd asked about the crystal before, and it didn't sound like that had changed. *So the others can't find it?* she asked.

Correct. Under my arm, please.

Sardelle moved to the suggested spot, and he grew quite relaxed. Perhaps he would open up more now. *Did you find the information you sought in the crystal?*

His leg twitched with contentment as she continued to rub his scales.

I did. Twelve hundred years ago, there was heightened volcanic activity in what we call the Scales and Ridges Mountains, and it caused the temperatures to drop globally for several centuries.

The seemingly random information puzzled Sardelle, but she nodded. *The Little Ice Age. We have records of it. The glaciers in the Ice Blades extended all the way into the foothills and valleys around the range.*

Yes. My kind do not flourish in the cold. We can fly through the mountains and spend time in freezing temperatures, but we are not fertile in such environments.

That will teach you to give a dragon a belly rub, Jaxi said. *Now you've got him talking about fertility.*

Actually, I'm rubbing his armpit.

Perhaps that's a sexually sensitive area for a dragon.

Sardelle frowned down at Jaxi. *Ssh. I want to hear the rest of the story.*

My kind gravitated toward the equatorial regions, Bhrava Saruth continued, *but they grew crowded with so many territorial dragons in such a small space. There were wars and daily battles. A group of bronze dragons who were tired of being on the bottom when it came to resources and mates got together and studied other planes of existence. Over the course of a century or two, they experimented and finally created a portal that allowed travel to one of these other existences, one that may or may have not been less crowded. They had no way to know since it was a one-way trip. Unless someone was able to build a portal on the other side, any dragon who went through could never come back.*

But they risked it anyway?

Actually, they tricked everyone else into risking it. They pretended that it was a big secret while leaking information about it, information that promised a bountiful and warm climate with room for all the dragons in the world. Like mindless lemmings, the dragons sailed down to the arctic where the portal had been made and flew through it. Bhrava Saruth sniffed. *Had I been awake at the time, I wouldn't have fallen for that ruse.*

All of the dragons went through? What happened then?

Not all of them. The six bronze dragons who had created the portal closed it, buried it, and kept Serankil for themselves.

Serankil? That's the dragon name for this world, right?

Yes. One of the dragon scientists who remained here was the one to create the repository that you found for me. Bhrava Saruth rolled his head sideways on the grass and made an approving sound.

Sardelle took that as a thank you. He twitched his claw, and she went back to rubbing his side.

His entries read almost like a confession, Bhrava Saruth said. *I think he came to regret that he'd played a part in getting rid of all of the other dragons, especially when years passed and none of them returned. He questioned whether they had truly found another plane of existence to send them to, or if he and his cohorts had tricked them into flying to their deaths. He wanted to reopen the portal to see if they could find the others or invite some of them back, but his colleagues refused to allow it. They liked sharing the world amongst themselves. I don't know what happened to those last six bronzes, but can only assume they eventually died, leaving the world bereft of dragons.*

Bereft, Jaxi said, *as if the rest of the world was mourning the loss. People were probably delighted that nobody was eating their sheep and burning down their barns anymore.*

Not all *dragons did those things,* Bhrava Saruth said, hearing Jaxi's comment even though it had been directed at Sardelle.

You don't eat sheep? I don't believe you. I can see wool in your teeth.

Not sheep that belong to humans. High priestess, your sword is being mouthy again. I believe she should be punished.

Sardelle laid a hand on Jaxi's pommel. *Can you wait until after we find Ridge to provoke him? Unless you want him to use you as a toothpick to clean around the gums.*

Jaxi made an incoherent grumbling noise.

Bhrava Saruth, Sardelle asked, *why hide the crystal? Why not share what you learned with the other dragons? Don't you think they would like to know?*

They might do something foolish. Like seek out the portal and try to open it again. I believe there are a perfect number of dragons in the world now. There's no need to open a portal and invite others to return. Besides, those were the dragons who condemned me to that prison for thousands of years. Let them stay where they are.

It sounds like your god wants to keep Iskandia all to himself, Jaxi said.

Sardelle did not know whether she objected to the idea or not. The world had to be a safer place without dragons involved in and instigating wars, but she didn't know if she or Bhrava Saruth had the right to decide that.

Therrik is coming, so you may want to save the philosophical questions for later, Jaxi said.

Sardelle shifted so she could see down the road. A minute later, Therrik jogged into view, Kasandral's hilt visible over his shoulder. Bhrava Saruth, still on his back with his head upside down, made a noise between a grumble and a sigh.

I guess he doesn't enjoy seeing that sword returning, Sardelle thought.

Therrik has actually been doing an admirable job of sublimating the urges Kasandral is sending him as we ride around on Bhrava Saruth's back, Jaxi said.

Are you praising him? I wouldn't have guessed I'd ever hear that.

Just making an observation. Now that he's aware of the sword's influence over him, he's fighting to keep it at bay. Maybe he's the rightful wielder for Kasandral.

Maybe we'll convince Eversong to leave Iskandia, and there will be no need for anyone *to wield Kasandral.*

I think the only way that will happen is with a sword through the heart.

Bhrava Saruth did not bother to right himself as Therrik approached. Sardelle lowered her hand, and the dragon sighed, his twitching tail flopping to the grass.

"What are you doing to that dragon?" Therrik came to a halt

in the road, frowning over at them.

"Rubbing his belly. Has Ridge been to the town? Was there a flier?"

Therrik mouthed *rubbing his belly* incredulously before answering the other questions.

"Yes, we just missed him. The retired colonel there let him take his flier. He took off at dawn." His face twisted into an odd expression. "With the woman in his lap."

"His *lap*?" Why was he flying with some *other* woman in his lap? He'd only done that with her once, and only to save her when the flying fortress had been crashing. Sardelle forced her feelings down, searching for the logical explanation. "Because it wasn't a two-seat flier, I assume. And he had to take her with him because..." Because *why*?

"Because the bitch is controlling him and has been all along," Therrik growled.

"We don't know that."

"What's the other possibility? That he's found a new sorceress he's screwing, and he couldn't wait to give her a tour of the countryside?"

Sardelle winced at the blunt language—and the unpleasant images it put into her mind. "Let's just catch up with them and find out," she said, forcing herself to react reasonably.

Bhrava Saruth rolled to his feet, dropping to his belly so they could climb on.

"Either way, I'm sticking this sword into her," Therrik said.

I'll hold her down so he can do it, Jaxi said. *Assuming I can get past her soulblade to do so.*

Sardelle climbed up to what she was starting to think of as her place over Bhrava Saruth's shoulder blades. She waved Therrik up to the base of the dragon's neck, wanting him in front of her, no matter what praise Jaxi offered for his control.

If the soulblade is who's responsible for controlling Ridge... Sardelle balked at the idea that he was under someone's control, but she pressed on. *We might need you to hold it down. Him,* she corrected. *It was a him, wasn't it?*

Wreltad, yes. Maybe I can distract him by making fun of his name.

A soulblade battle tactic I'm not familiar with?

It's only applicable in certain battles. Such as when your foe has a three-thousand-year-old name. Maybe I'll call him Tad. Or Taddy.

Bhrava Saruth leaped into the air, wings flapping. As soon as he cleared the trees, he turned toward the capital.

Can we catch them in time? Sardelle wondered. It was a couple of hours past dawn. What if Ridge and the sorceress had landed in the capital?

I will do my best, high priestess. I am much faster than the human flying contraptions.

Are we going to barrel into the city on his back? Jaxi asked. *That might alarm the people a tad.* She snickered. *Tad.*

Refining insults to use on him? We'll stay high, out of gunfire range. And hope we can catch Ridge before he reaches the capital.

Yes, they are going to the big city, Bhrava Saruth said. *I can sense them in the air many miles ahead of us.*

You can? All along, Sardelle had been disturbed that none of them could sense Ridge—or the sorceress—ahead of them. Her range was limited, but dragons could see much farther, both with their eyes and their minds.

In a creative manner, yes. She's able to hide her presence, and that of the human male with her, so I haven't felt her during this journey, but a flier is an odd thing to pass through the skies, at least from the perspective of an animal or bird. I started reaching out to the birds ahead of us, which I can sense, even at a distance of many miles. I can see the world through their eyes, and several are fleeing from the noisy flying machine. Through the birds, I can track your mate.

Good work. Sardelle patted the scales under her. She assumed Ridge would head straight for the butte so he could land on the flier runway, but it would be useful to know if he deviated from that route.

Yes. Bhrava Saruth beamed pleasure at this praise. *I will find your mate for you, high priestess. Then he will become my first true worshipper in this time.*

Sardelle forced a smile. She recalled that she had implied to the dragon that Ridge might be a potential worshipper, back when she had been trying to finagle his help the first time.

How Ridge would feel about that, she didn't know, but it was a problem to worry about once she had pried him away from Eversong, and he was safe in *her* arms.

* * *

Before Tolemek opened his eyes, he grew aware of something heavy pressing on his chest. A boot. Stabs of pain pulsed at the back of his head. He could feel the deck under him rocking with the motion of the sea. When had they come down out of the air?

His eyes crossed as the muzzle of a rifle came to rest on the bridge of his nose. He was still in the passageway near the boiler room, and he could glimpse support beams broken all about him, but he was more concerned about all of the faces staring down at him. Several guards in the emperor's colors, dark gray and purple, loomed over him. The boot belonged to the emperor himself. He glowered down at Tolemek, his head shaven, his white goatee bound by beads.

Smoke clogged the passageway, and dozens of holes reminiscent of teeth marks let light in through the bulkhead, but the emperor did not appear worried. Indeed, the battle had grown still out there, the cannonballs and machine guns quiet. How much time had passed? Had Kaika's explosion destroyed the engine? Was the ship sinking into the bay, even now?

Tolemek berated himself, knowing it had been his insistence to pull the firemen out that had delayed them, kept them from getting far enough away from the boiler room. If they hadn't been caught by the explosion, they might have been the ones to come across the emperor, catching him off guard or on the deck.

He lifted his head to see if the guards had Kaika too. The rifle muzzle pressed against his nose, pushing his head back down. Not before he glimpsed her on her knees behind the emperor, her hands bounded behind her back, a rifle jabbed into the side of her neck.

Tylie? Tolemek called.

Your sister and your friends cannot help you, a female voice said into his mind. The dragon. He recognized her from before. *Nor can this gray-scaled cockroach.*

Phelistoth?

He is weak. He thought the empire would want an alliance with him, when I am here, Yisharnesh the Mighty.

What can the empire do for you, Yisharnesh? Why ally with humans?

The emperor recognizes my power and greatness. His people will treat me well for my occasional help, provide an excellent lair and see to my needs and whims. I will find a suitable mate and breed babies, making many dragons. My offspring will rule the world as my ancestors once did.

"You look like a baboon with all of that hair, Targoson," the emperor said.

"Thank you, Your Highness. I prefer it to the melon-head look." Tolemek had heard a story that the reason Cofah soldiers had been required to shave their heads was because the emperor himself had gone prematurely bald and hadn't wanted his troops to have more hair than he. It might just be a story, but the emperor's lips flattened in satisfying annoyance.

"I was just going to have you shot when my men found you lying here, especially since the Iskandian assassins have proven lackadaisical when it comes to killing you. You know, it's irritated me greatly that you chose to work for those obstinate rebels."

"Only because the empire turned its back on me."

"You deserved to be ostracized after Camp Eveningson."

Tolemek gritted his teeth. Angulus had forgiven him for Tanglewood, and he had twice the heart as Salatak, so those deaths must have stung him even more. As he stared up at the man sneering down at him, he realized for the second time that day that his heart had chosen Iskandia long before his brain had. He might never be beloved by the people there, but he was welcomed by some. That was enough. He had a home. He only hoped he might find a way to return to see it again. And to see Cas again. Was she still out there? Still alive?

"Since I've endured a great deal of loss, both financially and in manpower, here because of you, I'm going to have my new ally scour your brain before I kill you." The emperor lifted his head, as if calling to the heavens. "Dragon? Tell me if he knows where my daughter is, and also, I implore you, steal all of his secrets from him, all of his recipes for his formulas, his salves, all that he has used for good and ill."

Tolemek hoped the call might go unanswered, that the dragon was busy or would scoff at his demands. Instead harsh fingernails scraped through his brain, making his skull hurt from the inside out. If he had been standing, he would have fallen. As it was, all he could do was thump his head back against the deck, his entire body stiffening as the dragon ruthlessly stole everything from his mind. He tried to think of anything but what the creature sought—he even tried to feed her memories of finding Phelistoth in a Cofah lab, his blood being sucked out by the vial full, to show her what kind of "ally" the emperor might be—but it was hard to do more than writhe in pain at the harshness of the intrusion.

"Maybe he'll die just from having a dragon pawing at his brain," someone said with a snicker.

"I hope so. We crashed, thanks to him and that witch."

The emperor remained silent. Tolemek wanted to protest that Kaika wasn't a witch, but it hurt too much to talk, too much to think. Only the knowledge that they'd brought the ship down made him feel slightly better, but if it was still seaworthy, they hadn't done enough.

"The dragon informs me that she has the information," the emperor said. "But you do not know where my daughter is. That is unfortunate." He turned slightly. "Check the other one."

A moment later, Tolemek heard Kaika gasp and knew the dragon was rifling through her thoughts too. He turned his head as much as he could with the rifle pinning him down. He wanted to catch her gaze, to apologize, if only with his eyes.

Kaika wasn't looking at him. Her chin was to her chest, as if in defeat, but Tolemek noticed something that surprised him. Either her hands hadn't been tied behind her back, after all, or she had somehow slipped one free, perhaps disguising the movement as a reaction of pain when the dragon had jumped into her head. Now, she slid that hand past her belt and into her trousers, using her shoulders to hide the action from the guards standing behind her. When she withdrew her hand again, something compact was hidden by her palm. She met his eyes, giving him a bleak but determined smile.

Without a doubt, Tolemek knew she had pulled out an explosive. Her words from the jail flashed into his mind, "I can't believe they didn't bother stripping us." The guards must not have even searched her yet, or nobody had been brazen enough to check her crotch. Maybe they foolishly thought Tolemek was the more dangerous of the two people they'd found here.

He might have laughed in triumph, but he realized there was only one thing she could do with that bomb from that position. Detonate it and kill everyone around her, including the emperor. Including him.

Tylie, he thought, having no idea if she could hear him. *I love you. Tell Cas I love her too.*

Kaika nodded at Tolemek and shifted her thumb. She'd armed the explosive.

Weapon! the female dragon cried into his mind—into all of their minds. Everyone spun about, startled and confused.

Kaika threw the grenade at the hull next to the emperor's head. The guard standing over Tolemek with the rifle jumped to protect his supreme commander. With the weapon no longer pointed at his face, Tolemek flipped to his hands and knees and tried to get out of the way. Other guards were leaping in, hurling the emperor to the deck, covering him with their bodies. The passage was a cluster of chaos. Tolemek crashed into the back of someone's legs as he jumped to his feet. Expecting the guard to stop him, Tolemek lowered his shoulder to ram the man. But this guard was trying to run away too. Tolemek hit nothing but air, and he almost stumbled to the floor again. He only made it a few more steps before the grenade went off.

For the second time that day, an explosion behind him hurled him into the air. It felt like a battering ram smashing between his shoulder blades. His feet left the ground, and he crashed into the guard who had also been running. Light flooded the area, and water washed into the passageway. Tolemek landed in several inches of it instead of on the hard decking. More water surged in, a wave crashing over his head. Cold, salty water enveloped him, and he sputtered as it rolled into his mouth.

Someone grabbed his shoulder. He didn't know if it was a guard trying to gather up prisoners or someone who couldn't swim hoping for a handhold. After a glance over his shoulder to make sure it wasn't Kaika, he rammed his elbow backward, catching the person in the ribs. His sleeve tangled with something. He started to jerk his arm back, but recognized the butt of a pistol in a holster. He groped, found it with his hand, and yanked it out. The bullets would probably be too waterlogged to fire, but he could clobber people with it if he needed to.

His feet found something hard—the wall? The ceiling?—and he pushed off through the gaping hole in the hull. His entire body hurt, and he might have a concussion, but he recognized his chance to escape and had to use it. He swam toward the light.

A guard sputtered nearby. "Getting away!"

"Where's the emperor?"

Tolemek swam, squinting into the morning light, searching for the closest shoreline. He spotted land, but two ships blocked the way.

Someone gasped a few meters away. It sounded like a woman. He paused. Kaika? Had she survived that? He had been sure she wouldn't with the guards fencing her in, keeping her from fleeing up the passageway.

Tolemek turned, only to come face to face with a shaven-headed man. The figure was grabbing something, not looking at Tolemek, but he would surely attack as soon as he realized Tolemek was there.

"—off me, you—" That was Kaika's voice again. She gasped and was shoved under water before she could finish. Two guards wrestled with her.

Tolemek lifted the pistol and clubbed the one in front of him. He had to get to Kaika to help.

His target cried out in anger and disgruntlement. Tolemek barely avoided being elbowed. The water made everyone slower.

As the man turned, he surged in, wrapping an arm around his neck and clubbing him again. He wished he had a knockout grenade, a more elegant and less devastating solution, but the emperor's men had removed all of his tools.

After he struck the man a third time, the fellow gave up. He thrashed and tried to escape. Boots planted into Tolemek's abdomen, as the guard pushed off. Tolemek grunted, all of his air driven out of his lungs. Since the guard didn't look like he wanted any more of the fight, Tolemek let him get away.

He paddled toward where he'd seen Kaika struggling, but his arm smacked against someone else coming up for air. Another bald head. He almost clubbed that head right away, but he paused before striking. The face that turned toward him, blood streaming from the nostrils and the eyes glassy, belonged to the emperor.

Tolemek grabbed him, not sure yet what he intended to do, but options spun through his mind. He could trade the man for Kaika or use him for a shield. Though he expected a fight, the emperor was barely conscious. He batted feebly at the water.

A gunshot fired, the sound muffled by water. Maybe all of the bullets weren't waterlogged, after all.

Tolemek hooked one am under the emperor's armpit and across his chest to keep him afloat. He started to paddle in Kaika's direction, but her head came up first. She gasped, flinging hair out of her face with one hand. Her pistol came up and she spun around, looking for her enemies. But she seemed to have dealt with them all, for the moment. Aside from the guard who had given up and was swimming away, nobody remained to oppose them.

Before Tolemek could grow too elated about that, he noticed boats heading their way. *Many* boats. Packed rowboats carved through the choppy waters of the bay, dozens of soldiers aiming rifles at Tolemek and Kaika.

"Get close to me," Tolemek whispered, wanting to make sure none of them risked shooting out of fear of hitting the emperor.

Not that it mattered. The soldiers rowed with fervor, closing the distance fast, coming at them from all sides. There was no escape.

A shadow fell across the water. Tolemek hoped it might belong to a flier, swooping in to rescue them, but the only propellers he heard were in the distance.

Massive wings spread above him, blocking out the sky. Talons stretched toward him. Thinking it was the gold dragon, he almost ducked, but silver scales covered the belly above them.

As Phelistoth's talons wrapped around Tolemek, bullets fired from a dozen directions. Nothing hit him. As he was pulled into the air, Tolemek tightened his grip around the emperor, realizing that this was their chance, assuming Phelistoth had switched back to their side. He couldn't be positive of that, but he wrapped both arms around his prisoner. The talons gripping him were like vises, tightening to keep him from falling, nearly crushing his ribs in the process.

The dragon's other foot extended and wrapped around Kaika, pulling her up into the air as well. More rifles fired, but Phelistoth flapped his wings, the bullets bouncing away when they struck his invisible barrier. He took them into the sky, then surprised and terrified Tolemek by flinging him up toward his back. With his arms wrapped around the emperor, he couldn't reach out to grab anything, not that the smooth scales offered any handholds.

But some magic directed him, levitating him in the air until he could right himself. He landed astride Phelistoth's back with the emperor flopping onto his stomach in front of him. Blood dripped from the dragon's sides where long, deep scratches had gouged into him, tearing away scales and exposing bluish pink flesh. There were many wounds, and Phelistoth must have felt as battered as Tolemek, but he flew without a hitch, his powerful wingbeats taking them away from the water. Kaika landed in front of Tolemek, flailing and cursing until she touched down. She dropped to her stomach and spread her arms, fingers doing their best to grip the dragon's smooth scales.

Maybe Tolemek should have been scared too—they had already risen a hundred feet or more, with the sounds of gunshots growing faint. But he felt the magic holding them in place, and he'd seen Tylie ride Phelistoth enough times to know she was never in danger up here. So long as the dragon *wanted* them here, they should be fine. He just hoped that was the case and that Phelistoth wasn't taking them up to one of the imperial airships to sell them to the empire. He craned his neck, trying to see if Cas and the others were harassing the Cofah craft and spotted three fliers breaking away, flying toward the city. Phelistoth had already flown out over the sea, and Tolemek couldn't tell who was piloting them.

No, I am not taking you to their ships. The empire does not want my help. Bitterness flavoring Phelistoth's telepathic words. *They have aligned with Yisharnesh and prefer to work with* gold *dragons.*

Tolemek almost scoffed at the dragon's problem, but was uneasily reminded of himself. *They don't want me either. Just my knowledge.* It rankled that the gold dragon apparently now knew everything he knew about chemistry and science. He hoped she had a poor memory and forgot it all.

I offered the emperor his daughter as an act of good faith, so he would see my value, since I recovered her for him, and he accused me of kidnapping her just so I could bargain with her.

He's not known for being a reasonable man. Tolemek looked down at their prisoner, but he had fallen unconscious—or he was pretending to be unconscious—and was either ignoring this conversation or wasn't aware of it.

Kaika had glanced at Tolemek a few times, and he thought Phelistoth might also be sharing his words with her.

As I was attempting to change his mind and inform him that Tylie should be permitted to study in Cofahre and live with her family, as is healthy for young humans, Yisharnesh came and drove me off. She forbade me, a lowly silver dragon, to speak with an emperor who rules over millions. As if any human is better than a dragon!

Tolemek kept his mind still, lest he make a sarcastic comment. The last thing he wanted was to drive Phelistoth and his fickle loyalties back toward land.

The emperor heard all of this, and he said nothing to gainsay it. He stood there with that haughty expression on his face, agreeing and believing that aligning with a gold dragon, one offering to breed and make an army of dragons, meant there would be no room for Tylie and me to have a home in the empire.

That alliance may prove foolish for him, given that Yisharnesh came out of that cavern of criminals. She may have been lying to him about much. Tolemek wondered if an alliance would continue if they succeeded at making the emperor disappear. The idea of an army of gold dragons was alarming.

I told him that! He chose not to believe me. Yisharnesh purred in his ear like a fat, content cat.

I believe King Angulus would not be so arrogant as to object to multiple dragons living in his country. Tolemek almost laughed, realizing he was negotiating on behalf of the country he hadn't even decided would be his long-term home. Or maybe he had. He smiled when he thought of his lab and of Cas. He wished he had a way to communicate with her now, to tell her that he was on his way home and hoped she was too.

Oh, I know that. Angulus is transparent in what he wishes. But sharing such a small continent with Bhrava Saruth. The dragon made a grumbling noise in Tolemek's head.

Tolemek snorted. *Trust me, I felt the same way about sharing it with Zirkander.*

Yes, Phelistoth said slowly. *It is odd, but we are similar, I suppose. Outcasts. Never again to fly over the homeland where we grew up.* He shared images of that flying, of crossing mountains and plains, lakes and forests. They weren't quite the same as the Cofahre Tolemek remembered—for one thing, the empire was much more populated now, and there were far fewer wildernesses left—but the terrain was familiar, and a twinge of homesickness stirred in his breast. He pushed it away and thought of Cas again.

The difference between a homeland and a home is that one is a place and one is people. It's the people that matter.

My people are gone.

You have new people, if you're willing to accept them. Tolemek thought of Tylie and also of the comrades he had made since entering Iskandia, people who had freed Phelistoth from his prison and from the Cofah scientists. This wasn't the first time the empire had treated him poorly.

Phelistoth sighed. *Do you think Angulus would give me a region to myself, where Bhrava Saruth isn't allowed to go?*

Perhaps you could negotiate that with him. I'm sure he would be more open to dealing than Salatak.

Perhaps.

When the dragon fell silent, Tolemek's thoughts returned to Cas and how he had come to think of Iskandia as home. He wished he could check on her, to see if she was all right. He had seen three fliers but not all four.

Tylie? he asked in his mind, not expecting a response, since he believed they'd already gone many miles. *Are you out there?*

Yes, came her cheerful response. *I heard you talking to Phel.*

She must have been linked to him in a way that enhanced her telepathic range.

Good. Are you all right? Is Cas all right?

I'm flying with Cas now, Tylie added brightly. *We are both happy you and Captain Kaika are safe.*

Are you heading our way? Tolemek looked toward land again, but they were now too far away to see even the hulking airships. He saw no sign of the fliers.

Not yet. We're following Wasley and Farris into the city to look for Zia. Who and who? Was that Duck and Pimples? *Colonel Abram isn't happy about it, but I told him we couldn't keep up with the dragons anyway. He sent Captain Blazer to accompany you and Captain Kaika. Phel is much faster, so we'll arrive home later than you.*

Home, Tolemek mused. Tylie was calling Iskandia that too.

We'll come as soon as we can. Colonel Abram is adamant that you keep an eye on the emperor. Did you really get the emperor, Tolie? That's amazing. Is he angry? Will he punish Mother and Father?

I'm not sure. We're hoping he won't be able to punish anyone if we can escape cleanly. Can you tell if there's pursuit? Is the gold dragon coming?

Not yet, but if she realizes what's going on, she might come after you. To help the emperor. Tylie stuck out her tongue in her mind.

Where is she now?

I ensured she was busy, Phelistoth announced, sounding smug.

He shared imagery with Tolemek, perhaps with everybody, showing him fleeing the bay with the gold dragon in close pursuit. He flew over the trees along the coast and dipped toward the city, soaring over the rope bridges and diving and weaving among the treetop structures. He goaded Yisharnesh, laughing at her because she wasn't any faster than a puny silver dragon. Infuriated, she hurled waves of energy while streaming gouts of flame after Phelistoth. Several times, he was clipped by her power, or her fire hammered against his shields, but the city suffered the most from their air battle. Entire structures were knocked from the treetops. Wood and rope bridges burst into flames. Observers leaped from elevated platforms and bridges and into the river or marsh waters to avoid being struck.

And the city, believing itself in terrible danger, retaliated. Paddle boats with cannons and shamans came out into the wide delta, doing their best to defend against and even sling attacks at the gold dragon. Phelistoth led her close to them, somehow avoiding being shot at himself. Yisharnesh was in little danger of being killed or seriously wounded by the townspeople, even the shamans, but Phelistoth attacked her while the humans distracted and harried her. The shamans fired a launcher, and a magically imbued net flew into the air, spreading wide enough to entangle the gold dragon. Phelistoth took his chance to escape, leaving her to deal with the determined citizens while he took off to check in on the battle. He spotted Tolemek and Kaika in the water and, at Tylie's urging, swept in to grab them.

So she's back there now, laying destruction to the city where Cas and Tylie are going? Tolemek scowled.

Nobody answered him. The sea stretched below, the shoreline growing distant behind them. They must have flown out of Tylie's range. Tolemek turned his scowl back toward land. Even though they had, against all odds, achieved their objective and kidnapped the emperor, he couldn't help but feel he was running away from people who needed his help.

Chapter 16

FLAMES LEAPED FROM NUMEROUS SPOTS in the city as Cas flew above the trees and the delta came into view. Charred boards floated in the river, some with people clinging to them. Other survivors swam for the riverbanks. Buildings that had perched elegantly in the trees were now smashed with only broken platforms remaining. Several of those trees were on fire, and a number of homes on stilts along the banks had been destroyed, the roofs caved in.

Cas let Pimples take the lead as they flew along the river, but she stayed close, hugging his left wing, not sure what to expect. After the air battle over the bay, they had landed briefly so Blazer could fix something that had been rattling in Cas's flier. Quataldo had then sent the captain off to catch up with Tolemek, Kaika, and Phelistoth with orders to keep an eye on them and report to General Ort if the rest of the squadron was delayed retrieving Zia. Quataldo had almost gone with Blazer, but he'd seemed reluctant to leave lieutenants in charge of finding the Cofah princess and had climbed in with Pimples, his stomach still queasy, perhaps, after experiencing Cas's dragon-shaking tactics. Cas now had Tylie, and Duck flew off Pimples' other wing, his back seat empty. He was also sticking close, since he did not have a communication crystal.

Tylie leaned over the side of the flier, peering down at the city, smoke wafting up from all directions. She had alerted them as they approached the city that the gold dragon was attacking Tildar Dem, fooled into doing so by Phelistoth. Cas was relieved that Tolemek and Kaika had gotten away, but she worried they might have condemned the princess to a horrible fate by leaving her behind. Had Zia reached the city yet? Maybe she was still out on that raft and hadn't been caught up in this.

As they flew closer, the gold dragon came into view, and

Cas gawked. She was tangled in a net and thrashing in the river. Several boats were out in the water around her, firing cannons and harpoons. On two of those boats, men in strange clothing made from alligator hides stood in the bows, their hands outstretched. Shamans? Neither magical nor mundane attacks seemed to be harming the dragon, but for some reason, she couldn't escape that net. Why couldn't she simply incinerate it with her flames?

It's magical, Tylie spoke into her mind as Cas flew over the scene, looking for sign of Zia. *And very old, I think. It feels so strong, so much more magical than my brother's potions and other items I've seen. Almost like Kasandral. Or Jaxi!*

The net doesn't talk, does it?

Tylie giggled. *I don't think so. But it may be an artifact from ancient times, something made when dragon wars were common and sorcerers were very powerful and could create powerful things. Phel's told me much about those times. He misses them so much!*

Cas did not care about Phelistoth's homesickness. She wanted to find Pimples' new girlfriend and get out of here.

"I don't see Zia anywhere," Pimples said over the crystal. "Can Tylie tell where she is?"

She's coming, Tylie announced.

"Coming? Coming from where?" Cas and the others had flown past the city, so she turned back toward it. She watched the ground, both to look for Zia and because she worried that those riverboat shamans might think the fliers were hostile and open fire. So far, the people down there had been too busy with the dragon to notice them, but that might not last.

Down the river, Tylie said.

Cas flew out over the waterway, then cursed when she spotted Zia. She was still on the raft. Of course—where else would she be since she couldn't leave that log? She must have been caught up in the current, or maybe she hadn't been able to steer toward a landing place with so many bridges and platforms being destroyed.

"She's heading straight toward the dragon and the boats," Pimples shouted.

Yes, she was. And Cas had no idea how to do anything about it. She had rope in her storage compartment and might be able to dangle the end down so Zia could grab it, but how could that help if she couldn't be pulled from that log? There was no way their aircraft could lift a heavy raft out of the water and fly it off somewhere.

Her breath caught. They shouldn't have to.

"Pimples," she said, "get your rope out. I'm doing the same thing. If she can grab the end or hook it to the raft, maybe we can pull her up the river or over to the bank."

Cas eyed the trees on either side, wondering if they could possibly do what she imagined. The only place there was clear enough air for them to fly low was right above the water, and even then, branches stretched out, branches that could catch their wings and impede them—or cause them to crash.

"That could kill her," Pimples said. "At our speed, we'd tear the raft to pieces as we dragged it upriver, and her with it. I mean, we could switch to thrusters, but then we'd quickly lose our forward momentum."

Even though she was listening to him, Cas had dug out her rope. She tied it off using the base of her seat and flung the end over the side. "I'm going to try. I'll switch to thrusters as I come in. All I need is enough momentum to drag her to the shore. Tylie, can you tell her my intent?"

"Raptor," Pimples said, "it's too dangerous."

"So is crashing into a furious dragon."

The dragon punctuated her last words by spewing flames from her snout, bathing the closest riverboat. The net held, but the people on the deck flung themselves into the water, all save for a shaman that stayed, his hands raised and his head bowed. At first, the flames beat against an invisible concave shield around him, but as Cas circled over the river, finding an angle where she could dive toward Zia, the shaman's shield faltered and disappeared. He tried to leap off the deck, as the others had done, but the dragon's fire engulfed him. A charred, unmoving body hit the water.

Cas swore, hardly noticing when Tylie tapped her shoulder.

"Do it, Raptor," Pimples said. "Better to have the raft ripped apart than to die like that."

That raft was in the middle of the river heading inexorably downstream, straight toward the trapped dragon. Zia kept trying to find ground to push off with her pole, but the water was too deep. She had no way to steer.

Free me, a voice commanded.

It was so jarring and so full of power that Cas found herself turning toward the source—the dragon—before she caught herself. Images of flying down and somehow cutting through the net crashed into her mind. She recognized the mental compulsion for what it was but still struggled to push it aside. Down in the water, people swam toward the dragon. Cas had no idea if they would be able to help, or if the creature would even let them. What if she was so furious that the dragon simply burned them alive?

"Raptor?" Pimples said. "I'm going to come in behind you. Zia's raft is almost to the dragon. I'm lowering my rope too. Can Tylie tell Zia to grab it and tie it to a log? We'll only get one shot, and she's going to have to tie quickly. Otherwise, we'll be past her, ripping the rope from her hands before... damn it, this is never going to work."

Cas forced her attention back to the waterway and the raft. "We'll try. Tylie?"

I told her. She believes your plan is crazy and thinks what she's heard about Iskandians is true.

Cas decided not to ask what that might be. There wasn't time. She flew over the dragon, watching to make sure she didn't raise her head and breathe fire through the net at her, then dipped as low as she could, making the rope dangle into the water. Cas lined up her approach so that it would trail across the raft.

Zia tossed aside her useless pole, then braced herself and reached out toward the rope.

Cas cut the power to the propeller and let her hand hover over the switch that activated the thrusters. Even though she was still twenty or thirty feet above Zia, she worried their heat would reach her. It might not be as deadly as the dragon fire, but it wouldn't feel good.

Zia reached for the rope, but as Cas had feared, even with her propeller off, her momentum took her past too quickly. Zia barely got her hands around it before it was torn from her grip.

"I was afraid of that," Pimples groaned, the same thing happening on his run. "I knew this wouldn't work. Damn it."

Cas activated her thrusters and looked for a spot to land amid the trees and branches. Going back for another try would be useless, but maybe they could come down somewhere ahead of the raft, leave their fliers, and run along the bank and throw a rope out to Zia.

As she turned toward the riverbank, Cas craned her neck to check on the dragon. Dozens of people were in the water around her, pulling off the net. Zia's raft couldn't have been more than ten meters away. Maybe it would bounce off and keep going past the dragon. With all those people in the water, Yisharnesh might not even notice.

The dragon's head escaped the net as Cas landed on a narrow beach, her wheels more in the water than in the silt. She unfastened her harness and untied the rope as quickly as she could. The dragon roared, the power of the cry rattling tree branches on either side of the river. The humans that she had commanded to help were thrown into the air. Some sailed fifteen or twenty feet before landing in the water again. With the dragon blocking her view, Cas couldn't see what happened to the raft.

"Zia, no!" Pimples cried. Still farther upriver, he had a better view. Or maybe a worse one.

Logs flew into the air, just as the humans had. Pieces of the raft, Cas realized.

Pimples landed his flier in the water and flung himself from his cockpit, not caring that his flier wasn't on solid ground. Colonel Quataldo, still in the back seat, shouted something at him. Pimples, already swimming toward the dragon, did not respond. Quataldo scrambled into the cockpit as the flier drifted down the river, scraping and bumping against the ground underneath it. Right now, it wasn't far from the bank, but it would pick up speed, and Cas doubted Quataldo had any experience flying the craft.

Cas raced along the bank toward it. She trusted Pimples would heroically rescue Zia—if she had survived that blast—but Quataldo would write demerits for all of them if *he* had to be heroically rescued, or if they lost a flier. They didn't have enough extra seats for them all to make it home *without* that flier.

Cas waded into the water as the craft floated toward her. She pushed off the bottom and swam toward it. It was already picking up speed, heading toward the center of the river. She imagined it passing her and floating out to sea. If she hadn't been so busy paddling, she would have cursed Pimples.

She veered, trying to cut it off. Quataldo saw her coming and leaned out, thrusting the butt of his rifle toward her. Cas lunged and grasped it. Quataldo pulled her in and hoisted her into the air as if she weighed nothing. He plopped her down into the cockpit, a cockpit that had an alarming amount of water in the bottom. More sloshed over the sides.

"I trust you have more of an idea of what to do up there than I do," Quataldo said.

Cas activated the thrusters, hoping they would work. She had never tried to take off from the water before. The power from the crystal was more forgiving than other sources of energy, and no spark of ignition was required to start the propeller, but she did not know how the machinery itself would hold up.

Nothing happened. The banks floated by as the delta widened. The sea spread out before them, waves breaking across the mouth of the river.

"Lieutenant Ahn, I would prefer it if we don't float home."

"Yes, sir. Me too."

The power crystal beamed happily from its spot under the controls. Cas glared at it and tried to start the thrusters again. If this didn't work and she got swept out to sea, she would kill Pimples. However long it took her to find her way back to Iskandia to do it.

On the fifth try, water bubbles rose up around the flier, and a sick gurgling noise came from under the craft. Finally, she felt some lift. They rose sluggishly, but she allowed herself to hope that once they cleared the water, the components would dry out and work better. She wished Blazer had stayed with them, since she had more tools—and knew what to do with them.

The flier cleared the surface, something clanked angrily, and water spewed out of orifices Cas hadn't known the craft possessed. The thrusters groaned but picked up power. Soon, they lifted a couple of inches. Just as she was wondering if they would have to hover all the way back home, she thought to try the propeller. Water flew from its blades, but it started right away. They skimmed across the surface, heading toward the higher waves of the ocean, and she tried pulling up on the flight stick. Finally, the craft rose, still dripping and spewing water.

Cas turned them back toward the river to check on the others. The gold dragon was flying straight toward her.

"Lieutenant," Quataldo warned, a rare hint of panic in his voice.

Already diving toward the water again, Cas said, "I see her."

Free from the netting, the dragon flapped toward them. Cas had no idea what she could do to defend herself except get out of the way. When she dipped back toward the river mouth, the belly of the flier almost skimming the water again, the dragon did not follow. She didn't even glance back. With powerful, determined wingbeats, the creature headed out to sea, water glistening on scales alight in the morning sun. For a heartbeat or two, Cas admired the beauty, but then a jolt of panic went through her.

"Tolemek," she rasped.

"Did you say something?" Quataldo asked.

"If she's going out to sea, I'm afraid she's going after the emperor. Phelistoth is carrying three people, and he's injured." Cas let her head thud back against her seat. She reached for the communication crystal, thinking to warn the others and say that they needed to get going immediately, but remembered Duck didn't have a crystal and that she was in Pimples' flier, so the only person she could call was Tylie. No, even Tylie had climbed out, Cas saw as she flew closer to the city. She appeared to be helping some of the people who had been thrown across the river in the dragon's burst of power. Cas commended the effort, but they couldn't stay here. They had to get back across the ocean as soon as possible. It was bad enough that the fliers couldn't keep up with the dragons in an even race. The longer they remained here, the farther behind they would fall, leaving poor Tolemek and the others to deal with an irritated gold dragon out in the middle of the ocean.

In the end, she did thumb the crystal on. "Captain Blazer? Are you still in range?"

Cas spotted Pimples slogging out of the river, a woman in his arms. Zia, presumably. Cas was too far away to tell if she was conscious.

"Captain Blazer?"

"Yes, I'm still here," Blazer said. "Flying across the ocean by myself because that silver dragon didn't want to wait on me. I'm not sure he even knows I'm behind him."

"I hope he's flying as quickly as he can, because he's going to have trouble soon. The gold dragon just left, and she's heading in that direction." Cas wanted to ask Blazer to help, to try to delay the dragon, but what would that do? Get her killed, most likely. "You might want to stay out of the way, ma'am. We'll be along as soon as we can collect everyone."

"You get that princess?"

"We have her. I'm not sure what her status is."

"You might want to make sure her status is healthy and happy. In case we need to barter her to someone for our lives. And the lives of everyone in Iskandia."

"Yes, ma'am. I'll try."

* * *

As the flier soared toward the capital, tree-filled wilderness transitioning to cleared farmlands below, Ridge grew more and more certain that he was taking an assassin to see the king. What could he do? Land early and insist she get out? Flip them upside down and let go of her? Since she sat sideways in his lap, with her arm looped over his shoulders, Mara had no harness to keep her in the seat the way he did. He rejected that idea almost as soon as it came, the notion of letting a woman fall to her death horrifying him, enemy or not.

Mara smiled and patted him on the back of the head. "Besides, I can hang on very, very tightly."

Ridge stared straight ahead, trying to pretend he wasn't appalled that she could read his mind. How was he supposed to outmaneuver someone who knew his thoughts as soon as he did?

"You know," she mused, playing with his hair, "as well liked as you are in every town we go to, you yourself could be a popular king." Her smile flattened into a smirk. "If something were to happen to the existing one."

"I don't think popularity has much to do with how the succession is determined." He kept his voice calm, but inside, his heart beat as rapidly as the propeller blades. She was as much as admitting that she intended to kill Angulus now.

"Perhaps not, but sometimes usurpers have come along, slain the old monarch and inserted themselves upon the throne. It's happened in the empire, and I'm sure it's happened here."

"Usurpers who like paperwork and being chained to a desk. Running a country isn't an easy job, I'm sure."

"It could be, for someone who was just a figurehead. He could go off and be popular and fly his little contraptions, while someone else handled the real work and enjoyed the power of the position and the way history would admire her for having so boldly taken that position."

"Someone?" Ridge choked. "You?"

"Perhaps." Mara's eyes gleamed with this vision, and her fingernails dug into his scalp.

"Either you're delusional, or—" He stopped, not knowing how to articulate the *or*. Or what? Or she was far more powerful than he could imagine?

"Let's find out, shall we?" She nodded toward the horizon. "I believe that's your capital city coming into view." The grid of streets, houses, and buildings was indeed visible now. Beyond that and slightly to the south of their flight path lay the harbor, the butte that held the hangars at one end and the hill of black rocks that held the castle at the other. "Take us straight to the castle," she added.

"We can't do that." Ridge's voice came out impressively calm, considering all the flailing his mind was doing.

"Why not?"

"This isn't a military craft, and I don't have permission to fly into the castle whenever I like. We'd be shot down as we approached."

Mara played with his hair, as if the threat bored her. "I'm willing to risk that."

"I'm not. Besides, we'd crash if we tried to land this flier within the castle walls. It's an old model. No thrusters. We need a runway so we can decelerate."

There, even she would have to see that logic. And it was the truth. What was he supposed to do? Use the courtyard as a runway? They would smash into a wall before he could brake fully, probably after taking out one of the king's fancy fountains.

"I've seen you fly. You're talented. You can make it work."

"You've seen me *crash*. I wouldn't think that would give you confidence in my abilities." He frowned at her. "Or had we met before that?" Seven gods, was *that* why Wreltad had stolen his memories? Because they had met in battle before? Because he would have recognized her and known her for an enemy from the beginning?

Mara smiled cryptically. "I believe you need to turn now if we're going to land in the castle."

Yes, that was true, but his gaze snagged on the dark blue of the ocean, the sunlight gleaming off its surface. Instead of turning toward the capital, Ridge kept them on a path that would take them out over the ocean. There, he could crash them into the waves with enough speed that neither of them would be rescued and nursed back to health.

You would kill yourself to keep an enemy from reaching your king's doors? Wreltad asked.

Wouldn't a Cofah soldier do that?

A private or a corporal perhaps. One thinks of officers as being less

expendable. And of thinking themselves less expendable.
I couldn't be a pilot with an attitude like that.

Ridge set his jaw and steered toward the open ocean. At least, he tried to steer in that direction. His eyes widened as his hand, operating of its own accord, tilted the flier to head south, straight for the harbor and the city. And the castle.

He fought the invisible power that controlled him, but he couldn't twitch so much as a finger. He glared at Mara out of the side of his eyes—his eyes were all that he could move.

"You *will* take us to the castle," she said.

He couldn't speak to respond. *Fine*, he thought, letting go of all his resistance, *let's see if you can land this flier where you want it on your own.*

She chuckled. "Do all men think themselves indispensable?"

Again, he couldn't respond. A prisoner inside his own body, all he could do was watch as the flier descended toward the castle.

CHAPTER 17

As they descended, the vibrations of the old propeller trying to shake his teeth out of his jaw, Ridge hoped the guards would mistake him for a Cofah invader and shoot the flier down. He still did not have control of his body, and there was no other way to ensure Mara did not land and attack Angulus. Unless they crashed so spectacularly that neither of them walked away from it. That *was* a possibility. He was very aware that this craft did not have thrusters as they lined up their approach.

Out of habit, he dipped his hand toward the pocket where he often kept his dragon luck charm. Belatedly, he remembered that he had lost it. There would be no luck for him today.

Have faith. We will not allow this contraption to crash while we're aboard it.

Wonderful. Ridge glanced down at Mara's waist. He had yet to see Wreltad's true form—the sheathed knife digging into his thigh did not match the image Wreltad had shown Ridge of an elegant sword. It hardly mattered. He did not doubt that his enemies had magic, not when it was keeping him from flying freely.

Whichever one of them was restricting his movements allowed him enough leeway to adjust the flight stick. It appeared that he was going to be responsible for this landing. Once again, he thought of veering away from the castle and taking them out to sea—or at least to some deserted beach that could serve as a runaway. A sharp pain in the back of his head punished him, and he lost all ability to move for a few seconds. A warning.

This isn't very honorable, he grumbled to Wreltad.

By now, Ridge doubted Mara had any honor, but he wondered if he might appeal to the soul in the sword. He seemed more reasonable.

No, Wreltad said, a hint of sorrow in his voice, *but if you stay out of the way, you might yet survive this. Tarshalyn enjoyed fornicating with you and believes she would have an easier time ruling here if you stood beside her. She would even let you be king, so long as she had most of the power.*

If you can see in my head, you know I'd never agree to that. The king has my oath. I would be forsworn if I did anything but my best to defend him and protect my country. You say you understand honor. You must understand this.

I do, but if you stand against her, she will kill you. As she has killed many others who stood against her.

How many?

Too many to count.

Did she enjoy fornicating with them too?

Only with a few. None of them had your sense of humor.

What a wonderful accolade. As far as I've noticed, she doesn't value that much.

I've found it refreshing. I believe I will miss you.

Ridge had no idea what to say to that. It was more eulogy than flattery. *Please give me back my memories, Wreltad. Maybe it will change something.*

It won't.

Frustration burned in Ridge's veins as he took them down, the sea air whipping at the flier's wings, and the kingdom flag snapping on its pole in the courtyard. He steadied the craft, gauging the distance between their wheels and the top of the wall, wanting to cut it as close as he could. The sooner those wheels touched down, the more room he would have to brake. He was aiming at the longest strip of lawn within the walls, a side yard that stretched from the front to the back, broken only by a row of low hedges. He deemed the hedges more desirable to hit than a stone wall.

Two shots fired, and Ridge instinctively ducked. Even though being shot down might save Angulus from Mara, he couldn't bring himself to wave and invite fire. To his surprise, there were no follow-up shots.

Several people ran for the stairs leading down from the

wall, men on their way to warn the head of security that an unauthorized flier approached. He wished they knew that an *assassin* approached.

On the forward wall, men dropped to their bellies as the flier cruised over their heads, the wheels just missing the crenellated parapet. The craft hit the grass a third of the way into the courtyard, the bump that jostled them far lighter than seemed appropriate for someone crashing. Of course, it wasn't the landing that was hard here—it was halting before they hit the wall.

Ridge pulled on the brake, grimacing as the hedges came up far too quickly. Without a harness, Mara might have been thrown from the cockpit, but he wrapped an arm around her, reacting on instinct before he could consider the merits of letting her go.

Such a gentleman, a female voice said into his mind—her voice. She grinned and lifted a hand, fingers splayed toward the windshield.

The hedges flew out of the way, bushes torn from their roots and flung into the air before the nose of the flier smashed into them. Broken branches and stray leaves smacked against the windshield, and Ridge nearly caught a twig in the eye. They neared the back wall quickly. He couldn't pull the brake any harder. His feet pressed against the floorboard, and his back was molded to the seat, with Mara molded to *him*.

Whether it was luck or her applying some of her magic, the flier stopped inches from the wall. Mara seemed supremely unconcerned. She slung her legs over the side of the craft and dropped to the ground.

Aware of guards streaming from the walls and out of one of the castle side doors, Ridge unbuckled his harness. His legs were rubbery, but he had to get out, to try to keep Mara from hurting anyone. He glanced toward what remained of the hedges. It wasn't much. Had she done that with her *mind*? Or some gods-given power?

"General Zirkander?" a man asked.

No less than twenty guards formed lines behind the tail of the craft, their rifles pointing toward Mara's chest. A couple of those rifles pointed at the unorthodox flier, too, with its distinct lack of military or royal paint colors. Ridge was surprised nobody was pointing a weapon at him. Nonetheless, he climbed down slowly without making any abrupt movements.

The man who had addressed him wore a guard captain's triple gold sword rank pin on his uniform collar and a brimmed cap with a matching emblem on the front. He alternated frowning at Ridge and at Mara, who wore a vacant expression, as if none of this was of concern and her thoughts were elsewhere.

With a jolt, he realized that might be the exact case. Could she search for Angulus with more than her eyes?

"General?" the captain asked again, focusing his frown on Ridge. "Are you... *you*?"

What was Ridge supposed to say to that? With his missing memories, he wasn't sure he could honestly answer that with a yes. His hesitation seemed to worry the guards, because they shifted their weight and traded uneasy glances.

"More or less," Ridge said and tried a smile. He was, after all, known for his irreverence. "Am I not on the king's appointment calendar?"

"Sir... you're supposed to be dead."

"In a crash in the Ice Blades?"

The captain nodded, glanced at Mara, then looked expectantly at Ridge.

Mara wasn't acknowledging Ridge or any of them. Was he to be left to the introductions, then? What would happen if he blurted out that she was a witch? He wasn't about to walk her to the king's office. But if all of these men attacked her, would she attack back? To greater detriment? What choice did he have? He wasn't going to help her along in this. He'd already been too much assistance, whether intended or not.

"I survived the crash," Ridge said. "This, ah, lady—" was lady the correct term for someone who could tear up hedges with her mind? "—is my—" He tried to say captor, very blunt, very unmistakable. But the word would not come out. It was as if an anchor tied his tongue to the bottom of his mouth.

Maybe the captain had seen those hedges fly from their roots, because the frown he turned toward Mara was extremely suspicious. "Sardelle went looking for you, General. She didn't find you?"

"Who?" Ridge asked.

The captain's gaze lurched back to his face, his eyes widening.

The lieutenant next to him leaned close and whispered, "Maybe it's not him. Maybe it's a dragon. They're supposed to be able to turn into humans."

Even though he'd heard about dragons multiple times now, the statement stunned Ridge so much that he was late defending himself. The notion that they existed still struck him as crazy, and how could one possibly turn into a human? That didn't make sense.

"You are wasting your time with us," Mara told the guards. "There's a dragon coming, a *real* one."

"Sure there is," the captain said, then hissed at a couple of men whose concerned expressions had lurched skyward.

An alarm wailed from somewhere in the city, and Ridge stiffened. That alarm was only sounded when Cofah airships or pirates were spotted on the horizon.

"I told you," Mara said smugly, crossing her arms over her chest. "There's a dragon approaching from the direction of the mountains. Go look. We'll wait." Her gaze flicked toward the side door that the guards had streamed out of, and Ridge had the distinct impression that she would *not* wait, that she would go inside and hunt down Angulus.

Another alarm blared, this time from the direction of the front wall of the castle, its wail echoing that of the one in the city. The captain ordered a few of his men up to the wall to check, but he kept his rifle pointed toward Mara.

"Sir, who did you say this is?" the captained asked.

Mara lifted a hand, and Ridge stepped toward her, worried that she would fling these men aside as she had the hedges. Weaponless, he did not know what he could do, but maybe if he surprised her, he could knock her down and run into the castle to warn the king.

Even as he reached for her, she flicked a finger, and the remaining guards flew backward. Rifles fired, but the bullets did not strike anyone. Ridge tried to grab Mara's wrist, but she spun toward him, and a wave of power sent him stumbling back.

"You owe me your life," she growled at him.

"I owe the king my allegiance," Ridge said. "And wasn't it your *sword* that saved me?"

"You want to help the king? The castle? Maybe you should fly up there and try to stop that dragon."

As soon as her last words came out, a cry came from atop the wall, one of the captain's guards. "There *is* a dragon coming," the man verified. "It's not Phelistoth. It's a huge gold dragon. And it's coming right at us."

Ridge had no idea who Phelistoth was, but fear and worry coursed through his veins at the thought of a dragon attacking the castle.

Go take care of it, Wreltad said. *Better you not be in the castle for this.*

For this? Ridge clenched his fist and tried to grab Mara, but once again, he was pushed back by some invisible power. *The assassination of my king?*

She won't let you stop her, Wreltad warned. Then, he changed tacks. *Isn't a dragon more of a threat to your people than a lone assassin could ever be?*

You tell me. Is it?

Go see for yourself.

"Go deal with it, Zirkander," Mara said, waving her hand toward the flier. If she knew about the conversation Wreltad was having with Ridge, she did not show it. Not that it mattered. Her words were compelling, far more than they should be, and he found himself walking toward the craft. He forgot the threat she represented; all he could think about was the dragon that was coming.

There weren't any other fliers parked on the landing pad behind the castle. The soldiers on the walls had cannons, rocket launchers, and big artillery guns, but he was the only one here who could fly up and confront a dragon face to face. It sounded like a suicide mission—would a dragon be susceptible to bullets or would they bounce off? The various paintings and statues he had seen that immortalized the ancient creatures had always shown them as huge, nearly indestructible.

"To the guns," the captain ordered, shouting to be heard over the wailing alarm. "Enemy dragon incoming."

It all felt surreal, like some strange dream—or nightmare.

Go, Wreltad said again. *Go deal with that dragon and its riders.*

Ridge could not disobey the order. He wasn't even sure he should. He jumped up to the cockpit once again and maneuvered the flier away from the wall. As soon as he turned toward the torn strip of grass ahead of him, he realized the obvious, that he would not have enough room to take off. Without thrusters, he would never achieve lift in time.

I'll see to it that you do, Wreltad said. *Just get out of here.*

Mara was jogging for the side door, completely unopposed since all of the guards had raced up to defend the walls. Ridge realized that Wreltad might be trying to save him from Mara. At the least, he was trying to get Ridge out of the way. Was there *truly* a dragon out there? Or was this some diversion? A witch's illusion?

He worried that he was being fooled and that his king would be killed while he was dithering in the sky, but the same compulsion that had forced him into the cockpit now forced him to take off. Before the craft had crossed half of the courtyard, it lifted into the sky.

The gold dragon came into view as soon as he cleared the wall, a powerful creature flapping massive wings as it soared over the city. The sight stunned him, the first dragon he'd ever seen. Or at least, the first dragon he could *remember* seeing. Either way, it did not look like an illusion. Maybe Wreltad truly had wanted him to fly up to protect his people, not just to get him out of Mara's way.

How Ridge might offer that protection, he did not know. Terror flowed through his limbs as his flier buzzed away from the castle, heading straight toward the dragon. Down in the streets, people screamed. Sirens continued to wail.

Ridge tightened his grip on his flight stick. He didn't know if it was in his power to stop the dragon, but he would do everything he could to try.

* * *

The houses of the capital city sprawled out below them as Bhrava Saruth carried Sardelle and Therrik toward the harbor. They had closed the distance, but had not yet caught sight of Ridge's flier in the air ahead of him. Bhrava Saruth was confident that the alarmed birds in the sky had told him the truth of Ridge's position, which was why they were angling toward Harborgard Castle instead of the flier base.

An alarm wailed in the city, and Sardelle shook her head bleakly, positive that it was for the dragon's approach instead of for the enemy who had apparently flown into town on Ridge's lap.

You're not going to get over that, are you? Jaxi asked. *Will you forgive him if Taddy is controlling him?*

I'll forgive him if the soulblade is controlling him—Sardelle refused to call an ancient sorcerer's soul Taddy—*but I doubt I'm an evolved enough human being to forget it completely.*

I'm not either. I plan to do my best to melt Taddy into a steaming pile of molten ore. If I can't do that, I'll at least mock him horribly while Kasandral cleaves him in half.

Sardelle thought about pointing out that Jaxi and Kasandral had clashed in battle once and that soulblades were strong enough to defy cleaving, even from dragon-slaying swords, but she spotted a flier rising above the castle walls and all thoughts except for one vanished from her mind.

Ridge.

She squinted. Was it him? It had to be—that flier wasn't painted bronze like the military ones.

The one-man craft turned toward them. She reached out as the figure came within range of her senses and confirmed it was Ridge before her eyes could verify that determination. A wave of giddiness washed over her, and she bit her lip.

Ridge! she called into his mind, certain that he was coming to greet them, perhaps to guide them in to the castle so the artillerymen on the walls wouldn't be tempted to fire.

But instead of returning her telepathic greeting with a pleased cry of her own name, alarm flared in Ridge's thoughts. Alarm and *fear*, as if he believed her some enemy out to kill him.

Another voice? he wondered. *Now who? Are you the dragon?*

No, it's me. Sardelle.

How many damned witches are there in the world now? Frustration and confusion swamped him, but he gripped his flight stick with determination, heading straight for Bhrava Saruth, his other hand reaching for his machine gun triggers.

Sardelle closed her eyes, hurt even though logic told her not to be, that he was naturally frustrated if he'd been dealing with Eversong and had never known—couldn't remember—her.

Jaxi? Is there any chance you can fix him? Sardelle was the healer and might have a better chance of that, but she would need to be close enough to touch him to get a feel of how the sorceress—or her soulblade—had affected Ridge's mind. Jaxi had the superior range, so maybe she could see the influence first and discern how to break it.

Jaxi did not answer immediately, and Ridge's flier drew closer quickly. Bhrava Saruth had not altered his course, and they would collide if neither of them diverted.

I don't think so, Jaxi said. *I don't even know what I'm looking for exactly. You know my specialty is burning things into ashes, not fixing brains.*

Yes, sorry. Sardelle kept her disappointment to herself. It had been too much to hope for.

All I can tell is that he's positive this dragon is his enemy. I'm not sure he's put any thought into who the two people riding on his back are.

Bhrava Saruth, Sardelle thought. *Please prepare to shield yourself. He's—*

The first blast of gunfire interrupted her. Ridge's bullets streaked straight toward them. They bounced off an invisible shield, but that did not keep the dragon from making a disgruntled comment.

High priestess, your mate is shooting at me.

Yes, I noticed. I'm sorry. We believe the sorceress is controlling him somehow. Please don't do anything to hurt him.

Ridge fired again, his flier almost upon them now. He veered upward and to the side to avoid crashing into Bhrava Saruth. He looked down at them as he flew past, meeting Sardelle's eyes for a second. The lack of recognition in his face stung her to the core. She had expected something similar to the expression Cas had worn when under Kasandral's control, one that showed her wrestling with herself, her horror at how she was being used. But Ridge didn't know her at all. It was like meeting the eyes of a stranger, a stranger who thought she was the enemy and someone to be killed.

"What are you doing, you idiot?" Therrik shouted as the flier streaked past.

Aren't you supposed to call him General Idiot? Jaxi asked, presumably speaking to both of them.

Not now, Jaxi. Sardelle was in no mood for jokes. *Bhrava Saruth, can you capture him somehow?*

It was a ludicrous request—since the bullets couldn't break through Bhrava Saruth's shields, they should simply continue on to the castle and confront Eversong. But she couldn't help but think that if she had Ridge here beside her, she might be able to get a better look at what they had done to him. Also, he could become an ally instead of another threat to worry about.

The noise of his propeller changed as he banked, coming back toward them. Bhrava Saruth could have outdistanced him, but instead he turned to face the charge. A boom came from below—a cannon firing from the castle wall. They had almost reached the building.

Bhrava Saruth flapped his wings and picked up speed.

Careful, Sardelle added. *It would be best if we didn't destroy the flier.* She didn't want to do anything that would cause those castle guards to grow more agitated and unload all of their weapons at them. Also, she knew how valuable fliers were to the military. This seemed such a foolish way for one to be destroyed.

The dragon's wing beats faltered. *High priestess, will it not fall out of the sky once its rider is gone?*

Yes, you're right. Just capture him without destroying it, please. Jaxi and I will worry about the flier.

Oh? Jaxi asked. *Lucky us.*

Ridge fired again. Sardelle could feel his frustration as his bullets bounced off the dragon's shield. Frustration, bleakness, and surprise, as if he hadn't known this would happen. Didn't he remember his battle with Morishtomaric?

I don't think he remembers much of anything, Jaxi said.

Sardelle tried not to think about what she would do if that turned out to be a permanent situation, if Ridge remembered nothing of her or of them together. Would he be able to fall in love with her again? Without the unique circumstances that had brought them together at the mining outpost?

The flier veered downward, this time heading under Bhrava Saruth's belly. Maybe Ridge thought he could shoot the dragon from below and find a vulnerability?

Bhrava Saruth twisted, moving impossibly fast. His head lashed out, his maw opened, and fear blasted through Sardelle. Even though she knew better, it was hard to see that as anything other than an attack. She couldn't see as well as she would have liked—Bhrava Saruth's body was in the way—but she felt what happened with her other senses. Ridge ducked and tried to veer away as the dragon's head snapped toward him. He almost succeeded, but Bhrava Saruth used magic to aid him, throwing a wall of wind at the nose of the flier. It gave him enough time to grasp Ridge in his mouth.

Ridge's startled cry was like a dagger thrusting into Sardelle's soul, and she felt certain those sharp fangs were hurting him. Bhrava Saruth's neck came up, twisting, and he dropped Ridge atop his shoulder blades, right in front of Therrik. Ridge's eyes bulged with fear, and his hand darted toward his waist, but he had neither a belt nor a weapon there.

Sardelle started to reach past Therrik, wanting to touch Ridge and let him know he was with friends, but Jaxi spoke into her mind.

The flier?

Sardelle cursed, remembering that they were going to keep it from crashing. Without a hand on the stick, it had veered off course and was descending toward the city. Sardelle steadied the stick with her mind, though she found that steering it wasn't as intuitive as she thought. The idea of landing it on the butte on the opposite side of the harbor daunted her—she didn't think she could extend her range that far and continue to control it.

How about that road in front of the castle? Jaxi suggested. *I'll help.*

The curving cobblestone road with sharp bends? At the speed it's flying, it will need a runway, room to slow down.

I will halt it, high priestess, Bhrava Saruth said.

Sardelle should have asked how, but was distracted by Ridge. Sitting astride Bhrava Saruth in front of Therrik, he was looking to either side, like a trapped animal. They were hundreds of feet above the castle. He wouldn't be so foolish as to jump, would he?

"We're not your enemies, Ridge," Sardelle said, resisting the urge to speak the same words into his mind. If he'd forgotten her, he wouldn't find telepathic contact reassuring.

Ridge stared at her without recognition. His brow furrowed, as if he was *trying* to remember.

"Relax, Zirkander," Therrik said. "We're here to kill the sorceress, not you."

Ridge mouthed the word *kill* as he looked at Therrik's chest—his uniform. The concern stamped on his face lessened slightly. Sardelle told herself it didn't matter how that came about and refused to feel stung that it was Therrik that put Ridge at ease, not her.

"Colonel Therrik," Ridge said, reading the nametag. "Do I know you?"

"Looks like she didn't take away his ability to read," Therrik said over his shoulder with an eye roll, "but that's all we can count on." To Ridge, he said, "You and your sarcastic mouth have been annoying me for the last three months."

"That does sound like me." He peered hard at Therrik's face, as if willing himself to remember.

"And this is your woman." Therrik jerked his thumb over his shoulder at Sardelle. "She's almost as much of a pest as you are."

Ridge's mouth dangled open. Sardelle tried a tentative smile, though she doubted that introduction would do anything to warm Ridge's heart toward her.

"But she's a witch," he blurted. "She talked to me in my head." He touched his temple, his expression dazed.

"Yeah, she does that. The dragon does too. Also her sword. It's a bizarre world you live in, Zirkander."

I guess Therrik has gotten over his interest in me, Sardelle thought, while trying not to feel hurt by Ridge's, "she's a witch," condemnation.

That was more like lust than interest in a relationship, and not entirely. You're lucky he didn't drag you to the back of one of those caves. His mind is an uncomfortable place. Controlling himself is probably as hard as controlling the sword.

Sardelle was more interested in figuring out *Ridge's* mind. Now that he was closer, she tried to get a sense of what had been done while ignoring that he had that look on his face again, like he thought jumping might be better than being up here with them.

Figuring out his mind might need to wait for later, Jaxi said. *Bhrava Saruth just removed the power from the flier's crystal. Also, there's smoke coming from the castle.*

I have temporarily halted the energy, Bhrava Saruth said, *so I can land the contraption. The machine parts are too confusing, but I recognize the magic. Watch.*

The flier had stopped moving, and it was floating in the air above the castle. Terrified guards gawked at it. A couple of people shot at it. Far more weapons were aimed toward Bhrava Saruth. He was circling the castle, not going down yet. Despite the threat of a dragon in the skies, several guards were racing from the castle walls and toward the main building. Smoke was, indeed, wafting from windows on one corner of it. That was the end where Angulus's office lay.

Can you put it down, Bhrava Saruth? Sardelle asked. *And then take us down to the courtyard? Therrik and I should be able to get the people to stop shooting at you when we're down there.*

They do not understand that I only wish to help, Bhrava Saruth replied mournfully.

I know. After we deal with the sorceress, I hope we can change their opinions of you.

"How did you end up on a dragon, Colonel?" Ridge asked.

Even though Therrik had insulted him, and Sardelle had smiled at him, he seemed to find it more comforting to focus on his fellow officer than on the woman who loved him.

"Angulus's orders. Sardelle?" Therrik looked back again. "Assuming the sorceress can control Zirkander at any time, maybe we should drop him off somewhere out of the way while we go deal with her. Better not to worry about him switching sides."

Sardelle grimaced at the idea of thrusting Ridge "out of the way," especially when she hadn't even gotten to touch him yet, but she remembered how Apex had gotten in the way during their first battle with Kasandral, an innocent taken down by the merciless sword. She couldn't lose Ridge before she'd had a chance to win him back.

"Probably a good idea," she admitted, meeting Ridge's eyes, his bewildered expression tearing at her.

Bhrava Saruth? she asked.

I've landed the contraption. Look!

Don't look, Jaxi suggested.

The flier was now perched atop one of the castle towers, its propeller still, its wheels half up on the low wall surrounding the roof. The tower guards were fleeing down the stairs, a few pointing backward at it and shouting warnings.

That's, uhm, very good, Bhrava Saruth, Sardelle said. They would have to get him to help remove it later. *Would you mind flying over to that butte? We should set Ridge down over there before coming back to the castle.* She eyed the plumes of smoke wafting out the windows and hoped the delay wouldn't endanger the king.

If we wish to stop the sorceress, there may not be time, high priestess. More dragons are coming.

What?

Her first thought was that even more dragons had found their way out of that cavern of statues, but Bhrava Saruth shared a vision with her. Phelistoth was flying across the ocean, the harbor and capital city in the distance ahead of him. Kaika and Tolemek on his back, along with a third person who lay face down, his legs and hands tied. Sardelle couldn't see his face, but he was clearly a prisoner.

She was about to tell Bhrava Saruth that they shouldn't need to worry about Phelistoth when a second dragon came into view behind them, a gold dragon. She was chasing Phelistoth, gaining on him.

That's Yisharnesh, Bhrava Saruth said, *the female that escaped imprisonment at the same time as I. She threatened to eat me if I didn't let her have the repository of knowledge. I had to fight her to drive her from Iskandia and claim this land as my own. She's not a nice dragon.*

Are you stronger than she is? Sardelle thought Bhrava Saruth and Phelistoth might be a match for the female dragon, but her side had more to lose, since they were over the city, a city she didn't want to see destroyed in some epic dragon battle.

I'm craftier than she is!

That sounds like a no, Jaxi observed.

"Get behind me, Zirkander," Therrik said. "I'm going to need room to use this sword." He jerked his thumb toward Kasandral's hilt. Bhrava Saruth must have also shared the vision of incoming dragons with him.

"How will I do that exactly?" Ridge looked down on either side of Bhrava Saruth's body—they were still circling, well above the castle—then raised his brows toward Therrik's broad form.

"I don't care. Climb over me. Just get out of my way." Therrik leaned forward, flattening his chest to the dragon's back.

"When I woke up," Ridge said, "this wasn't how I imagined my day going."

"Just hurry up, Zirkander. Angulus is down in that castle, probably in trouble because you delivered a witch to his doorstep."

A grimace crossed Ridge's face. He might not remember who Sardelle and Therrik were, but he seemed to realize he had done exactly that. He clambered over Therrik, grabbing him to keep from falling. Sardelle scooted back to give him more room.

Phelistoth needs my assistance, high priestess. He is injured and will be no match for a gold female, and he must worry about those he carries on his back.

Sardelle looked at Therrik's back and at Kasandral. Therrik might be able to assist in a dragon battle, but could she and Ridge do anything? *Am I right in that you would have an easier time fighting without* us *on your back?*

Very likely. I can put you down someplace safe.

Sardelle would have loved to be deposited someplace safe, where she would have time to figure out how to fix Ridge—and to give him a hug, damn it. But smoke was pouring out of more windows of the castle, and when she checked again, one corner of the roof had burst into flame.

Put us down in the courtyard, please. She looked at Therrik's back. Ridge had climbed past him, and he had drawn Kasandral. *We'll deal with the sorceress.*

She was confident that Therrik would attack the sorceress. She was less confident that she could trust Ridge to help. What if Eversong waved her hand and asserted her control over him? Turned him against Sardelle? Battling Cas had been horrifying enough. To think of striking at Ridge—it hurt all the way to her marrow.

"I'm sorry... ma'am," he said, noticing her gaze—it was hard not to when they sat astride Bhrava Saruth's back, facing each other. "I don't remember you."

"I know. I hope Jaxi and I can figure out a way to return your memories to you."

"Who?"

"Ah, my sword. She's a soulblade." Sardelle touched Jaxi's pommel.

He doesn't even remember me? That's disheartening. Jaxi made her pommel flare cherry red for a few seconds.

"Another one?" Ridge looked over his shoulder at Therrik, as if expecting him to explain.

Therrik was busy staring down at the courtyard. Bhrava Saruth was descending now, and more signs of chaos came into view. Most of the soldiers had left the walls and run into the castle. A few remained and turned firearms toward the dragon, firing uselessly, the rounds bouncing off his shields. Phelistoth and the female had yet to come into visual range.

"We met at the Magroth Crystal Mines," Sardelle said, "where you were stationed as the commander."

His brow wrinkled. "That sounds unlikely. I'm a—"

"A pilot, I know. Wolf Squadron. But you punched a diplomat, and General Ort and King Angulus decided to teach you a lesson."

"That sounds more likely."

One of his wry smiles ghosted across his lips, and it tugged at Sardelle's heart. She wanted so much to wrap her arms around him and bury her face in his shoulder, to tell him how much she had missed him and how she had worried that he was gone forever.

Instead, she slipped her hand into her pocket. "I found something that you left behind when you crashed."

His eyebrows rose.

Careful to get a good grip on it—he would never forgive her if she dropped it into the harbor—Sardelle withdrew his wooden dragon charm. "This might be a good time to rub it," she said, tilting her head toward the castle.

Ridge stared at it. For a moment, he didn't react, but then he blinked a few times, moisture filming his eyes. He reached for it, but hesitated, as if not certain he could take it.

Sardelle pressed it into his hand.

"Thank you," he whispered and stroked it with his thumb a few times before meeting her eyes again, his expression faintly sheepish.

"I already rubbed it," she told him, knowing he was self-conscious about his superstitious streak. But it was the truth. She had taken it out of her pocket to hold several times on the trip down from the mountains, not certain if she would ever find him. "We'll need all the luck we can get."

Bhrava Saruth landed on one of the walls, talons grasping the crenellations. *Phelistoth is almost here and Yisharnesh too,* he announced, *so I must go immediately. She has thoughts of razing the city in her mind, because—ah, that is the Cofah emperor they have stolen. How delightful!*

Therrik leaped from Bhrava Saruth's back, running for the nearest set of stairs.

Ridge and Sardelle slid off too.

She paused to rest a hand on Bhrava Saruth's scaled side. *Be careful.*

Most assuredly, high priestess. You be careful too. A wave of power flushed through Sardelle's body.

Judging by the way Ridge staggered back a step, he must have received it too. Sardelle did not know what it was, but she immediately felt strong and invigorated.

A god has blessed you, Bhrava Saruth said and leaped into the air.

"Should I find that alarming?" Ridge asked.

"Not until later, when he asks you to be his worshipper." Sardelle gripped his arm—it was the first time she had presumed to touch him—and nodded toward the stairs Therrik had gone down. "We need to stay with the colonel. That sword is the only weapon that's proven it can damage dragons, and it should be able to hurt a powerful sorceress too."

She thought he might balk at the idea of going to hurt Eversong, but he nodded once and followed right behind her.

"Tell me what I can do to help."

Sardelle wished she knew. Her thoughts of him being used against her or getting into Kasandral's swing path returned to mind, and she almost told him to stay right there. But she wanted him with her, where she could keep an eye on him, and protect him if need be.

Chapter 18

Tolemek could almost feel the female dragon's breath heating his back. Or maybe she had started shooting flames. He didn't want to look back and find out for certain. The dragons had crossed the ocean far more quickly than fliers could, and the Iskandian shoreline had come into view, but he was not certain it represented hope.

Yisharnesh has the power to destroy the city, Phelistoth informed him, and perhaps he spoke to Kaika, too, because she looked at their prisoner. The emperor was tied and gagged between them, though he had regained consciousness hours earlier. Now and then, he looked toward the rear. His expression had grown quite hopeful since the gold dragon had come into view behind them. *She is threatening to do that, after she slays us*, Phelistoth added. *I also sense... I could be mistaken, as it's quite far away, but I believe there may be a second dragon after us.*

What? We never saw another dragon in Dakrovia.

Three came out of that cavern. Bhrava Saruth is here in Iskandia, as is the female, and there was a second male. It's possible Yisharnesh has made him her mate and requested his help in this matter.

Two *enemy* dragons? Tolemek slid his hand down his face. It had taken everything they'd had just to kill one dragon at Galmok Mountain. And that had been with Phelistoth's help. He was in no condition to engage in another battle now. He had poured all of his energy into keeping ahead of Yisharnesh on the flight across the ocean, and he hadn't managed to heal his wounds yet.

Is there anyone in the city who can help? Tolemek asked, though he couldn't imagine who might be there. Sardelle? She couldn't do anything against a dragon.

There is no one I wish to ask for help.

What did *that* mean?

"Ask anyway," Kaika said. "We're not giving our prisoner back, not after all we went through to get him."

The emperor made an indignant noise that was muffled by the gag.

"If we did give him back, would the female take her mate and go away?" Tolemek asked.

So she says, Phelistoth responded. *I do not believe her. I...* Something akin to a groan sounded in Tolemek's mind.

Problem?

Help is coming.

That's good, isn't it? Tolemek wondered what constituted help. A flier squadron?

He peered toward the shoreline, which had resolved itself into the familiar terrain features of the capital, the harbor, the bluff, and the inland sprawl of the city. He *did* see fliers taking off from the bluff.

No, not them. They can do nothing.

Then who?

Phelistoth kept flapping his wings, but he turned slightly, and Harborgard Castle came into view. A gold dragon flew up from its walls, startling Tolemek. He glanced back, half-expecting that their pursuer had leaped ahead of them somehow and had reached the city first. But no, there were two dragons in the sky now in addition to Phelistoth.

"Is that Sardelle's dragon?" Kaika asked.

The emperor twisted his head, which dangled down Phelistoth's back, to look away from *his* dragon and to the one rising from the castle.

"I think it's more that Sardelle is his person, but it must be." Tolemek couldn't imagine a human laying claim to a dragon, but he allowed himself to feel hope. Would the dragon—Bhrava Saruth, that was his name—be a match for this female? From this distance, it was hard to gauge which one was bigger.

Females are always bigger and stronger, Phelistoth said.

"So, we have help, but there's no guarantee that he'll be able to drive her away before the enemy male shows up? Or at all?" Tolemek almost asked if Phelistoth and Bhrava Saruth together would be able to beat the female, but they couldn't ask Phelistoth to go into combat while he carried three people on his back, especially when one was such a valuable prisoner.

Absolutely not. Bhrava Saruth is flaky. I'm surprised he isn't on a mountaintop somewhere, stroking his crystal.

Tolemek did not know whether his irritation with the other dragon had to do with the crystal or just that Bhrava Saruth claimed an Iskandian heritage. If the latter, he would have to get past that if he wanted to live here.

It is I, the god Bhrava Saruth, a new voice resonated in Tolemek's head. *I am here to assist you. Would you like to become my worshippers? I will bless you before we go into glorious battle together!*

Maybe it would be better *if he was on a mountaintop, stroking his crystal,* Phelistoth grumbled.

"What's a blessing?" Kaika asked. "I might worship a dragon for something that would protect me from explosives, bullets, and dragon fire."

A roar came from behind and Tolemek grimaced. The female had closed the gap. Another ten meters, and she could reach out and snap down on Phelistoth's tail as it streamed behind them. Her maw opened and flames shot out. They struck a shield just behind that tail, curling around it, cupping them with fire.

It seems she wants to get us before our help arrives, Phelistoth said.

He had scarcely finished the last word before a wave of power slammed into him. Tolemek felt it, too, but some counter magic kept him from being hurled from the dragon's back. However, the wave *did* affect Phelistoth, knocking him to the side and from his course.

"Can you drop the emperor off at the castle, Phelistoth?" Kaika shouted. "Maybe we can get some pilots and come back up to help. Oh, Tolemek, do you have any more of those bullets?"

"No, but I have some of the dragon-scale eating acid at my lab," he said.

"Castle, then lab, please." Kaika leaned down and kissed one of Phelistoth's scales as he righted himself, recovering from the attack and dipping toward the harbor.

"Are you *flirting* with the dragon?" Tolemek asked.

"Just trying to be a pleasant passenger."

More flames battered the back of Phelistoth's shield as he dove toward the castle. It might have been Tolemek's imagination, but the fire seemed to come closer before that shield deflected it, almost to the tip of Phelistoth's tail. After battling the female back in Dakrovia and flying across the ocean, he must be tired. How many attacks could he withstand?

The flames stopped abruptly as a golden form streaked past. Bhrava Saruth crashed into the female, and they flew sideways, somersaulting through the air. Phelistoth flapped his wings faster and did not look back.

Yisharnesh, Bhrava Saruth cried. *You've come back to me. You wish to dance with me, after all.*

The irritated roar did not sound like an agreement to dance. Tolemek focused on the castle and the courtyard, hoping Bhrava Saruth would either drive the female away or buy them enough time so they could craft weapons that would work. He also couldn't wait to hand the emperor off to Angulus and his guards.

His hope of depositing Salatak in someone else's lap faded when he saw how much smoke was streaming out of the castle. One of the towers had been destroyed, and flames leaped from many of the windows.

"What's going on down there?" Kaika asked.

"I don't know, but it doesn't look good." He thought about saying they should bypass the castle and go straight to his lab, but what would they do with the emperor? Tolemek doubted he could go to some of the scientists on the floor and ask them to babysit a kidnap victim.

A sorceress is causing destruction, Phelistoth announced.

"It can't be Sardelle." She didn't run around, causing havoc. "The Cofah one?" Tolemek asked. "Eversong?"

I do not know the names of all the humans you deal with. Do you still wish me to land?

Several bodies lay in the courtyard. Tolemek pushed his hair out of his face with a frustrated hand swipe. There was nobody down there to whom they could hand off the emperor.

"Yes," Kaika said, with a sigh. "I'll watch him." She looked back to Tolemek. "You'll have to help the dragons by yourself. I lost all of my explosives during our swim anyway."

Tolemek nodded. Yes, if anyone could handle a prisoner, it would be Kaika. If nothing else, she could flirt with him.

Phelistoth swooped down and alighted on one of the few towers that were not in flames. Kaika slid off, grabbing the emperor's arm. He tried to struggle, but they had tied him well, and he could barely stand. Kaika saluted Tolemek—or maybe that salute was for Phelistoth—and tugged her prisoner toward the stairs.

Up in the sky over the harbor, the two gold dragons fought, diving and raking each other with claws. Definitely not dancing. For the moment, the fight appeared even, but what would happen if that second male showed up?

"To the lab, please," Tolemek said.

Phelistoth sprang into the air again, stealing the location from Tolemek's mind and flying into the city.

* * *

Ridge was not an expert on barging into castles to defeat malevolent sorceresses, but felt he should have a weapon. Not that a firearm would be of any use to him if he came face to face with Mara again. He had been powerless to keep from delivering her to the castle. If anything happened to Angulus—or anyone else here—it would be his fault. So far, the halls had been empty, but they were full of smoke, and he dreaded the moment when they stumbled across wounded or dead guards. Given the shouts coming from deeper inside the castle, that moment seemed inevitable.

A door banged somewhere behind him. His hand darted to where his pistol should have been. He clenched his fist, annoyed that he was defenseless. He hated to rely solely on the two people ahead of him in the hall, not when he had no memory of Colonel

Therrik or the person Therrik had introduced as "your woman." Sardelle. His mind boggled at the notion that he might have a relationship with her. With a *witch*.

Even if she had been a normal woman, his mind might have boggled. He was not sure he could imagine them as a couple. Oh, she was beautiful, even in simple travel clothes and with her dark hair pulled back in a braid, but she had a dignified and proper mien. She did not seem like someone who would appreciate his irreverence and immaturity. Still, she *had* brought him his luck charm and had humored him when he rubbed it. He'd been teased about that habit before, by men and women. Sardelle had smiled gently at him, and he'd felt an inexplicable warmth toward her. Her admission to having witch powers had thrown him, but he had to admit there was a faint familiarity about her. He couldn't remember her, but the thought of trusting her seemed... right.

"This way, Sergeant," someone barked from the direction of the door that had banged.

Three castle guards ran up behind them. Ridge's first instinct was to get out of their way, since they seemed to have more of a clue than he did, but he spotted a young private holding a rifle and held up a hand.

"Soldier, I need to borrow your firearm."

Sardelle paused to look back at him. Therrik, who had been throwing open doors and raising his sword to kill the first suspicious person he saw, kept at it, advancing systematically down the hall.

The trio of guards halted and took in his dirt-stained uniform with half of the buttons gone. No, he didn't look like a competent and highly decorated officer, not today. Fortunately, they couldn't see that he was still missing a sock.

"It's General Zirkander," the sergeant said. "Give it to him, Madds."

"But the witch—"

"We'll get you another one."

"Yes, sir." The private handed Ridge the rifle.

"Ammo too." Ridge pointed at the kid's ammo pouch. "You boys seen the king, by chance?"

"No, sir. He was at a secret meeting with the council heads. Only his personal guards know where. We were told to find—" the sergeant's voice lowered to a whisper, "—a witch, sir."

"Yes, we're looking for her, too, if you want to come along." Ridge did not wait to see if they would. Now that he was armed, he hustled to catch up with Therrik.

Sardelle had been waiting for him, and she joined him, jogging at his side, as if that was her usual place. Was it? He wished he knew.

"I didn't know if that would work," he admitted when he caught her glancing at him. He held up the rifle he had been given.

"I've noticed that young men are smitten with you. It's the older ones—your superior officers—who find you less charming."

Huh, she *did* know him. "Have you met General Ort?"

"Oh, yes."

"You sure it's wise to arm him?" Therrik growled, stomping out of a room, his gaze flicking toward Ridge's new firearm. He did not wait for an answer. He proceeded to check the next room.

"Apparently, some lower-ranking officers find me less than charming too," Ridge said.

"You were both colonels when you met. You drugged him and left him beside a road, so you could lead a mission to Cofahre without his help."

Therrik stalked out of the room and headed for a stairwell, one set of steps leading up and another down. Smoke clouded the air on the higher level, but after casting a glower in Ridge's direction, Therrik headed down the stairs descending to a basement level.

"I would say that doesn't sound like something I'd do," Ridge said, "but I might as well be honest with you. The other witch was able to read my mind." He also didn't feel compelled to lie to her or withhold truths the way he had Mara. Even if he still couldn't believe they had the relationship Therrik had bluntly spoken of, he didn't get the sense that she wanted to use or manipulate him. If she wanted anything at all from him, he couldn't see it.

The calm reserve she carried about herself seemed to suggest independence, that she didn't need anything from anyone, woman or man.

"Sorceress, please," Sardelle said.

"Pardon?"

"The term witch is considered derogatory."

"Oh. Sorry. Is it all right to call our enemy a witch?" Ridge stepped ahead of her to follow Therrik down the stairs, having the sense that the person with the rifle should go ahead of the woman with the sword.

"I won't object to that. She's tried to kill both of us before."

An ominous thought, that. Would she try to kill both of them now when they found her?

While Therrik searched another room, Ridge paused at the bottom of the stairs and dug into his pocket. He withdrew his dragon figurine and ran his thumb along the smooth wood. On a whim, he offered it to Sardelle, in case she might like to do the same.

"Rub it for luck?" he whispered.

Sardelle smiled sadly and rested her hand on the charm for a moment, her fingers brushing his palm. A shiver went through him at the touch, as chaste as it was. She withdrew her hand, and the words *too soon* came to mind.

"I usually do it more vigorously," he said.

"Pardon?"

"The rubbing." Ridge flushed and stuck the figurine back in his pocket. What an idiotic time for flirting.

"I see." Her expression was hard to read, almost appearing sad, but for a second, he thought he also glimpsed amusement in there. Could one be amused and sad at the same time? "Does it work better then?" she asked.

"I hope so. I..."

Ridge stopped, pressing a hand against the wall for support, as some foreign sensation came over him. His skull itched from the inside, and it felt as if a thousand ants were crawling around on his brain. He leaned his rifle against the wall, afraid he would drop it.

A hand touched his back and a feeling of reassurance came over him. "Ridge?" Sardelle asked from behind him. "Are you all right?"

It's me, Wreltad spoke into his mind, his voice hard and angry. *She's gone too far. I choose death.*

What? With the ants still crawling all over his brain, Ridge could barely concentrate on the words.

When a soulblade breaks the bond with his handler, he accepts that the magic keeping his eternal essence tied to this world will fade, and he will die. Before that happens, I am giving you back your memories.

"I—" The crawling sensation in his head intensified, more like an attack than a gift, and Ridge grabbed his temples. He stumbled back, dizziness assailing him, numbness afflicting his limbs. He was aware of tumbling and falling against Sardelle, but he couldn't stop himself.

"Ridge?"

Her voice came to him, as if from a great distance, even though he could see her face as she knelt at his side, cradling his head in her arms. He saw her in a snowy landscape, smiling at him from beneath the fur-lined hood of a parka several sizes too large for her. He saw her smiling in a cave, bending over him and tending wounds on his chest. He saw her in the back of a flier, helping him fight against Cofah invaders. He saw her naked, limbs entangled with his at his mother's house. He saw her lying in his arms, telling him he would be a better father than he'd ever imagined. They were together in all of the visions, not always entangled, but always together, always supporting each other.

Tears came to his eyes. Seven gods, how had he forgotten her? How had he not remembered that someone so patient and understanding and sexy and beautiful had come into his life, taking away the loneliness in his life and showing him what it was to have a soul mate?

"Sardelle?" he rasped.

She was stroking his face, her hand tender and caring, the touch of a healer, the touch of someone who loved him. And of someone whom he loved back.

"What happened?" she whispered. "I sensed something. Was it an attack?"

"It was—" He didn't have the words. He slid his arms around her and pulled her down to him, hardly noticing that the edges of the stairs were biting into his back. He buried his face in her neck, inhaling her womanly scent, a scent that was once again familiar. Tears ran down his cheeks, but he didn't care. "I'm sorry," he whispered.

"For what?" Though she seemed surprised, she did not hesitate to return the embrace.

"Forgetting."

There were tears in her own eyes when she lifted her head enough to look at his face. She touched him, not with her fingers this time but with her mind, tentatively, an uncertain whisper. *You remember now?*

Words, tangled up in his emotions, seemed too complicated, too difficult to get out, even in his head, so he kissed her instead. This wasn't the place for it—they needed to find and protect Angulus—but it was faster than explaining, and it was something he hadn't known just how much he missed.

You do remember, she thought. It wasn't a question this time. Her tears mingled with his on their cheeks.

She returned his kiss, all of her emotions coming through a link that he had missed as much as the physical elements of their relationship. He experienced all of the horror she had felt when they'd found his crash site, her fear that he was dead, her refusal to stop looking for him, her longing for a joyous reunion, the ecstasy she'd known when she'd realized he was alive, the betrayal she'd felt when she'd heard he was flying off with another woman, the way it had hurt when he hadn't recognized her. When he'd called her a witch. He stroked her hair, tears of shame falling as he silently apologized for hurting her, for being an obtuse fool. He wished they could spend a month like this, and that he could truly apologize to her, but he knew they couldn't.

"What in all the hells is this?" Therrik demanded, slamming a door shut behind him. "I thought you were here to help me kill that damned sorceress, not hump each other on the king's stairs like horny baboons."

Reluctantly, Ridge pulled his mouth from Sardelle's. He

lamented that his memories of Therrik had returned along with the ones of Sardelle. He could have done without remembering the surly colonel.

Sardelle blushed and drew back, to Ridge's further lament.

"Sir," Ridge told Therrik.

"What?"

"I now remember getting this rank." He waved at the pins on his travel-stained uniform. "I'd appreciate it if you remembered it too." Ridge pushed himself to his feet and offered Sardelle a hand up. "And I believe the rule is that generals can hump whenever and whomever they like. It's in the officers' handbook."

"Not when there are enemies in the castle," Therrik growled. "*Sir.*"

Ridge waved him toward the hallway. "Go then. Find her. You're the one with the sword that can hurt her."

"You're the one whose mind she was poking in. What military secrets did you let her access?" Therrik's scowl deepened. "Does she know what the king's emergency plans are?"

"I don't even know what his plans are." Ridge wanted to sound indignant and say that he'd given the woman nothing, but she—or Wreltad—might *have* sucked military secrets from his mind, and that chilled him. He might not be the highest-ranking officer in the army, or the one most likely to be entrusted with confidences, but he knew enough to endanger his whole country.

Without letting go of Sardelle's hand—he had no wish to ever do that again—he picked up his borrowed rifle. He didn't know why he bothered. He was now more certain than ever that it would be useless against Mara. Eversong. Tarshalyn. Gods, he remembered her now, in all of her incarnations, including the one with the dark hair and the ancient armor. That bitch had tried to fry him with a fireball. And he'd *slept* with her. He tripped over a carpet runner. Damn it. She'd drugged him and it hadn't been his fault, but still. His blood boiled at the memory of how easily he had been led along—and led into that barn. And Sardelle would know, too, if she didn't already.

He gave her an anguished look as they walked side by side, following Therrik deeper into the castle. Even if it hadn't been his fault, how could that not hurt her? Hells, he'd been thinking of sleeping with Mayford's granddaughter, too, after knowing her for all of ten minutes. Did it matter that he hadn't been aware of Sardelle's existence? Yes, of course, but he still felt chagrined for being so... licentious. That was the term, wasn't it?

I was thinking slutty, but if you prefer to make a vocabulary word out of it, by all means.

Jaxi. Ridge would have admitted to missing her if he hadn't felt so guilty. She probably knew all his thoughts.

Yes, I see you've not only been rutting with other women, but you've been bonding with other swords.

He snorted, his humor piqued despite his morose thoughts. She sounded more affronted by his relationship with Wreltad.

Sardelle raised her eyebrows.

"Jaxi is reestablishing her relationship with me," he said, keeping his voice down, aware of Therrik alternately checking rooms and glaring back at him.

"She missed you." Sardelle squeezed his hand. "I did too." Maybe she hadn't dipped into his thoughts yet and gotten the details about his trailside dalliances.

Something to worry about later. After they found Angulus. He shuddered to think what Wreltad had meant with his comment that Mara—Eversong had gone too far. It occurred to him that Wreltad must have known exactly who was coming on that dragon, and he must have also known that Ridge wouldn't be able to damage the creature. Had he known that Sardelle wouldn't allow it to damage *him*? He must have suspected. Maybe he truly had wanted to get him out of the way to protect him. Ridge wished that solicitude had extended to Angulus.

Sardelle wrinkled her nose. Even though the smoke had been thicker on the level above, it lingered here, as well, and the air was hot. In places, the wood-paneled walls were charred.

Someone screamed in the distance, and Therrik paused, looking back toward the stairs. But he frowned down at his sword, shook his head, and continued deeper into the castle. That wasn't just any sword, Ridge realized. With his memories back, he recognized Kasandral. It glowed a faint green as Therrik stalked the corridors. However had he and Sardelle traveled together without it luring him into attacking her?

Where is he, my Iskandian hero? a woman's voice sounded in Ridge's head. Eversong.

He jumped before realizing she wasn't with them in the passage. She could be talking to him from anywhere in the castle.

He glanced at Sardelle, wondering if she could hear Eversong communicating with him. She returned his look, raising her eyebrows in inquiry. She knew him well enough to know something had happened, but she didn't seem to know what. He shook his head, hoping that ignoring the sorceress would cause her to leave him be.

Something stirred in Ridge's mind. It didn't hurt—it almost felt like an itch inside his skull—but it wasn't friendly. He could tell this was Eversong. He should repel her, but he didn't know how. She rifled through his thoughts, hunting for information on Angulus's whereabouts. As if Ridge knew where the king hid when invaders came. In a tower? In the basement? In a privy?

I checked there, she said dryly.

He found it reassuring that Eversong hadn't found Angulus yet, but wondered if Therrik had a clue as to where he was going. The wood paneling gave way to old stone walls and doors leading to storage areas. Ridge had never been in the basement of the castle, but thought it strange that none of the guards he'd seen streaming off the walls and inside were about. Despite his invitation, the three who had given him the rifle had chosen a different intersection.

I gave them much to keep them occupied upstairs, Eversong said.

The ground shivered as a thunderous crack came from another part of the castle. Distant screams of fear mingled with shouts of rage. A crash followed—walls coming down?

Ridge eyed the arched stone ceiling above them. If Eversong knew where he was, how simple would it be for her to drop the ceiling on their heads? Maybe he shouldn't think about that and give her ideas. He wondered if Wreltad was fighting her at all, or if she had thumped him with her mind and left him stuck in the ground somewhere.

Between one step and the next, her presence in his mind disappeared. Sardelle had drawn Jaxi, and her blade glowed a silvery blue.

"Sorry," she whispered. "I didn't realize she was contacting you."

Therrik whirled around. "What?" He speared Ridge with his gaze.

"Not by my choice," Ridge said.

"I told you she might continue to control him," Therrik told Sardelle, ignoring Ridge.

"She's not controlling him, and I'll keep her from contacting him again." Sardelle lifted her sword. "Jaxi will do her best to obscure our location from her."

It was strange having them communicate with each other instead of through him, as they had in the past. Ridge eyed Kasandral—the blade's glow had grown more pronounced when Therrik turned to face Sardelle and Jaxi—and stepped forward to stand between them, just in case.

Therrik sneered, turned his back, and continued down the hallway. He walked around a corner, disappearing from sight for a moment.

"We're fine," Sardelle whispered. "We have an understanding."

"That your sword is bigger than his?" Ridge asked, not bothering to whisper.

More that her dragon is bigger than his, Jaxi said, smirking into his mind.

Sardelle smiled and shook her head. *I'll explain the dragon later.*

He touched her on the back, comforted by how she always knew what he was thinking, whether she was using her telepathic skills or not. How lonely it had been in his head without her presence. He hadn't even known to miss it.

You missed my presence, too, right? Jaxi asked.

Of course. Ridge walked around the corner with Sardelle.

Therrik had not continued far. He stood before an ornate wooden door with grapevines carved along the edges. He pushed it open, stared inside for a long second, then held up his hand as

Sardelle approached, a warning not to come closer.

"There's nothing you can do for them," he said, reaching for the doorknob.

She frowned and blocked his hand so she could look inside. Her entire body slumped, as if with great weariness. Or sadness.

Dread settled in Ridge's stomach as he leaned around the doorjamb. A meeting room lay inside, a massive oak table in the center, with men and women occupying chairs around it, their bodies flopped forward, blood leaked from their noses, their eyes closed or glassy and open in death. They were *all* dead. As were at least ten guards stationed around the room, now toppled to the floor, only a couple having drawn pistols or swords before dying in the same manner as the others.

Ridge turned away, leaning against the wall, his eyes burning, his stomach twisting. He had caused this. *He* had brought Eversong here.

"You're right," Sardelle whispered. "It's too late. They died too quickly for a healer to help."

"The witch did this?" Therrik snarled.

"It was done with magic, yes."

"That's Lord Arton," Therrik said, pointing. "And Lady Morishan."

Ridge leaned back in for another look and realized that he also recognized some of the faces, mostly from newspaper articles. "It's the whole council, isn't it?" he said numbly. "The leaders of every county. I'd forgotten they would be here this week. I…"

He stared at the bodies until his eyes burned, his throat tight with regret and recrimination. *Had* he forgotten? Or had he known they would be here for this meeting? Had the information been in his head, in the part he couldn't access but that Eversong and Wreltad could? He sagged against the wall, the cold stone harsh against his shoulder. How had he allowed himself to be used so? Because they had saved his life? His life wasn't worth the lives of all of the country's government leaders. Who would they find dead next? Angulus? If Eversong killed him, who would be left to rule Iskandia?

Sardelle clasped his hand.

He resisted the urge to flinch away. He did not deserve to be comforted, but he could not bring himself to pull away from her. There had been too much *away* already.

Therrik shut the door. "This is frustrating."

"An understatement," Ridge whispered.

"I was tracking her with the sword, and she was down here, I was sure of it." Therrik frowned at Kasandral, the blade still glowing a pale green.

"She was clearly here," Sardelle said quietly.

"Yes, that's what the sword thought."

"I didn't realize it had the ability to track a specific person. In the past, it's been distracted by the closest magical target." Sardelle touched her chest.

Distracted by, Jaxi said. *Obsessed with...*

"I'm a tracker. I told it to track what I wanted it to track if it didn't want to be thrown in a chasm. It was doing a good job, but now..." Therrik's gaze shifted toward one wall, then the floor, and then toward the other wall. "Over there." He waved at the wall opposite the door. "She's still down in this basement level, I think, but she's all the way on the other side of the castle. Give me a second. This thing is—gods, that's creepy. It's communicating with me." He stared down at the sword, looking more like a man thinking of hurling it across the harbor than someone *communicating*.

Another great crash came from somewhere above. "Sounds like the castle is coming down all around us," Ridge said.

"It is," Sardelle said. "The dragons are fighting."

"*Here?*"

"I guess they got tired of doing it in the air." She frowned toward the ceiling, her eyes growing distant, and a worried crease formed between her eyebrows. "It's not going well for Bhrava Saruth," she whispered.

Ridge reached up and touched her face, wanting to smooth that worry away. She blinked and looked at him. He pulled his hand away. He had probably interrupted her concentration. She might not want him fondling her face right now, anyway. They had Angulus to find and he was... tainted. In more ways than one.

"This way." Therrik gave them a dark look. "I think she knows we're after her and is trying misdirection. Either that or Angulus is the one doing the misdirection, leading her around the castle the same way *you* fly." His gaze pierced Ridge as he stalked past, heading back toward the last intersection they had passed.

"How is that?" Ridge asked.

"Like you're drunk, deranged, and scratching your butt at the same time."

Another time, Ridge might have defended himself, but another crash came from somewhere above, and dust trickled down from the ceiling. Therrik broke into a run, with Sardelle following right behind. Ridge raced after them, his grip tight on his borrowed rifle.

"Can you tell if Angulus is still alive?" Therrik asked over his shoulder.

"I've been trying, but she's been dampening my senses," Sardelle said. "I haven't been able to detect anyone down here."

"Try again," Therrik ordered.

"Just follow your sword," Ridge growled, bristling at his presumptuousness. Even the king didn't give Sardelle orders.

Sardelle was following nonetheless. She had that familiar, distracted look in her eyes, as she called upon her magic, even as they followed Therrik up a set of stairs and into a hall on the ground floor.

"A flier squadron is in the air," Sardelle said. "They're on their way to join the dragon battle."

Ridge looked toward a window, but there was nothing to see out of it yet.

"The *dragons* aren't my concern right now," Therrik growled.

"I can't sense Angulus, but others have seen him alive recently," she said. "He was by himself, yelling for them to get out of the castle, to find safety."

"Why wasn't *he* doing that?" Ridge asked.

"And where were his guards?" Therrik added.

Dead on the floor of that meeting room, Ridge thought. He didn't say it, didn't even want to think about it. Later, if they survived this, he could mourn those deaths—and his role in bringing them about.

Therrik turned left down a wide hallway, only to stop abruptly. The way ahead was collapsed, sunlight streaming in through the missing roof. A dark shadow flew past, gone as quickly as it had appeared. One of the dragons?

"It's a damned maze." Therrik cursed and ran back into the first hall, searching for another way around. "She could already have him."

Ridge wished he could do something more than running behind Therrik. He felt so useless. But he couldn't imagine what that something might be. A flier wouldn't help here, and the only one nearby was parked on a tower in the courtyard.

Kasandral started glowing more brightly, and Therrik picked up his pace. They ran through the garden in the interior courtyard. Ridge gaped at the destruction around them. An entire wing of the castle had been flattened. Barely glancing in that direction, Therrik led them through a door on the far side. He charged down a set of stairs, the treads littered with rubble. He leaped the stones, barely slowing. They were under the kitchens, and they passed storage rooms full of barrels and crates that offered dozens of hiding places. Therrik kept going. He seemed positive about his destination now.

A great boom came from ahead, and Therrik faltered for the first time. Ridge had to grab the wall to keep from falling. Sardelle tumbled against him and he caught her, supporting her to keep her upright.

"That wasn't the dragons," she said, her voice barely audible. Somewhere up ahead, it sounded like a building was collapsing.

"A bomb," Ridge guessed. Would Eversong have used a bomb? Or was Captain Kaika up there with the fliers, hurling explosives at the dragons? He clenched his fist. Finding Angulus had to be the priority, but he felt he should be up there, commanding that squadron.

A cloud of dust rolled down the hall toward them. Therrik swatted at it with Kasandral and ran into it. Most of the wall lamps had gone out or fallen to the floor, but Ridge could see by the unearthly green glow of that sword. The tiny group rounded a corner, entering a storage room so large that one might have kept a dragon in it. The back half had crumbled, a wall and several ceiling arches collapsing. Therrik stopped several feet from the pile, the glow of the sword playing across it. It rose higher than his head, and the level above was visible through the massive hole in the ceiling.

Ridge waited near the hallway, expecting Therrik to turn again to look for another way around. Then a rock shifted in the pile. More dust wafted up, mingling with what already lingered in the air. Ridge dabbed at his watering eyes and resisted the urge to cough.

Sardelle backed away from the sprawling debris pile. She put her hand on Ridge's chest, taking him with her, toward the wall most distant from the rocks. He wanted to resist—he wasn't some coward to hide in the corner—but the concern on her face warned him to go with her. She had power he did not, and if she was worried about what was coming out of that rock pile, what could he and his little rifle do?

Therrik shouted, startling Ridge, and ran to the rubble, slashing downward with Kasandral.

Ridge expected him to hit the rocks with a clang that would break the blade. Instead, the sword sank in, cleaving a huge slab from the ceiling in half. From higher in the pile, rocks tumbled out of place, clattering down the slope toward Therrik.

He jumped back, just avoiding one that nearly slammed onto his foot. Other rocks stopped before tumbling off the pile, coincidentally—or not—covering the slab he had cut into with the sword. Protecting what lay beneath it?

"She shouldn't be able to harm him directly," Sardelle said, "not while he holds Kasandral, but—"

A boulder the size of a man's torso flew from the pile. It would have struck Therrik in the head had he not ducked quickly enough, moving with amazing speed for a big man. The boulder slammed into the wall beside Sardelle with enough force to shake it and the floor below.

"She can harm him indirectly," Sardelle finished.

"Good to know." Therrik grunted and danced away from another large boulder that flew at him. Had it struck, the speed would have broken bones—maybe his skull.

This one's trajectory took it into the ceiling, where it thudded loudly, then toppled to the ground ten feet from Sardelle. She might not be as much of a target as Therrik, but just being a spectator here could get them killed. Ridge grabbed her hand, thinking to pull her into the hallway for protection as more rocks flew through the air, but she shook her head and rooted her feet.

"I have to help him. Therrik, try again. I'll do my best to shield you."

Therrik did not hesitate. He charged toward the rubble mountain, again aiming for that broken slab. As he cut downward, another boulder sprang from the back of the pile, spinning as it zipped toward his head. He started to duck, aborting his attack, but it bounced off an invisible barrier several feet in front of Therrik. He stared as a few more rocks crashed into the barrier, then nodded and hefted his sword.

Sardelle stood without moving, her gaze focused on him.

A snapping noise sounded in the ceiling above her.

Ridge grabbed her hand again, this time pulling too hard for her to resist. He yanked her off her feet and dragged her toward the hallway. More snaps came from the ceiling, and rocks tumbled down where she had been standing. Therrik yelled as a head-sized rock slammed into his shoulder, knocking the sword from his hands. With Sardelle distracted, the barrier around him had disappeared.

Therrik lunged for the sword right away, but his fingers never reached it. He was lifted from his feet, as if caught in a tsunami, and hurled all the way to the back of the room. He struck so hard that Ridge was certain he would be knocked out, if not killed outright.

Before he consciously knew what he was doing, Ridge sprinted across the chamber and dove for Kasandral. He was terrified it might turn Sardelle into an enemy to him, but he prayed he could keep it focused on Eversong.

As he landed, an angry force tightened around his windpipe, invisible fingers wrapping around his neck. A vision of his head being torn off flashed into his mind, but his hand wrapped around the sword hilt first. It flared to life, pale green light bathing the rubble pile. The force around Ridge's throat disappeared, and he scrambled to his feet, the weapon in hand.

Rage and hunger filled his mind, emotions that did not originate with him. They came from the sword, along with instructions that beckoned him to attack the rock pile. Without hesitating, he thrust the weapon into the boulders, thinking he might skewer the sorceress buried within, the sorceress who had killed everyone in that room. The point dove in as if thrusting into a pile of sand instead of a pile of solid rock.

Don't make this choice, Eversong's voice spoke into his head. *I will kill you.*

Ridge hoped that was a bluff, that Kasandral would protect him, that she wouldn't be able to touch him or manipulate him. Still, afraid some mental attack was forthcoming, he stabbed faster, harder. It did not seem honorable, thrusting a sword at a wounded foe, but this foe could hurl rocks—and people—even while buried. A hunger coursed through him, again seeming to come from the sword, and he didn't know if he could have stopped if he had wanted to.

After one of his strikes, a muffled gasp came from somewhere under the rocks. Several boulders lifted from the back of the pile, and Ridge ducked. They flew toward him, but struck a barrier and bounced off before coming close. Sardelle stepped up beside him, her face caked with dust, but her eyes clear and bright. An angry feeling flowed up his arms from the blade, and for a second, Ridge struggled to see her as an ally.

"Keep going," she said. "I *will* protect you." She glared at the rubble, then spread her hands toward it, fingers splayed, intense concentration burning in her eyes.

She is *an ally*, Ridge told the sword, though he had no idea if it understood. With will as much as with muscle, he thrust the blade into the pile, aiming for the spot where the gasp had originated.

The entire pile trembled, as if an earthquake were striking. Even the floor shook. Would all of those boulders fly at him at once? Could Sardelle's shield stop that?

She growled deep in her throat, her eyes squinted shut as she made a tamping motion with her hands. Air swirled past Ridge, as if a breeze blew through the room, and the rocks settled.

Ridge thrust into them again. For a moment, nothing happened, and he thought Sardelle had won some victory. Then wind blew past Ridge again, this time more like a hurricane than a breeze. Strangely, it did not affect him, but Sardelle was flung backward, just as Therrik had been. Ridge reached for her, but was too late. She slammed into the wall and crumpled to the ground next to Therrik.

Therrik had risen to his hands and knees, but another wave of energy pushed him back against the wall. He might as well have been shackled there.

Sardelle surprised him by rising to her feet. She stared at the open area above the rubble pile where a ceiling had once been. Her eyes narrowed and a gust of wind swirled through the room. Dust and fine bits of rock swirled through the air, pelting everyone's skin. Then the force seemed to sharpen and focus. It struck the ceiling on the floor above theirs. Groans and snaps sounded, and more and more rocks tumbled down onto the pile.

Ridge staggered back, pulling the sword out and shielding his eyes from flying shards of rock. As he did so, he glimpsed blood on the tip of the glowing blade.

"She's injured," he said, scarcely hearing his own voice over the roar of falling rock.

Squinting, he stumbled back toward the pile. Maybe dropping more stone on her head would finish her off, but they couldn't assume that. Only the sword had proven that it could hurt her.

He drew back his arm for a mighty thrust when a new attack came. Not rocks or wind this time. A torrent of images cascaded into his mind. He was aware of Sardelle gasping behind him, but the images felt like daggers scraping across his brain, and he couldn't do anything to help her. He fell to his knees in front of the settling rocks, grit and stone jabbing through his trousers. He barely noticed. His mind was locked in the past, in the barn that Mara had lured him into, to the hay bales that she had pushed him against. He saw what he'd forgotten from that night, them tearing off their clothes and having sex, her whispering into his ear, promising to make him king. Even though the engagement had been lust-filled rather than love-filled, it made him question what he was doing. Was he truly trying to thrust a sword into the woman he had slept with? What kind of monster was he?

His determination to kill her wavered, the sword drooping in his hands. Rocks shifted and tumbled away from the spot where he had been stabbing. A blood-streaked and dust-caked hand reached up from the pile.

"Ridge," Sardelle whispered from behind him. "You have to finish it. She'll kill us all if you don't."

"I..." More images rushed into his mind of him entwined with Mara, of kisses shared, of thrusts of desire met with eagerness.

"Angulus is buried under there too," Sardelle said stepping up behind him. "He arranged this trap, risked his own life to bury her under the rocks, in an attempt to kill her, to protect the castle and this country. He's still alive, but he won't be if she crawls out of there. Remember, she killed all of the council leaders already. She doesn't care about you. Even if she did—"

Ridge swallowed. "I know." She was manipulating him, as she had that night. None of this was real.

Kasandral thrummed in his hands, almost pulsing with indignation. Indignation and rage. It wanted him to kill the sorceress. Images of the dead councilmen leaped into his head, mixing with the scenes of his night with Mara. Through the confusion, Ridge managed to keep enough of his wherewithal to thrust the sword into the rocks one more time.

A scream sounded, as the blade cut into more than stone this time.

Horrified, his mind still full of images of him and Mara naked on the hay, Ridge dropped the weapon and stumbled back. As soon as Kasandral tumbled from his grip, he knew he had made a mistake. He reached for it, but it was too late. The images disappeared from his mind at the same time as an invisible force struck him. As it had with the others, it hurled him all the way across the chamber.

The landing drove all of the air from his lungs as he slid down the wall to the floor. His body wouldn't work, and he couldn't breathe or even think about getting up. He couldn't do anything except feel pain and look helplessly toward the rubble he'd been flung away from.

Sardelle was still there, on one knee, also having suffered some attack. She glanced at the sword, its glow dim now that nobody held it, but she didn't reach for it, *couldn't* reach for it.

More rocks sloughed away from the pile. The hand that had reached out turned into a head, and then Mara's dusty upper body rose into sight. Only it wasn't Mara, not the Mara he had known. Her skin and hair were darker under the dust. This was the woman from the flying fortress, the woman who had tried to kill him and his squadron. She lifted a sword that Ridge hadn't seen since that day. Wreltad. The blade wasn't glowing, not the way Kasandral's was, and he remembered Wreltad's parting words, that he would choose death over continuing to work with her. Did she know yet? Did she care?

Blood trickled from Eversong's mouth and saturated the front of her shirt, but she found the strength to attack Sardelle. Ridge couldn't *see* that attack, but Sardelle's response was unmistakable. She dropped onto her back, clutching at her throat. She tried to gasp for air, but only a gurgling sound came out.

Ridge tried to make his body respond, wanting nothing more than to run back over there and pick up the sword. But his numb limbs would not heed his command. Eversong looked over at him, a triumphant sneer on her lips.

Therrik was the one to climb to his feet and sprint out of the shadows for the blade. Eversong saw him and lifted an arm, but too late. His hands wrapped around Kasandral's hilt, and with impossible speed, he lunged for her. He swept the blade at her so quickly, Ridge barely registered the movement. It was only when her head tumbled off, cleanly removed from her neck, that he realized what had happened. The soulblade fell from her fingers, clanked down the rubble pile, and lay still.

Ridge tore his gaze away from it and avoided looking at the decapitated body. He felt cowardly, but he was relieved that Therrik had been the one to kill her. Even knowing all he knew about her now, he doubted he could have done it. He looked toward Sardelle, his heart breaking at seeing her on the floor, though at least she had lowered her hand from her throat and no longer seemed to be in pain. He longed to go to her and engulf her in a hug.

"Seven gods, Zirkander," Therrik panted, wiping the sword off on his trousers. "You screwed that witch *too*?"

Silence filled the room after that statement. At first, Ridge could only look at him in confusion, but from the way Therrik and Sardelle stared at him, he realized they knew every detail. Eversong hadn't just shared those images with him. She had flung them out into the room. They had been meant to manipulate him. He wasn't sure why they'd been foisted on the others. To make them hate him? To not trust him? To hurt Sardelle?

He winced and forced himself to meet Sardelle's gaze. Even though that night hadn't been his choice, and he believed she would understand, that didn't keep the sorrow and hurt from her eyes now. He wanted to slither under that rubble pile and disappear. Sardelle blinked several times and looked away from him.

"The king is still alive under here," she said, a slight quaver to her voice. She wiped her eyes and swallowed before continuing. "I suggest we figure out how to get him out."

A distant crash came from somewhere above, the walls shivering in response. Ridge forced his sore body into motion and pushed himself to his feet. If more of the castle fell atop this room, they might never find Angulus.

Chapter 19

Sweat ran down Sardelle's spine as she lifted rock after rock off the pile, forming cushions of air under them to levitate them across the chamber. After the battle, her entire body ached, though not as much as she would have expected. She almost felt invigorated and wondered if she had Bhrava Saruth's so-called blessing to thank. Still, after that mental battle, she wanted nothing more than to collapse somewhere and relax—and to forget the images Eversong had stuck into her head. She'd seen enough of Ridge's thoughts earlier to know Eversong had drugged him to get him in that barn, but that didn't make those images any less vivid.

Ridge dragged rocks away by hand, his face hard to read. He hadn't spoken since Therrik blurted that accusation. Now and then, he paused to rub his back and watch the boulder-sized slabs drifting past, but he avoided Sardelle's gaze when she looked at him. She didn't blame him for what had happened, and had been warned earlier when she had gotten the gist from Ridge's surface thoughts, but it was still hard to accept with any degree of equanimity, especially when the damned woman had shared everything in vivid detail.

Therrik hadn't put away Kasandral yet. He stood in a wide-legged stance, breathing heavily and glaring down at Eversong's soulblade. He kept mumbling under his breath. The control words for Kasandral? Sardelle did not like the way the dragon-slaying sword continued to glow green. Was its thirst still not quenched? Was it trying to convince Therrik to attack Sardelle too? Or maybe it wanted to find a way up to the courtyard—what remained of it—to attack the dragons?

She could feel Bhrava Saruth fighting the female up there. A flier squadron was also in the air, trying to find a way to help. She worried the pilots would do more harm than good, confusing friendly dragons for enemies. As soon as she could, she had to go help, if only by telling whoever led that team to get out of the dragons' way. But for now, her senses told her that Angulus still lived under the rocks at the back of the pile, as impossible as that seemed. She couldn't leave until they recovered him.

"Will the sword do anything?" Therrik asked, sneering slightly as another boulder floated by. He would probably never get used to having magical allies.

"The soulblade?" Sardelle wiped her damp brow. "Possibly, yes. They've been known to finish battles when their handlers have died, though eventually they lose their power and go dormant without a link to another sorcerer."

Jaxi, can you tell if Wreltad is making sinister plans toward us?

Taddy isn't talking to me. Perhaps because I call him Taddy. He prefers to talk to your soul snozzle.

Ridge?

"He won't attack us," Ridge said quietly. "He could have helped Eversong there in the end, but he didn't."

"Why not?" Therrik prodded the soulblade with Kasandral. Light flashed around both swords, the air snapping and hissing angrily, like when droplets of water were flung into a hot pan. Therrik stumbled back. He switched Kasandral to his other hand and shook out the right. "It's definitely not dormant," he said.

"No, that would take some time." Manipulating the air, Sardelle moved another rock off the top and floated it into her pile. Her head was starting to hurt from the effort of using so much power. Angulus was at the far rear of the rockfall. It almost seemed like he was in the wall. "Soulblades had to last long enough to be transferred to new handlers. It was often weeks or months before someone acceptable was chosen."

Sardelle smiled, thinking of the ceremony where she had received Jaxi. She had been so proud to earn a soulblade at such a young age. The feeling of pride had faltered slightly with Jaxi's first sarcastic comment, it being quite the opposite of what Sardelle had expected from a wise and venerable soul embedded in a sword.

I wasn't that tickled with the match at first, either, as you'll recall. You had ink on your fingers and smelled of parchment. I was sure I'd spend your entire life being used as a paperweight on a library table and that you'd never take me out to smite things.

That would have been a tragedy. Sardelle glanced at Eversong's body.

Yes.

"Should I try to destroy it?" Therrik looked like he wanted to prod the soulblade again, or perhaps lift Kasandral overhead and cleave it in half. "It's Cofah, right?"

"Don't," Ridge said. "He was willing to accept death over continuing to help her any further. That's what he said when he gave me my memories back."

Therrik curled a skeptical lip.

Sardelle wasn't skeptical, but she was surprised, even though she had known something unusual had happened when Ridge's memories suddenly returned. "Why would he have chosen you over his handler?"

"He had a sense of honor. She didn't." Ridge shrugged.

Also, he likes your soul snozzle, Jaxi added. *Rather more, I gather, than he liked Eversong. If Ridge wants a soulblade, Wreltad would probably accept him as a handler.*

Sardelle gaped. Had that ever even been done? A soublade linking to someone without dragon blood?

I don't know, but I think it could work. A soul is a soul.

Ridge had been pushing rocks aside, but he paused to look over at them, a puzzled expression on his face. Had Jaxi shared her words with him too?

Yes, Jaxi said.

Ridge's gaze shifted toward the dusty sword on the ground. "Doesn't Tylie need a soulblade?"

"Uh." Sardelle *had* wanted to get her one to help with her teaching, but a Cofah soulblade? It was what Phelistoth had wanted, but that wasn't necessarily a good thing. She had hoped to find an Iskandian one for Tylie, one that would tie her to this continent rather than tempting her away. Even if Wreltad agreed to stay here and join with Tylie, if he had come from the same era as Eversong, he might have as much strength and raw power as she had possessed. Sardelle shuddered at the idea of such a weapon in a teenager's hands.

I would have to meet her first, a subdued male voice spoke into her head.

Startled, Sardelle dropped the rock she had been moving. It landed with a noisy clunk in the middle of the chamber, and Therrik and Ridge looked at her.

"Sorry," she said. "I was thinking about the answer to Ridge's question."

"Well, don't think when one of those boulders is over my head," Therrik grumbled.

A distant, muffled shout reached her ears. Sardelle jumped. Angulus.

She returned her attention to moving the rocks.

"Wreltad?" Ridge asked, looking to the blade again. "Could you help with these rocks?"

Whatever his answer was, he gave it only to Ridge, who nodded and stepped back from the pile. He waved for Sardelle and Therrik to do the same, and they retreated to the hallway.

With a great grinding of rock and shifting of dust, half of the rubble pile lifted up and moved across the chamber. Sardelle stared in awe. She wouldn't have been surprised if a dragon could do that, but a soulblade that had once been human?

A disdainful sniff sounded in Sardelle's mind.

Envious, Jaxi?

No. I could move a mountain of rubble too.

Oh?

Just not all at once.

The rocks settled on the far side of the chamber. As the second half of the pile rose, Sardelle realized Wreltad could have done this at any point when Therrik and Ridge had been hacking at Eversong through the stones. He could also have protected her when they first fell. Maybe Ridge was right and he truly had abandoned his handler.

After the rocks had been moved, Sardelle squinted into the settling dust. At first, she did not see anyone on the ground or against the wall, as her senses had promised her there would be. Then a man sneezed.

"Sire?" Therrik walked toward an old stone fireplace in the corner, the hearth half hidden by smashed crates.

Another sneeze answered him. A boot appeared from the dim recesses of the hearth, kicking away some of the broken crates. Therrik and Ridge rushed forward and shoved away the rest of the debris.

King Angulus, wearing his dark robes of office and even his crown, crawled out from the old firebox. Dust coated his clothing and his hair, and the crown had fresh dents in it. In addition to his formal regalia, he clenched a pistol in one hand and wore a bandolier with explosives in it.

"Did you do this, Sire?" Ridge waved at the rubble.

"Yes. Don't tell Kaika that I trapped myself along with our invader." Angulus scowled at Therrik and Ridge. "That's an order."

Therrik's eyebrows drew together in confusion. For the first time that day, he looked less enlightened than Ridge. Apparently, gossip of that relationship hadn't made it to Magroth.

"Did I defeat her by chance?" Angulus pointed at Eversong's body, but then frowned, looked for the head, and found it against the wall. "Never mind. Unless the rocks knocked her head off, I see I did not. My ego must remain small, I fear. Who decapitated her?"

Therrik lifted his chin, his eyes gleaming with the hope of some praise from his monarch.

"She was buried in the rubble when we got here, Sire," Sardelle explained, "but still had power left to use on us. It was a close battle. Therrik was the one who killed her."

She watched Therrik warily, certain he didn't want praise from *her*. How would he react? Therrik's gaze flickered toward her, but not for long. He remained intent on his king.

"I see." Angulus shuffled forward, sloughing stone dust from his clothing, and patted Therrik on the shoulder. "Good work, Colonel."

Therrik nodded curtly, as if the job had been simple and the praise didn't mean nearly as much as it did. "Thank you, Sire."

Angulus glowered at the body. "That *witch* killed several of my guards and one of my pages." His tone switched from anger to anguish as he added, "The girl was twelve. She was just trying to get out of the way."

Standing this close to him, Sardelle felt that anguish wrapping around Angulus, caught a glimpse of his surface thoughts, of a fireball annihilating the guards, of the girl caught in the crossfire. She gulped and drew in her senses, locking them behind a barrier. Hearing about the incident was painful enough. Seeing it through his horrified eyes made her want to curl up in a ball and weep. Later, maybe she would. Hopefully not alone this time. She looked to Ridge.

He was studying Wreltad, the blade still lying on the dusty floor. She could not tell if the soulblade was speaking with him or not. Maybe seeing Eversong kill the young page had been the moment that had pushed Wreltad over the edge.

Angulus sighed and removed his crown. He looked like he wanted to stick it in a pocket or maybe toss it somewhere, but he merely held it. "I was in a meeting with the council members when news came of the arrival of an unannounced non-military flier." His focus shifted toward Ridge.

Unlike Therrik, Ridge had no reason to hold his head high, and he dropped his gaze. Sardelle stepped closer to him, brushing his arm in silent support. It hadn't been his fault.

"I had a hunch it was trouble, but stayed with the others, as my bodyguards requested, until the fires started. I suspected magic must be involved, though I hadn't yet realized that it was our nemesis from the flying fortress. There were numerous guards in the meeting room with us." Angulus waved toward the other side of the castle, and Sardelle realized he did not yet know his councilmen were dead.

She closed her eyes, not wanting to be the one to give him more devastating news.

"The witch spoke into my mind and said that dragons were coming and that the end was inevitable for me," Angulus went on, looking at Sardelle rather than Ridge and Therrik.

Grimly, she realized she probably *was* going to have to be the one to tell him. Ridge remained quiet, his eyes downcast, and she could feel his chagrin even with her senses locked down. She shared the emotion. Even if she hadn't helped Eversong in any way, she had been too late to stop this destruction.

"I figured she would have no trouble finding me," Angulus said, "even though we'd chosen one of the more secluded and private meeting rooms to discuss the Cofah threat and other problems around the nation. My guards were adamant that they'd be able to stop her, but I knew better. I grabbed a few of them, since they wouldn't have let me leave the room without an escort. I didn't know I was taking them to their deaths." He kicked a rock across the room, frustration making his movements stiff. "We headed to the armory. There were fires everywhere on that side of the castle—I had the distinct impression she was trying to flush me out. I grabbed a few explosives from Kaika's special stash and ran back down here. I couldn't imagine that just throwing a bomb at Eversong would work, but I thought that if I was willing to sacrifice some of the castle, I might be able to trap her. She glimpsed me when I was on my way down into the basement and threw an attack at us." Angulus touched the back of his head, and his fingers came away bloody.

Sardelle stepped forward, realizing he needed her services. Angulus let her come close and rest a hand on his head as he continued to explain. His words sounded half-dazed as they came out. He probably had a concussion.

"My men ran back to face her," he said, "giving me time to escape. They wanted me to get out of the castle, hide in the city, but how do you hide from someone who can speak into your mind?"

Ridge stirred at the question, but he didn't say anything.

"I was sure she'd find me, no matter where I went," Angulus went on. "So I came down here, to this distant corner of the castle, hoping I wouldn't hurt anyone else with my trap." He waved toward the rock pile. "I set explosives around this storage room, then crouched and waited, pulling those crates in front of the old hearth. When she came, I detonated everything." His gaze shifted upward, toward the destroyed ceiling. With the rubble pile moved, they could see up to the level above and the one above that too. "A lot of them. I wanted to drop the entire castle on her. I hoped it would be enough to stop her." He shrugged, his broad shoulders slumping low. "I appreciate you three coming to finish her off and dig me out. We should look at the carnage elsewhere. I need to see how many of my people survived. And how many did not."

Sardelle was examining his wound, but she paused to meet Ridge's grim eyes. Therrik's earlier triumphant expression had faded.

"Sire," Ridge said, taking a deep breath. "She found the meeting room. Your council leaders are dead. So are the men who guarded them."

For a long, stunned moment, Angulus said nothing, only staring at Ridge. Then his fingers curled into fists, and he glared down at Eversong's body again.

"Why?" he whispered. "What did she want? Did the emperor order this?"

"She wanted to rule Iskandia," Ridge said. "She needed the existing government gone, so she could put a figurehead on the throne and rule through him."

"What figurehead? I don't have any descendants."

"Uhm." Ridge stuck his hands in his pockets. "She thought the people might be open to choosing someone who wasn't royal, but who was somewhat popular with the press."

Angulus's eyebrows shot up.

"It doesn't matter," Ridge said. "He wouldn't have done it. There would have been a lot of paperwork."

"That's not very damned funny, Zirkander. Not now. Gods."

"No, Sire. I know." Ridge looked like he wanted to crawl into that hearth and disappear from sight.

Sardelle wanted to wrap an arm around him, but she had to tend to Angulus's injuries first—she could still sense the dragons in the sky above the castle and knew they weren't safe yet.

"She was manipulating him, Sire," Sardelle said as she worked, staunching the blood and helping the wound scab over. "She and her soulblade were the ones who controlled all those Cofah soldiers in the airships, remember."

Angulus's scowl wasn't fading. Ridge stared bleakly at the floor, his shoulders hunched.

"He didn't accept the offer," Sardelle said. "Manipulation or not, he could have."

Ridge shook his head, denying that he could have under any circumstances.

"So he just brought her here to destroy my people. And my castle."

"Not of his own will," Sardelle said firmly. She understood Angulus was frustrated over the loss of his people, people who had helped him rule the nation for decades in some cases, but it wasn't fair to blame Ridge.

I have some news that might cheer him up, Jaxi said.

We could use cheerful news.

Phelistoth dropped Kaika and a prisoner off in the courtyard before going off somewhere with Tolemek.

A prisoner?

The Cofah emperor.

"Sire." Sardelle hesitated to tell him before she had finished sealing the gash in the back of his head, but she didn't want him to continue glaring at Ridge either. For whatever reason, Angulus seemed to find the idea of King Zirkander more alarming and likely than it should have been, especially with the sorceress dead. "Kaika is somewhere in the castle. Part of the team that went to Dakrovia has returned. She has the emperor with her."

Angulus's head spun toward her. "What? Where is she?"

Jaxi?

Trying to dig herself out of a tower that collapsed when a dragon crashed into it. Jaxi shared the image with Sardelle. It was a corner tower along the back wall.

"She's all right," Sardelle said, careful to emphasize that first, "but stuck in a tower that was damaged."

"Damaged?" Concern haunted his eyes.

Utterly collapsed is the more appropriate description, Jaxi thought. *It's a good thing she hauled him into the basement level before that happened.*

"Damaged," Sardelle said. "I'll help you get them out."

"I have burly soldiers for that." Angulus nodded toward Therrik and headed for the hallway. He pointedly did not look at Ridge.

Uh, you may want to find a way to help Bhrava Saruth. He's getting pummeled by the female, and there's a second gold coming.

What?

The other male that escaped the cavern when Bhrava Saruth did. I'm guessing he's the female's mate now and came to help.

How far out is he?

Maybe five minutes.

Therrik walked out after Angulus, his hand on Kasandral's blade, as if he meant to cut Kaika out of the tower. Maybe he did. There was no hangdog look about him. He'd gotten a *good work* from Angulus. For once, Ridge wasn't the hero, and he seemed lost in that knowledge.

Sardelle knew there wasn't much time, but she went to him and wrapped her arms around him. He stood there dejectedly. He lifted an arm to return the hug, but then let it drop, defeat cloaking him.

I don't deserve your... you.

I don't accept that as true, but even if it is, I deserve you, Ridge. I thought you were dead.

Oh, he thought, the word very small. He returned the hug, resting his cheek against hers and stroking her hair with one hand. "I'm sorry," he whispered, though he didn't seem to be able to get thoughts of the dead out of his mind. *You're sure you don't deserve someone less self-absorbed?*

I don't want anyone else, so you'll just have to get over that. I love you. She was glad she didn't have to use her voice to speak with him, because she wouldn't have trusted it to work. Tears leaked from her eyes, dampening the shoulder of his uniform jacket. He smelled of dust and stone and the road, and they had more problems to deal with, but she couldn't bring herself to let him go. She wanted to stand there, with his arms around her, something she hadn't known if she would ever experience again.

The castle shuddered around them, and someone screamed

in the courtyard up above. Sardelle lifted her head from Ridge's shoulder and reluctantly lowered her arms, though she couldn't resist a few selfish thoughts. Hadn't they done enough? Couldn't someone else deal with the dragons while she stayed here?

Ridge might have been thinking the same thing, because he did not release her right away. He lifted his palm to the side of her face, wiping tears from her cheeks with his thumb.

"Thank you for coming for me," he said, gazing into her eyes.

She leaned her cheek into his hand. "I always will."

He kissed her, his tangle of feelings washing over her: gratitude, sorrow, love, regret. Later, she hoped to inspire less mixed emotions in him, but for now, she tried to return the kiss in such a way that everyone else he had ever kissed, including enemy sorceresses and farm girls, would be a disappointment in comparison.

Two minutes, Jaxi said quietly. *That was Bhrava Saruth being thrown against a tower.*

Understood.

Sardelle pulled away from Ridge, feeling slightly smug at the dazed and breathless expression on his face.

"And I'll always rub your dragon too." She squeezed his butt before releasing him fully and walking over to pick up the soulblade.

"The figurine, right?" A faint smile ghosted across his lips.

"That too." The ancient sword, the hilt more intricate than Jaxi's, with a big sapphire jewel on the end, lay quiet in her hand, neither objecting to being touched nor offering a sign of acceptance. She held the hilt out toward Ridge. "Will you carry him for now? I can feel Jaxi glowering at him, and she might get jealous if I tote around a former nemesis."

I'm not glowering. I'm just informing him that Tylie is too sweet for him, and we might want to bury him in the crystal mines and select another soulblade for her.

So, you're being personable and charming.

Yes.

Remember, we blew up all the tunnels in those mines. Finding another soulblade in there would be a long-term project.

It's worth waiting for the right soulblade. An Iskandian one.
But Tylie is Cofah.
Tylie is a kid. She doesn't know or care what she is. She just wants friends.
She's older than you were when you went into your blade, Sardelle said.
All I wanted at that age was to have friends too. And to light things on fire.
Naturally.

Ridge's expression turned dubious as he regarded the soulblade. "An honor? Or my penance?"

"You don't deserve penance, Ridge. You helped kill a dragon that was destroying villages—and people. You almost died defending your country. You've selflessly risked your life for Iskandia countless times. Nothing from the last week changes that. You're an asset to the king and this nation. Angulus will get over his grumpiness—" maybe sometime after he had a new castle built, "—and see that again soon."

He sighed, more in defeat than agreement, and grasped the sword's hilt. "Want to go fight a dragon, Wreltad?"

The soulblade flared silver, driving back the shadows in the room and highlighting Ridge's face. Sardelle wondered anew at Jaxi's suggestion that Wreltad might consider linking with Ridge. That wouldn't help Tylie, but the sword could help keep Ridge alive when he was streaking suicidally through the skies.

He would be twice as reckless with a soulblade of his own. Jaxi sniffed derisively into Sardelle's mind.

I'm sure Wreltad's presence wouldn't keep him from talking to you, Sardelle said, guessing that Jaxi's objection had more to do with possessiveness than anything else.

Of course not. I'm fun and interesting. Who wouldn't *want to talk to me?*

"I guess he's agreeable to the idea," Ridge said. He looked at the scabbard on Eversong's waist, but flicked his fingers, apparently deciding to leave it for someone else to extract.

"Yes, but it's actually two dragons," Sardelle said.

"Two?"

"If we can find you a flier, I brought back the rest of your bullets from the Morishtomaric fight. They're in my pack where we landed up above."

"You brought my bullets *and* my lucky dragon?" Ridge's eyes brightened for the first time since they had reunited. "You are a magnificent woman."

He offered his free arm and nodded toward the hallway.

She linked her arm with his and walked out with him, pleased by his warm gaze.

"I believe I must offer to rub something of yours as a sign of my gratitude," he murmured, and a little shiver went through her.

"I don't have a dragon."

"We'll find something else."

"I'm open to that."

They walked up the stairs together, Sardelle struggling to keep her mind on the battle waiting for them, a battle they had to survive before they could rub each other's anything.

Chapter 20

TOLEMEK RACED INTO THE LAB, jumping over the floor-cleaning automaton that idled away in the hallway, the device unaware of the dragons battling over the city's harbor. As far as human workers went, the front desk wasn't staffed, and he didn't spot any open doors.

"Good thing I didn't bring the emperor here," he muttered.

Captain Kaika seems capable of guarding a human, Phelistoth said, trotting behind him.

Tolemek had been surprised when the dragon shifted into human form to follow him into the lab. He'd expected Phelistoth to wait for him on the roof. Maybe he thought the other dragons would be less likely to notice him if he was in this innocuous form.

I am growing weary of having my talons cut off by golds, Phelistoth grumbled. *Why are there no bronze dragons left in the world?*

As Tolemek opened the door to his lab, he decided not to point out that more than Phelistoth's talons had been cut in the numerous scrapes he had been in, first with Morishtomaric and then with the female.

It is an expression. Phelistoth strode in behind him. *Where is—*

He halted, staring at several large tables that had been pushed together in the center of the lab, taking up so much space that it was hard to maneuver around them. A dragon skull rested atop them, the scales, muscle, and brain material having been dissected and removed for preservation before Tolemek left.

"I requested that Morishtomaric's remains be brought in for me to study," Tolemek explained hastily, aware of the incredulous and somewhat threatening look that Phelistoth leveled at him. He had forgotten that the skull was still in his lab.

Study? For what purpose?

"To better learn the anatomy and biochemistry of dragons so we can defend ourselves against them in the future. Against hostile ones, only." Tolemek kept himself from asking if Phelistoth was about to *become* a hostile dragon.

Phelistoth curled his lip at the skull, then turned his back on it. *Where is this weapon that will affect dragons? I will gladly change back in order to hurl it at Yisharnesh.*

Tolemek skirted the table to reach a locked cabinet. He turned the dial to the combination, opened the door, and withdrew a ceramic jar surrounded with padding. "I had time to make more than I needed for the last confrontation, but I haven't had time to craft a delivery system."

Without a gunsmith nearby, he couldn't make bullets again. He looked down at the jar dubiously, imagining that the battle would not go well if he simply ran up and threw it at a dragon.

It will go well if I throw it, I assure you.

"Er, I suppose that could work." Tolemek could still imagine the jar missing or bouncing off the dragon's shields and falling uselessly into the ocean. This was all he had of the compound. He looked toward his cabinet of empty jars and vials. Perhaps if he split it into several containers, they would have more chances to—

There is no time. Yisharnesh is not enjoying Bhrava Saruth's dance moves, and her mate comes.

"Her *mate*?" Tolemek gaped toward the window, but it looked out over the city instead of toward the castle.

The other gold dragon that escaped from the cavern. It appears Yisharnesh has forgotten about the emperor and is focusing on Bhrava Saruth. She is irritated at him because he dropped a glacier on her head back in the mountains. When your irritation rises, sensible thoughts sometimes fall out of your head.

"Yes, I've noticed that happens with dragons." Tolemek held out the jar.

Keep it until we are poised to throw. The mate may leave if we convince Yisharnesh to leave. He is aloof and has no interest in humans, emperors or otherwise. I will instruct Bhrava Saruth to put all of his energy into lowering Yisharnesh's defenses, and then I will hurl the jar at her. Phelistoth ran back into the hallway, heading for the stairs leading to the rooftop.

Tolemek ran after him, asking, "Will that work?"

If Bhrava Saruth is strong enough. And if he'll follow my orders.

Tolemek tried to reassure himself that both of those things could happen.

* * *

Ridge didn't let go of Sardelle until they escaped the maze of toppled walls and flattened hallways that was all that remained of the castle. As soon as they stepped into the rubble-littered courtyard, he spotted four soldiers running toward a collapsed tower from the direction of the landing pad, where two Wolf Squadron fliers must have just settled down. General Ort led the group, alternately yelling for the king and glancing toward the sky. Three gold dragons wheeled and fought above the harbor, while a dozen fliers swooped about, like gnats in comparison to the mighty creatures. The fight was taking place at an uncomfortably low altitude. With two of the courtyard walls flattened, Ridge could see them easily, as they battled near the docks. One of the golds blew a stream of flames from its maw. The fire missed its target—that must be the dragon Sardelle had been riding—and bathed ships docked in the harbor. They burst into flame instantly.

Ridge spun toward Sardelle. "Bullets?"

She was already jogging toward the spot where Bhrava Saruth had dropped them off. "I'll get them and meet you at the fliers."

Ridge sprinted for the half-collapsed tower where Ort gesticulated wildly as he spoke to Angulus. Angulus barely seemed to be listening. He was digging frantically, trying to clear the doorway of the tower. Kaika must be trapped down there. Therrik and several guards were helping, but the men kept glancing toward the battle in the sky. As much as Ridge cared about Kaika, the entire city was at risk from those dragons.

"Sire," he blurted as he drew close. "General Ort. I need one of those fliers."

Ort's eyebrows climbed up his forehead when he saw Ridge, and for a moment, he looked like he might hug him, but he broke off the gesture and shook his head instead. "Those fliers are to get the king out of the city. Our people have been in the air for the last ten minutes, and all that's happening is they're getting knocked down. They can't hurt the dragons at all." His gaze drifted downward as he spoke, locking on the soulblade in Ridge's hand.

Wreltad hadn't stopped glowing. He wanted a battle, not to flee, and Ridge felt the same way.

"We have some bullets that can get through," Ridge said, pointing at Sardelle, who was waving a pack as she ran toward the landing pad. That was all the permission Ridge needed. "We'll leave you one of the fliers," he shouted, chopped the air with a salute, and ran to join her.

"Zirkander!" Ort yelled after him.

A cacophonous crash came from the direction of the harbor, and Ridge didn't hear anything else the general said. He wouldn't have slowed down regardless.

Sardelle waited next to the flier and tossed him the band of ammunition before he even slowed down. There wasn't much of it. He leaped up, pulling himself head first into the cockpit, not bothering to yank the rest of his body in before feeding the ammo into the guns. He stuck Wreltad down beside the seat, hoping the sword could truly help them. It would have to be with magic, because it wasn't as if Ridge could swing a blade while piloting.

"Zirkander," someone yelled, the voice obscured by the fact that his head was dangling into the cockpit.

Ridge didn't stop what he was doing. Nobody was going to deny him this chance to... to... he didn't know exactly. Protect the city. Make amends. Stop feeling like a feeble-minded ass who didn't deserve to live. "Yeah, say it like it is, Ridge," he muttered to himself as he pulled the rest of his body into the cockpit.

Sardelle already sat in the back seat, strapped into the harness, Jaxi in her hand.

"You say you want to come along?" He grinned at her, the anticipation of battle thrumming through his veins, pushing aside his dark thoughts.

"You're not fighting a dragon again without me."

"I was hoping you would say that." He hit the switch, and the power crystal flared to life.

"Zirkander, stop, damn you." Therrik raced up to the side of the flier, Kasandral clenched in his hand.

"Damn you, *sir*," Ridge said, hitting the ignition for the thrusters. "At least until Angulus decides to revoke my rank."

Therrik pointed at Sardelle, or maybe at the back seat. "Take me up with you. I can hurt those bastards."

Ridge hesitated. He did have Kasandral. But no, Ridge wasn't going after another dragon without Sardelle at his back.

"Good. Get Ort to bring you." Ridge shooed Therrik away from the thrusters as he piloted the flier off the landing pad.

Ort was busy arguing with Angulus, trying to pull him toward the empty flier so the king could escape, not join in a battle. By now, Ort ought to know that Angulus wasn't someone to flee in the face of trouble. Or if he did, it was only until he could drop a bomb on that trouble. Kaika was a good influence on him.

Therrik cursed colorfully and lividly as the flier rose, then shouted, "Here, you idiot!"

He threw Kasandral at the cockpit. Ridge yelped, thinking it an attack, but Therrik was throwing the weapon *to* him, not at him. He managed to catch it without cutting off any of his fingers. The selfless gesture surprised Ridge, though a livid scowl accompanied it. Therrik might still cut off Ridge's fingers once he landed again.

Wreltad throbbed blue. *We do not need that* inferior *weapon.*

"Nope, I didn't think so," Ridge said, jamming Kasandral between the seat and the hull on the opposite side of the soulblade. "We'll just use him to tighten any screws that might fly loose in battle. You're sitting on top of my toolbox."

Wreltad made a noise that might have been a snort. At the least, he didn't sound quite so indignant.

Which sword are you talking to? Sardelle asked, sounding amused.

Wreltad. Kasandral hasn't seen fit to talk to me yet. Ridge took them out of the courtyard, heading out to sea and picking up altitude before flying toward the dragons.

Sardelle rested her hand on his shoulder. Gods, it felt good to have her back there again. With all that had happened, it felt like it had been months since they had been in the sky together, not weeks. He squeezed her hand before turning them toward the battle.

Two large gold dragons were chasing a slightly smaller gold dragon around the harbor.

That's Bhrava Saruth. Sardelle's hand tightened on his shoulder before she seemed to realize what she was doing and released him.

The smaller dragon did not appear any faster than the others. He whipped between buildings in the city, curled around spires, and dove behind clock towers, dodging flames and magic hurled at him left and right. Ridge grimaced as more than one building crumbled under the assault. Several fliers were in the air, half of the squadron circling over the castle in a guard position, while the other half chased the dragons, shooting when they could.

I'm surprised the dragons aren't attacking the castle and trying to get the emperor instead, Ridge thought, trusting that Sardelle was monitoring him.

Bhrava Saruth is deliberately drawing them away, but he wasn't expecting two. He's gotten in a few bites, but he's already injured. He can't beat them. All he can do is buy time.

That's the dragon that picked me up by the scruff of my neck, right?

Yes, I hope you won't hold that against him. I want to help him. Sardelle paused, then added, *He thinks I'm his high priestess.*

Uhm, are you?

I'm not really qualified for that position.

That was not, Ridge noted, a no. He was flying through the city now, rounding a clock tower and doing his best to catch up with the rearmost dragon, so he couldn't properly gawk back at Sardelle. *Your week sounds like it was more interesting than mine.*

Two fliers dropped to his altitude, taking up positions off his wings. "General Zirkander, is that *you*?" Lieutenant Beeline asked over the communication crystal. Then, much more loudly, he shouted, "General Zirkander's alive!"

"Good to see you Beeline, Crash." Ridge nodded at the second pilot. A hearty cheer went up, a dozen voices talking and blurting greetings at once. He was closing in on the rearmost dragon and wanted to get some information, but he had to quash his impatience, reminding himself that they had all believed him dead. Later, he would take delight in the display of caring and enthusiasm, but now, as soon as he could, he asked, "Does anybody else have any of Tolemek's bullets?"

"No, sir. Our bullets bounce right off those shiny yellow hides."

"All right." Ridge tapped Kasandral's pommel, wishing he could hand off the blade to one of the other fliers. He had the bullets, and he had Sardelle. It would be better to spread around weapons that could actually harm the dragons, but none of the other pilots had passengers with them, passengers who could be pressed into sword-fighting duty. "I hate to say this, but I'm the only one here with a weapon that can hurt the dragons. The rest of you are just putting yourselves at risk. You better go to the castle and see if you can help while we—"

Blue light leaped from the top of Wreltad's pommel, arced around the propeller, and zapped the rear dragon in the backside. The creature screeched and wheeled about instantly. Blazing yellow eyes fixed on Ridge, and the dragon opened his maw.

"Get yourself killed by an angry dragon, sir?" Crash asked.

Ridge was too busy choosing a target to respond. Every instinct told him to steer clear of the stream of fire that had to be coming, but he had a perfect view of dragon tonsils and a big pink dragon throat. Surely, the creature would be vulnerable if he could fire a few of Tolemek's special bullets down its gullet.

Into valiant battle we go, Wreltad cried into Ridge's mind, sending more lightning around the propeller and at the dragon.

Valiant battle? Jaxi asked. *Is he joking, or does he really talk like that?*

Shields? Ridge asked, the question for Sardelle, Jaxi, Wreltad, or even Kasandral. Not waiting for an answer, he drove straight toward the dragon, even as it flew straight toward him. Smoke came out of its nostrils, and the maw stretched wide, flames boiling up from the back of its throat.

You have to stop firing before we raise a shield, or the bullets will bounce back at us, Sardelle said into his mind, fear making the words tumble out quickly. *If you're touching Kasandral, you might be safe from fire, but I doubt the flier will be.*

Ridge thumbed the trigger, loosing five precise shots. He didn't want to risk more than that—he doubted he had more than thirty bullets to spare. More lightning streaked from Wreltad, striking the dragon in the mouth, bouncing between its massive fangs, and curling down its throat. Ridge knew his bullets landed, but the lightning may very well have done more damage.

"Done," he announced, pulling up so the fire would strike the belly of his craft instead of roiling into the cockpit, though hoped Sardelle could shield them, so nothing was struck.

For a few seconds, nothing but orange existed in the world. The dragon had turned its head, tracking them. Flames crackled all around the flier. Ridge did not feel the heat, but he saw the air wavering as the inferno parted around them, around the bubble someone was shielding them with.

"Thank you," he said calmly, not sure whether he had Sardelle or one of the swords to thank, but grateful to have so much help. When compared to the last time he had been up here facing a dragon...

He shook his head, not wanting to think about it. Instead, he took them around, trying to get behind the dragon, so they would be safe from fire. He knew that deflecting such power took a toll on Sardelle.

The creature rolled, spinning a somersault in the air to deny Ridge the angle of attack he wanted. It roared, the noise deep and angry as it battered at his eardrums. Was this the male or the female? Ridge couldn't tell. Only one was fighting him. The other was still chasing Bhrava Saruth. That roar devolved into a sputter—a cough? Was it wounded? Maybe the bullets or lightning had damaged it.

Ridge dove toward that exposed throat, hoping the dragon couldn't hurl flames when it was coughing. He fired four more shots. This time, they bounced off before coming anywhere close to the creature's head. He broke off the engagement, veering to the side. After being grabbed out of his cockpit by Sardelle's dragon, he was careful not to go anywhere near those talons—or those teeth.

He's realized you can hurt him, Sardelle thought. *His defenses are up fully now.*

Wreltad sent more branches of lightning at the dragon, but they forked around an invisible barrier, Sardelle's words proving true.

Another flier swept down, firing at the dragon. Two more followed it, unloading bullets.

Ridge snorted. His people followed orders every bit as well as he did. There would be a talk later, but for now, he wrapped his hand around Kasandral's hilt as he guided his craft after the dragon with his other hand.

"We're taking that shield down," he announced to whomever was listening.

Yes, Wreltad agreed. *I'll be ready.*

Ridge hefted Kasandral, as Cas had once done. He would only get one shot, but a dragon was a large target. They were over the harbor now. If he had to, he would go diving for Kasandral later, once the dragons were dead.

The dragon wasn't flying straight, more like a drunken bumblebee. Dare he hope they had hurt it enough to take it out of the fight?

One of the Wolf Squadron fliers cut toward the side of the creature, shooting at its neck. Ridge shook his head as the bullets bounced uselessly off. The dragon must have noticed the attack, because the tail lashed out. It caught the wing of the flier as the pilot veered away. Even the glancing blow had the strength to send the craft tumbling. Worse, the dragon's head whipped around, and he sent a stream of fire after the flier.

Ridge clenched his jaw, worried for the pilot—was that Lieutenant Pigpen?—and frustrated with his team for not staying back, as he'd ordered. Even if he knew he would respond in exactly the same way, there was no point in risking death when one couldn't do anything.

"I'm going in," he said. "Everyone else, stay *back*."

Ridge bore down, picking his angle so he could come down from above. The dragon's tail lashed out like a whip, trying to knock his propeller off. Keeping his touch light, he avoided it, almost dancing with it, a dip here, a loop here. Finally, he was flying above the dragon's back, the harbor a blur of blue below them.

"I'm throwing the sword, Sardelle," he said, not wanting her shield to get in the way, though Kasandral could probably cut through it, the same as he had done to Morishtomaric's defenses.

Excellent, Wreltad said at the same time as Jaxi made a cheering noise in Ridge's head.

"Sorry, Kasandral," Ridge said. "Don't think anyone likes you." He hurled the sword like a spear, aiming at the dragon's broad back.

"Is the general talking to a sword?" someone asked over the crystal.

"Three of them," Ridge muttered. He wanted to watch the blade's descent, to see if it cut through the dragon's shield and worked, but he dove as soon as he threw it, hoping he could recover it if he missed or if it bounced off. He didn't truly want to go swimming for that sword later.

A flash of light came when Kasandral cut through the dragon's shield, followed by a surge of power rolling off the dragon. Ridge's flier's wings wobbled slightly, but Sardelle was shielding them again. The sword reached the dragon's golden scales and sank in. Wreltad sent more lightning streaking toward the creature, the bright blue branches biting into its hide now that its defenses were gone. A fireball the size of a house launched from behind Ridge, and he felt the heat of the sun on the back of his neck before it sped away. Jaxi's enthusiastic work.

The dragon screamed and bucked under the combined assault, though Kasandral seemed to hurt it most of all. Had someone driven the sword into his back by hand, the blade might have stayed in, but under those violent undulations, it flew free.

Ridge was ready. His flier's nose was already pointed at the harbor below, and he was picking up speed. He glided toward the blade as it fell. He thought about trying to set himself so he could catch the hilt with his hand as it tumbled past, but he might cut off his arm doing that. Instead, he got under it, then leveled to catch it with his wing, the blade slicing into the taut canvas frame and sticking.

"I'll get him later," Ridge said, pulling the nose up further so they wouldn't smash into the water. As it was, he thought he could feel the misty air above the waves as they swooped back upward.

"Everyone all right?" He glanced back at Sardelle and noticed her with a hand outstretched, utter concentration on her face.

Not fifty meters away, the flier that had been damaged by the dragon tail was landing, the entire framework charred from fire. A wide-eyed Lieutenant Pigpen sat behind the controls as he was levitated onto a dock.

"Thank you, Sardelle," Ridge said.

Her hand relaxed as the flier settled into a safe spot, and she nodded toward him. *You're welcome. They had a hard time obeying your orders to leave the dragons alone.*

It's hard to resist the allure of a dragon-sized target.

I think they just want to protect their general.

Ridge pointed his nose upward again, looking for the dragon Kasandral had poked. Two others—Bhrava Saruth and the female—were still fighting in the air behind the castle.

He's flying away, Wreltad said smugly. *That was excellent. This flying contraption is almost as pleasurable to fight from as the back of a dragon.*

Almost? Ridge asked, affronted on behalf of the fine craft.

Don't worry, Jaxi said. *I'll tell him he's being too uppity for the new sword.*

Thank you. I think.

Sardelle laid her hand on his shoulder again. He clasped it, glad to have her back there with him again.

Which one of us is going to climb out on the wing and bring in

Kasandra? he asked, turning the flier back toward the castle, aware that a battle continued over there.

He won't let me touch him, Sardelle said.

I can't touch him either, Jaxi said.

Nor I, Wreltad added.

Oh, I guess that means I'm nominated. Ridge thought about asking Sardelle to keep the stick steady with her mind, but they were still close to the docks. He would take them to land. It would be easier that way, and it would only take a moment. Then they could head over to the castle to help with the last enemy dragon.

Chapter 21

IT DID NOT TAKE LONG to fly from the lab back to the castle, but Tolemek frowned, finding the air unexpectedly clear of dragons over the city and the harbor. A few fliers circled over the water, but they had nothing to shoot at currently. Had the female changed into human form and gone in to retrieve the emperor? The flier pilots wouldn't be able to fire into the castle courtyard, with guards presumably all over the place.

The male flees, Phelistoth announced. *Look.*

Tolemek lacked a dragon's sharp sight, but with Phelistoth directing, he finally glimpsed a gold dragon in the distance, barely discernible from the waves on the horizon.

He has a sword-shaped hole in his back, Phelistoth said.

"Good. And the female? Is she gone too?" Tolemek's grip tightened on the jar of acid he carried. Maybe his formula would not be needed, after all.

No. She and Bhrava Saruth continue to battle. They crashed.

Where? The harbor?

No.

Phelistoth did not explain further. As his wingbeats took them up to the hill that held Harborgard Castle, Tolemek saw that the explanation was not needed. He gaped down at the two massive forms wrestling about, destroying everything they crashed into, within the courtyard walls. One of those walls had already fallen, nothing but a pile of rubble remaining, a lone cannon lying on top of it. Two of the castle towers had also been reduced to rubble, and as Phelistoth circled, another wall went down, this one belonging to the castle itself. Tolemek hoped Kaika had found someplace safe to take the emperor, though he couldn't guess where that might be right now.

I am trying to tell Bhrava Saruth to break apart from her, Phelistoth said as he circled above the castle. *I could throw the weapon at both of them.*

Don't do that, please. Sardelle likes that dragon.

He is a buffoon.

Maybe so, but he's trying to protect Iskandia and bought us time to get my jar.

Phelistoth grumbled again. *You tell him to break apart then. He's not listening to me.*

Tolemek doubted it was a matter of not listening as not having the opportunity to pay attention. Yisharnesh was the aggressor, fangs and talons sinking in, shaking her head as she tried to gnaw off the smaller dragon's shoulder. It was as if thousands of years of anger were being unleashed at once. Maybe she was angry that her mate had left her—or maybe she was too enraged to even be aware of it. Tolemek barely knew Bhrava Saruth, but he regretted that they hadn't found a way to bring back the emperor without bringing this trouble back with them.

Another tower toppled, as if some giant had batted it with the back of his hand. The dragons were not near it and did not strike it physically, but Tolemek recognized the power being unleashed, a wave of energy that could have killed a man instantly. Yisharnesh stumbled back, releasing her grip, and Tolemek assumed that Bhrava Saruth had hurled that attack.

"Now's our chance," he said, holding the jar in front of him. "Are her defenses down?"

Phelistoth dove toward the courtyard.

Yisharnesh recovered and retaliated before they reached her. She launched a counterattack with her mind, and Bhrava Saruth was hurled over the roof of the castle and toward the interior courtyard. He smashed into the top of Angulus's atrium, glass shattering everywhere. Leaves and broken branches flew upward as he slammed onto the table inside.

"Now," Tolemek ordered. Yisharnesh stood alone in the yard, but already she crouched to spring after her foe. Was she aware of them coming? Were her defenses up?

The air between Phelistoth and the female dragon seemed to ripple, and Tolemek sensed the power flowing outward.

Phelistoth's attack was not meant to hurl her about, but to batter at her mind, perhaps to lower her shields. All Tolemek could do was guess.

The female shook her body like a dog knocking off water droplets, not bothering to look at them.

The ceramic jar rose out of Tolemek's hands. It floated into the air above Phelistoth's head. Yisharnesh sprang toward the atrium where Bhrava Saruth struggled to rise. Tolemek groaned, certain they were too late, and also certain that her defenses were still up.

The jar hurtled through the air. It struck Yisharnesh in the back as she flew over the rooftop. A logger swinging an axe at the jar couldn't have broken it into more pieces. Tolemek winced as some of those shards flew into the side of the building and out onto the rooftop. Dragon scales weren't the only things that acid could eat through. But much of the formula struck her, spreading across her back like jam on toast.

Relieved her defenses had been down and it had gotten through, Tolemek thumped Phelistoth on the back. "That'll do it."

She does not appear harmed, Phelistoth responded.

Yisharnesh had been midair when the jar struck, and she continued along her arc, sailing out of their sight as she jumped down into the atrium. Phelistoth landed on the rooftop, careful to avoid smoking places where some of the acid had landed.

A shriek rang out with such power that it rattled every bone in Tolemek's body. Yisharnesh leaped into the air, almost crashing into them. He ducked as she flew over his head. Bhrava Saruth followed her. They clashed in the air once again. He landed a few good bites, but she flung him aside, the physical blow augmented with magic. He was hurled all the way to the front courtyard wall where he slammed into it and crumpled to the ground. Phelistoth, at the very edge of that magical attack, stumbled. He would have fallen off the roof, if he hadn't flapped his wings and taken to the air again.

Tolemek hung on, confused. He knew Yisharnesh had been hit. Why was she still fighting? Was it taking time to sink in?

She had shrieked. Had that been pain? Or fury? What if his acid hadn't worked on her for some reason?

He expected her to go after Bhrava Saruth, to finish him off, or perhaps to attack Phelistoth. Instead, she shrieked again and dropped to the grass in the courtyard. She flung herself onto her back and rolled about, legs and wings in the air, as if she were trying to rub biting ants off her scales.

Tolemek clenched a fist. "It *did* work."

If I attacked her, might some of the acid touch me and harm me? Phelistoth asked.

"It shouldn't. But..." He trailed off, watching as Yisharnesh sprang into the air. He doubted rolling on the grass would have done anything to help, but he waited warily, afraid of another attack.

All she did was fly over the courtyard wall and out to sea. Phelistoth sprang up to the top of a tower with a flier sitting perched oddly upon it, giving Tolemek a view of the big dragon flapping away. She dove into the waves, came out, flew upward, and then dove in again. Like a dolphin, she went in and out of the water as she fled toward the horizon.

It slowly dawned on Tolemek that his goo had worked and that she wouldn't be coming back, not anytime soon. He looked down at the destruction in the courtyard, two of the four walls completely leveled. At least half of the castle had fallen to the same fate, and other portions still smoked and burned. Bhrava Saruth wasn't moving—he lay crumpled on his back next to the wall. Tolemek couldn't tell if he even breathed.

On wobbly legs, he slid off Phelistoth's back. "I'm going to find Captain Kaika, make sure she still has the emperor."

If they lost their prisoner, all of this would have been too high a price to pay.

* * *

Sardelle kept her hand on Ridge's shoulder as they left the harbor and flew toward the castle, in part because she wanted him to know he had her support, in this and in everything, and in part because she didn't want to let go. At his order, the rest of Wolf Squadron had waited for him to collect Kasandral before heading back to the castle. Now they streamed out behind him, ready to help in whatever way they could. As the demolished courtyard came into view, the female dragon streaked into the sky. Ridge's finger tightened on his machine gun trigger, but she did not fly toward his squadron. Instead, she raced straight out to sea, diving into the waves as she put distance between herself and the coast.

Tolemek found some of his acid, Sardelle said into Ridge's mind as she used her senses—and common sense—to piece together what had happened.

Ah. Ridge sounded more disappointed than relieved, perhaps having hoped to send the second dragon fleeing himself, with Angulus looking on.

She squeezed his shoulder. They had done enough. It was better not to have to continue the fight, especially since he seemed extra reckless today. She had been tempted to jump out of the flier when he had been diving straight for that dragon's throat.

Ridge nodded and patted her hand again. *Yes, being done with the fighting is a good thing.* Out loud, he said, "Crash and Beeline, follow me down to the castle, so we can check on the king. Everyone else, stay in the air and keep watch for now. I understand our people brought back an important prisoner. It's possible some Cofah might be heading this way."

As they descended, Sardelle noticed the collapsed tower where Angulus was still directing the digging—he had recruited more people. She also spotted Bhrava Saruth at the opposite end of the courtyard, and her heart sank. He lay against the remains of a crumbling wall, stones littering the ground all around his supine form. With his legs crooked in the air and his wings limp at his sides, he looked much as he had when he had requested a belly rub beside the road. This time, his eyes weren't open, and he was far too wounded to appear content, with bloody gashes on his sides, neck, and head where the female dragon's talons had bit in. Was he even alive? Several of the castle staff who hadn't been assigned to dig had drifted over to him, to gawk and to touch.

As soon as the flier touched down, Sardelle leaped from the cockpit, not even waiting for the thrusters to die down fully. Ridge hopped down, too, but he jogged toward the king and General Ort, Kasandral in one hand and Wreltad in his other. His head was higher than it had been when Angulus had been berating him, but he still carried himself with wariness, not certain of the reception he would receive from his king or from General Ort.

Normally, Sardelle would have stood at his side as he faced them, but she had to check on Bhrava Saruth.

As she ran in his direction, guilt swelled in her chest. This hadn't even been his fight. He had deliberately battled the female for the sake of the humans in the castle and in the city. What if he had been mortally wounded?

When she drew close, she raised her hands, intending to shoo away the castle staff—one man was standing on his wing, damn it. But she paused when she heard a couple of the people talking.

"Did you see him drive the other dragon away?" a woman in an apron asked, touching one of his rear legs reverently.

"He fought to protect us. Got himself killed doing it. That other dragons wanted to destroy us all."

Killed? Sardelle's eyes widened with alarm, and she checked Bhrava Saruth with her senses. No, he wasn't dead. To her surprise, though his eyes were closed, he didn't even seem to be unconscious.

Unnoticed by those regarding him, Sardelle walked around to his head, which lay upside down on the earth beside the wall.

"Bhrava Saruth?" she asked. "Are you all right?"

A single green eye opened part way, focusing on her. *Ssh. Pardon?*

Since I am so grievously wounded, these humans are admiring the sacrifice I made for them. They do not fear me like this.

Are you grievously wounded?

I could get up if I wished.

But you're lying here, feigning death instead, so they'll sympathize with you?

Not death, just grievous injury. I am healing myself while they admire me. And touch me. Will you tell them that recovering dragons need belly rubs?

Sardelle's first instinct was to say that she certainly would not, but that green eye gazed imploringly at her. He *had* fought bravely for them, even when he had no real reason to risk himself to defend the king and the castle. It wasn't as if this was *his* king and castle. In addition to the battle, he had been helping her all week.

She rested a hand on his head, then cleared her throat, drawing the eyes of the people gathered around him. "This is Bhrava Saruth. He's a noble dragon who likes to help humans. When he has recovered from his injuries, he would be willing to heal you of any injuries you may have received. That goes for all of those in the castle, I'm certain. All he hopes for in exchange is your regard." She couldn't bring herself to mention worshipping.

Bhrava Saruth cleared his throat in her mind. *Belly rubs.*

"Ah, yes. He also likes to have his belly rubbed."

Several eyebrows rose at this statement.

"It's good luck," Sardelle added.

That might work on Ridge. She wasn't sure if it would on castle servants.

"Oh," the woman in the apron said. "Like putting a lucky dragon statue above your hearth."

"Exactly like that," Sardelle said. She wouldn't mention how Ridge's last house had been blown up while a lucky dragon statue perched on his hearth. "There you go," she encouraged as a couple of the women stepped forward and ran their hands along his scales. "Yes, there's room for more. Don't step on his wings, please."

A soft contented sound drifted from the dragon's vocal chords. Not quite a purr, but something akin to one.

I believe you have officially accepted the job of high priestess, Jaxi observed. *Either that, or you're his procuress.*

I don't remember signing a form promising I would be either.

Tacit assent. Resign yourself to getting a robe. And building a temple. Maybe Ridge will help you. It will give you time to reacquaint yourselves with each other. Of course, given the way Angulus keeps glowering at him, he may get assigned to a very distant duty station next. Do you think Bhrava Saruth minds if his temple is next to the crystal mines?

I better get over there to make sure that doesn't happen. Sardelle gave Bhrava Saruth a parting pat and trusted that his needs were being met.

Maybe you can comfort Ridge with more hugs and kisses.

I wouldn't mind that.

Though he seems to be busy chatting with Therrik right now.

Chatting? Sardelle wouldn't classify any of the conversations Ridge had with Therrik as chats.

When she reached the gathering, Sardelle found Ridge holding up Wreltad while rocks shifted and floated away from the collapsed tower. Tolemek was staying out of the way, pacing and looking toward the sky above the sea. Phelistoth perched on one of the more distant towers, also looking out toward the sea.

Therrik stood next to Ridge. He had either taken back Kasandral or Ridge had given the sword to him.

"That witch was far more of a pest than the dragon," Therrik said.

"We barely knew the dragon," Ridge said. "He could have become a pest."

"Once cut, he fled like a whipped hound. It took far more courage to strike down the witch."

"The witch was already wounded and barely standing when you cut her down. The dragon was a bigger threat."

"Had you taken *me* up there and let *me* wield the sword, I would have killed the dragon, not just driven him away."

"You would have been too busy throwing up in my back seat to kill anything except my upholstery."

"What's going on?" Sardelle asked, coming up and linking her arm with Ridge's, though she had gotten the gist of the *chat*.

I believe they're arguing over whose penis is larger, Jaxi said.

Humans have changed very little in three thousand years, Wreltad remarked.

The soulblades must have shared their words with Ridge, as well as Sardelle, because one of his eyebrows cocked as he looked down at Wreltad. Oddly, Jaxi did not get a similar look.

He's used to my keen observations.

Angulus paced as Wreltad continued to move rocks, barely acknowledging the arguing men or shaking off the comforting words Ort offered. Judging by his bleeding nails and fingers caked with dust, he'd had to be pulled bodily away from the rubble, and he had probably only allowed it because the magic was more efficient.

"Will our dragon ally live?" Ridge asked Sardelle, adjusting their linked arms so that the sides of their bodies touched.

She leaned against him, pleased to be close, and looked toward Bhrava Saruth. He still lay in the supine position, but no less than ten people were stroking his scales at various points on his body. Now that she knew that his injuries were not too serious, she could see that he was far more relaxed than tense. His tail twitched in contentment as the strokes continued.

"He'll live," Sardelle said.

Jaxi started moving rocks, too, and the pace picked up, boulders whizzing past so that people had to scoot back lest they be brained. About half of that was Jaxi and half Wreltad. Sardelle decided Therrik and Ridge weren't the only ones comparing the size of their... attributes.

A disdainful *Hmmph* sounded in her mind.

Sardelle smiled.

Wreltad pulsed a handsome shade of silvery blue, blowing up some of the boulders as they whizzed past while shielding them within invisible bubbles so the shards wouldn't fly away and hurt anyone. It made for quite an impressive display, having an artistic aesthetic.

I've changed my mind, Jaxi said. *I think Wreltad would be perfect for Tylie.*

Because they're both creative? Or because you're jealous that Ridge is waving around another soulblade?

He better not start oiling Taddy's blade.

Sardelle let her senses trickle through the dwindling pile of rubble blocking the base of the tower and stairs leading down to a basement level. She located Kaika's aura and smiled, finding her more annoyed with the situation than injured. The second person was even more annoyed. Sardelle's first brush with the Cofah emperor struck her as strange, if only for its utter mundaneness. There wasn't any dragon blood in his veins, nor did she sense anything special or unique about him. He was just a man in his sixties, whose feelings vacillated between righteous indignation and outright fear. Nobody had told him yet whether he was to be allowed to live or whether he would be interrogated and forced into signing treaties, and all Kaika was doing was glowering at him and fondling her grenades.

No, you'll only be exiled, Sardelle thought, but did not share the words with him. He would find out soon enough.

As the final stones were removed from the stairs to the lower level of the tower, she sensed more fliers arriving, these coming from the direction of the ocean. She checked the pilots, worried the Cofah had sent air and sea forces to retrieve their emperor.

Four fliers cruised toward the harbor, none of them belonging to the enemy.

Tolemek met Sardelle's eyes. "Is that Cas?"

Sardelle nodded. "Cas, Blazer, Pimples, Duck, Tylie, an officer I haven't met, and a young woman I also haven't met."

"That would be Colonel Quataldo and Princess Zilandria," Tolemek said.

"Princess *who?*" Angulus had been forced to step back, his guards insisting on going first down the stairs and into the dark tower basement. "My orders didn't say anything about kidnapping a princess."

Tolemek held up his hands. "You'll have to take that up with Farris."

Ridge lowered Wreltad, a bemused expression on his face. "Pimples went along on a covert overseas mission? Was math required?"

"My understanding is that the math interest helped in securing the rather bookish princess," Tolemek said. "Cas has more details. Pimples even more."

Ridge's puzzled expression did not fade. Sardelle, also knowing nothing about what had transpired over there, could not enlighten him.

"Out of my way," came Kaika's voice from the bottom of the stairs. "If I wanted your paws all over me, I would have let you know when we first met. Scoot, move."

A thump sounded, someone being shoved against the stone wall as Kaika barreled past, her prisoner in tow. Covered with dust and soot, she burst into view, barely slowing as she thrust the bound and gagged emperor at two guards, then launched herself at Angulus.

Therrik stepped forward, raising Kasandral, as if to defend his monarch from a fellow officer who had gone mad. Ridge halted him with a smirk—and an iron grip.

Angulus spread his arms, and a second later, he and Kaika stood with limbs entwined, locked in a kiss that could have woken a man—or woman—from the dead. The guards sighed and looked at the ground.

Therrik gaped.

Ridge's smirk widened. "Good to see some things didn't change while I was gone."

Therrik didn't stop staring, but he did manage to close his mouth and fix it into his usual scowl. He stalked over and took over guarding the emperor, who had been struggling to escape the guards.

Are there any Cofah coming in behind our people's fliers, Jaxi? Sardelle dreaded the idea of another fight, but she wouldn't be surprised if more than dragons had been sent to recover the emperor—and his daughter.

None on the horizon yet, Jaxi said. *Though maybe you want to ask Bhrava Saruth about that. His range is a lot farther than mine. That is, if he can pull himself away from that massage.* Jaxi sniffed. *I had no idea dragons were so needy.*

Just that one. I've never seen Phelistoth request belly rubs.

We don't know what he asks Tylie for when we're not around.

Sardelle didn't want to contemplate that.

"Therrik," Angulus said, finally breaking his kiss with Kaika, though he hadn't let her go yet—a challenge when she had one leg wrapped around him. "Take a couple of guards and find someplace to lock up our prisoner until I can have him taken to the new home I've prepared for him. We may need to take over the old citadel for the time being."

The emperor's eyebrows drew together in a V, and he looked like he wanted to speak, but nobody had removed his gag.

"Yes, Sire," Therrik said.

"See to it that he has food and something to drink, whatever small comforts we can offer, considering..." Angulus extended a hand toward the ruined castle.

"Yes, Sire."

As Cas and the others soared over the castle, looking for places to land their fliers—a challenge in the demolished courtyard—Therrik strode off with his head high, Kasandral sheathed on his back, and his prisoner gripped firmly in hand. While they waited, Kaika walked over to Ridge, a satisfied grin on her face, and thumped him on the shoulder.

"Good to see you alive, General."

"Good to see your lip muscles haven't atrophied while we've all been away, Captain."

"I keep them well exercised."

Ridge opened his mouth, caught Angulus looking at him through slitted eyes, and shut it before anything else came out. Maybe the last couple of weeks had left him a little wiser.

Just subdued, I think, Jaxi said. *I'm sure his mouth will be back to normal once you forgive him for lip wrestling with other women.*

I've already forgiven him.

Don't tell him that right away. Tonight, he plans to very passionately and vigorously demonstrate to you that you are the only woman he loves.

I do enjoy his vigor.

Now, if I can just get him to put that scruffy Cofah soulblade aside. With vigor.

After landing, the flier pilots and their passengers headed directly to the king and the growing group around the collapsed tower. Unlike her father, who was no longer in the area, the young dark-haired Cofah princess was not bound or gagged. She followed Pimples and looked around with large, uncertain eyes.

Cas ran ahead of the group, reaching them first. After a hasty salute for the king and a grin and a salute for Ridge, she went to Tolemek for an embrace that wasn't quite as molten as Angulus and Kaika's but which, given their usual preference for privacy, surprised Sardelle in its thoroughness. Ridge usually sighed and rolled his eyes when his lieutenant showed affection for Tolemek, but he merely smiled and pulled Sardelle closer.

After a suitable time had passed, and while Angulus greeted the princess formally and respectfully, Cas left Tolemek's embrace and came over to stand in front of Ridge.

"It's good to see you alive, sir." She saluted him solemnly and hesitated, glancing at Sardelle.

Sardelle inclined her head and stepped to the side. Cas bit her lip and hugged Ridge. His eyebrows rose in surprise, but he returned the embrace and patted her on the back.

"Are you all right, Ahn?" he asked quietly.

"Yes, sir." Cas cleared her throat and backed up, her cheeks flushing slightly. "We all thought you were dead."

"I'm glad to disabuse you of that thought then. Now, before you leave, could you explain to me why that young woman—a Cofah princess, I understand?—is holding Pimples' hand?"

Her eyes crinkled. "I'm not sure I *can* explain that, sir."

Epilogue

CAS AND TOLEMEK RODE ON horseback down a tree-lined lane in a quiet part of the city. A steam wagon rolled along beside them, driven by Pimples and Beeline, both of whom were sharing ridiculously pleased grins. Several other Wolf Squadron pilots sat in the back, keeping an eye on the precious cargo.

"Are we sure we want to arrive with this?" Tolemek muttered to Cas and tilted his head toward the wagon bed.

The large group was on the way to General Zirkander's house for one of his legendary brisk-ball and beer gatherings, the likes of which hadn't been seen since the previous summer. Now, with the late spring weather finally warm and sunny, and no Cofah warships lurking off Iskandia's shoreline, the time for gatherings had apparently come. Cas, not much of a partygoer, had only been to one of them. She recalled drunken colleagues wandering around the yard, wearing nothing but curtains. She also recalled their repeated efforts to convince General Ort to go over and kiss the neighbor's aged grandmother. Now that Sardelle and Ridge had moved off base, the latter shouldn't be a problem. Cas wasn't sure about the former. She was fairly certain the general's new house had curtains.

"As appalling as it is," Cas said, "I suspect General Zirkander will like it."

Tolemek was still looking dubiously toward a tarp covering a couch in the back of the wagon. "I was thinking more of Sardelle's likes."

"She can ask a dragon to incinerate it if she hates it. Now that she has two living there most of the time, that shouldn't be a problem."

"I don't think they're there *most* of the time," Tolemek said.

Cas was less certain. She'd heard the neighbors on the street had moved out of their houses. That might just be a rumor. She had also heard that a growing number of people in the city had heard about how Bhrava Saruth had helped defend the castle in an attack and wanted to come touch him for luck.

"They just visit," Tolemek said. "They don't live there all the time. I have been feeling guilty about foisting Tylie off on Sardelle so often, but now that we're getting a house..." He smiled shyly at Cas. They had discussed it again a few days ago and were now looking in earnest for something that suited their joint needs.

She smiled back. "Tylie and her dragon can spend time there?"

"*She* can. I'm not sure about having dragons around. If we do end up leasing a place, I'd like to get the damage deposit back someday."

"I thought Phelistoth didn't breathe fire."

"He doesn't, but he's been teaching Tylie how to levitate things. Sometimes there are concentration lapses."

"Ah."

Cas looked forward to sharing more than a room with Tolemek and shopping for a place of their own, rather than simply staying in the barracks or in the room near the lab that the king provided, but she got the impression that Tylie liked staying out here, with woods and a pond next to the house. She seemed to enjoy nature, even when she wasn't convincing trees to lean this way or that.

"I trust my gift will be well-received," Colonel Quataldo said from the side of the road. He was walking instead of riding, keeping up with the group easily. He carried a brown box with a bow tied around it.

"Is that the egg you found in Dakrovia?" Tolemek asked.

"Now with a dragon carved into the shell, yes."

"Sardelle should like that," Cas said.

"So long as it doesn't hatch," Tolemek muttered.

Cas wasn't close enough to swat him, but she flicked her fingers in his direction.

"As I told you in the swamps," Quataldo said, "it wasn't fertilized."

Giggles came from the front of the wagon as Pimples and Beeline made the final turn onto the general's street. Judging by excited shouts that drifted from the yard at the end, the athletic activities had already begun. Cas would join in later, once the targets were half drunk. She had better aim than most, and people were quick to claim her for their team, but the *other* team always targeted her first, often three at a time. When she got pegged with one of those big leather brisk-balls, it was enough to knock her on her butt—and leave a bruise the size of her butt.

"Almost there," Beeline crooned, the rim of his oversized cap pulled down almost to his nose.

"Won't you feel guilty delivering that thing to your C.O., Farris?" Tolemek asked Pimples.

"Not at all. I need a few laughs to keep my mind off..." He sighed dramatically—melodramatically, Cas would have said—and gazed toward the western sky.

"Still missing your princess?" Tolemek asked.

"Yes. I know we have her to thank for the fact that the Cofah aren't trying to obliterate the city right now, any more than it's already been obliterated, but I wish she hadn't had to go home." He brightened. "She did send me a letter recently. She wants to come to visit."

"To visit you or visit her father?"

"Me, of course. She doesn't know where her father is. None of us do. The Cofah actually seem fairly certain that he died in the Dakrovia dragon attack. They're not entirely sure who to blame, but they know we were there. We're lucky nobody's retaliating."

"I understand that Angulus implied the princess's return was a peace offering," Cas said.

Pimples sniffed. "She came with me willingly. We wouldn't have kept her here against her wishes."

"I don't think the king felt the need to make that clear."

There were so many vehicles already parked in front of Zirkander's house that the couch delivery team struggled to find a route to the lawn. A couple of the fancier steam carriages looked like they had come from the king's garage, and Cas glimpsed a few bodyguards in uniforms patrolling the premises.

Unlike most of the other guests, they did not carry mugs of beer in their hands.

Tolemek guided his horse away from Pimples and Beeline, perhaps wanting to distance himself from Wolf Squadron's carefully selected gift. He headed toward the side yard where an impromptu corral had been set up. Cas went with him, also not wishing to take credit for any part of that gift. She had dutifully chipped in on it, but she had been on the losing side of the vote, wanting to get Zirkander and Sardelle a nice couch akin to the one that had been obliterated by the dragon.

Tolemek handed his reins to a youth who looked like he might have been borrowed from the castle for the job. If the king was here, this was a much more prestigious gathering than usual. Cas hoped his presence meant that Angulus had forgiven Zirkander for allowing the sorceress access to the castle. She hadn't heard the entire story, but she remembered the uncharacteristic hangdog look the general had worn that afternoon when she first landed. The next day, he'd shown up at work with his expression more sure, but he still seemed subdued, not as cocky and irreverent as usual. Of course, it had only been three weeks. Time would likely heal any wounds on his soul and return him to his typical self.

"Uhm, Cas?" Tolemek asked, his tone odd. He had dismounted first and stood looking toward the backyard. The shouts, grunts, and thumps of a brisk-ball game came from that direction.

Cas slid off her horse, handing the reins to the stable boy. "Yes?"

"Should I be worried? Or perhaps armed?" Tolemek lowered his voice. "I didn't bring any knockout grenades. I didn't think I would need them at a barbecue."

"Are you talking about for the game?"

"Ah, no."

Cas, too short to see over her horse's back, had to walk around to find out what Tolemek was talking about. She paused to stare, not certain whether to share his alarm, to be pleased, or to feel wary. Maybe all three?

She patted Tolemek on the chest, hoping the gesture reassured him that he wasn't in danger—and hoping she was right. Her father watched them from the corner of the house. In stark contrast to most of the barbecue attendees, who wore brightly patterned and often clashing shirts that left one grateful that uniforms were mandatory at work, her father was dressed in his usual black and gray, the drab colors indifferent to the sun's cheer. Most likely, he had numerous weapons stashed about his person, though none of them were visible today. Cas walked toward him, deciding to find the lack of obvious weaponry reassuring. The king's guards meandering around the property were equally reassuring, though if her father was truly determined to kill someone, guards wouldn't stop him. He could strike and disappear into the woods behind the house quickly.

"Caslin." Her father nodded gravely. His jaw tightened when he glanced at Tolemek, who was following behind her, but he did nothing worse.

"Father," Cas said, knowing she sounded as stiff as he did, but never knowing how to change that. She couldn't ever be comfortable with the man. "I wasn't expecting you here."

"No?" His sandy brows arched slightly. "General Zirkander invited me."

"It looks like he invited *everyone*." Cas glanced toward the king's men. "It's possible he's considering this a belated housewarming party and expects gifts."

Her father gazed at her without comment, his eyebrows settling into their normal position. It occurred to Cas that her comment might have been an insult.

"I mean, I'm not surprised that he invited you," she said, not sure that was any better. "But why did you come?"

"To see you. You haven't been by since returning from Dakrovia."

A mission he shouldn't have known about, but his knowledge of such things did not surprise her.

"I'm sorry. I didn't realize you were expecting me." The last time she had visited the house had been the first time in years. She wouldn't have guessed that he expected her to return, though he had mentioned something about them target shooting together.

"I wish to let you know that the bounty on your pirate's head is no longer in effect," her father said.

"We guessed that, but it's good to know." She glanced at Tolemek, not sure if she should introduce him or encourage him to run away before her father spoke to him. "His name is Tolemek, Father. He's no longer a pirate. He's working for the king as a scientist."

She was sure he knew all of that, but she did not know what else to say for an introduction. Tolemek and her father had never met face to face. Tolemek stood quietly, with his hands clasped behind his back, almost in a military stance. He hadn't reacted to the *your pirate* comment. He'd heard much worse here, she knew.

"Is the pay adequate?" her father asked him. His mouth turned downward slightly. "Your apartment is... modest."

Leave it to her father to subtly let him know that he knew where he lived—and that he thought it wasn't good enough.

"It's a reasonable monthly income," Tolemek said, "and Cas and I are planning to look for a bigger place together, something that's truly ours. I have a side deal going with a pharmaceutical company that's proving quite lucrative. I suppose we could eventually look for a house up in your neighborhood, assuming they let foreigners buy land around here."

"You didn't tell me about that," Cas said.

"No." Tolemek smiled agreeably.

She lowered her voice and murmured, "Not because it's something dangerous that I wouldn't approve of and that you shouldn't approve of either, right?" She was certain he did not want to make anything that could be used to harm people anymore, but she wondered why he hadn't mentioned the side project. They had been together often of late.

"It's not dangerous. It's not glamorous either. Your Lieutenant Averstash was in an early trial." He nodded but said nothing more. Not wanting to go into details in front of her father?

She sensed a hint of embarrassment from him. What would Pimples have agreed to use in a trial? Even as she wondered, Pimples jogged past on his way to talk to Captain Blazer and Captain Crash, who were minding the barbecue pit and the smoker in the backyard.

"We're going to do the unveiling soon," he told them. "Can you finish up and join us out front, sir, ma'am?"

As Pimples ran back past Cas, giving her an inviting wave, she noticed that his face lacked the telltale acne that had resulted in his nickname. He'd said something about avoiding the mess hall food lately, but maybe that wasn't it at all. She squinted at Tolemek. His smile broadened. Seven gods, had he used his scientific gift to make some kind of pimple cream?

"Maybe that has something to do with his newfound luck with princesses," Cas said.

Tolemek winked. "Likely so."

"Father, will you join us for the, ah, unveiling?" Cas gestured toward the front yard.

He twitched his nose in that direction, not appearing enthused at the prospect. "General Zirkander said there would be brisk-ball."

"You're not interested in playing, are you?"

"I would be interested in watching *you* play. It's been many years since you competed in marksmanship competitions and brought home medals."

No, she just brought home pirates now. Ex-pirates.

"I'd be particularly pleased if you placed yourself on the team opposing Zirkander," her father said, an unholy gleam in his eyes.

"I'd like to see that too." Tolemek grinned.

"As a leader, he should be targeted early and removed from the game," her father said.

"Absolutely," Tolemek said.

The two men met each other's eyes over Cas's head, and she had the sense of some kind of strange bonding passing between them due to this mutual agreement. Had she known the idea of Zirkander with a big bruise on his butt could bring these two together, she would have suggested a game months ago.

"I can't promise to hit him," she warned as they walked toward the front yard. "He's almost as squirrelly on the ground as he is in the air, and he knows to target *me* first too."

"It should be an interesting match then," her father said.

"Indeed so." Tolemek slid an arm around Cas's back as they walked.

Her father noted it, but he did not object or even look all that irritated. Perhaps the promise of Tolemek growing wealthy off pimple cream had elevated him to a new status, one good enough for his daughter. Cas shook her head. Parents were odd.

* * *

"Out here, sir," Beeline called through the front door of the house. "Wolf Squadron has something for you."

Ridge had been about to carry a plate of meat patties and sausages out for his captains to cook, but he set the plate on the counter instead. "He sounds tickled about whatever he has for me."

"I wish I was as tickled," Sardelle said as she sliced radishes, carrots, and lettuce on a cutting board. Women always seemed to think vegetables should be involved in meals.

"Have you been peeking into people's minds and spying on them?" He waggled his eyebrows at her.

"Under tarps, actually."

"Then you can come outside with me and hold my hand, to keep me from being overwhelmed by the surprise."

"*You'll* probably like it." Her mouth twisted wryly as she set down the knife and wiped her hands.

He smiled, not in a hurry to go outside. He'd been finding this shared domestic moment quite pleasant. Sardelle had managed to shoo the dragons away for the day, the soulblades were in the bedroom, and Ridge could pretend they led a cozy, normal life.

"It's here," came a squeal from the open back door. Tylie raced through the kitchen on bare feet, wearing a paint-stained sundress and carrying a turtle, the latest woodland creature she had befriended.

An *almost* normal life, Ridge amended as she grinned at them and continued into the living room and out the front door.

"Shall we see what they've brought you?" Sardelle offered a serene smile and extended her hand.

Instead of clasping it, he stepped forward and hugged her, still amazed that she had forgiven him for forgetting about her and for traipsing through the mountains with the enemy. *More than traipsing.* He knew Sardelle wouldn't forget, no matter what she said, but she was too good of a person to blame him for it.

"I know what you said, but I really don't deserve you," he mumbled, feeling a little abashed by his emotions. General Ort and the king had kept him busy at work these last weeks—Angulus in particular feeling Ridge should pay handsomely for being offered the throne by a nutcase sorceress—and Sardelle had been flying around the country, collecting candidates for the sorcery school she was planning, so they hadn't had many quiet moments like this.

"Is it because I'm a high priestess now?" she teased, ignoring his darker thoughts, though he was sure she knew what was on his mind. She seemed to enjoy their hug and did not rush to pull away, even though pilots kept poking their noses through the front doorway to check on them.

"That *does* make you quite intimidating."

As far as he knew, she hadn't formally accepted that position and thought the idea of a dragon god silly, but Bhrava Saruth introduced her as his high priestess to everyone he encountered—everyone he encountered who would listen to a dragon. Rumors were spreading far and wide about her and her god. Ridge was just glad people weren't trying to drown her for being a witch. The average Iskandian subject still feared magic or did not believe in it, but having a dragon looming over her shoulder gave her a status that few could ignore.

"So long as *you* aren't intimidated when he shows up." Sardelle kissed his neck, which aroused thoughts that had nothing to do with going outside to spend time with his colleagues.

"It's hard to be intimidated by a dragon that rolls onto his back and asks for belly rubs when I come up the walkway."

"He's decided he's quite fond of you. I think it's because you carry that figurine around in your pocket. I may have convinced him early on that it depicted him."

"Maybe it *does*. He came from the past, right? Maybe my father used some dragon in a book as a model when he carved it, and it was a picture of him."

Sardelle leaned back so that she could look him in the eye. Too bad. He'd been enjoying the neck nuzzling. "You don't sound that alarmed by the idea."

"I'll happily worship him, if he'll help us defend the city from future attacks. I'll even bring him cheese."

"I haven't noticed that Bhrava Saruth has Phelistoth's taste for cheese wheels. He is fond of those mango tarts you brought back from your inspection down south."

Ridge frowned toward the cupboard where he had been storing those. "The mango tarts I brought back to share with everyone here? I promised I'd have one for Angulus if he came."

"Ah. How *big* of one?"

"It's supposed to be a bribe. I'm trying to get him to forgive me for causing the destruction of a thousands-of-years-old castle which happened to be the oldest structure on the city's historical landmarks register."

"He's no longer irked at Kaika for nearly doing the same a few months ago," Sardelle said. "Perhaps you could ask what methods she employed to earn his forgiveness."

"I'm not capable of using *her* methods of earning forgiveness."

"Sure, you are." Her eyes twinkled, and she ran her hands up his chest. "In fact, you had me in quite a forgiving mood the night after the battle. And also on the horse ride that brought us home from it, it being a shame that the stable boy could only scrounge up the one horse and we had to share."

"Yes, but I love you. I have no interest in sharing horses with other people." He was pleased that he could say that honestly, that even when his brain had been annoyingly vacant, he had avoided that intimacy with the sorceress.

"Mm." She melted back against his chest, more at the proclamation of love than the horse-sharing promise, he suspected. "Perhaps Angulus would be satisfied with a nice cheese wheel instead?"

Ridge wrapped his arms back around her, enjoying the

moment and no longer thinking of kings, dragons, or tarts. They managed a kiss that once again had him thinking of escaping to the bedroom before the next interruption came and forced him to tuck those thoughts away for later.

"Ridge?" a voice called from the front door. The voice that did not belong to any of his pilots.

Ridge released Sardelle and peered into the living room. His mother and father stood on the threshold, Mom in a patchwork dress that she had likely made herself and Dad in his usual adventuring clothes, which consisted of more pockets than seemed mathematically possible for garments of that size. He clutched his journal in his hand, but he managed to look Ridge in the eyes without scribbling notes in it or looking up something. Mom clutched his other hand and pulled him firmly inside. She carried a basket with an embroidered cloth covering the contents.

"Mom." Ridge laid a parting hand on Sardelle's back, then strode out to greet them. "You came. I wasn't expecting you."

They had shared a weepy reunion the day after the dragon battle, one that had moved Ridge to tears, even though *he* had never believed himself dead. The hugs, gifts, and offers of beer he'd received from his comrades had moved him, as well, making him appreciate all of his friends and colleagues in a way that one sometimes forgot to do in non-crisis day-to-day life.

Since he'd seen his mother a few times since then, he gave her a less emotional hug now, then offered an arm to include his father. As usual, Dad had been overseas during Ridge's supposed death, so he hadn't had to deal with any gut-wrenching emotions, if he even had the capacity for them. Ridge had never been sure. Now, Dad patted him absently on the back while peering around the house, as if looking for fascinating ancient artifacts in a forgotten temple. At least he had come.

"Your father showed up a few days ago," Mom said. "I wanted him to see your new home. And I wanted to spend time with the lovely Sardelle of course." Mom beamed over at her, practically oozing thoughts of pregnancy and children. If she'd heard that some dragon was claiming Sardelle as a high priestess, she didn't show it. It was possible she hadn't decided to believe in dragons yet.

"Days ago?" Ridge asked, waving Sardelle over to join them. She had hung back in the kitchen doorway, clearly not wanting to intrude. "Why didn't you come sooner?"

"Because I had to lock your father in the bedroom and make him satisfy a year's worth of womanly urges, Ridge."

"I... I... *Mom*. I don't want to hear about your *urges*." He gave Sardelle a horrified and apologetic look, certain that she didn't want to hear about his parents' urges either. She only smiled back at him, her eyes twinkling.

"Then you shouldn't have asked, dear." Mom patted him on the cheek and pulled back the cloth on her basket. "Soap?"

"Are they carved into cat shapes?" Ridge scrutinized the basket. No, those didn't look like cats.

"They're dragon-shaped," Mom said. "There's a story going around about how dragons were involved in the Cofah attack on the castle earlier this month and how one apparently fought on our side. So silly! I'm certain it was just you and your flier squadron, right? Either way, dragons are incredibly trendy now. Dragon patterns are on all of the fabrics at the market, and well, you can see the results of my new soap molds."

Ridge looked at Sardelle, again wanting to apologize, this time for the fact that they would be washing their armpits with dragon soap for the next five years.

Bhrava Saruth will be pleased, she said into his mind.

Maybe I should introduce him to my mom.

He's quite handsome when in human form. She might get urges.

Ridge couldn't hold back a choking noise. He wasn't sure whether the idea of his mom and her urges bothered him more than the fact that Sardelle had *noticed* that the faithful dragon who followed her around made a handsome human. They were both disturbing ideas.

You want disturbing, ask him to shape-shift into your *form*, Jaxi said.

Dragons are not always familiar with what humans consider tact, Wreltad said.

Jaxi and Wreltad were being stored out of sight for this gathering, but that didn't keep them from popping into Ridge's head now and then. Wreltad might be in the process of bonding to Tylie now, but he liked to chat with Ridge as much as Jaxi did.

I do believe Sardelle was most drawn to him in his ferret form, Jaxi said.

People have been enjoying the company of soft, furry creatures since long before my time, Wreltad added.

"All you all right, dear?" his mother asked, touching his arm.

"Yes, I'm just choked up with emotion. It's good to see you two together in the same room again."

Mom smiled and hugged Dad, who gave her a squeeze back, but then leaned forward conspiratorially. "Ridge, is it true that you went to a cavern full of dragon artifacts?"

"Uhm." He'd gone to a cavern full of *dragons*. "In a manner of speaking."

"Could you take me there?"

"The king ordered it sealed, and the Cofah dropped bombs onto it a few weeks later. We're fairly certain it's collapsed and the rest of the... artifacts won't be escaping."

"*Sealed? Bombed?*" Dad staggered back, resting a hand on the wall for support. "Governments do *not* know how to treat ancient and sacred ruin sites."

"Sacred?"

The god Bhrava Saruth did come out of it, Sardelle shared with him.

Ridge's groan was hidden by a knock on the open door. Expecting a couple of pilots trying to drag him out for whatever was waiting out front, Ridge waved the person in without looking. He was busy sharing a disgruntled look with Sardelle, whose eyes were twinkling even more now.

"Afternoon, General," Kaika said, strolling in, also with a covered basket dangling from one hand. Seven gods, she hadn't been making soaps, too, had she? "General's parents." She offered them a non-regulation salute, then walked around them and toward Sardelle.

Ridge waited to see if the king would follow her in, but he

did not. The last he had seen, Angulus had been sitting at a picnic table and speaking with General Ort. From what Ridge had heard, Angulus hadn't slept much in the last few weeks, as he and Ort had traveled all over the country, finding and instating replacements for the council leaders who had been lost in the attack. When Angulus was back in the capital, he was overseeing the rebuilding of the castle while dealing with historians and bureaucrats who demanded that as much of the original structure be saved as possible. Handling those people was probably more stressful than enduring Cofah attacks. Ridge hoped Kaika was helping Angulus find a few moments of relaxation—or invigoration, might be the better word—when he was home. They had gone back to being discreet about their relationship since that passionate reunion kiss in front of the collapsed tower, but Ridge couldn't imagine their affair was much of a secret within the castle walls—what remained of them.

"How are you doing, Captain Kaika?" Sardelle asked when Kaika stopped in front of her. Her gaze dipped to the basket, and one eyebrow arched. "I trust you're not in need of my services."

"No, I'm fit enough for spirited exercise, I assure you." Kaika winked. "I haven't been injured in nearly four weeks, but I've been wanting to thank you for the times you rendered those services to me. Multiple times."

Tylie appeared on the threshold of the front door. She smiled shyly at Ridge, but her gaze locked onto the basket. The turtle in her arms had been replaced by a small golden-furred creature that Ridge hadn't seen before.

Jaxi sniggered into his mind.

That's not a ferret, is it? Ridge asked.

I am the god Bhrava Saruth, the dragon's voice rang into Ridge's head, not diminished at all by the fact that it was being projected from a ferret. *I heard you speaking about me,* he added.

We were discussing dragon soaps.

Icons of me? Most acceptable.

The ferret chittered, then jumped out of Tylie's arms as she crept closer to Kaika and the basket.

Ridge stepped back, but that didn't keep the golden-furred

creature from landing on his arm and climbing up to his shoulder. It chirped in his ear, and he rubbed its fur obligingly.

"Oh my," his mother said. "What a feisty thing."

The ferret cooed at her until she came forward and petted it. It made contented noises and draped itself over Ridge's shoulder, oozing sybaritic satisfaction.

Had Ridge been thinking his life normal earlier? How odd of him to have had that delusion, even for a moment.

"I've been meaning to give you a gift," Kaika told Sardelle. "I went back and forth between something useful, like explosives to plant around the house in case aerial invaders come again—" Mom's expression grew confused, and she glanced toward a window, "—and then I considered baked goods, since someone I know now has access to a very talented chef, who did, you'll be pleased to know, survive the attack on the castle."

"That's good," Sardelle murmured.

"But it seemed sad to give a gift that might simply be eaten by your frequent houseguests. I trust this will not be eaten." Kaika frowned over at the ferret.

Have no fear of that, Bhrava Saruth said. *Predators do not taste good. I prefer sheep and cows.*

And the occasional tart? Ridge asked.

The ferret rubbed Ridge's jaw with his head.

Kaika apparently heard the conversation, because she smirked. Sardelle did too. Ridge hoped the dragon wasn't talking to his parents. Mom wasn't ready for that.

The blanket on the basket stirred slightly. Ridge had a feeling he was going to end up with as many animals roaming around his house as his mother had. That was a distressing thought.

"Anyway, here." Kaika thrust the basket toward Sardelle. "I'm told that it comes from a long line of mousers, so it should be useful around here."

Sardelle accepted the basket and peeled back the blanket, revealing a cute black and white spotted kitten.

"It?" Fern asked, coming forward. "You didn't look at the sex?"

"I don't care to snoop into an animal's genitalia," Kaika said.

"She reserves that for human relations," Ridge said.

Ridge, Sardelle admonished him silently.

Kaika only grinned.

Fern took the kitten out of the basket, eliciting a few tiny mews, and headed for the kitchen. She linked Sardelle's arm with hers, perforce taking her along.

"Come on, dear. Let's find Spots some milk."

"Spots?" Sardelle asked.

Tylie trailed after them, probably looking for a new animal to carry around, since her ferret had left her.

As Ridge headed for the door, figuring he should find out what his pilots wanted, the ferret ran down his back, nails sinking in along the way, and scampered across the floor and into the kitchen. Dad watched the creature go through narrowed eyes. Mom might not be ready to believe in dragons, but Dad might put the puzzle pieces together sooner.

"Sir!" several voices greeted him when he stepped into the sunlight.

"*Finally*," someone in the back said. "Help me get this tarp off."

Captain Blazer was the one to amble up to him, padding over the grass that hadn't quite grown back after Morishtomaric's attack the month before, and stopping on the walkway. She removed her cigar and gave him a lazy salute. "I'm pleased to announce that Wolf Squadron chipped in to get you a housewarming gift."

"That's very thoughtful, Captain." Ridge watched as Pimples, Beeline, and Duck wrestled a large tarp-covered item out of the back of a wagon parked across the street. He was aware of Angulus and Ort watching from the picnic table overlooking the pond beside the house. Neither appeared enlightened.

"Yes, sir," Blazer said. "Much thought went into this. We hope you enjoy it." She grinned wickedly.

By the time the tarp-covered object was heading up the walkway, Pimples, Beeline, and Duck cursing under the awkward weight, Ridge was fairly certain he was getting a new couch. He wondered how Sardelle would feel about it. She'd been so fond of the one that she and his mom had picked out.

"Here it is, sir," Pimples said. The trio of lieutenants set it down in front of Ridge, their hands resting on the tarp. "Ready?" he asked his conspirators, who held other corners of the tarp.

Ridge dropped his chin to his fist and waited for the unveiling.

The tarp was torn back, revealing what appeared to be, at first glance, the remains of a crashed flier. On second glance, it looked much the same, though Ridge also recognized the outline of a large couch. The frame was made from uneven pieces of bronze metal, flier scrap parts to be specific, that were riddled with bullet holes. The upholstery, if one could give it such a lofty label, was thick, shaggy, and had a unique greenish coloring that reminded him of squished caterpillars.

"That's, ah, quite fine," Ridge said, glancing back to make sure Sardelle was not witness to this. Would she move out if the couch came to be the focal point of their living room? It couldn't be any worse than dragons, cats, and turtles lounging around the house, right?

I might move out, Jaxi commented. *Don't even think of laying my scabbard on those cushions.*

"Shall we bring it in, sir?" Pimples asked.

"Ah, certainly. Just watch out for..."

"Alarmed screams from women?" Angulus suggested from his table.

General Ort had his face in his hand and was shaking his head. Ridge recalled that he had approved of the sedate suede couch that had been incinerated, even if he had never seen it in person.

Pimples, Duck, and Beeline hefted the couch—it certainly was big—and turned it on its side to stuff it through the doorway.

"Interesting how you boys don't show such enthusiasm for physicality when it's time for P.T.," Ridge observed as they passed.

"Our muscles have been bolstered by beer," Duck said before they disappeared inside.

Ahn wandered over from the side of the house, carrying a leather brisk-ball at her side. "You up for a game, sir?"

Tolemek and her father stood back, watching with smiles

on their faces. Ridge promptly had the sense that he was being set up for something. Ahn's father *never* smiled. A part of him was pleased that the man had actually come to the gathering, for Ahn's sake, of course, but more of him regarded this approach with wariness.

"That depends, Ahn. Are we on the same side or opposing sides?" Ridge had assumed everyone would want to eat and drink before hurling balls at each other. The game was more entertaining after a few beers.

"Opposing, sir. Apparently, my father wants to see you pummeled."

"How shocking."

Judging by Tolemek's grin, he wouldn't mind seeing that either. He walked over and draped an arm around Ahn's shoulders. "Can I join in? I'm not that familiar with this game, but I believe I could be useful. On Cas's team."

"You don't have knockout grenades in your pockets, do you?" Ridge asked.

"I don't think those will be necessary."

"I'll join in," came an unexpected voice from the side. Angulus left the table and walked over, rolling up his sleeves as he came.

"On my side, Sire?"

Angulus's eyes glinted. "No."

"Er." Ridge tried not to feel too bleak that so many people wanted to see him pummeled, though it was hard not to let an expression of distress creep onto his face. "Doesn't anyone want to join my team?" he asked, afraid the words sounded more pitiful than intended.

"Against Raptor?" Pimples asked. "No."

"Is it even *allowed* to throw a ball at the king?" Beeline whispered to Blazer.

She shrugged back at him.

"I'll join you," someone said from behind him. A young man with mussy golden hair that hung in his eyes ambled out the door and winked at Ridge. "I saw a version of this game played in my youth."

Ridge recognized Bhrava Saruth in human form from Sardelle's descriptions, but most of his guests frowned curiously at him. Angulus's eyes narrowed to slits. Maybe he'd seen the dragon as a human before. Or he could guess more quickly than the others who this was. Ahn and Tolemek also wore shrewd, suspicious looks.

"Well, that should make things a little more fair," Ridge said, smiling slightly.

As he'd always believed, rubbing a dragon charm could bring good luck. Apparently, rubbing a dragon could bring good luck too.

THE END

Printed in Great Britain
by Amazon